EVEREST
1811

AHMET ÜMİT

Born in 1960 in the city of Gaziantep in southern Turkey. He moved to Istanbul in 1978 to attend university. In 1983, he both graduated from the Public Administration Faculty of Marmara University, and wrote his very first story. An active member of the Turkish Communist Party from 1974 until 1989, Ümit took part in the underground movement for democracy while Turkey was under the rule of a military dictatorship between 1980-1990. In 1985-86, he illegally attended the Academy for Social Sciences in Moscow. He has one daughter, Gül. Since 1989, Ümit has published one volume of poetry, three volumes of short stories, a book of fairytales, one novella, and six novels. One of Turkey's most renowned contemporary authors, Ümit is especially well known for his mastery of the mystery genre, as reflected in many of his bestselling novels and short story volumes. Drawing upon the unique political and historical background of his home country, Ümit delves into the psyches of his well-wrought characters as he weaves enthralling tales of murder and political intrigue.

ELKE DIXON

Born in Tacoma, WA in 1969. From 1988 to 1994, she studied Art History and Literature in Washington State and Puerto Rico. After numerous visits to Istanbul between 1990 and 1996, she settled there more permanently, and has since been involved in a variety of projects, from translations to visual arts.

THE FLOCK

Ahmet Ümit

Translated by
Elke Dixon

Publication No. 1811
Contemporary Turkish Literature 30

The Flock
Ahmet Ümit

Original Title:
Kavim

Translated by Elke Dixon
Proofreading: Alan Scott
Cover Design by Füsun Turcan Elmasoğlu
Page Layout by M. Aslıhan Özçelik

© 2018, Ahmet Ümit
© 2018; Everest Publications. All rights reserved.

1. Edition: December 2018

ISBN: 978 - 605 - 185 - 319 - 2
Certifacate No: 10905

EVEREST PUBLICATIONS
Ticarethane Sokak No: 15 Cağaloğlu/ISTANBUL
Tel: +90 (212) 513 34 20-21 Fax: +90 (212) 512 33 76
e-mail: info@everestyayinlari.com
www.everestyayinlari.com
www.twitter.com/everestkitap

Printed by Melisa Matbaacılık
Certifacate No: 12088
Çiftehavuzlar Yolu Acar Sanayi Sitesi No: 8
Tel: +90 (0212) 674 97 23 Fax: +90 (0212) 674 97 29

Everest is a trademark of the Alfa Publishing Group.

Chapter 0

A nasal-burning odor woke him. He knew this smell. The smell of a church that had remained shut for years. Of oil lamps, crumbling stone, corroded marble, rotting wood, tattered pages and moldering corpses. He should have been horrified but he just gazed around. He glimpsed a gently stirring black figure. A formless, vague shape... A jet-black silhouette... He smiled at it.

"Mor Gabriel," he murmured.

The figure drew closer, and as it approached, it assumed human form. A person in black. A person who came up to him and whispered in his ear:

"Do you know me?"

"Mor Gabriel," he murmured again. As the name Mor Gabriel spilled from his mouth, he heard music: Liturgical music coming from deep, deep within. A mumble of recurring passion in a language he didn't know, the rhyme of a person in raptures. Just then he noticed the cross. A cross of silver. As he tried to discern whether the man carried it in his hand or on his chest, a flash of light split the emptiness in two. He felt a stab of pain. The light flashed again, the pain disappeared and relief spread throughout his entire body. The sound receded. First the colors in the room faded, then the black shape vanished, and then the room, and then the light...

Chapter 1
This strange creature called man has neither the power nor the law to keep evil at bay.

The interrogation room is dimly lit. Nazmi is seated at the end of the long table, I'm in the chair to his left and Ali is standing. The overhead light illuminates only Nazmi's face. There's a wan glare on Nazmi's broad forehead, his eyes retreat into their sockets, in darkness...

"Head up," Ali warns. He isn't angry; his voice just carries the authority of a policeman doing his job. Nazmi is in no state to oppose him. He slowly lifts his head and his hazel eyes appear, devoid of joy. The light must have hit him hard; he's blinking. A beard of at least two weeks on his face. The scar under the pit of his eye sits like a black stain a finger-width above the line where his beard starts. It's our Ali's words that break the silence of the interrogation room. Indicating the black Browning on the table, he asks, "Did you shoot yourself with this too?"

Nazmi's meek gaze turns first to the Browning, then to Ali. He nods, confirming it.

"Yes, with that."

"It's your service pistol?" I cut in.

"My service pistol..."

"Nice gun," I say. "Seems you were popular in the police force. I've read your file, the acknowledgements, the awards... Your superiors are very pleased. Everyone speaks well of you."

Nazmi just listens without a peep. At one point his eyes shift to the cigarette packet on the table. I pick it up and hold it out to him.

"Have one..."

With trembling hands, he pulls out a cigarette and settles it onto the edge of his dry lip. I reach out and light it. "Nobody believes you did it," I say, as he takes a deep drag on the cigarette. "How did this thing happen?"

His murky eyes wander idly round my face. He draws the cigarette smoke deep into his lungs again as if that were a solution.

"I don't know, Chief Inspector..." he finally says. "I don't know," he repeats, as the smoke forgotten in his lungs ineluctably seeps out. "It just did."

"You mean you did it?"

He answers in a bitter, regretful voice.

"I did it."

Why are we questioning him? The truth is plain as day. Anyhow, the man isn't denying it. Why should we torment him more? But Director Cengiz has a warning. The recent unsavory write-ups in the press about the police call for us to go over everything with a fine-toothed comb. Ali must agree with Director Cengiz because he takes to questioning again.

"Why did you do it?"

Nazmi buries himself in his cigarette rather than answer. But Ali doesn't let up.

"Did you argue with your wife the night of the murder?"

Nazmi answers Ali without looking him in the face.

"Yes, we argued."

"What about?"

"I don't remember. We were always arguing lately..."

Ali hovered over Nazmi like a hunter looking for a means to lure his prey, trying to catch a weak spot.

"Were you jealous of your wife?"

Even I find Ali's question strange, and I think Nazmi's going to protest but he doesn't.

"Yes, I was jealous," he says. His voice reflects a man who is drained, without hope, at the end of his tether. "It tickled her, my being jealous..."

He smiles forlornly, as if inwardly speaking to his murdered wife. This doesn't last long.

"You're on the wrong track, Inspector," he says. He's lifted his head and is looking at Ali. On his face is the strength of his convictions. "I didn't kill my wife because I was jealous. It's not what you think..."

"So then what is it?"

"It just happened," says Nazmi. "Fate..."

He takes another drag on his cigarette.

"How so?" says Ali.

"Fate. You know..." There's the tenacity of a man beyond caring in his voice. He turns to me. "Chief, you would know better. It's difficult in our line of work."

I corroborate by staying silent. Ali disagrees with me.

"Police work is difficult," he grumbles, but we don't up and murder our wives or daughters, he wants to say, but can't. He turns his gaze from Nazmi, concluding, "...but we don't draw our guns and shoot our loved ones any old time we lose our temper."

Nazmi's confidence disappears all at once and he chooses to hang his head to conceal his eyes. Ali has no intention of giving him an opportunity.

"Why did you shoot them?" He relentlessly repeats the question.

Nazmi is deadpan; he neither stirs nor responds. Ali is going to really lay into him. I intervene so as to not let him.

"Look, Nazmi, we are obliged to complete this inquiry. You'd do best to explain what happened."

He lifts his head again, his movements so slow it seems it hurts him to budge.

"I already explained, Chief. But since you want me to, I'll do it again: That night I came home. Dinner still wasn't ready. Aynur was asking, the neighbors have a dishwasher, when are we going to get one. I'd been on duty for twenty-four hours. Some muggers had snatched a diplomat's wife's bag. We pursued the mugger in Tarlabaşı all day. They shot at us. One of my friends was wounded and I would have been hit too if I hadn't ducked. Anyhow, we surrounded the street. We rounded up whoever we saw but we couldn't find the woman's bag. When we got back to the station that evening, we got bawled out by the director. For everything from incompetence to idiocy. That's the state I came home in, you'll understand. My wife greeted me with, 'When are we going to get a dishwasher?' We still haven't finished paying off the TV we just bought. I didn't want to argue... I walked in. My daughter was inside, crying. She was two years old... She must have been hungry. I wasn't hungry; I was tired. My head was buzzing like a beehive. My wife said, 'Pick that child up. Can't you see I'm making dinner?' I frowned. My wife assumed I didn't want to pick up my daughter. Really I was just tired. I wanted to hold my daughter and go to sleep. I took her onto my lap but she wouldn't quiet down. And neither would my wife. I wasn't listening to them, didn't want to hear them; I just wanted to sleep and for the buzzing in my head to stop. It didn't. It just got worse as if someone had poked a stick into the hive. I put the child on to the bed and covered my ears with my hands. Rather than letting up, it just got louder. No, I couldn't hear my kid's or my wife's voices anymore. Even though my daughter was bawling her head off, and my wife had planted herself in front of me, pointing at the child and yelling away. I told her to be quiet... Maybe I didn't say it but I thought I did, and she just stepped up to me. Started slapping me. I don't know, maybe she didn't hit me but it seemed to me like she did. Even if she did hit me I didn't care, wouldn't care... It was my wife I wanted free of, not my daughter, the bees buzzing in my head... I don't know when my hand went for my gun, when I took it out of its sheath and pulled the trigger. I just know I kept shooting till the noise of the bullets firing one after the other scared the bees away. I wasn't shooting at my wife and daughter, I just wanted to chase away the bees. But when I opened my eyes, I was faced with their bodies writhing around all bloody. I didn't know what to do, so this time I turned the gun on myself and pulled the trigger. But it didn't work. I didn't die. It's God who decides who lives or dies in the end."

He stays quiet for a bit, then sets his eyes on my face and concludes, "That's how it is, Inspector. That's the truth. But let the records show it however it pleases you. What do I have to lose? No judge can give me a harsher punishment than I've given myself."

I'm looking at Ali; is this okay, is this what we wanted to hear? But that stern policeman look on Ali's face, which I know so well, doesn't change. As if he means to say, "Fine, Inspector, but what fault is it of that poor woman and that innocent two-year-old child?" He's right; right but young. Especially young for our profession. He believes he can prevent crime and evil by catching killers and applying the law. As for me, I've learned from the direct experience of the hundreds of cases I've encountered that catching a killer to stop crime, applying the law to uphold justice, doesn't work. I wish I hadn't learned that, I often say. I wish that, even if it were a lie, I could believe that there existed a thing called justice in the world. But I can't believe it. Because this strange creature called man has neither the power nor the law to keep evil at bay. The door opens as I'm mulling this over. And from the opening door appears the dreary light of the fluorescents, followed by Zeynep's pretty face.

"Inspector, we have a situation," she says. Her sculpted eyebrows furrow and her dark eyes stare solemnly into my face. Her gaze is about to slip over to Ali. My question coincides with that moment.

"What is it?"

"There's been a murder in Elmadağ. Peculiar circumstances..."

We're not in a position to discuss what's peculiar about it in front of Nazmi. In any event, I'd like to get out of here.

"We're coming," I say.

Ali looks at me in disappointment.

"We'll take a written statement later. Nazmi's explained it all anyhow."

Ali doesn't insist. He puts his jacket on and follows me out. "Hope you feel better," I say, turning to Nazmi as I walk out the door.

A pained smile appears on Nazmi's lips.

"Thanks, Chief. But I won't."

Chapter 2
The murder he's been searching for all these years awaits him.

Night meets us as we pull out onto the street. A cold, damp, dark winter night. A night made thoroughly gloomy by the hazy brake lights of cars advancing along the avenue. Tiny water droplets appear on the car's windshield. As Ali works at wiping them away, he peers out and states, "It's so dark out. It's not even five o'clock."

"That's normal," says Zeynep. "It's December. Winter nights are long."

Ali doesn't respond. He just throws Zeynep, sitting in the seat next to his, a look. She doesn't bother about his intense gaze; she pulls her coat snugly about her, cold because the heater has only just started warming up. I'm in the back, and every bit as cold as Zeynep. My overcoat is too thin and I'm hunkering into the corner of the seat. Our only music is the crackling of the radio.

"Inspector Şefik from CSI informed us," she starts to say. She's half turned towards me and I get a faint whiff of her perfume. I see her face in profile. She's quite a beauty, our

Zeynep. She inadvertently looks at Ali as she explains, but it's like she doesn't see him. "They've found some unusual evidence at the crime scene."

"Unusual how?"

She's trying to look at me but she can't turn her neck enough.

"He didn't go into detail, Chief. But he said we'd better come straight over."

She looks back at Ali and this time she does see him. She smiles and continues.

"And he left a special message for you. 'Tell Ali the murder he's been searching for all these years awaits him,' he said."

Ali doesn't take his eyes off the road. It seems he still hasn't come to terms with our dropping Nazmi's interrogation and going to another job.

"He always says that," he mumbles discontentedly. "But it always turns out to be one of the mundane ones."

"I think it's different this time around. His voice was jittery when he told me there were some things we needed to see."

"I doubt it. Şefik gets shook up whenever he sees a corpse."

Ali is being unfair. Şefik is one of CSI's most experienced inspectors. He works with the fastidiousness of a jeweler; no detail escapes him. Many a time he's helped us find a killer based on a strand of hair, a bit of saliva or a single drop of blood. Not just us - the medical examiners speak gratefully of him too. And our beloved criminologist Zeynep always sings his praises. But for whatever reason, this time she chooses to keep quiet. Perhaps she thinks what we'll see at the crime scene will be impressive enough. Or she doesn't want to talk without being certain. Honestly, I don't have it in me to argue with Ali either. I would do better to rest my eyes until we got to the scene. After all, I'd be going to Evgenia's *meyhane* from there. I haven't been to see her in ages. She must be very perturbed. I'd got a real tongue-lashing yesterday. I have to go conciliate.

I snuggle into my overcoat, and as I prepare to make the most of our not-so-long trip, Ali grumbles, "I hope that child killer hasn't gone into action." However disinterested he appeared, Şefik's words must have started to affect him. Ali's speculation rouses me, but I keep my eyes shut. In the darkness under my closed lids appear the bodies of three seven-year-old boys. First they'd been raped, then strangled. They look into my face with fear seared into their pupils, necks twisted like broken dolls... It's Zeynep's voice that scatters the image.

"I don't think this is the Candyman's handiwork."

"Why? Did Şefik say something?" Ali asks.

Our people called him the Candyman, yet we'd found no candy wrappers on the murdered kids, nor sweets in their stomachs. I don't remember who had coined the moniker. Must have started out with the cliché of perverts luring children with sweets. Not terribly creative, clearly. But that the Candyman nickname had proved useful was equally true.

"No, dear. All Şefik said is it's an interesting murder. Like always, he didn't clarify. I don't think it's the Candyman because the dates don't match up."

"They don't?"

"No, they don't," Zeynep repeats. "It hasn't been three months since the last murder. And besides, today's not Friday."

"Maybe the guy's broken the rules. Who's to say he'll always kill according to the date?"

He doesn't believe it himself; his voice has a ring of uncertainty. I'm picturing a man from a world that is darker than inside my closed eyelids. I keep repeating 'that we've confirmed', because there may be other children whose bodies weren't found. Three murders, committed three months apart, on the final Friday of the third month. What kind of person rapes and kills a seven-year-old on the last Friday of every third month? "It could be someone who was raped at the same age," Zeynep had posited. But why at three-month intervals, and why the last Friday of the month? The murderer must have his reason. A reason justifiable to him, however pointless and bizarre and ludicrous to us. I wonder if one day we'll learn. Perhaps. But I know this: whatever we find out, it will not bring back those murdered boys. It would stop the Candyman from murdering any other children... But only the Candyman. Other murderers would continue to murder, be it children, young adults or the elderly. So it has been since the world was formed, and unfortunately, so it would be... This is the first and most important truth that events teach us. And as for the definitive truth of the incident we were currently on our way to, despite my not having seen the crime scene yet, this murder was not the Candyman's stunt. As all this is going through my head, my phone begins to ring. I see our director's number on the screen and pick up.

"Hello. Yes, Director?"

Hearing me say 'Director', Ali and Zeynep prick up their ears.

"Hi, Nevzat," says Cengiz. "Where are you?"

"On my way to Elmadağ, to a crime scene. There's been a murder."

"There's always a murder," he says. His voice is tired, perhaps a bit weary. "Where after that?"

I don't feel like telling him to Kurtuluş, to Evgenia's *meyhane*.

"I don't know. Depends on the situation at the scene."

He finally comes out with it. "Nevzat, I wanted to have a little chat with you. Why don't we get a couple drinks this evening?"

Oh, great. I had to find some way to get out of it right away or Evgenia would kill me.

"That would be really nice, sir, but it looks like things are going to take a while. Could we have this talk in your room tomorrow morning?"

There's a brief silence. I realize I've upset him. But it beats breaking Evgenia's heart.

"All right," Cengiz finally says. "We'll meet in my room tomorrow. The *rakı* isn't meant to be. We'll have coffee."

"Okay. I'll be there."

"Good luck."

"Thanks, sir."

As I ring off, I wonder what it is he wants to talk to me about. We aren't that close. In fact, I like Cengiz. He doesn't just follow protocol. He'll go out on a limb for the members of his team. And he is what has kept me from retiring. Otherwise they would have given me the boot long ago. The subject of Cengiz's appointment has been on everyone's tongue lately. He is expected to be promoted. Is that what he's going to talk about, I wonder? Fine, but I don't understand these things. And our higher-ups aren't so hot on me either. Well, we'll see.

"Director Cengiz, Chief?" asks Ali.

He must also be curious about the reason for the call.

"Yeah, it was him."

"Is he asking about the murder?"

"No, he wants to have a chat."

Ali laughs affectionately.

"He's a good guy, our Director."

"We've never seen him put a foot wrong," I say.

"Nope, Chief. He's a very good man. None better..." He pauses. "Unless we count you, of course."

He isn't kissing up to me. I know it's heartfelt. But I still don't like him talking this way, because I know that I'm not such a good person. There's no use debating that now. I put my cell phone into my coat pocket and close my eyes again. Sleep would pay off, in whatever form.

Chapter 3
Awake, O sword, against my shepherd, and against the man that is my fellow.

"This is the Vatican Consulate, isn't it?"

At Zeynep's question, my eyes part. I must have drifted off. Floating images pass before my eyes, and after that the glow of the streetlights. As I sit up and look out the window, I ask, "Where?"

Zeynep points to the building we're passing.

"Here, Chief."

I'm looking but all I see are long, high walls. Ali changes the subject, in any case.

"Look, there's the ambulance. And behind it CSI's van. Must be that apartment building up there we're looking for."

As I look in the direction Ali has indicated, I notice the flashing lights of the ambulance at the bottom of the street.

"Apparently, they haven't taken the body, since the ambulance is still here," Ali continues.

This is good. It means the prosecutor and forensic practitioners haven't come yet. Seeing the crime scene before they've moved the corpse would work to our advantage. The positioning of the body, state of surrounding objects and detection of contusions were all crucial. And traces of evidence can be lost while lifting a body.

Ali parks the car in front of the ambulance. As we get out, a uniformed officer comes over. He is about to tell us we can't park here, but then pulls respectfully aside after I show my ID.

"This way, Chief Inspector."

I point at the building where the ambulance is parked.

"This place?"

"Yes, here, Inspector. The murder was perpetrated in the flat on the top floor."

I look up at the building. It must be at least a hundred years old. Not even the new beige paint job can hide its age. A large double door, wide steps... There's no one at the windows. Either they haven't noticed or they are over the shock. Otherwise the apartment residents would be hovering around us like flies to honey. We go in. The officer accompanying us shows us to an antique wooden elevator.

"The stairs are steep. You'd better use the lift, Chief Inspector."

We cram into the wooden elevator, which none of us have much confidence in. It starts up, emitting strange noises. It's so slow, if one of us had chosen to walk, we'd be up there before the lift was. In any case, we get to the fourth floor in one piece. CSI's seasoned inspector, Şefik, meets us at the door of the lift, his usual sardonic smile on his face. He had taken off the special outfit he wears when he enters a crime scene.

"Where have you been, Chief? If you'd been any later, we were going..."

I smile and extend a hand.

"You wouldn't have left." As Şefik squeezes my hand, I ask, "So what is this compelling incident?"

"A murder, Chief..."

"Well I'll be damned," Ali jokes. "Is there blood then, too?"

"Stop messing around, Ali!" Şefik is no longer smiling. "I swear, it's the darndest thing. The perpetrator left religious tokens..."

"Religious tokens?"

"Yes. A cross, a bible and such... I guess related to Christianity." After looking each of us in the face, he gives up explaining. "Better see it with your own eyes," he says, showing us to the door.

We pull plastic gloves over our hands and booties over our feet. An overpowering scent hits us as soon as we've stepped inside.

"Incense?" I mumble.

"Incense," Şefik confirms. "It's from one of those censers used in churches."

It isn't just incense; there's another smell. Şefik explains before I have to ask.

"And there was cannabis being smoked. The smell has permeated the place."

"They were smoking hash, eh?" There is no surprise in Ali's voice. "So they were on a spree, you mean. One got high and killed the other... What's so interesting about that?"

Şefik turns round and looks at Ali, grave and a bit tense.

"It's not that simple. You'll see."

Ali doesn't object this time.

"Who found the body?" I say, as we pass through a short corridor.

"The custodian's wife. She was wiping down the stairwells and noticed the door was open. She rang the bell and when she didn't get an answer, she went in and..."

"Where is she now?"

"She was terrified. We sent her to the hospital so they could calm her down. But I've already told you what she knew."

"When did she find the body?"

"Two hours ago."

At the end of the corridor is a spacious living room. The body is there, lying on a sofa. The room's curtains are drawn. On the table in the middle is a large book.

"The Holy Book," Şefik divulges.

"The Bible?"

"Holy Scripture is what's written on it."

For a moment, I can't decide whether to look at the Holy Scripture or the corpse, but then I approach the book. I settle my spectacles on the tip of my nose and take a look. The black letters are laid out on yellow paper.

"Both the Old and New Testaments," Şefik clarifies. He sees my puzzled look and carries on. "I mean the books before Jesus, like the Torah and the Psalms... and also the Bible."

"How do you know all this?" Ali reverently croons.

"It's written in the book, Ali. But the important thing for us is this highlighted line." Şefik points to a place in the second verse that's been underlined in a dark black liquid. Ali reads it aloud.

"Awake, O sword, against my shepherd, and against the man that is my fellow."***1

He gives me a blank look, to which I say nothing because I don't understand either. He reads the line again.

"'Awake, O sword, against my shepherd, and against the man that is my fellow." This time he looks at Şefik. "Now what does that mean?"

"I don't know," says Şefik, again pointing at the highlighted line. "But my guess is it's been underlined with the victim's blood. The red gradually got darker." He looks at Zeynep as he continues. "It doesn't really look like ink."

Zeynep examines the line, which appears drawn with a ruler.

"Possibly, but it's not right to say before a lab analysis... Did you see this?"

Zeynep points to the words "Mor Gabriel" written vertically in the margin of the right-hand page in the same reddish ink, blood, or whatever fluid it was.

"We saw that," says Şefik. "It's very clean-cut, not like handwriting - more like they used a stamp. But who Mor Gabriel is, that we don't know."

"Must be someone like a prophet or a saint," Zeynep reasons. Her questioning gaze is locked on Şefik's face.

"Don't look at me," says Şefik. "I don't understand anything about religion, Christianity least of all."

I choose to hold my tongue, as I've never heard of a saint named Mor Gabriel either.

"And what's this?"

Ali indicates the censer next to the Holy Book, which at first glance resembles a slim pitcher.

"An incense burner," I explain. "They're used during church rituals."

The silver censer is ornamented in colorful stones and has a handle on its side and a dome-like cap. Three chains hang from the side of the cap, with nine tiny bells attached to the chains. The elegance of the censer has Zeynep's attention too.

"Exquisite craftsmanship... The filigree is masterful," she coos.

"Filigree?" Ali asks, intrigued.

"A kind of silverwork, albeit a very tricky one. It's like embroidering with threads of silver... A very delicate business, I mean."

"Well, I don't know about filigree or whatever, but the smell of incense in the room came from this smoke burner," Ali says, turning to me. "If they use smoke burners in church rituals, then we can assume a ritual has been performed here."

A ritual? Neither Christians nor Jews kill people in their rituals, I think it's safe to say. But it's too early to jump to any conclusions on the subject. I wave a hand towards a lamp that's still lit.

"The lights. Did you turn them on?"

"The custodian's wife did. The curtains were closed so it was dark inside."

"She didn't touch the body or any objects, did she?"

"Touch them? She took one look at the corpse and went mental. Started screaming and ran over to the neighbor's. The man is a retired officer; he got the woman and took her outside. He's the one who called us."

After all this information, I finally approach the body on the sofa. The first thing to catch my eye is a metal cross. It gleams under the light reflected from the room's lamp. At first, I think the corpse is holding the cross in its hand. Like he understood he was going to die, and so sought refuge in the Lord at the last minute, surrendering his life as such. But when I get closer I see I was mistaken. The metal under the cross has been stuck into the man's heart.

"I didn't pull it out," Şefik explains, pointing. "I wanted you to see it. Forensics and the prosecutor too, of course..."

"You did well," I say, turning back to the body.

He wasn't too tall but he was built. His large frame took up the whole maroon sofa. A forty, forty-five-year-old, dark and handsome. Despite the pale yellow that spread through his face, not even death had spoiled his masculine good looks. Short salt-and-pepper hair, thick eyebrows, straight nose and a strong chin. On his thin lips is the innocent smile only seen on those who are at peace. His eyes rest on the cross lodged in his heart and there's an expression of gratitude on his face. As if he were given a gift. The left side of his grey, sleeveless t-shirt, however, is entirely stained red. The drying blood has pasted the t-shirt to the victim's muscular body. On closer look, I see another wound about two centimeters under the cruciform-handled knife.

"The perpetrator took two stabs," explains Zeynep, standing immediately next to me. "Both were aiming for the heart. The attacker stabbed with intent to kill."

"The victim must have known his murderer, Chief," says Ali, joining the discussion. "There are no signs of a struggle in the room."

"You're right, Ali," says Şefik. "And the door shows no sign of forced entry. The victim must have let him in himself."

"Maybe the man also knew he was going to be killed," Ali continues. His eyes are on the victim's mouth. "Just look how he's smiling. Like he's happy to die. Could he have hired the killer himself?"

It wasn't unheard of. Some people just don't have the guts to kill themselves, and they could pay a hitman to do it. I'd encountered a similar situation in Yeşilköy ten years ago. A bankrupt contractor had had himself killed like that. However, Zeynep felt differently.

"A victim's smile doesn't show the emotional state at the moment of dying. When the impact of the nervous system on the muscles post-death ceases, the victim's face may not reflect what he felt at the moment of or just before death."

"Well, I don't know," says Ali. "The man doesn't seem like he suffered at all..."

"The house is pretty tidy," I say, turning to Şefik. "Was he single?"

"The neighbors say he was. He was the quiet type. There was a woman who came from time to time, but the neighbors never saw anyone else. We haven't probed too deeply, though. We don't intend to deprive you of your job."

As I speak with Şefik, Zeynep bends down and starts taking a closer look at the corpse. Ali has stopped listening to us and goes to the table at the victim's head.

"Are these his papers?" he asks about the transparent bag on the table. Şefik nods and then feels he has to elucidate.

"His national ID card and his driver's license."

"What's his name?" I ask, as Ali removes the contents of the bag.

Ali reads off the ID card in his hand.

"Yusuf Akdağ, born in Midyat, 1970."

"Midyat. Isn't that a district of Mardin? It's a region where Assyrians live, if I'm not wrong. What does it say in the religion field?"

"Christian. Were these Assyrians Christians?"

Zeynep, studying the victim's neck, answers.

"Yes. I read that somewhere. If I'm not mistaken, they were the first Christians."

"The first Christians, huh?" Ali says, intrigued.

The pitch of his voice has risen. Is he beginning to get excited, our Ali?

"I'm not sure," Zeynep replies. "But our victim's being from Midyat better explains the filigree censer. This craft of filigree is only found around Mardin."

"So then the man's name written on the side of the Holy Book... Mor Gabriel, was it?"

"Yes, Mor Gabriel," Zeynep confirms.

"Then that's him!" Ali says with the enthusiasm of having reached a crucial conclusion. "So he's an Assyrian saint."

Noticing my expression of doubt, he rephrases.

"Most probably an Assyrian saint, I mean."

We won't find answers to these questions without consulting an expert, so we should concentrate on the questions we can answer.

"You say he was born in 1970?" I ask Ali.

He takes another look at the ID to be sure.

"Yes, 1970. Thirtieth of September."

I look at the victim as I say, "So that makes him thirty-five then. He looks older."

Zeynep, examining his eyes, steps back a bit and studies his face.

"Yeah, he looks at least forty."

"Any other information on the man?" I ask Şefik.

"There's just the national ID card and the license, nothing else. No diploma, no property deeds, no photos..."

"What, you mean no photos at all in the house?"

"Apart from the headshots, none. We haven't come across a single photo taken with family or friends."

"Interesting. What did he do, this man?"

"The next-door neighbors said he's in commerce."

Şefik answers my question and turns to Zeynep.

"Did you see the mark on his wrist?"

Zeynep hasn't seen it. "Where?" she asks.

"On the right wrist, at the pulse line."

Zeynep turns over the right hand, and yes, there it is. On the inside of the man's wrist is a mark the shape of a strawberry. "Is it a tattoo?" asks Şefik. Zeynep examines it.

"I don't think so," she says. "It looks like a birthmark." She lets go of the man's wrist. She looks up, first at Şefik and then at me. "It could also be an erased tattoo."

"An erased tattoo would be a boon to us, Zeynep, my dear. Let's find out, can we?"

"Sure, Chief. We'll check it out."

Ali is looking at the cell phone on the table. He almost touches it.

"It hasn't been dusted for fingerprints yet," Şefik warns. "Careful or you'll smudge them."

"I'm just looking. Is it the victim's?"

"Unless the perpetrator was stupid enough to forget his own phone, it's the victim's."

Ali glowers at him and is about to answer back when an officer steps in, preventing it.

"Chief, there's a man at the door. He's asking about Yusuf Akdağ."

Well this is good, a man here to see the victim.

Chapter 4
A person with so many questions in their head, they don't believe in any religion.

The man who has come to see the victim is standing in the kitchen. He sees Ali and me come in and turns towards us. The first thing I notice is a pair of big hazel eyes behind wire-framed glasses. He's young. His short blonde hair is naturally wavy and he's not so tall, but slightly hunchbacked. This is what makes him appear weaker than he is. A frail momma's boy type... Or is he? Because when he sees us, he stoops over a bit more and bravely fixes his eyes on my face, his attitude one of someone who has sensed something is wrong and is ready to take it on.

"What's going on here? Where's Yusuf Abi?"

"Have a seat," I say, showing him to one of the three chairs at the kitchen table. "We'll talk more comfortably."

He ignores my offer and remains standing.

"Where's Yusuf Abi?"

His voice is harsh, almost threatening. There was a time it would have irked me, but I don't get bothered anymore. The smell of food from the window into the apartment's airshaft is distracting. For a moment I forget about the man opposite me and remember my old home. My wife's smile, my daughter's cheerful voice... I get a knot in my throat. This small kitchen, this man with the metal-rimmed glasses, the corpse, Ali standing beside me... I feel alienated from everyone and I want to leave. Ali's question to the man brings me round again.

"Who are you to Yusuf?"

His voice is just as hard as the man's, just as domineering. The man stands opposite the door, bewildered.

"A friend... Kind of a friend."

Ali gets right up into his face.

"A friend? Or kind of a friend?"

"A friend. I'm his friend."

Without waiting longer, I join the conversation.

"What's your name?"

"Caner."

"Caner what?"

"Caner Nusayr Türkgil."

Interesting name. Ali must be thinking what I'm thinking because he immediately sticks the question, "Are you Christian?"

"No, I'm not."

"Are you Muslim?"

"I'm agnostic."

Ali and I exchange a look.

"Pardon me?" Ali asks flippantly.

"Agnostic," Caner repeats, undaunted.

"And what is that?"

"A skeptic," he hastily explains. "A person with doubts about religion, about God. With so many questions in their head, they don't believe in any religion."

"Why not just say 'non-believer'?"

"No, we don't presume there isn't a god, either. As I said, we are uncertain. A lot of questions. Neither a complete unbeliever, nor a believer."

Ali doesn't get it and thus the man rubs him the wrong way. He scowls at him, saying "What did you say your middle name was?"

"Nusayr."

"Yes, Nusayr? What does that mean?"

"It's the name of a mountain in Syria."

Now how did Syria get into this?

"Where are you from, Caner? I mean, where were you born?"

"In Istanbul. But if you must know, I'll tell you. My mother and father are from Antioch. So I'm Arab." His voice gets louder as he explains. In the end he can't take it and starts asking, "Why are you treating me this way? What are you asking these questions for? Has something happened to Yusuf Abi?"

Instead of an answer, he gets Ali's question.

"Was something meant to happen to Yusuf?"

Consternation flashes through the eyes of Caner Nusayr.

"No, nothing's meant to happen to him, but..."

"So then why would you ask that?"

As Caner panics, he panics more.

"I don't know. You... All these police... It's normal for a person to worry."

His hazel eyes seem to ask whether that's not so. I ignore it.

"How long have you known Yusuf?"

"A year... Maybe a bit longer..."

"A year, maybe longer?" Ali cuts in again, his manner a mix of roughneck and authority. "You are mincing your words, brother."

The alarm on Caner's face is turning to fear. His confidence is collapsing but he doesn't stop resisting.

"How should I know? I don't remember from one day to the next. And what's going on anyhow? Where is Yusuf Abi?"

"Yusuf was murdered," I disclose.

I'm studying Caner while I tell him. My words cause his smooth face to distort, his eyes to narrow, his lips to part.

"Murdered?"

"Yes, murdered. He's inside, a knife stuck in his heart."

For a moment he has a hard time believing it, but then it sinks in. No, I don't think it's sadness he feels; he seems surprised. Or trying to look it. I point to the chair and repeat my offer.

"Have a seat."

"When did this happen?" he chooses to ask, instead of sitting.

"We don't know yet. I can say it was hours ago."

Caner's eyes intensify, as if he's going to recall an important detail. Ali doesn't back off.

"When did you last see him?"

"Pardon? What did you say?"

Did he not understand or was he trying to buy time?

"Yusuf, I'm saying. When did you see him last?"

Caner takes his time answering, plunking down in the chair I've offered as if he's just remembered it. Then he manages to croak, "A few days ago... in Malik Amca's shop."

"Who is Malik?"

"An antique dealer. He has a shop called Orontes in the Grand Bazaar. I met him through Yusuf Abi."

"Are you an antique dealer too?"

"No, I'm at the university. Mimar Sinan Fine Arts..."

"Are you a student?"

"An assistant professor."

"A teacher, huh? So what do you teach?"

"Art history."

"What's your relationship with this Malik?"

"I help him occasionally. As an expert."

"What do you mean by expert?"

"On the subject of old texts. Texts from the first age of Christianity. I know Greek and Latin. And Aramaic."

"And Yusuf? Was he also at the university?"

"Yusuf Abi? No. He wasn't."

"Was he in antiques?"

"Not really..."

"What was he doing with Malik?"

Caner swallows.

"Yusuf was interested in old books, religious texts on Christianity," he tries to explain. "That's how we got to be friends. After hearing my profession, he wouldn't let me go."

"Wouldn't let you go."

"I mean, he's the one who wanted to meet. 'I have things to ask, I need to talk to you' he said."

"What did he want to talk about?"

"Christianity related issues."

"Particularly the Assyrians, am I right?" I interrupt.

"Yes, he was interested in Assyrian history too." He suddenly plants his eyes on my face. "Who killed Yusuf Abi?" When no answer is forthcoming, he makes his own guess. "His killer hasn't been caught."

My assistant doesn't let the opportunity slip.

"Who said he wasn't caught?" Caner doesn't get it. He looks confused and Ali spells it out. "Maybe we're talking to him right now."

Caner looks like he's been slapped. He tries to get up from the chair he's sitting on to protest.

"Me... You suspect me?"

With a hand to the chest, Ali pushes Caner to sit back down. The young man starts to defend himself as he sits.

"You're wrong. I'm no murderer. If I were, what would I be doing here?"

Ali is having fun. He doesn't much care for this intellectual snob, and continues to toy with him.

"There's a widespread belief at Homicide. Murderers return to their crime scenes."

"No, I didn't kill anyone. And why should I kill Yusuf Abi?"

"I don't know. We'll find that out."

The interrogation is floundering so I jump in again.

"Yusuf was Assyrian, right?"

"Yes, he was. But he didn't know much about Assyrian Christianity." He looks us in the face, then carries on explaining before we ask him to. "They left Midyat when he was really little. He lost his mother and father in a traffic accident. His relatives looked after him for a while, then he came to Istanbul when he was still quite young. Here he lost his ties with the Syriac community. That's why he knew nothing about them or any other Christian denomination. He wanted to learn. He would always ask me questions."

"All right then. Let us benefit from this knowledge of yours too," says Ali, rejoining the inquest. "Now, you say there are a lot of Christian denominations. Was there any sect that Yusuf didn't get on with, or was hostile to?"

I look at Ali and realize this is the first time in ages he's had such an appetite for conducting an investigation. I guess he's also finally been convinced. This time he believes he's snagged quite a riveting murder case. As I watch him, I remember my own youth. Of course I was very different from Ali. The manners I was taught, the environments I was raised in, were considerably different. By different I don't mean better, just different. Our clothes, our hairstyles, even the way we carried our guns was different. And naturally, our reasoning. Was mine better, or his, I really don't know. The world wasn't such a nice place before. Nor is it now. But back then I was more optimistic, at least as much as Ali. The same fire that burns in his eyes right now once burned in my eyes. But that was in the past, a long time ago.

"Well, why aren't you answering?" says Ali. It was as if he were asking me, rather than Caner. *So, Chief, why don't you get excited anymore?*

I also pull myself together, along with Caner.

"I don't understand," Caner says. "I mean, are you saying a Christian cult killed Yusuf Abi?"

"We aren't saying that," says Ali. "We are asking if it's feasible. Not overlooking the possibility that you are the murderer, of course."

Caner's eyebrows furrow. In a reaction neither Ali nor I expect, he warns us, "Look. If I'm guilty, arrest me. And I will call my lawyer."

Caner is right. I look at Ali to see how he'll respond. My assistant answers without hesitation.

"You can call your lawyer right now but that won't take suspicion off you. You'd need some pretty good excuses to get rid of that. Even more importantly, we need to believe those excuses."

In reality, he is talking through his hat. Even so, his words have an effect on a well-educated man like Caner. He tries to explain in a more conciliatory tone.

"I'm innocent. I am ready to help in any way I can in order to catch Yusuf Abi's killer. But I cannot understand why you see me as a suspect. My only crime is knowing Yusuf Abi. Are you going to be suspicious of everyone who knew him?"

"Yes, we will suspect everyone," says Ali. "But let's not forget that it's you visiting the crime scene. Maybe you came to take some belonging you dropped. Maybe you were going to destroy evidence..."

"You're mistaken. I just came to see Yusuf Abi. We were supposed to meet this afternoon but he didn't show up. I called him but he didn't answer, so I got up and came to his house."

"Do you realize, Caner," I cut in again, "that although you say you are ready to help us, you still haven't answered Ali's question?"

"Which question?"

"Could a secret Christian sect have murdered Yusuf?"

He ponders this a while before responding.

"I don't think so," he says, though he has doubts. "It's true that there are a lot of Christian sects. But why would they kill Yusuf? And I'm not even sure there is such a cult."

"Maybe not a cult, but a fanatical Christian..." my assistant prompts.

A glimmer appears in his hazel eyes and I think he is going to elucidate, but he doesn't. The light goes out just as quickly as it has appeared.

"I don't know... I don't think Yusuf has an enemy like that. If he does, I don't know about it."

As soon as he finishes his sentence, he averts his eyes. Is he hiding something from us or is it just the stress of the interrogation?

"Okay, tell us a little about this Yusuf," says Ali, picking up the questioning again. "Who is this man? What does he do?"

"As I said, he has no family in Istanbul. Just a few relatives left in Mardin. He opened a textile shop in Merter at one point, then realized it wasn't for him and gave it up. I mean that's what he told me."

Ali voices the question in my head.

"Where does his money come from?"

"He says he inherited it. His parents died in a car crash, you know, so when he came of age he went to Mardin, sold his vineyards and whatnot, and divvied out the money among relatives. He was left with a pretty hefty sum. I've never seen him struggle. He always had cash in his pocket."

"Was he single?"

"Yes."

"Girlfriend?"

"He had a girlfriend. Meryem."

"Meryem," I mumble, smiling. "Interesting name. Like the prophet Jesus' mother."

"Yes, like Jesus' mother." A mischievous expression appears on his face. "And Yusuf was the name of Jesus' father. I mean if we don't assume God as such."

Ali's hopes rise, and for that matter it rubs off on me.

"And?"

"No, no. This is all entirely coincidental," corrects Caner. "Yusuf Abi's interest in Christianity has nothing to do with his girlfriend's being named Meryem."

"All right. Where is this Meryem now?"

"At the bar. She runs a venue in Ortaköy called Nazareth."

"Nazar et," Ali repeats. "Strange name. People say '*Nazar etme*' to stop the evil eye, but these guys name their place the opposite, as if to summon it."

An expression of condescension towards Ali flashes in Caner's eyes.

"Not 'Nazar et'. Nazareth. It has nothing to do with the evil eye. Nazareth is the name of a place where Jesus lived at one time. He was known as Jesus of Nazareth for many years."

"Isn't that Nasıra?" I shoot back. "As I know it, the prophet Jesus was called Jesus of Nasıra."

Throwing me a look as if to ask how I know that, Caner answers, "You're right. I used the English name because that's what they call the bar." He gets that mischievous look on his face again. "That the bar is named Nazareth is no coincidence like the other names. Meryem opened the Ortaköy bar six months ago. And it was Yusuf Abi who named it."

Chapter 5
Mary Magdalene sits weeping beneath Jesus' bloody feet.

It's not hard to find Nazareth in Ortaköy. The bar is situated on one of the narrow streets that stretches from a main road which shakes with the flood of traffic all hours, down to the sea. Finding Nazareth is easy but accessing it is hard. The narrow lane, just like the avenue, is packed. Ali and I let ourselves be swept along by the crowd. Zeynep is not with us. She has stayed at the crime scene and will wait for the prosecutor and forensic practitioners, then shuttle any evidence that needs examining to the laboratory. She might just work through the night to turn up new data and shed some light on the murder. As for Caner, we let him go on the condition he doesn't leave town. Interesting young man, Caner. He's hiding something from us for sure, but for now it's hard to say if he's implicated in the murder. Ali must feel the same, because even if he doesn't really like him he lets him waltz out. And Caner might be of use to us in the case. That is, if it's as complicated as it looks... I've seen my share of cases that start out with mystifying connections, which in a couple of days turn out to be simple matters of money. Anyone outside this line of work would think we're always dealing with freakish circumstances. Murders so complex they're unsolvable, the world's craftiest killers, blood-curdling hidden intrigues... Plenty of young people passionately throw themselves into the profession in order to solve cases like these. To unravel the most complicated crimes, uncover the genuine killer, deliver justice... Such are the grand ideals of young people whose lives haven't yet been messed up, dirtied or beaten down. Of course, not everyone who wants to be police has these ideals. In this country, where money doesn't grow on trees, the vast majority enroll in the Academy to land a guaranteed job. Not only will they receive a salary, they'll carry the power of the state in those flashy uniforms. They'll do their jobs, catch criminals, and fight bad guys. But whether they become policemen for idealism or just to have a profession, the feeling won't last long. The policeman dream ends when he steps onto the streets. That's what generally happens. Doubtless there are some who maintain the first day's excitement till the end, who don't abuse the opportunities for the power they possess. But they are few and far between. The real heroes, I mean. And Ali seems one of them for now. I say 'for now' because he's so young. If he isn't killed - and daredevils like Ali don't live too long - we'll all see together what kind of policeman he'll become.

Ali walks excitedly beside me, unaware of my thoughts. Dragged along with the throng, I spot 'Nazareth' written in red neon letters in front of an old, wooden door. The 't' in Nazareth is slightly bigger than the other letters and designed as a cross. Ali pauses a moment and points at the writing as if to ask, did you see it, Chief? I nod in response. He doesn't understand why I'm unenthusiastic and he gives me a funny look. He's finally found that complex murder he's searched for all these years and wonders why I don't share his exuberance. But I just can't. Ali starts walking towards the bar again. He isn't waiting for me anymore; he hurriedly cuts through the crowd a few steps ahead of me. Still, he can't help looking back at me occasionally. "You're falling behind, Chief." I understand him. His gut is boiling; he's rushing to get at all the info on this incident as soon as he can, whereas once again I carry the anxiety of having to tell a person their loved one has died. Despite having done it many times, it's one of the routines of the job that I can't get used to. Meaning that doing a job tons of times isn't necessarily enough to get used to it.

When we get to the front of Nazareth, we're met by two hulking men dressed in black with shaved heads. One is horse-faced, the other has a stubbly beard. Not the trustworthy sort, you'll understand. They must not have liked the look of us either because they are assertively blocking the antique-looking door with their bulky frames. Ali pays them no mind, quickly diving between them. But the guys are determined, and almost double Ali's size.

"Hey, brother," says the stubbly one. "Where you going like this, without even a 'hello'?"

Ali frowns in lieu of an answer and backs up a step. There's such rage in his eyes that I think to myself *oh no, he's going to punch him*. But it's not as I fear. Ali contents himself with a nod, then pulls out his ID and flashes it.

"Police. Step aside."

The expression on the hulk's face instantly softens.

"Sorry, officer. We didn't know."

"Not officer," Ali rebuffs. He shows his ID again. "Inspector... Don't you know how to read?"

In fact, Ali is not one to care about rank, but he doesn't like the guy so he's going to torment him.

The stubbly one is grinning smugly, the horse-face has the same stupid smile.

"What's your name?" I ask the stubbly one.

"Tonguç, sir."

"Is Meryem Hanım inside, Tonguç?"

Tonguç doesn't know what to say. He looks to his friend for help but he's also unsure. What should they say now? What if the boss woman is in trouble with the police? Seeing they hesitate this much, she must be inside. Without waiting for their response, we dive in. Tonguç follows us, making a point of calling out to his friend at the same time.

"I'll be right back, Tayyar."

Once we've stepped through the door, a dim entrance opens before us. Music from within rings in our ears as we enter the corridor. It sounds like a dirge, like a really old hymn. The song sounds familiar even if I've never heard it before. My gaze shifts to the two walls running parallel up the hall. Just like the music we're hearing, they give the impression of being left over from much older times. There are pictures lit by spotlights on the walls. The lights illuminating the pictures aren't strong, but soft rather, almost like beams radiating from a divine source. I'm mulling this over when I notice that each wall is a fresco. On close inspection, I understand they are pictures of the prophet Jesus' life. Mary and the baby Jesus... Jesus being baptized by John... Jesus resurrecting Lazarus... Jesus walking on water... the Last Supper... Judas betraying Jesus on the Mount of Olives... Jesus bearing his own cross... falling to the ground... being crucified in the place they call Golgotha... women at the head of his empty tomb... Mary Magdalene's encounter with him...the consecration of the disciples... Jesus' ascension to heaven... Now don't assume by my identification of the pictures that I have any deep knowledge on the subject of Christianity. And no, Evgenia didn't explain all these either. Evgenia is Orthodox but she doesn't really have much to do with religion. She'll occasionally go to church, light a candle or two, make a wish and that's it. It was Uncle Dimitri who told me about Christianity. He was the priest at the Patriarchate in Balat. Everyone called him Papaz Efendi, but I called him Uncle Dimitri. He and his wife Madame Sula lived in a small house with a garden. In summer there were plums, apricots, and mulberries, and in winter big juicy quinces. Madame Sula made excellent quince jam. And candied pumpkin. They had no children, and in the summer months I never left that garden. I learned all about Jesus from Uncle Dimitri. No, he didn't tell me so as to convert me to Christianity. In fact, he avoided my prying questions for quite a while. I suppose he was afraid my family would misunderstand. But I was such a willful child, and I wouldn't leave the poor man alone until I'd learned every known aspect of Jesus' life. Then I forgot all about it. However, I can still recall enough of what I learned to decipher what these pictures depicted.

As we leave the narrow entrance a big surprise awaits us. It isn't a bar we're walking into but a virtual church. Ali spreads his hands in consternation and says, "What the hell is this?" He turns to Tonguç. "What is this here? A bar or a chapel?"

"It's a bar, Inspector."

"How is this a bar? It's a church, plain and simple."

Tonguç swallows, "Nah, Inspector, what church?" He tries to explain. "Alhamdulillah, we are all Muslims."

"Sure, we are Muslims, brother, but what is this? Are you doing missionary work here?"

"Would we do that? We are a people committed to our book and our flag, praise Allah. But folks love eccentric stuff like this. Books about Jesus are all the rage these days. Meryem Abla created this atmosphere. If you ask me, it's a waste of time. It didn't increase our customers or anything, but Meryem Abla wanted it like this."

As Tonguç continues his explanation, I slip inside. The columns which were obviously a late addition, the ornamented dome, fake tombstones seemingly buried in the walls... Even the seating had been arranged like that of a church. No stools, just pews. The only anomaly is the pews aren't positioned in rows but facing each other, with enough room between them to place tables of course. All the tables are wooden and humble. Suited to the overall decor, in other words. Only two of the tables are occupied. Not much demand for this place from the crowds outside, ostensibly. There are three customers at the first table and four at the other, all speaking amongst themselves. Not really speaking, more like whispering. You know how out of respect you keep your voice down in a mosque or a church? Well, like that. The bar counter is just opposite. I mean, in the place where the priest or the pastor's pulpit would be found. There's a barman in black at the head of the counter. Directly behind him is a huge window at least two meters high and one and a half wide. The intersecting slats holding the four panes together have been painted a phosphorescent red, forming a natural cross. There's even a wooden confessional box to the left of the bar. But I can't see anything like an administrative office around.

"Eh, where is this boss of yours?" I say to Tonguç.

He points to the confessional.

"Her office is behind that little room."

Ali laughs.

"So, then your boss takes confessions here."

Tonguç takes advantage of our pause and makes a slight move to pass in front of us.

"I'll let her know you're here," he says. He lifts the dark lace curtain of the confession booth and dives in. We aren't just going to stand here; we follow him in. Inside we see another wooden door opening on to another room. We walk in behind Tonguç. The area is small but better lit than the bar. A woman sits in front of a black wooden table. In front of the table are four black chairs. The woman is in her thirties, red hair, beautiful. Or not beautiful exactly, but alluring. She sees us come in and is returning our stare. It's grief in her face more than surprise. But the bar security doesn't grasp her situation and tries to explain.

"Meryem Abla, these gentlemen are police."

She looks neither startled nor flustered. She just sits there staring at us.

"All right," she says, and then in a shaky voice, "Show them in."

Her voice is shaking! Yes, this woman has been crying. The kerchief in her hand confirms my verdict.

"Have a seat," she says, sniffling. She tries to appear stoic. "I suppose you've come about Yusuf."

As we sit in the chairs she shows us, I think to myself, *so you've heard*. I wonder who from? The same question must pass through Ali's mind because we both feel the need to exchange a glance. But there's one way to find out: Ask. Ali does just that.

"Who did you hear it from?"

"What does that matter?" says Meryem. "Now that Yusuf is dead..." She can't keep it up any longer; she covers her mouth with her kerchief and starts to silently cry again.

"Yusuf is dead?" Tonguç asks in amazement. "He was just here last week."

Ali gestures to be quiet. My assistant's manner is so assertive, Tonguç smothers his curiosity and shuts up. So what if he doesn't? The only one who can answer him is Meryem, and she is currently trying to suppress the hiccups frothing up inside her. It can't be said she's succeeding. Ali and I sit in opposite chairs, Tonguç stands, and we are waiting for the woman to calm down. Meanwhile, my gaze slips over to the fresco on the wall behind her. It depicts the scene of the Crucifixion. There are four women in front of the crucifix. One is Jesus' mother, Mary. Two of the others I don't recognize but the one with red hair I know to be Mary Magdalene. She sits weeping beneath Jesus' bloody feet. Directly under the picture, in the place where art ends and reality begins, our Assyrian Yusuf's lover, the red-haired Meryem, sits crying. There's undoubtedly no connection between Meryem of Ortaköy and Mary of Magdalene, but I still can't help the strange feeling coming over me. Eventually Ortaköy Meryem recovers, wiping her nose and face with the handkerchief. When she lowers it, I have a better chance to study her face. She's attractive, but how can I put it? There's an impudent - not impudent but defiant, look to her face. Audacious black eyes, pert thick lips and a sharp nose, nostrils flaring with passion as she speaks... But it does seem there's something artificial about her nose, that most likely she's been under a plastic surgeon's knife.

"I'm sorry," Meryem stammers, embarrassed by my inquisitive stare. "Sobbing like this... in front of you."

The woman has very real grief. My stomach wrenches.

"First let me say how sorry I am," I tell her. Meryem responds with a deep sigh. She'll start to cry again if I let her. "I apologize; we came so unexpectedly. But you'll want the murderer to be caught straight away too."

Her face changes, her nostrils flare in anger again and the grief in her eyes gives way to profound hatred.

"Is it clear who killed him?"

"It isn't. We're hoping for your help."

She starts to think. Her olive-black corneas inside the bloodshot whites of her eyes are restless and twitchy like fish that don't know where they are going.

"Has he got any enemies? Anyone he's fighting with?" asks Ali. "Any money issues? Affairs of the heart?"

Meryem is glowering. She got stuck on the last four words. "It is not affairs of the heart," she says stiffly. "He had no debts and was owed no money."

Ali didn't give two shakes about her agitation.

"And this place? Were you business partners? I suppose Yusuf gave the bar its name."

"We weren't business partners," she snapped. "Whatever I have was Yusuf's too."

"Was everything Yusuf had yours as well?"

"What are you implying?"

"Not a thing. Just trying to understand."

It was time for me to interrupt as good cop.

"Did Yusuf come to the bar often?"

Meryem turns to me but she hasn't understood the question.

"What?"

Tonguç tries to answer for her.

"Yusuf Abi stopped by every other day." He pauses, his eyes fill up and he's nearly crying. "He was a good guy..." A teardrop forms in his right eye. "A man like Yusuf Abi comes along once in a blue moon."

Meryem looks at the bouncer, not with anger but rather affection, though she still doesn't cede control. The grief in her face may not dissipate, but she does return to her role of sovereign boss.

"Come on, Tonguç. Out with you." Her tone is commanding and confident. Tonguç heads for the door without a peep, but the boss calls out after him again, "Wait, wait." She turns to us. "Excuse me, I forgot to ask. What will you have to drink?"

"Nothing, thanks," I start to say.

"It doesn't have to be alcoholic. We have tea and coffee too."

"In that case, a Turkish coffee, no sugar."

"And you?" she says to Ali.

"I'll drink a strong instant coffee if you have it."

"Tell Yeşim to bring them in," says Meryem to Tonguç. Standing at attention in the middle of the room with tears in his eyes, he bows respectfully.

"All right, abla."

As soon as Tonguç walks out, I repeat my question.

"I'm talking about Yusuf. Did he come to the bar often?"

"As Tonguç said, he'd visit every other day, but he didn't interfere with my business."

"You say he didn't interfere," says Ali, "but Yusuf took an interest in everything in the bar, from the decor to its name."

Meryem is trying to keep her cool.

"He never balked at helping me when necessary. His desire to help with the bar came from me, not him. He came here, not for bar business, but to see me."

"Yet he didn't stop by for a week," says Ali. Maybe he doesn't mean it, but there's a mocking tone to his voice. Noticing the sparks of rage in Meryem's eyes, he has to clarify. "Your man said that. Yusuf last came here a week ago."

Meryem's anger seems to pass.

"True... He hasn't come by since last week." There's a brief silence but Meryem doesn't drag it out; she answers before we ask. "We argued. He got cross with me..." She can't speak. Tears well up in her eyes again. She keeps talking as she dries the wetness running from her lashes to her cheeks. "I hurt his feelings for nothing. Business was going badly. I was stressed out. I made a fuss. And he walked out. I couldn't swallow my pride and call him, and he couldn't either. If I'd known..."

The woman chokes back her tears again and we wait for her to regain her composure. It doesn't take long. Meryem sniffles and picks the cigarette packet up from the table. She tries to take one out and then pauses, holds it out to us as if she's just thought of it.

"Smoke?"

We decline. Meryem lights up. She takes several deep drags in succession. As the smell of tobacco spreads through the room, "Yusuf was pretty knowledgeable on the subject of Christianity," I say. I study her to see how she'll react to my words. "We found a copy of the Torah and the Bible in his house. And a censer."

She thinks back and smiles wistfully.

"Yes, he loved the smell of incense."

"Did he burn it because he liked it or to cover up the smell of other things?"

Meryem is speechless for a moment. Ali elucidates, very sure of himself.

"Cannabis was being smoked in Yusuf's house. Did Yusuf light incense to mask the smell of cannabis?"

"No," says Meryem. "He liked the smell, that's why."

"And you?"

"I also like the smell of incense."

"And marijuana?"

"I don't smoke marijuana. Just cigarettes."

"But Yusuf did?"

"I don't know that, but I don't."

There was no sense in bickering.

"About this Christianity, Meryem Hanım..."

Happy to close the subject of cannabis, she turns to me and I finish my question. "Are you also Christian?"

"No," she says, placing the cigarette on the ashtray in front of her. "And Yusuf wasn't religious like that either. I've never seen him go to a church or anything."

Ali picks up on the woman's circumvention and immediately poses his question.

"And yet he didn't hesitate to design this place as a church."

"Why would he? We're shopkeepers. We're doing business here. Whatever catches on, whatever the customer wants, we arrange our bar accordingly."

"I guess this time it didn't catch on so well."

"It's still early. Our customer base isn't used to it." She leans in and takes the cigarette from the ashtray. After a few drags, she explains. "And sometimes things just don't catch on."

"Did Caner come here too?" I say, getting back to the subject. "You know Caner, right?"

Meryem stays quiet a moment.

"You know, the guy from Antioch," I have to clarify. "The alleged expert on Christianity. We met at Yusuf's house. According to him, they were good friends."

"They were," Meryem confirms. "Caner's a good man. He's got a heart of gold."

"And you heard from him that Yusuf was killed, didn't you?"

As you can guess, the needling question comes from Ali.

"Yes, I heard it from Caner. Is that a crime?"

"No... Why would it be? Did he also explain how he died?"

"No, just that he was stabbed. Isn't that right?"

Meryem looks confused. She nearly loses her composure again.

"Regrettably so," I say. Meryem takes refuge in her cigarette. I use the opportunity to move on. "You say Yusuf didn't go to church often, but he was a Christian. And as I understand it, he was preoccupied with Christianity. That's how he and Caner became friends, isn't that right?"

Meryem confirms it with a nod and I carry on.

"What I'm saying is, couldn't he have had a run-in with some Christian sect while doing this research? Was there any cult or zealot among them that might have felt animosity towards him?"

Before answering, she weighs my words in her head.

"No," she says, "I don't think so. He didn't really know any Christians. The closest Christian to him was Malik."

"Malik the jeweler?"

"The antique dealer," Meryem corrects me. "He has a shop in the Grand Bazaar. Interesting guy. It's like he lives in a dream world. When he talks, you can't understand what's real and what's fantasy. He's obsessed with Christianity. He is not a normal man."

Ali's face tenses as if he's stumbled onto an interesting find.

"Not normal how?"

Meryem seems to know what's going through his mind.

"It's not what you think. Malik couldn't kill anybody. And he was very fond of Yusuf."

"How did he meet him?"

"That I don't know. In any case, you'll talk to Malik, and he'll tell you."

I take over questioning duty again.

"Didn't Yusuf know any other Christians? Maybe he didn't go to church much but on holidays, special occasions, he'd go, wouldn't he?"

"We went together once. To that big church in Beyoğlu. You know, the one past Galatasaray Lycée on the left as you go towards Tünel?"

"Saint Antoine?"

"Yes, that's the one. It's the biggest church on the street. Lovely inside, too. There are places to light candles on either side. Yusuf prayed and I made a wish."

Afraid Ali will tactlessly attempt to ask the woman what she'd wished for, I cautiously continue with the questions.

"Was there anyone at that church he knew? A priest or a father? I mean any kind of holy man?"

"I don't think so. If there was, I didn't know about it."

"Didn't you hear any names at all during your talks with Yusuf?"

As Meryem tries to recall, there's a knock at the door. A young lady carrying a tray with our coffees enters. As soon as she steps in, her eyes lock on our handsome Ali.

"Is the instant coffee yours?"

He understands the girl fancies him and puffs up, but it isn't contrived, it's innate. Well, he's young. He sees me watching him, collects himself and answers her, "The instant is mine, the Turkish coffee is the Chief's."

The young woman ignores Ali's Chief, giving Ali his coffee first before giving me mine. Meryem keeps smoking, also watching them, but she's unaware of what's taking place, most likely concentrating on whether or not Yusuf knew any other Christians. After the waitress has left our coffees in the room, along with her head, Meryem Hanım speaks.

"Actually, there was someone Yusuf often spoke of. But I don't know whether he was Christian." She finally stubs out the cigarette butt. "I'm trying to remember his name. Oh, yes! Timuçin. That's it. Timuçin. Yusuf would mention him when we talked."

"I don't think anyone named Timuçin would be Christian," says Ali, taking a sip of his coffee. "How could a Turk be a Christian?"

"You're wrong," says Meryem. "There are thousands of Turkish Christians in the world."

Ali is confused. He's ready to object but I have no intention of letting him.

"So, who is this Timuçin?"

"I don't know. In fact, we never spoke about the man. A couple of times, Yusuf said, 'I'm busy tomorrow. I'm going to meet Timuçin Abi.' And once we had a problem with permits and he said, 'I'll tell Timuçin about it. He'll handle it.'"

"Did he handle it?" I ask.

"He did. I guess Yusuf saw him from time to time. They may have had a business connection."

Timuçin could be an important link in solving this murder. Ali must be on the same page because he keeps on that track.

"But you never saw this Timuçin?"

His voice is full of suspicion, as if he thinks she's lying.

"No, never," says Meryem. She's caught his implication and her voice comes out stern. "I don't know who he is, how old, what he does..."

"Yusuf," I say, "Did he like Timuçin? Maybe you never saw him but you were with Yusuf when they spoke on the phone. You must have understood how Yusuf felt about him."

"Or maybe Yusuf told you," Ali adds.

Meryem is watching Ali, but there's no anger in her eyes anymore.

"He didn't explain much, but I suppose he was a bit intimidated. And he respected him. I always thought he was someone important to Yusuf."

I wasn't sure if this information would help us but it was better than nothing. I take my first sip from my coffee, which has gone cold. It's not very good.

"Didn't you ask Yusuf who this Timuçin was?" Ali continues.

"No, I didn't. We had an unspoken agreement. We never spoke about our past."

Without taking a breath, Ali raises his second question. "Why not?"

Meryem frowns. "I don't believe that concerns you."

I know Ali's going to insist, and maybe we'll learn something useful, but for the time being there is no sense in turning the woman against us.

"So not just Timuçin. You don't know too much about Yusuf either," I say.

"Exactly."

"See, I don't get that," says Ali, as if in protest. "How can you be friends with someone you don't know well?"

Meryem squints and scrutinizes Ali. There's no animosity in her eyes, but there is disdain, a bit of mockery.

"Have you got a girlfriend?" she asks.

Ali composes himself. I don't expect him to respond but he does.

"No."

"I'm not surprised. If you keep on like this, you never will."

He gives her a blank stare.

"Have one," Meryem continues. "Because there's no one in this world you can completely know." Ali's silence encourages her. "Tell me, how well do you know each other?" She gestures towards me. "You have your superior with you. I am sure you have courted danger and faced death with him. What your job entails, I mean. How well do you know him, for example?" Meryem shakes her head from side to side. "Nobody can know anybody. We think we know them. We believe them as far as we know them. But if we really knew them, forget about love, nobody could even be friends with each other."

I don't know how true what she's saying is, but she's obviously been around. What's also obvious is that Ali is affected, because he's tongue-tied, staring at Meryem without a clue how to respond. It's up to me to ask the question.

"You're right, Meryem Hanım," I say. "But there's something niggling at me. I'm sorry, and don't answer if you don't want to, but weren't you curious about Yusuf? Who this man really is. Who he sees, what he gets up to..."

After a brief indecisiveness, Meryem answers.

"I knew some of it, anyhow. And of course I was curious about people I'd never met, friends I'd never seen, like Timuçin. I'm sure Yusuf was also curious about my life before I met him. But he never asked and neither did I. If I must say, I was a little afraid of what I'd hear. Afraid it wouldn't match the Yusuf in my head and in my heart." She turns her gaze to Ali and confidently explains, "The truth is not always nice. Sometimes the less you know, the better."

Chapter 6
You're selling bacon in a Muslim neighborhood.

I hear that music coming from deep inside again as we leave Meryem's room. The smell of incense plays in my nose just like at Yusuf's house. We haven't taken but a few steps when Tonguç appears beside us. His huge paws are locked respectfully in front of him, his mournful eyes on our faces.

"Here, let me show you out, Chief," he says.

I have no objections to that, and in fact I'm pleased because I have questions for him.

"Okay then, let's go."

Ali, his eyes scanning the bar, leans in to my ear and says, "Chief, let me have a word with the waitress."

It's hard to judge Ali's real intention but we could use all the information we can get.

"All right," I say. "Don't take too long. I'll wait at the door."

As Tonguç watches us with interest, I take his arm and drag the man, at least a head taller than me, towards the door.

"Come on. He'll catch up with us."

Tonguç's gaze stays on Ali. Without giving him an opportunity to ask a question, I open the subject.

"You loved Yusuf, didn't you?"

Tonguç stops and looks me in the eyes.

"Yes, I did, Chief," he says in an emotional voice incongruent with his physique. "I never saw such a brave, good man. He was calm and quiet, but solid."

We continue walking. "Who do you think did it?" I ask as we pass through the empty rows.

This time he doesn't stop. He shakes his bald head, which continues to shine even under the dim light, and answers, "I don't know, Chief. That's what I've been puzzling over. Who would want to kill Yusuf Abi? And let's say they did, how would they have the guts?"

"Why wouldn't they have the guts?"

"If you knew Yusuf Abi, you wouldn't ask, Chief. He wasn't your average man. Fearless, with a firm fist, he could take on an army. No one would want to mess with him."

I picture Yusuf's muscular body lying on the sofa.

"Well," I say, "There's always someone who can outdo you. Look, they killed him too."

"It's a dirty trick, Chief. They ambushed him. They couldn't have done it any other way."

"Could it have been someone you know? Someone from Nazareth, for instance?"

He gives me a look of surprise.

"No... No, Chief, there's no one here like that. And everyone here loved Yusuf Abi."

"Not least of all Meryem Hanım."

He nods his hairless head in agreement.

"Her least of all. She went to pieces. It may seem she has a stiff upper lip, but I don't know how she's going to recover."

"Things weren't so great between them. They hadn't seen each other in a week..."

Tonguç looks around as if worried someone will hear, then whispers, "It was Meryem Abla's fault. First she asked Yusuf Abi for help designing the bar as a church. And Yusuf Abi brought that blonde guy. The university prof or whatever."

"Caner?"

"Yes, Caner. That guy rubbed me up the wrong way. One of those elitist intellectual jerks. Full of himself. I couldn't figure out what business a man like Yusuf Abi had with an asshole like him."

"Anyhow," I say, "you were talking about decorating the bar..."

"That's right, Chief. When Meryem Abla insisted, this Caner guy came over. He had this wimpy architect with him. They drew up some plans, then brought the bar to this state. I said it back then, this is not going to catch on. 'You're selling bacon in a Muslim neighborhood,' I said. But Meryem Abla didn't listen. Turned out I was right. Look around, only two tables taken. It's like this every night. When it didn't take off, Meryem Abla lost her cool. She started moaning, as if Yusuf had suggested this. Yusuf is a self-respecting man and he wasn't having it. He grabbed his coat and stormed out. And Meryem has her pride. She couldn't get herself to call him and apologize. Such a shame. They weren't talking to each other."

We've passed through the entrance and are nearly at the end of the road. However, there are a few more things I want to learn.

"Have you heard of someone called Timuçin? He was Yusuf's friend."

Tonguç gives a strange look as if hearing it for the first time.

"Timuçin? No, Chief, never heard the name. If Yusuf had a friend like that I don't know about it."

"So did you meet Yusuf here?"

"No, not here. In Beyoğlu. We were running a bar in Beyoğlu those days. I mean, Meryem Abla was running it. Cazip Bar. A low-key place. Had a set clientele. We didn't do great business but it was better than here. It was on Süslü Saksı Street. A huge venue. It belonged to a Greek foundation or something like that, otherwise we couldn't have afforded it. That's where I met Yusuf Abi."

"Did he use to come alone?"

"Yes. Or that egghead Caner would sometimes tag along. Oh, and there was a man called Malik. Skinny bald guy with a beard. Talks real articulate. He's Arab or something. A little unhinged, but rich. They say he has a shop in the Grand Bazaar. He came with him too sometimes, but he usually came alone." He smiled and nodded. "At first I thought Yusuf Abi was a cop. Plain-clothes, or narcotics. He was coming and going, you know... I thought, man, he's an undercover cop but he's giving himself away. But then when we moved we realized he wasn't. He's a total romantic."

"What about the toughness, the courage?"

"He did sport in his youth. Martial arts and such. Said he still worked out a few hours every day."

"How did you know Yusuf was tough? Did he tell you himself?"

"No, Chief. I saw it with my own eyes. Yusuf Abi didn't like to talk about himself. Now I told you our Cazip Bar in Beyoğlu belonged to a Greek foundation, right? Well there's this Kurd from Bingöl that hung out on our street. Bingöllü Kadir. He used to be PKK but then he turned informant. It could be hearsay, but it's said someone higher up has got his back."

"Someone higher up?"

"I don't know, Chief. It's just what they say. The police or National Intelligence Organization... Maybe someone else. I mean that's what I heard. Bingöllü is spilling on everything that happens around Beyoğlu. Anyhow, Bingöllü caused all kinds of problems for us. He hounded us morning and night, telling us to get out, that he was going to rent the place. Meryem Abla tried to reason with him but it didn't sink in; night after night the guy was in our bar, at Meryem's desk. Eventually she lost her temper. She gave him the boot. Bingöllü was furious. The next day he came by the bar with four men as it was about to shut. We weren't expecting him to play so dirty so we weren't prepared. I went inside at midnight as the bar was closing. I suddenly felt a pressure on the back of my neck. One of Bingöllü's men had put a gun up against it. I froze. Tayyar, our other bouncer, was no different. A man behind him and a gun to his neck, too. I was just thinking, man, who are these guys, when I saw Bingöllü Kadir. Next to him two jackals, strutting over to Meryem's desk like they were the conquerors of Istanbul. Apart from us, there were five customers in the bar: Yusuf Abi sitting alone at the table in the corner and two couples at a window table. When the couples caught on to the situation, they tried to quietly clear out. But when Bingöllü shouted, 'Sit your asses down!' the poor things tucked their tails under and shrank into their seats. Yusuf Abi just calmly kept drinking his *rakı*. Bingöllü walked towards Meryem's desk and dared her to throw him out again.

"She gave him a onceover then reached for her *rakı* and took a sip. Bingöllü saw that she was ignoring him and got even angrier. He walked up, grabbed her by the chin and howled at her, 'Talk, bitch! Why can't you find your tongue?'"

"Bingöllü had barely shut his jaw when Meryem Abla picked up the *rakı* bottle and brought it down on his head. First I heard the bottle crack, then I saw the blood painting Bingöllü's big forehead red. Bingöllü reached up to it and then stepped back while the two behind him got over their surprise and jumped on Meryem Abla. Or I should say they tried to jump her, because Yusuf Abi was on the stage in a heartbeat. I don't know when he'd grabbed the chair and swung it at the guys but I did see both those jackals go down. One of them tried to get up, but Yusuf descended on them like a hawk. He started to bring the metal frame of the busted wooden chair down onto his head. But the other one was unattended, right? So he pulled out a huge hunting knife. Yusuf's back was to the man and he was beating on the other guy. If Meryem hadn't shouted at him to watch out, the guy might have skewered him. But Yusuf scooted aside as soon as he heard her voice. The jackal's knife missed him. Yusuf swung the piece of chair at that guy too. The man ducked sideways, the chair hit him in the shoulder and then fell to the floor. The guy staggered a bit but then recovered fast. When he saw Yusuf Abi's hands were empty, he gave him a dirty smirk. He weighed the knife in his hand and attacked again. And that was the critical moment. Yusuf glided smoothly to the left, caught the man by the wrist and pulled up real hard. Bingöllü, the men, Tayyar and Meryem, the customers, me, I mean everyone in the bar heard the sound of his arm cracking. The knife fell to the floor and Yusuf Abi took a swing at him from the left. The guy hit the floor like a sack of potatoes. And he didn't get up. Meanwhile, Bingöllü wiped the blood off his face and set to attacking Yusuf. Yusuf sent him flying into the other corner with one kick. The guy who had me was in shock. He'd pulled the gun off my neck, not sure whether to shoot or not, and just stared around. I took that opportunity to turn around fast and with my left hand pushed the barrel away from me, and with a shout I headed him right in the middle of his fat nose. I saw the blood emptying from his nose and then he went down. As he was falling I grabbed his gun. I looked over and that other asshole that had Tayyar had pointed his gun at Yusuf. 'Drop it!' I shouted. 'Drop it or I will fuck you up!'

"That totally took that asshole by surprise. Our Tayyar is a sharp guy. He immediately turned round and grabbed the gun. The other guy just still looking. Now these men had come into our venue like this so it wouldn't do to let them go without decorating them a bit. Tayyar knocked him on the chin with the gun handle. He swung to the left but Tayyar didn't let up. He held him by the shoulder and kneed him in the testicles. The guy doubled over but Tayyar was still pissed. He grabbed him by the ears and this time put his knee in his face. The guy fell onto his back on the bar's polished wooden floor. Tayyar and I turned our guns towards Bingöllü, who was trying to wipe away the blood blurring his vision and keep on his feet at the same time. Meryem Abla approached Bingöllü, the broken bottle still in her hand. He lifted his right hand to protect his face, thinking she was going to hit him, but she didn't.

"'Look, Bingöllü' she said. 'I can finish you right here and now. But I'm not going to. I'll leave you in one piece so you can explain it to these cocky punks. But if you ever so much as step foot in this bar again, I'll slice you and your jackals up and feed you to Beyoğlu's street dogs.'

"Bingöllü is listening but his eyes, gleaming through their bloody lashes, are still on the broken *rakı* bottle. Meryem Abla doesn't intend to hit him. Better to scare the dog than kill him, they say. And that's what Meryem did. 'Do you understand?' she asked, walking towards him. Bingöllü backed up a couple steps. Then she shouted at him to fuck off out of there.

"Bingöllü backed up slowly then turned round and left the bar. Meryem Abla looked at us, pointed the bottle at the guys rolling around on floor and told us, 'Toss these jackasses out.' And that's it, Chief. Yusuf Abi was a sound guy."

"What happened after that? You said the police were protecting Bingöllü. Didn't he retaliate?"

"No, Chief. He didn't. He couldn't. Meryem Abla may be a woman but she also has powerful people behind her. Maybe you've heard of Burnt Fehmi? One of the old tough guys? Meryem is his daughter. She's known as Henna Meryem in their world. She can hold her own with the men. I mean, she's a pretty tough cookie herself."

"That's how she became friends with Yusuf?"

Tonguç looked embarrassed.

"That's right, Chief," he said, averting his eyes. "As you might guess, there was a love interest too."

My mind is on this hack mafia guy.

"Bingöllü," I ask, "couldn't he have wanted revenge? Once everyone's forgotten this incident and Yusuf had let his guard down..."

Tonguç thinks a moment before answering.

"Nah," he said, shaking his head. "No, Chief. Bingöllü couldn't risk it. If Bingöllü were that brave, he wouldn't have let us get away with it." He thinks. "But then... No, it's not possible."

"What's not possible?"

"Chief, you know this bar of ours in Beyoğlu?"

"Cazip Bar?"

"Yes, where all this stuff happened. Right now someone else is running it. But the contract is in our name. The men rent from us. Meryem was explaining recently that this Bingöllü had paid a visit to the man who manages it. Told him to get out and whatnot. And the man rang us. Meryem sent word to Bingöllü not to be a bastard. Bingöllü withdrew to his corner again. I mean, I don't know, this Bingöllü..."

"I understand, Tonguç. We'll look into him. Look, this is all really important. If there's anything else you know..."

"That's all of it, Chief."

I take my card out of my pocket and hold it out to him.

"Here are my contact numbers. If you remember anything, something else comes up, ring me straight away. Okay? Day or night, it doesn't matter."

"All right, Chief."

Ali catches up with us as Tonguç is putting my card in his pocket. We leave Tonguç with his horse-faced friend Tayyar and exit the bar. Outside the weather has grown frosty. A shiver runs through my body. Pulling my coat around me, I ask Ali, "So what did you find out?"

"Nothing yet, Chief. The girl's shift ends at one. I'll come pick her up."

"In the middle of the night?"

He looks at me with a teasing expression.

"Chief, did you forget? This is Istanbul, a city that lives twenty-four hours a day."

"How could I forget?" I answer, half-joking, half-serious. "But you also shouldn't forget that if you say you'll live twenty-four hours and then you oversleep, there will be hell to pay. I expect you in my office at eight tomorrow."

Like a spoiled child, he immediately retorts, "Would I do that, Chief? When have I ever been late?"

I'm about to give an answer when my phone rings. It's Evgenia calling.

"Where have you been?" she says. Her voice sounds full of reproach. "Or are you going to stand me up again?"

It bothers me having to talk in front of Ali but there's no other choice.

"Of course not, Evgenia. I'm on my way. I'm coming."

When Ali hears me say Evgenia, he pricks up his ears. Thankfully he doesn't hear what Evgenia has said.

"I know all about your 'I'm on my way's," she continues.

"No, no. I *am* on my way," I say, trying to close the subject. "I'll be in Kurtuluş in fifteen minutes."

The admonishment in her voice gives way to a sweet sassiness.

"Don't be late or the *mezes* will run out. Look, I had some shrimp *börek* made for you."

"Is there liver stew too?"

"But of course! I've got my eyes on the door; hurry it up."

As we hang up, I catch the smirk beneath Ali's mustache. As though the dog is saying, "sure, I get in trouble when I flirt, but when you do it, it's no problem.' He can't say it out loud yet, but if things carry on this way, before too long he'll take the liberty. I need to muzzle him a bit.

"What do you think?" I ask.

For a moment he doesn't know what I'm talking about. He thinks I'm referring to his under-moustache grin.

"What? How's that, Chief?"

"Meryem," I say. "Do you think she's hiding something from us?"

He immediately relaxes, the dog.

"Meryem? Actually, her behavior seems weird. Don't you think so? The man she loves was murdered. She hears about it but continues to sit in her bar. Wouldn't most people go directly to Yusuf's house?"

"I didn't make much of that. People can behave strangely at a time like this. But I don't think the woman's told us everything."

"You mean she knows who killed Yusuf?"

"I wouldn't go that far."

"Still, it's obvious she's a powerful woman. This business is not unfamiliar to her."

"Of course it's not. She's Burnt Fehmi's girl."

"Isn't Burnt Fehmi that thug who was murdered a couple years back?"

"Yep. His daughter. And she has a nickname too. Henna Meryem."

"Henna Meryem, huh? I think I've heard the name before, Chief. So then she's from the mafia world."

"And there's another guy from that world. Bingöllü Kadir. A former terrorist turned informant. Now he's playing tough guy in Beyoğlu. He and Yusuf went at it a few months back."

Ali rubs his hands together. "Go on, say it, Chief. We're involved in an organized crime case," he says eagerly.

Like I said, this kid isn't going to die a natural death.

"It looks that way, but don't go diving in head first. We're going to do everything slowly and by the book."

"Don't worry, Chief," he says, though he's already copped an attitude. He squints and shakes his head. "This Bingöllü thing sounds interesting. Why didn't Meryem mention it?"

"She didn't think it possible the guy would attempt such a thing. She thought she had totally scared Bingöllü off."

"I don't know, Chief. If it were me, he'd be the first one I suspected. Am I wrong?"

"I'm not of the same mind, Ali. This kind of men are no-nonsense. Kill someone, then mislead the police with a Torah, a Bible and such, the Christian set-up... It lacks logic to me. These guys' minds don't work with such finesse."

"But the man was PKK. If he's from the cultured team..."

"I seriously doubt it. The guy's an ordinary hatchet man. What business would an educated man have with mafia?"

"That's also true. But let's not forget, Meryem doesn't know what we found at the crime scene. All she knows is Yusuf was stabbed to death. She isn't aware of the knife handle made from a cross, or the Holy Book's underlined verses. Despite not knowing these things, she still didn't talk about Bingöllü."

There is nothing to say. Ali is right.

"The next time we meet up, we'll make our first order of business to ask Meryem about this matter," I suffice in saying.

"This Malik is an odd one too, Chief. The guy is Christian, and they say he's obsessed. Maybe he did it..."

"Maybe. Before interrogating him, it's hard to say. And let's not forget Caner."

"I think he's the first one who needs interrogating. Oh, and then there's Timuçin. This faceless friend..."

"Ah yes. Him too. We'll have to investigate all these individuals in detail." My expression is loaded as I look at my assistant. "So when I said to come early in the morning, Ali, I wasn't joking. We have a lot to do tomorrow."

"As you wish, Chief. I'll be in your office bright and early." He pauses. That impish smile appears on his lips again. "Maybe you shouldn't stay out too late either. As you said, tomorrow's going to be a hard day."

He's still kidding around, the punk. I'm not really angry with him. In fact, I enjoy this sneaky jabbing at each other, so long as it's not taken too far.

Chapter 7
Müzeyyen Senar's melancholic voice fills my ears.

Evgenia's *meyhane* is at the end of Kurtuluş Avenue, in the street stretching off to the right before reaching the square. The *meyhane* is named Tatavla, the old name for the neighborhood of Kurtuluş. Stepping in, the heat spreading from the huge wood stove installed in the center of the *meyhane* licks my face. I search for Evgenia among the imbibing night owls at tables choked in cigarette smoke. Müzeyyen Senar's melancholic voice fills my ears.

A smile spreads across my lips. This *meyhane* has such an atmosphere; from the first step inside it changes a man.

"Nevzat," says that voice I recognize so well from behind me. "Nevzat..."

It's the only voice I'd want to hear after Müzeyyen Senar's. Evgenia's voice, clear as a drop of water.

As I turn in the direction of the voice, I hide behind my back the red roses I bought from the gypsies in Taksim Square. I see Evgenia leave two middle-aged, likely Greek women at a table near the window and come towards me. She's smiling, but then I've never seen her not smile. She was smiling in Urfa, at the police station on that hot summer day we first met, and years later on that rainy spring night in Istanbul, when we met again. Or maybe she wasn't smiling, but the light in her face made me think she was. Really, Evgenia always has a light in her face. Whether the light was cast from her sandy brown hair, her broad forehead or her large green eyes, you couldn't say. Evgenia's face radiated all around as if there were a divine light inside her head. No, I'm not talking about a halo like those around the heads of Jesus or the saints. It is not an otherworldly glow, but just the opposite, a light full of life that says the world is a beautiful place. The loveliest, most meaningful and sacred light that can spread from a human body. Evgenia looks out from a light like this. And when I tell her, Evgenia says, "To a raven its babies look like hawks," rebuffing me in that charming Istanbul Turkish – yes, Evgenia speaks Turkish without an accent despite being Greek. But I can't brush it off. Whenever I see her, I want to bask for a while in her light, in the giddiness, the ecstasy of it. And that's what I do. As Evgenia approaches, I happily watch her, not missing a single movement of her body. Evgenia is coming, her light draws me in and she gives me a firm hug. I smell her subtle perfume, reminiscent of wildflowers, and then feel her warmth.

"I missed you so much," she whispers.

"Me too," I say. We stay that way for a bit. Then I notice we are standing in the center of the *meyhane*, customers watching us with curiosity. I feel strange here in the middle of the restaurant, Evgenia's arms wrapped around my neck and my right hand trying to hide the roses behind my back. If I must admit it, I'm embarrassed. Evgenia isn't in the least. She doesn't care one whit about our audience. I slowly extricate myself from her embrace. But she's not letting go. Once her body is free, she hooks my arm. That's when she sees the flowers.

"For me?"

I hold them out to her.

"Who else would they be for?"

She handles them gently, afraid to touch them, as if each rose were a living entity that could be harmed.

"They're beautiful," she coos. Her skin reflects the redness of the roses as she puts them to her face. "Thank you," she says, turning back to me again and planting a huge kiss on my cheek. Then she takes me by the hand and drags me to the table in the left-hand corner of the *meyhane*, but as she does, she doesn't neglect to needle me. "The poor *mezes* have been waiting for you for hours."

I pick up my step, wanting to escape the prying gazes of the customers as quickly as possible, while at the same time listing off my excuses to redeem myself with Evgenia.

"It was last minute business. I was just on my way... Don't look at me like that; I swear it's true. I meant to be here by seven at the latest."

"What last minute business?"

"Never mind. You don't want to hear it."

"Why don't I want to hear it?"

"Because it involves a murder, that's why." Something suddenly occurs to me. "Evgenia, what do you know about Assyrians?"

"Not much. I know a few people and that's it. Why do you ask?"

"An Assyrian man was murdered. I thought maybe you knew some of them."

"Oh, there are so many denominations of Christians... it's impossible to know them all."

We get to the table. Seeing the *mezes* dotting it, I forget all about the dead man and the Assyrian connection. A deep sheepishness overcomes me. The table is covered with Greek and Armenian mezes, from salted bonito and *topik* to *tarator* and sautéed chicory. There's samphire, roasted peppers, stuffed mackerel and dried mackerel salad, octopus, and calamari salad. And I know it won't be long before the shrimp *börek* and stewed liver will grace our table as the hot appetizers course. That's how Evgenia is. Whatever she does, she makes you feel like a VIP.

"You sit," she says. "Let me find a vase for these girls," she adds, indicating the roses.

I settle into my chair, my gaze slipping over to the carafe of *rakı*. I'm really craving it. I take two *rakı* glasses and place them side by side. I pick up the carafe and fill the glasses an equal amount. I add water to mine and the blessed substance turns as white as mastic. I leave Evgenia's as is. She likes her *rakı* neat. And as I'm filling our water glasses, my light-footed Evgenia comes to the table, the roses in a white vase with brown trim she bought last summer in Athens.

"Everyone's eyes are on the roses..." she says, placing the vase on the table. "Where do you find such lovely flowers?"

"From the cemetery at the top of Kurtuluş."

She hesitates as she's about to sit. She thinks I may be serious. That's Evgenia for you. When she loves someone, she's inclined to believe their every word. But the teasing tone in my voice gives me away. Her eyes are on my face. She knows I was joking, or at least suspects it. She shakes her head and sits down opposite me.

"You're pulling my leg. How would you get into the cemetery at this time of night?"

"Have you forgotten? I'm a cop. I go wherever I want."

For a moment she almost falls for it again. Then she breaks into laughter.

"Nevzat, you're terrible."

I hold up my glass.

"Okay then. To terribleness!"

She complies, raising her glass, but says, "Let's not drink to terribleness. May nothing ever be terrible."

"Now what have you done? I'll be out of a job."

"No you won't. And if you are, I'll look after you."

"Thank you. So what are we drinking to? To goodness?"

"No..." Her misty green eyes shift to the red roses. "Let's drink to beauty. What's beautiful is good."

I've seen my share of beautiful killers, and none of them were good, I want to say. But there's no sense in spoiling the mood.

"All right. To beauty then."

We drink. I close my eyes and savor the *rakı* burning my palate.

"Divine," I mutter. "Did you have a priest bless it or what?"

The grown woman giggles like a child.

"Priests won't have anything to do with *rakı*. Wine maybe..."

I open my eyes and look at the *mezes* again.

"The food is also great." I point at the music booth. "And Müzeyyen is singing particularly well tonight."

"Everything is wonderful tonight," she says, her green eyes planted on my tired face. "You are here, for one."

I watch Evgenia. When did she come into my life? It's like I've always known her. In fact, I remember it like it was yesterday: the first day I ever saw her, about ten years ago in that small room at the police station in Urfa, with nothing but a small cloth bag in her hand. Without waiting for the police officer who had brought her to my room to explain, she stepped up and said, "Help me." More than her words, what got my attention was how light the color of her eyes was against skin tanned by the angry Urfa sun. "Send me to Istanbul, or the Kerdani tribe will kill me."

She wasn't begging for help. She was standing in front of me with the determination of someone demanding her rights. I sat her down and tried to listen to her predicament. But there was no time to lose; she was afraid and wanted to escape the city at once.

"They're going to kill me," she'd said. "Help me get to Istanbul."

"Nobody can kill you. We'll protect you," I said, trying to comfort her. "But first, explain the situation."

She saw she had no other choice. She explained. Evgenia had fallen in love with a young Kurdish man named Murat who used to hang out in her father Yorgo's *meyhane*, I mean Tatavla, the very one we are sitting in now. Murat was the son of a prominent family from Urfa's Kerdani tribe. He'd run away because of a blood feud and come to Istanbul. He stayed with an uncle who ran a petrol station in Dolapdere. His uncle was a drinker, and he'd frequented Tatavla with his nephew. It was here Evgenia saw Murat. As soon as she laid eyes on the tall, dark, young Kurdish man, she was smitten. Evgenia's mother had died while she was in high school, and her father Yorgo didn't take kindly to this passion. When her father wouldn't condone it, it only fanned the flames. Evgenia and Murat began to meet secretly and live out their passion far from everyone's gaze. Which would have been fine, but then the day came when the wounds healed between the Kerdani tribe and their adversaries. The blood feud in Urfa came to a peaceful conclusion. Consequently, Murat was meant to return to Urfa. Evgenia hadn't wanted the man she loved to go, but Murat was obliged to.

"Come with me," Murat had said. "We can marry there."

Evgenia was very young back then. She believed life was love. Her head was in the clouds. She didn't want to hurt her father, but she knew he would never allow the marriage. For a while she was conflicted. On the one side was her father's protective gaze, his words of compassion, on the other Murat's warm hands, his thrilling voice, his dark, penetrating eyes. They say love outweighs everything, and so it did again. In the end, Evgenia chose Murat. She left her aging father and the aging *meyhane* in Kurtuluş and set off with Murat for Urfa, which she'd never seen in her life, and about which she might not even have been curious enough to look at photos. Yes, in the blink of an eye, she risked changing her entire life, and what's more, without fully knowing the man she was going to live with.

That's how Evgenia is. When she loves someone, she hands over body and soul and her smile to them. She loves someone and she believes in them to the end. Even if life with its painful experiences shows over and over not to do this, she never gives up her belief in people. When I try to warn her, she says, "What should I do? What meaning is left to life if I don't believe in my loved ones? True, there have been times those I love have betrayed me, times I've been backstabbed by those I've considered friends, people who have let me down - but I will never give up on friends. If I do that, it would be like giving up on life. What's the value of life without having and sharing with those you love? Don't get angry but, Nevzat, feeling foolish is better than being alone."

Evgenia's world isn't built on castles in the sky or half-truths. She is in fact a very down-to-earth woman. But she goes by the saying: the patience of a saint, tolerance of a dervish and faith of a monk. "Listen so that they will listen, smile so that they will smile, give so that they will give back to you." Without a doubt, she has no equal in this area. Mostly the scales tip against Evgenia, but she doesn't let it get to her. She knows people are flawed, and because she holds that truth, she also empathizes more easily.

Anyhow, let's get back to our story. When Evgenia abandoned her elderly father Yorgo and ran off with Murat to Urfa, she left behind a letter with only a single line.

"Daddy, forgive me."

Her father, who passed away before I could meet him, was a good man. He forgave Evgenia from the moment she left him, although he couldn't help being scared for her. How could he not be worried? His one and only daughter, whom he'd cherished and doted on, was marrying into a people that were nothing like them, with different traditions, a different faith and creed. Yet he knew it was love, and he knew that overcoming Evgenia's obstinacy was impossible. Helpless, he accepted the situation.

However, it wasn't long before Yorgo's fears came to pass. The moment our two lovebirds arrived in Urfa, the problems began. Murat abruptly changed. He still loved Evgenia, but the Urfa Murat was not the Istanbul Murat. It was as though, as soon as the Urfa sun touched Murat's black hair, that naive, lighthearted young man she loved turned into someone else. Gone were his bashful grin and his charming glances. Murat's face had hardened like the stones of Urfa's castle, his eyes swallowed up their sparkle like dark caves, and his body grew heavy like an old sheepdog's.

At first Evgenia couldn't understand what was happening. Murat's two-story stone house with its nine rooms and vast garden was like a fairytale to her. She felt like the princess in a fairytale. In the unaccustomed atmosphere of this magical culture that stretched back thousands of years, she spent her first weeks in a half-dream, half-reality, always weaving pleasant fantasies and seeing things in a positive light. And the people in the house treated her with esteem for a while. Remarks like "She's a guest, a foreigner, an orphan, exotic, or poor thing" would ring through the stone walls of the rooms.

Evgenia loved the women's warmth and the people's candor. The men were hard, a bit distant, but she wasn't bothered. They would get used to her and accept her, she thought.

Initially, Murat married her in an unofficial religious ceremony. The marriage recognized by the state was to come later. But as soon as the religious ceremony was performed, the spell was broken. Evgenia's welcome was over. The household immediately changed its tune, and she was expected to be like the other women in the house. Although Evgenia didn't like this, she started to do what was asked of her. Whether it was the dishwashing, the cooking, or whatever else, she did her part without regarding it as a burden. The hardest thing was only being able to see Murat in the evenings. And only when everyone retired to their rooms. Intimacy around the family was looked down on. In the end, she pulled her husband aside and spoke up.

"Murat, what is happening?" she asked.

He couldn't grasp her meaning, stared blankly at her and repeated, "What's happening?"

Evgenia tried to explain.

"Murat, don't you see? We aren't together anymore."

Murat still didn't understand.

"Why? We sleep in the same bed every night."

Evgenia calmly explained her concerns.

"Murat sweetheart, I'm not happy here. I'm living a life of imprisonment."

Her young husband frowned. "Our house is not a prison. Are my mom and my sisters living in a prison?"

In his own way, Murat was right. That's how people around there lived. But Evgenia was also right. She was born and raised in Istanbul. Until now she'd lived freely, without any restrictions.

"They are used to it," she tried to clarify. "I can't live this way. I feel constricted. I'm suffocating, Murat."

"So then we'll take a trip to Balıklıgöl Lake this weekend," said Murat, brushing her off.

That night, Evgenia understood for the first time that they spoke different languages, but it was too late. Still, she tried to hang on to hope. For the sake of the love she felt for him, she tried to bear the troublesome days and nights that grew worse as time passed, but she failed. She finally understood that she couldn't live like this. In the meantime, the preparations for the civil marriage continued. A week before the wedding, she spoke to him again. This time she was more determined.

"This isn't working, Murat," she'd said.

Murat's dark eyes were watery with sadness. That expression Evgenia loved so much settled in. He suddenly became the man she loved again.

"You don't want me?" he asked, hanging his head.

She looked lovingly at him. "I do want you, Murat. I just don't want to live here."

Her offended young husband gazed downward and his thick lips pouted.

"You don't like my family," he said. "You look down on us."

"No, I don't. I love them, but I can't live like them. Let's go back to Istanbul. We can get married there."

Murat shook his head.

"Not possible."

"Then I'm going back alone," she said.

Murat shook his head again.

"That's not going to happen. You belong to me now. You can't go."

For the first time, she looked at the man she loved in fear.

"Murat, what are you saying?"

The man she loved was as uncompromising as parched earth.

"You came here and you married me. You can't just up and leave. What would we tell people? It's a matter of honor. A question of morality, the honor of the Kerdani tribe."

Evgenia had started to cry. Murat didn't even try to comfort her. He left his unofficial Greek wife in tears and went off. Evgenia cried all night. The love she'd felt for Murat emptied her body drop by drop along with her tears. When morning came, so as not to tip off the people in the house, she took only her small cloth purse and hurried to the station where I worked in those days.

And that's what Evgenia explained to me on that hot summer morning. What she said was very clear, yet I still couldn't help but ask, "Are you sure you want to go?"

She gave me a look of indignation.

"I am sure. Do you think I'm playing games?"

I called the chief of police straight away and explained the circumstances.

"It's a delicate situation, Nevzat," he said. "The men see this woman as a member of the family. They'll make it a matter of honor. Even if we send her back to Istanbul, they'll pursue her. We need to talk to the elders and take care of this from the top."

"Who will take care of this, sir?"

"Who else? You."

"But sir, I'm homicide."

"Great. This way you'll preempt a murder. What else could you possibly want?"

In the end, I was left bearing the brunt of it again. Although to be honest, we weren't so busy at the time. There was the case of a fifteen-year-old girl who was stoned to death for getting pregnant by her uncle's son, but we'd finished our investigation and submitted it to the prosecution. Still, if I'd wanted, some petty bureaucratic jobs could crop up and I could get out of this thing. I liked the chief of police though, and didn't want to let him down. And more importantly, I wanted to help my fellow Istanbullian who had got herself in trouble for the sake of love. First of all, I needed to talk to the head of the Kerdani tribe this Murat belonged to. Here there were other rules that were possibly more important than the laws imposed by the government. Rules going back how many thousands of years. Call them ceremonial, or call them tradition, people believed in these rules far more than state law. The rules were imposed by tribes, or sheikhs, or by daily life itself. It was imperative that any officer serving in Eastern Turkey first and foremost recognize this.

Once Evgenia was settled into a police safe house, I found Nebi, the head of the Kerdani tribe, drinking tea under a pergola on the edge of a vast cotton field. His latest model BMW jeep was parked like a black stallion beneath a walnut tree.

With his pitch-dark complexion and hazel eyes flecked with green, he couldn't have been forty yet. The tips of his black moustache had gone yellow from smoking. When he smiled, he bared blackened teeth, one of which was missing in front. He jumped to his feet the moment he saw me. "I'll send word to the village. Let's slaughter you a lamb, Chief," he said. I politely declined, although I did go on to drink a couple glasses of his mouth-puckering smuggled tea. I refused the pungent cigarette he'd hand-rolled from Bitlis tobacco and started to explain our predicament. The young chieftain listened to me without surprise.

"I tell you, Murat's father Mahmut is a headstrong man," he said. "You are our elder, and the government has come to our door, so we'll talk if you want, but Mahmut won't really pay us any heed."

"So what do we do?"

"Mahmut won't listen to us, but he is afraid of Sheik Mehdi. He doesn't go against his will. Let's visit our sheik."

Nebi and I headed off together to Sheik Mehdi's house. Sheik Mehdi was sitting in the smallest room of an adobe house in one of Urfa's poorer old neighborhoods. He wore the ankle-length white gown known as an *abiye* - that's right, what the fashionistas call an evening gown is what people in Urfa call this garment - and a white cloth on his head which the locals called a *kefi*, held in place by an *egal*, a ring made of black fabric. Sheik Mehdi sat on a humble cushion spread out on a straw mat. He was very old; he looked like a natural extension of the magical, centuries-old city. He was blind in one eye, with the scar of a huge Aleppo boil on the left side of his face, yet he wasn't grotesque. From the moment he spoke, charm beamed from his face. He treated us to a bit of *mırra*, bitter cardamom coffee, before asking us what we wanted. He didn't say a word as I explained, just trained his good eye on the straw mat and listened to the situation. When I'd finished, he looked up and turned to the boy sitting in front of the door.

"Go get this Mahmut and bring him to me," he said. "And his son Murat too," he added, as the young man made for the door.

He turned to us again.

"You be on your way now too. With God's license, I will handle this. Send the poor woman back to where she's from. From now on, no one will touch her."

To be honest, I didn't believe Sheik Mehdi at first, but when Murat came to the station the next morning with a suitcase of Evgenia's things, I was convinced. Even then, I didn't immediately let Murat go. I brought him a tea, wanting to understand his state of mind, his real intentions. Murat was sad, gloomy, crushed like a boy whose honor had been broken.

"Tell me, Murat. Have you really given up this woman?"

Murat gave me a look of helplessness.

"What else can I do, sir? Our sheik said, 'This woman is Christian and you are Muslim. She is impermissible for you. Not only is she Christian, she also doesn't want you, although you want her. Have you no self-respect? Why do you want her? What kind of man are you? What kind of Muslim? What kind of person?'

"After he said that, my father jumped on me too. 'You will divorce this wife immediately,' he said. 'I do not want the woman to enter my house again.' So what could I do? I had to accept it. If God doesn't want us to be together, if it isn't permissible in the eyes of my sheik, I said I would let her go. Yesterday our sheik divorced us in the eyes of God. Evgenia is no longer my wife."

"So you've completely given up."

"I have, sir. It wasn't working out anyhow. Istanbul is one thing and this place is another. She is an Istanbul girl. She wants to go out and have fun. Here, whoever does that is called a... pardon me... a whore. I don't know whether it's right or wrong either, Chief, but that's what they say. You are here too. You live here and you see. Maybe that's just what works best for us."

After Murat spoke like this, I relaxed. Now the woman was completely free. The following day, I got Evgenia a ticket for the night bus. I took her to the bus station in the squad car. Before she boarded, she thanked me and said, "If not for you, I couldn't have escaped here."

"If I hadn't been here someone else would have helped you. You still would have got away."

"No," she said. "I know it. There was a woman next door. An Assyrian woman. She'd sometimes come over to Murat's family's house and we would have a heart-to-heart. 'Forget about Istanbul, girl,' she'd say. 'You won't leave this house alive.' If it weren't for you, I'm sure I wouldn't have."

"Well, it's over now. Go back to Istanbul and start a new life. Feast your eyes on the sea for me."

"I will," said Evgenia. "In fact, I'll do even better. I'll have a glass for you."

"Drink up. Bon appetite."

Evgenia suddenly took my right hand. She opened it up and dropped a small cross into my palm.

"This cross is auspicious," she said. "My mother gave it to me, and her mother to her. It protects people from trouble. It saved me from my plight and I won't be needing it anymore, but you are always in danger. You have it."

I looked at the cross in my palm tentatively and she misunderstood.

"If it doesn't suit you, I mean you are Muslim…"

I smiled and took it.

"Thank you so much. We need all the luck we can get."

She shook my hand and got on the bus, returning to Istanbul and her elderly father. I didn't see her for ages. Five years passed, and I also returned to Istanbul. And then a year later, that horrific thing happened. I lost my wife and daughter in a bombing. At the funeral, a woman came from within the crowd and offered me her condolences. Her face rang a bell but I couldn't put my finger on it. At that point, I didn't even know who I was myself. It was like I'd lost my mind. A few months later, they told me a woman had called. I was chasing my wife and daughter's killer and in no state to deal with anyone. But when the woman kept calling, I got curious to know who it was. It was Evgenia. When I heard her name, I realized she'd been the woman from the funeral. I rang her back and we talked. She reiterated her condolences and asked if there was anything she could do. I thanked her. Her father had also died the previous year and she was running the *meyhane* now. "I'll expect you," she said.

"I can't come these days," I told her

"You should," she said. "Don't withdraw into yourself."

I didn't heed her words. I had to find my family's murderer at all costs. But I couldn't manage. Yes, look at the irony in life. I, who was known for solving complicated murders, could not find my own wife and daughter's butcher. And the painful thing was, I wasn't sure I'd ever be able to anymore. Then about a year later, one rainy spring day, Evgenia called again. "Why haven't you come?" she asked, as if we'd just spoken yesterday. She had dropped the formal language and addressed me like we were old friends. At first I found it strange, her speaking like this, but then it tickled me. Still, I didn't immediately accept her invitation.

"I can't make it tonight," I said. "I have an investigation."

"That's right. You are a police officer, aren't you?"

"Yes, I am. Did you forget? We met because I'm police."

"Of course I didn't forget. But you don't seem at all like police to me."

"What do I seem like?"

"Like a friend. An old friend who I've been through a lot with...."

I started to laugh.

"What's so funny?"

"You never learn your lesson."

"Never learn my lesson?"

"Think about it. Without fully knowing Murat, you got swept off to Urfa by him. And now you choose to be friends with some man you've seen all of three or four times."

She didn't speak for a bit, then in a wounded voice, whispered, "You're right. Why am I insisting so much?"

She was going to hang up...

"Wait, wait," I said. "Don't take it the wrong way. Since you see me as an old friend, you have to hear me out. What is it they say? True friends tell you the bitter truth." When I got no answer from Evgenia, I continued. "This evening I have things to do but I can come tomorrow. Go on, give me the address of this *meyhane*."

I got the address and dropped round to Tatavla early the following night. From that day forward, I was a regular of both Tatavla and Evgenia.

As I ponder all this, Evgenia watches me, her eyes sparkling with curiosity, and asks, "What is it, Chief? You've zoned out. What are you thinking?"

"Nothing..." I reply, lifting my glass again. Evgenia does the same but along with the curiosity in her eyes comes a self-satisfied joy.

"Let's drink to you," I say.

She doesn't care about that; her empty hand reaches out and covers my glass. She speaks boldly as if revealing an important fact.

"Tell the truth," she says. "You were thinking about me, weren't you?"

For some reason I was shy about looking her in the eye.

"What would I be thinking about you?" I say, liberating my glass from her hand. I take a considerable gulp from my *rakı*. She doesn't drink, but rather sits staring at me, glass in hand. It's like everything we've been through since we met is flashing before her eyes.

"Nevzat," she suddenly says, her posture, demeanor and facial expression unchanged. "Nevzat, why is it that you don't marry me?"

I'm reeling as if from a heavy blow. Before my eyes, I see my wife in her wedding dress. The modest wedding ceremony at the police lodgings. The music, the people's faces. A large crowd. A lot of noise. The noise gathers into a whizzing at first and then an explosion. The crowd scatters, and from within the scattering crowd is an exploding car. My wife! My daughter! Nausea rises within me. No, I can't do this to Evgenia. I shake my head and erase all the visions, the voices and the memories. *Rakı*. Yes, I take shelter in the healing power of this magical white substance again. As I slowly sip at it, I tell myself there's only one way out, and that is to make light of it. I try to smile as I set down my glass. My eyes burn as I grin and it's as if shards of glass prick my lips but I succeed. Evgenia sees me smile, if not a flawless smile. But it's not enough, and I need a line. The kind of funny, light-hearted, playful line a man without a care in the world would say. And I find that, as well.

"I will marry you but," I say, "you'll have to become a Muslim."

I must have saved the situation because Evgenia also regains her humor and joins the joke.

"Why am I turning Muslim? You turn Christian."

After she says this, she takes a sip off her *rakı* and sets her glass down on the table.

"You're the one who wants to get married," I say, dragging the game out. "You'll have to do the self-sacrificing."

"You mean I am the only one who wants to?"

"Well, you are the one who proposed."

The gleam in her eyes suddenly gives way to sadness again. Has she discerned my frame of mind?

"I'm not joking, Nevzat." Her voice is injured. "Seriously. Why aren't you marrying me?"

I relax; she hasn't caught on. In fact, we don't really talk about the feeling between us. We don't try to analyze it. Sometimes when it comes up, we employ simple language to say we're important to each other and leave it at that. But whatever happened, Evgenia has strange resolve tonight. Perhaps she's wanted to discuss this subject for days but just jumped straight in thanks to the tension of not being able to. And it doesn't look like she's giving up. There's no easy escape from these beautiful, questioning eyes. But I don't know what to say. To gain some time I look away and point to my depleted drink.

"What about those traditional Greek table manners," I say. "You always say the Greeks are more hospitable than the Turks, but here my glass is empty and instead of looking after the *rakı*, the lady is backing me into a corner."

"All right, the *rakı* is coming." She reaches for the carafe, and as she pours, she continues. "Here you are. And here's your water." She holds up her own glass and says, "And now, to you!"

We drink together. The glasses go back onto the table. Her eyes, grown deeper with despondency, are still planted on my face. As I said, tonight there's no escape for me.

"We can't get married because..." I start, but I can't follow through. There's a brief silence. Her green eyes open inwards like a sea preparing for a storm. I try again.

"We can't marry... I mean... Look, Evgenia, what I mean is this." She listens without laughing at this preamble, without blinking, without losing interest, with the same expression on her face. This persistence of hers is ruffling me. *Because I haven't forgotten my wife, and while she's here, while I have love for her, I cannot marry you*, I want to say. Then I realize it will be unfair to Evgenia... I realize it won't really reflect the truth so much. I want to tell her, *if I marry you, what will I do if they kill you, too*. I understand that this doesn't reflect reality either and I give up. And then the words pour out of my mouth spontaneously. I struggle to explain the real issue, without knowing what it is myself. "Life is not that beautiful," I start. "Or maybe it is, but it hasn't treated me so well. Maybe it has to do with my work. Every day a murder, every day death, every day evil... When I turn round and look back, there're not so many beautiful things. There were, there could have been, but it didn't happen. I don't know, but it seems that way to me. On the other hand, despite all this, it is worth it to live. But there are very few bonds tying me to life. And you are one of those bonds, Evgenia. Missing you is a beautiful thing. Missing you is what ties me to life, one of the feelings that proves life is still worth living. If I were to marry you, if we were together every day, if we met at this table every evening, I'm terrified of not missing you. Or even worse, I'm afraid you wouldn't miss me. In that case, I would have far fewer reasons to live. I'm not talking about killing myself. I hate suicide, but I suppose in that case life would become thoroughly unbearable."

The depth in Evgenia's eyes swells. It grows big enough to embrace me, this *meyhane* and the entire world. She reaches out to touch my hand. Her hand is hot.

"Thank you, Nevzat," she says, her voice is as warm as her hand. "Thank you."

Chapter 8
Again the phone calls interrupting my sleep, again the nighttime duties.

At close to midnight I come to the humble abode in Balat I inherited from my father. I've politely declined Evgenia's proposal that I stay with her, saying I have to get up early in the morning. Poor Evgenia, she's also got used to living like this. Still, she didn't hesitate to have a go at me, raising a final glass to, "all the beautiful nights we haven't spent together and won't be able to spend together." We drank a lot but I'm not drunk, just pleasantly tipsy.

I'm entering my two-story stone house wedged between ugly apartment buildings when I run into Bahtiyar. He's taken shelter from the cold on the stoop, his large, hairy body on my doormat. He doesn't bat an eye when he sees me. He just greets me with a gentle wag of the tail from where he lies. Bahtiyar is our neighborhood dog, the lucky offspring of a kangal mother and a stray father. I say lucky because there isn't anyone on our street who doesn't love and cherish him. This is also why our friend is a bit spoiled, brazen as a cat. He stretches out and sleeps wherever he pleases, just as he is sprawled out on my doorstep now. Let him sleep, I have no complaints, but I need to open the door.

"Come on, Bahtiyar. Up you go," I say sternly.

His brown eyes train on my face and then he takes his time to gingerly get up off the mat.

"Good boy."

Whether it's the permeating smell of the *mezes* or what, he sniffs at my hands and clothing. I stroke his head. He likes being petted but I have to go inside. I leave him and take out my key. As I open the door and go in I call out, "Come on, lie down. No one will bother you anymore."

He plants his brown eyes on me again. Before long though, he sniffs at the air as if he's got a whiff of some new, intriguing odor, then descends the small stairs to the street. "Where to, Bahtiyar?" I shout after him. He doesn't answer. Whatever it is he smells, it's made him forget the cold and go on down the street. There's nothing for me to do; I close the door and climb the stairs which creak at every step. It must be freezing inside but I'm not cold. I head for the bedroom without even turning on the light. I get undressed and throw myself straight into bed. Tomorrow will be a hard day. Still, I can't sleep right away because Evgenia's words are flying round my head. Now where did this talk of marriage come from? I toss and turn, unable to find a decent answer. And then somehow I envision Henna Meryem before my eyes. She's an impressive woman, not the kind of person you meet every day. Her father, Burnt Fehmi, was an old-style mafia type who, when he died, the papers called "The Last of the Istanbul Tough Guys". Those who knew him said he was a good man. But I don't know. You'd have to ask the families of those he'd killed, too.

I guess I slept after that, and I wake up to a ringing. The bedroom is wrapped in a blue light. The ringing is inside the room. From in front of the framed photo of my wife and daughter at my bedside, I pick up the phone's receiver.

"Hello?"

"Hi Chief..." Ali's voice. "Sorry to bother you this time of night."

"Not important, Ali. What's up?"

"They've shot Bingöllü Kadir, Chief."

Bingöllü Kadir? I can't place it.

"Who?"

"The guy Yusuf fought with... You know, Tonguç explained it. And you told me. They came to attack Meryem's bar in Beyoğlu and Yusuf beat the men up..."

I'm starting to wake up and understand.

"The PKK informant?"

"That's the one, Chief. He was shot as he was leaving the bar with an individual by the name of Ferhat. Bingöllü died at the scene. Ferhat was injured."

"Did he say who shot them?"

"We haven't taken his statement yet. He's at the hospital now. But the killer turned himself in."

I'm suddenly awake.

"Meryem?"

"Close. Tonguç."

Tonguç. How many hours since we'd talked to him? He didn't look like someone about to kill a man. Meryem... Henna Meryem must have put him up to it. How is she so sure this Bingöllü Kadir killed Yusuf? What weren't they telling us? What could the PKK informant Kadir possibly have to do with a Bible and a cross? My brain goes into overdrive. During my stint in Urfa, I'd overheard some transvestites talking about how people who were previously Armenian, Assyrian or Greek changed their names under pressure and became Muslims. Could Bingöllü be one of those? Maybe his family was Assyrian but had switched religions. And Kadir had returned to the fold of his faith and his people. But the man had turned informant, working for the state. So, so complicated...

"Chief," says Ali from the other end of the line. He hasn't understood this long pause. "You there?"

"Sorry, Ali. I was thinking. Where are you now?"

"At the Taksim Station. With Tonguç."

Shall I wait for you to interrogate him, is what he means.

"Okay, I'm coming too."

As I get out of bed, I glance over at my wife Güzide and daughter Aysun watching me from the photo on the nightstand. They'd had the photo taken when Aysun finished first grade. I'm not with them. Something had come up at the last minute and I wasn't able to go. Something was always coming up. Güzide and I had had our fair share of quarrels about that. But they aren't angry anymore. They're just watching from inside the photo, and never losing their smiles. I smile back at them, knowing they'll never notice.

"You see, don't you?" I mumble. "Nothing has changed. Again the phone calls interrupting my sleep, again the nighttime duties."

They silently hear me out as always. That's fine. I keep talking, and will keep talking to them, even if they don't answer. Aysun always complained that I didn't talk much. "Daddy, you never have time for us when you come home. You never talk." Now I talk, whether or not my daughter hears. Because if I didn't, I'd go mad.

I go into the bathroom. The cold water feels nice, carrying away the last crumbs of sleep, if not the grief inside me. Back in the room, the light covering the objects in a luminous blue gets my attention again. I look towards the window and see white flecks blowing about in the darkness. It's snowing. I used to love the snow. My mother used to say that snow brings good fortune. My father, solving crosswords in the paper, would look up over his glasses and answer her, "Ask the people who don't have firewood or coal to burn about that." I felt bad for the people without wood or coal, but I still loved the snow. Now it has absolutely no meaning for me. Nevertheless, I can't resist going up to the window to look out at the street. The snowflakes float calmly down under the street lamp. A couple of streets down from ours, the rooftops of the Greek Patriarchate, the run-down older houses and the newer, ungainly apartments are covered in a fine white veil. As is the street; without so much as asking permission or giving notice, nature has spread its blanket of white over the cobblestones.

I shiver as I go out onto the street and make a beeline for my faithful old Renault. I open the door and get in, but it's even colder inside. I insert the key in the ignition and turn it and it groans once or twice. Just as I thought it wasn't going to start, the old guy gives a weak cough and then revs up.

The streets are deserted. The falling snow adds a profound sadness to the desolation. Passing over the Unkapanı Bridge, I realize this forlornness has wrapped itself round all of Istanbul, making it a part of this old, fatigued, plundered city. To the right under the bridge, the still, dark waters of the Golden Horn stretch to the Marmara Sea, with Topkapı Palace like a fairy tale under the illumination of its red lights. In front of me, the Galata Tower resembles a thick spear skewering the sky, and to the left stand Pera's misshapen buildings, as if leaning on one another. On this winter night, the same mournful solitude rains down on them all, in the form of white flakes.

In contrast to the desolation of the street, the Taksim Police Station is bustling. Even at this hour of the night, it is as packed as any betting shop at five minutes to closing. A transvestite with a bloodied face catches my eye. Two uniformed police hold her by the arms and are trying to drag her up the corridor. She is seething; her upper body is bared and the blood from her mouth trickles down between her silicone breasts to her belly. The police are having a hard time holding on to her. When they lose their grip, they fly off the handle and thwack her.

"Stop that," she cries. "What are you hitting me for?" Then she turns to me. I don't have a uniform, you know, so she assumes I'm civilian. "These dogs wanted to fuck me..." she shouts. "I swear I didn't do anything. They wanted to fuck me... I told them not for free and they beat me up. Stop hitting me! Ah!"

I am about to lay into the officers but before I can even open my mouth, Muammer's booming voice resounds through the corridor.

"What's going on here?"

I turn to look in the direction of the voice and see Muammer's huge frame.

"What's all the commotion? What is this, a three-ring circus?"

The officers stop hitting the transvestite. She lurches towards fat Muammer as if she's found her savior but the police don't let go. She sinks to her knees although Muammer is only a few meters away.

"I have a complaint, Chief. These police attacked me."

Muammer looks at her in disgust.

"Keep your voice down," he admonishes. "Say what you have to say without yelling."

She points at the two police with a shaky hand.

"But they're beating me, Chief. How can I not yell? These two have no sense of decency. They keep hitting me."

"Get up, quick," says Muammer. "Don't you have a coat?"

"It's in the car," says one of the officers. "She took it off and threw it aside."

The transvestite cuts in straight away. "I want to speak, Chief."

"Okay, but don't shout." He turns to the officers. "Get her dressed, then bring her to me."

As he turns to go back inside, he sees me. I'm in the dark so he can't quite make out my face.

"Nevzat, is that you?"

"Yes, it's me," I say, smiling. "Good luck with that."

Muammer is also smiling.

"Good luck to us all."

We clasp hands.

"You're here about the man who shot Bingöllü, aren't you?"

"Yes. Aren't you?"

"Us too, us too..." He hooks my arm and drags me towards his room, adding, "He's in a holding cell waiting for you."

"Seriously, though. How did this thing play out?"

"I'll explain," he says, turning to a blond officer standing in the corridor. "Son, make us a couple of coffees."

"Yes, sir," the blond officer says.

"Hey, Blondie. You made it with sugar last time. I took one sip then left it. Nevzat and I both take it plain, so make it accordingly."

"All right, sir. Just leave it to me."

We head for his room again.

"Well Nevzat, it's a funny case you've got here," he says, returning to the subject. "Off to a complex start but then easily solved."

"What do you mean? Tell me."

"Now when our mobile team got to the crime scene they found Bingöllü and this other person, Ferhat, both of them bloodied up. Bingöllü was already long dead, Ferhat just unconscious. Lucky guy, the bullet grazed his head, and as he went to protect himself from a second one, he must have hit his head on something and passed out. When I heard the circumstances, I said okay, the PKK took the guy out. You know Bingöllü is a PKK informant. It wasn't an hour before the bald one showed up, the one called Tonguç. He turned himself in with his weapon. Actually, I don't get it. Why would he turn himself in? It's not like there are any eye witnesses. Just the injured guy, who maybe can clear some things up when he comes around, but there's no reason for this Tonguç to surrender."

Muammer is still talking while we go into his room. As he slides his big belly across the table to settle into his seat, I sit down on one of the chairs.

"There is a reason, actually," I say. "It's a kind of mafia reckoning."

"Well, all right then." He holds out a pack of Marlboros from on the desk. "Have one."

"No thanks. I gave up. If I'm going to die, it'll be from a bullet. I don't intend to get cancer."

"I'm going to stop too, but..." he says, taking one from the pack. He's finishing his sentence as he lights up. "I have to concentrate, so I just can't find the opportunity."

The acrid smoke fills the small room as he continues.

"And then this young inspector of yours came."

"Ali..."

"Yes, Ali... He's a good kid. A bit hot-tempered, but a good kid. I didn't know he worked with you. He came in, talking about 'our case' or whatever. I snapped at him, but then I looked and your name came up so I helped him."

"Thank you. Where is Ali now?"

"He went to the hospital a while ago. Ferhat, this man with Bingöllü Kadir has come to. He's going to get a statement."

"So he's awake. That's good news."

Muammer didn't understand. He looks me in the face.

"Why's that good news? What else have you got to learn? The perpetrator came in on his own two feet. The case is closed, so what are you still curious about?"

"It's complicated, Muammer."

Muammer's pudgy face tenses up, his blue eyes narrow. He takes a deep drag off his cigarette then asks, "Or is that bald guy not our murderer?"

"He might not be. I need to dig around a bit."

"Dig away. I am counting the days till this retirement comes and saves my neck. Come to think, why aren't you retiring, Nevzat? Didn't you start the profession before me?"

"They aren't letting me go, Muammer. I should have retired years ago. Our Director Cengiz said the institution needs me. So I stayed."

"I don't buy that. The institution needs you... They won't let you go... As if you don't want to stay. You've been ready to stay all along."

"No, Muammer, I swear I'm tired now. It won't be long; a year or two and I'll pack it in."

His eyes lack conviction as he stares at me.

"I really doubt that." He takes a deep drag. "This Ali, he was with me when he called you. You didn't have to come down here. You got up in the middle of the night and came over without balking."

"I have to interrogate the witness."

"Why are you doing it? You've got a lion of a kid with you. Can't he manage? No, Nevzat, don't give me that. You don't have it in you to leave this place. Mark my words. Don't fool yourself."

As I'm getting my comeback ready, there's a knock on the door. "Come in," Muammer says, assuming it's the coffee. But it's the transvestite and four officers who come in. Two are the officers who were hitting her, the others are an inspector and his assistant.

"What's up, Ragıp?" Muammer asks.

The inspector named Ragıp steps up.

"You wanted to see this individual, Chief."

Ragıp is a big guy, but his body is disproportioned. His legs are short and his chest looks too powerful.

"Were you with them too, Ragıp?" says Muammer.

"No, Chief. I wasn't. But you know, this is my team."

Muammer glowers at Ragıp. It's apparent he doesn't like him. He nods towards the transvestite and asks, as if rebuking, "All right, what's this one's problem?"

"She hangs around a bar in Harbiye, Chief. I mean, she finds clients there, for prostitution. The bar is near Vali Konağı Boulevard. We've told her before not to use that place but she didn't listen. When the team went to pick her up, she kicked up a storm. And now she's slandering the squad."

"No, sir," she interrupts. She's covered up now; she has on a woman's fur coat and she's cleaned her face. If we don't count the slight bruise under her left eye, she looks normal. "These guys tried to take me to the park in their car. With the intention of fucking me."

"Watch your language," Muammer growls. "This is a government office. No swearing."

"Sorry, sir. I mean, they wanted to have sexual intercourse with me."

"Who is 'they'?"

She points to the inspector and his assistant.

"Inspector Ragıp was one of them?"

For a moment she doesn't know what to say.

"No, he wasn't. Not this time, but before..."

Muammer sits up testily in his chair.

"So you're lying," he rumbles, before he himself forgets it's a government building and impulsively shouts out, "I'll have your ass in a sling. Tell it like it is."

She seems to back down for a moment but then recovers.

"I'm not lying, sir," she says, pointing to the commissioner. "Earlier, Blockhead Ragıp..." She swallows then explains. "We call him Blockhead Ragıp amongst ourselves. He's fucked me and my friends lots of times." As it dawns on her that she's sworn, she swallows again and corrects herself. "He's had sexual relations with us many times. And he didn't pay a penny. And in the squad car, no less. And now these ones too."

Muammer is fuming, but what can he say? If he shouts at his own men, they'll say he took the word of a prostitute and berated them. So he laid it on her.

"Look here. You will answer what I ask. Am I asking about Ragıp? I asked you about these men."

She doesn't know what to say. Already reeling from the bashing she's had, she is completely discombobulated. She tries to explain anyhow but Muammer doesn't let her.

"What's your name?"

"Camellia..."

"Camellia, is it? Give me your real name before I lose my patience."

"Abdurrahman..."

"Ha. There you go."

Muammer takes a last drag off his cigarette and after stubbing out the butt in the ashtray, he turns his bloodshot eyes on Abdurrahman.

"Look, Abdurrahman. Right now you are speaking pretty freely, right? I wouldn't do that. You know why? Because there are cameras on the street that have got you. Because the Governor lives there. Which means, everything that goes down, it's all recorded. I'll have the cameras brought over and we'll all watch it together here like a Turkish film. If you are lying, well then..."

Abdurrahman starts to shrink.

"What is it?" says Muammer. "Cat got your tongue?"

"Sir," says Abdurrahman, swallowing again. "We're just trying to make a living. These guys are getting in the way."

"Well go make a living some other place. Is that the only place in all of Istanbul with ass enthusiasts? The country is full of perverts. You'll have plenty of customers turn up wherever you set up shop. Stop putting us in this position. Get your ass fucked somewhere that doesn't get us in hot water."

In lieu of a response, Abdurrahman hangs his head.

"Hello, do you hear me?" Muammer persists. "You are not going to that bar. Got it?"

"All right," says Abdurrahman. "We won't go there, sir."

"Fine then, off you go. We can't get two words in with my friend here."

As they leave, Ragıp lags behind. Indicating Abdurrahman, he asks, "What are we going to do with him, Chief?"

"How should I know?" Muammer scolds. "If there's room for him in a cell, throw him in. If not, send him packing."

"I swear, I don't know what to do, Nevzat," he starts to complain when Ragıp closes the door. "Those officers are innocent, I know all of them, but Ragıp? He's a right son-of-a-bitch. He'll make his way through every last one of Istanbul's queers if we let him. He's that much of a scumbag, that much of a disgrace. And with a wife like a rose. Too delicate to even look at. But the man's a sicko. What that tranny said about him was true. He's getting his happy endings at the park in the squad car. I've had tons of complaints. But he's sneaky, that bastard. I'm just looking for an excuse. As soon as I find one, I'll give him the boot."

That's how it is in our profession. You don't just deal with outside evils, you have to deal with the dirtbags among us too. And it's much harder to control the internal slimeballs than the people on the outside, because everyone knows someone higher up, everyone has a relative. Everyone approaches their fellow cops with tolerance. They want their own mistakes inside the force overlooked, so what happens here stays here.

"Yes, Nevzat, that's how it is," Muammer continues. "Now if I catch this pervert in the act, if I have him discharged, I'll make a lot of enemies. Just look what you did to your colleague, they'll say. Isn't that right?"

"Yes, but that shouldn't deter you. If we don't clean out these types, how will we convince our citizens that we stand for justice? Even more importantly, how will *we* believe we stand for justice?"

"We can't believe it. And we can't convince anyone. Not even if we clean these guys out. Nobody thinks well of us. Don't delude yourself into thinking we are the saviors of the people, the unrelenting adversaries of criminals. There's no such thing. Citizens are also corrupt. If it's in their interest, they show us fear and respect, but as soon as we've turned around they curse us. You're in here, too; you know it's always the way. Could it be better? Maybe. But everywhere in the world it's like this. Police are not loved, my friend. That's the nature of things. Play with dirt and you get your hands dirty."

There's another knock on the door, and the blond officer enters with a tray of coffee without waiting for Muammer to tell him to.

"I made it just how you wanted, Chief," he says, looking at Muammer. The foam and the dregs are just right."

Muammer nods and smiles, as if he's suddenly forgotten all that just happened.

"Gloating doesn't become you, son," he says, messing with the young officer. "Wait, let us taste this coffee first and see how it is. If it's any good, we'll gloat for you."

The blond officer hands me my coffee and water first, then gives Muammer his. We bring the cups to our lips at the same time. The coffee really is very tasty. It is probably the best thing about this cold, eventful winter night. Muammer is sipping slowly. He shakes his head with the air of a forty-year coffee addict and says, "Good job, Blondie. You're starting to get the hang of this." He turns to me. "What do you say, Nevzat?"

"Delicious. Nicely done."

The blond officer's face radiates.

"Thanks, Chief," he says before going out. After another sip on my coffee, the time has come for what I'm actually wondering about.

"Muammer..." I say. "This Bingöllü Kadir, what's his deal? What do you know about him?"

Muammer takes another cigarette from the packet and answers before settling it onto his lip.

"Like I said, he's not really that important. One of those young men from the Southeast who turned PKK informant. When there was no need left for them in the region, he came to Istanbul. He found other troublemakers here like himself and started doing small dirty jobs." He lights his cigarette and takes a series of draws off it until the air in the room is thoroughly spoiled, then continues. "The people he mixes with are all criminals. The difference between Bingöllü and them is that he's closer to us. We said not to do something, he didn't do it. We wanted information on anyone, he provided it. He was always helpful to us. But ultimately, he's a dog. He'll help you one day, put a bullet in you the next."

"So how did you hook up with the guy? Did somebody higher up suggest it?"

His thin eyebrows furl.

"Huh? No. What higher up? Don't go digging for something that's not there, Nevzat. It's nothing like that. He told us himself when we first caught him. 'I'd be glad to help you out,' he said. We told him we'd see. He informed us on a couple small jobs. That's all. You just love to pick fights with our superiors. Keep them out of it. They have nothing to do with this, friend."

"Okay, okay. You sure spook easy."

"Yeah, I'm spooked all right. My retirement's just around the corner. Just because you're a crackpot, does that make me crazy too? I'm on the home stretch. Why should I sacrifice my retirement for some lowlife rat?"

"You're pouring it on a bit thick, Muammer. Don't worry. No one can throw you out of your job."

"So you think. But if they show us the door, that'll be it for us."

"Anyhow, does Bingöllü have a file or anything?"

"A file?" He takes a drag, then a sip off his coffee. "Yes, yes," he says. "I've read it."

"If you've read it, you'll know," I say. "Is this Bingöllü Muslim?"

He finds the question odd.

"Muslim? I suppose he is. How should I know? It'll be easy enough to find out. The stuff Bingöllü had on him is right here."

Muammer reaches over and opens the drawer. He pulls out an evidence bag. From the bag, he takes out an ID card with drops of blood on it. He can't see well so he grabs the light to read it.

"The man was Muslim. Take it and see for yourself."

I take the ID and look it over. As Muammer says, it writes Islam in the religion field.

"What exactly are you trying to find out, Nevzat?"

"What I want to find out is whether or not this man's family used to be Christian. Assyrian or something."

"Assyrian? Okay, but why would they be?"

"There was another murder committed last night, Muammer. The ones who killed Bingöllü thought he did it. Bingöllü was killed because he was suspected of that murder."

"Okay, it's possible, but what has it got to do with Assyrianism?"

"The man who was murdered yesterday was killed with a knife with a cruciform grip. The man was a Christian from Mardin. And there was a Holy Book next to him. The Torah or the Bible or whatever..."

Muammer's blue eyes begin to shine.

"Wow, it's like one of those American murder movies..." The allure doesn't last. "No, no, Nevzat. We don't get murders like that. You'll see. At the bottom of this will be a simple matter of money or some woman or something." Still, he can't be sure. My words must have confused him. "Isn't that so, Nevzat?"

"It is, and I feel the same way you do, but it would be worth looking into," I say, reaching for my coffee again. Muammer also goes for his coffee, though his hand stops on the cup handle. Same as Ali, he's begun to get swept up by these murders.

"I swear, Nevzat," he says, "I don't remember reading anything in the man's file like that. We'll get the files and take a look, but I doubt there'll be any information like that in there. We'll have to see his birth records or something. Maybe this Ferhat will give us something. Let's call Ali if you want and have him ask about that too."

It's a good idea. Ali answers his phone on the second ring.

"Yes, Chief?"

"Are you with Ferhat, Ali?"

"That's right, Chief."

"How is he?"

"Good. He can talk no problem."

"There's something important we have to learn from him. Whether Bingöllü's family is Assyrian or not... Ask him, without letting on, what Bingöllü's relation to religion was. Has he read the Bible or anything? You understand what I mean, right?"

"Sure, Chief. Don't worry. And there's a matter I want to tell you about. Ferhat says he saw a woman with Tonguç. He couldn't quite make out her face but most likely..."

"Meryem," I finish his sentence for him. "Henna Meryem. The picture is clear. Get all the details, Ali. And when you're done there, come back to the station. I'm waiting for you."

I hang up and turn to Muammer.

"So, shall I see this Tonguç now?"

"That'd be good. His lawyer is going to turn up soon."

"Seriously, where is the lawyer? Tonguç turned himself in, so his lawyer should also have been here a while ago."

Muammer laughs mischievously.

"Actually, he did come. I got rid of him. Told him we sent Tonguç to the Central Station. It won't be an hour till he's back, so make it quick.

"All right. Have this Tonguç brought in and let's talk."

Chapter 9
It's the era of men who are worthless pieces of trash

Once I've promised Muammer I'll pass on whatever I find out, he leaves his room to me and goes next door. I take the opportunity to open a window and air out the room. An icy wind fills the interior. I don't have much time to enjoy the fresh air; I have to go through the possessions Tonguç had on him. I dump out the contents of the envelope Muammer's given me on to the table. A skull keychain with three keys, a packet of Camel 100s, a black Zippo, silver prayer beads, a gold neck chain, ID card and driver's license. I check the religion field on the ID first; like Bingöllü's, it says Islam. My gaze slides to the place of birth field, and seeing Malatya, I am pleased. It'll be good ammunition for the interrogation. There's nothing else among Tonguç's things that gets my interest. I stuff everything back in the envelope. Anyhow, a few minutes later the blond officer who brought us coffee shoves a handcuffed Tonguç into the room. It's really cold inside now, so, as they come in I get up and close the window. When

I turn round, I catch Tonguç's eye. He sees me and the tense look on his face dissolves. He relaxes; in fact, he smiles.

"Come on over, Tonguç," I say. "Come and sit down."

"Hello, Chief. I guess we were fated to meet again."

His voice is cheerful as if he's seeing an old friend. Like he isn't the one who took the blame for killing one man and maiming another a few hours ago. He knows that his killing a lightweight mafia boss like Bingöllü Kadir will enhance his reputation, and he thinks Meryem Abla will look after him on the inside. Also because, as happens in this country every ten years, he believes there will be a general amnesty and he'll get out in no more than three to five years. His only concern is the handcuffs on his wrists. He strains as he sits in the chair opposite mine. I point at the cuffs.

"Are they pinching you?"

A beseeching expression appears on his face.

"Really bad, Chief."

"If you weren't connected to the PKK I'd take them off," I say. I wanted him to know I was resolute in my verdict on the subject, so without waiting for what Tonguç has to say, I turn to the blond officer. "Okay, you can go. I'll let you know when we're finished."

Tonguç's mirth suddenly turns into nervousness. "What PKK, Chief? I have nothing to do with the PKK," he says before the officer has even left the room.

The officer is looking at us. I gesture for him to leave. As soon as the door closes, I adopt an uncompromising expression and warn, "Don't play games with me, Tonguç. I know who you are and why you did this thing."

"Of course you know, Chief. These men here know too. I explained everything and handed over my weapon. Yes, I shot Bingöllü and that man. Because they killed Yusuf Abi."

"Is there a child in front of you, Tonguç? Are you playing with me?"

His head's all mixed up. He hasn't got the slightest idea what I'm talking about.

"No, of course not, Chief. Why would I do that?"

"Unless you were playing with me, you wouldn't talk rubbish like this." He stays quiet a moment. I take a deep breath and ask, "Tonguç, tell me. Who is Yusuf to you? Your brother? A relative? What has he done for you? Huh? Tell me, what did this Yusuf do that you got blood on your hands for the man?"

"Yusuf Abi..." he tries to elucidate.

"Don't you tell me how Yusuf Abi was a good man," I interrupt. "You won't convince me or anyone else of that. Look here, I am your only chance. You are in big trouble. After word got out about the incident, the phone calls keep rolling in. Everybody wants you."

"Who is everybody?"

I spread my arms like a man about to lose his temper and bawl, "Who do you think, Tonguç? MIT. Our very own National Intelligence Agency. Or Military Intelligence, or Gendarmerie Intelligence... They all want you. And right now, straight away."

He's completely stunned but he still doesn't understand what I'm trying to say. It's better this way; the stress should increase slowly, first doubts and misgivings, followed by fear and panic.

"Why do they want me, Chief?" poor Tonguç naively asks.

I open my eyes wide and give him a look as if to say, give it up already.

"Don't act like you don't know."

"I don't know, sir," he says, bowing his thick neck. "I really don't."

"How is it you don't know, Tonguç? Is Bingöllü Kadir not a PKK informant? The PKK has been after him for years. He's been attacked several times too. In the end you killed the man. And you say you don't know. Do people not know why they commit murder?"

Tonguç swallows hard. His mouth must be dry to the tonsils.

"You mean they think I am PKK?"

Instead of answering, I watch him with incredulous eyes.

"You... You too?" He stammers.

I don't need to talk anymore to drag Tonguç into fear; staying quiet is more effective.

"I'm not PKK, Chief," he says pleadingly. "I'm tied to my country, my citizenship and my flag. What business would I have with those bastards?"

Leaning back, confident of the answer I'll get, I ask, "Aren't you from Malatya, Tonguç?"

Tonguç doesn't understand where this is leading. Without mincing words, he explains, "My father is from Malatya. They came to Istanbul when I was little."

"At any rate, are you from Malatya or aren't you?"

"Yes, I am. What is wrong with that, sir?"

"Tonguç, man, are you really an idiot or are you trying to pull one over on me? What's wrong with that? There's PKK there, that's what. PKK. Aren't you Kurdish?"

Tonguç's face turns white, and then red.

"Kurdish? I'm... We're Turkish."

"Don't lie to me. I'll check the registry, find out your village and bring it out."

Now what can Tonguç do?

"All right, my grandfather was Kurdish. My father knows a bit of Kurdish but we always considered ourselves Turks. Anyhow my mother is from Maraş, a full-blooded Turk, I mean. I'm also Turkish, no Kurdishness in me. Plus, is there some rule that says every Kurd is PKK? Millions of people in this country are Kurdish and yet enemies of the PKK. Am I wrong?"

I breathe the deep sigh of someone encountering a difficult dilemma.

"I don't know, Tonguç. Are you telling the truth?"

"I am, Chief," he persists. "You know me."

"Whoa, wait a minute. Where did you get that from? I don't know you. Don't you go pointing to me as a witness in court or anything."

"Why, Chief?"

"Why? Because you duped me. When we first spoke, I believed you. I thought, this Tonguç is a good man. But not twelve hours after our conversation, you went and shot Bingöllü. Whereas while you were talking to me, you didn't show any sign. Is that a lie? Isn't that how it happened? No,

Tonguç. Don't you dare call me as a witness. I'm telling you, I'll speak out against you in court."

As he slumps down, disillusioned, I give him the line that will send him into a panic.

"Whether they'll give you a trial, that I'm not so sure of anyhow."

"What do you mean? Won't there be a trial?"

"Will there? Don't you know what the counter-terrorism units do with PKK gunmen? Didn't the men who instigated this tell you what would happen to you? If I turn you over to the fight against terrorism, there's no way out, Tonguç. Once you are in there, you can forget about a trial or prison. If you explain everything and give a straightforward confession, that's another story. I mean, if you grass on your friends from the organization, or even better, you yourself take part in the operation against them, maybe they'll do something for you. Otherwise, there's no escape. There are only two ways out of there. One is the hospital, the other is the boneyard..." I get a mournful expression. "You know that."

He flaps about like a flustered child.

"You mean they're going to kill me? Without a trial or anything?"

I look away, feigning a lack of interest.

"But I have rights... I'll get a lawyer..."

"Of course you have rights. And the organization can send you a lawyer. But that's all on paper. For the people who fight terrorism, traitors have zero rights. They'll finish you off in one night. It won't even be clear whether you ever lived or not." I suddenly raise my voice. "Don't you get it, friend? You killed someone who fought for this country and the flag. You killed a patriot."

My words are even too much for Tonguç.

"Who is the patriot, Chief?" he asks self-righteously. "Bingöllü? Come on. The man is mafia. Assault and battery, pimping women, operating purse-snatching rings, that's him... How is that patriotic?"

"The man is a hero, Tonguç," I say, carrying on the game. "I just read his file. He put his life on the line to protect the soldiers in the southeast. He's even decorated." I get that accusatory expression again. "Why am I telling you this? You know it already. It's because you know it that you shot him."

"You're making a big mistake," he tries to explain. His voice is full of pain and panic, like a man having his flesh ripped out. "I shot Bingöllü because he killed Yusuf Abi. What do I care about the PKK or the Kurds?"

I stare into his face with despondency for a bit, then standing up, say, "You can tell it all to JİTEM. You haven't convinced me, maybe you'll convince them."

Afraid I'll leave, he asks, "What is JİTEM?"

I watch him from above, a disdainful look on my face. "Don't pretend you don't know."

"I swear I don't, Chief. May God strike me dead, I don't know."

I throw him a look that says he can't fool me and then say, "You know all right, but okay, let me explain anyhow. JİTEM is the gendarmerie intelligence, but it isn't legitimate like MİT. Neither the General Staff nor the Gendarmerie Command ever admits its existence. But there's quite a trail of PKK corpses wherever JİTEM passes by. Bodies killed after they are tortured... Dozens of young men like you, or even braver. Because the existence of JİTEM isn't acknowledged, the murders committed by them aren't acknowledged either. You understand, right?"

He loses all control. I can now see the horror spreading under his skin.

"And I don't suppose they'll look kindly on the killer that butchers a man who has served them all these years, as Bingöllü Kadir has."

"You're making a huge mistake, sir," he says again. "I've got nothing to do with the PKK. I swear on my life."

"So then why did you kill Bingöllü?"

Just as he's about to speak, I warn him, "Look, you are going to say you loved Yusuf Abi, but don't bother. I've had my fill of that fabrication."

"Chief..." he says. I see the resistance in his eyes breaking down. "Sir," he repeats. But he still hasn't made a decision.

"Look, Tonguç," I say. "If you tell me the truth, you'll go straight to the prosecutor's office tomorrow. You'll tell the prosecutor the facts you've told me and head off to prison like a gentleman, do your time and get out. But if you continue to lie, I won't have any other choice. I'll turn you over to them within the hour."

He doesn't know what to do. He keeps averting his eyes. I need to encourage him a bit.

"And you had a female militant with you," I say, without taking my eyes off him. Tonguç is already completely agitated, on the edge of his chair. "Who was that woman? Was she the instigator?"

After a brief pause, he says, "That woman, she wasn't a militant. She wasn't a militant and I'm not PKK."

He's begun to unravel. Still, these are critical moments and a wrong question could ruin everything.

"So who was that woman?"

He looks round the table uneasily.

"A cigarette. Haven't you got a cigarette, Chief?"

It could take some time to extricate a Camel from the envelope, and I had to keep him feeling trapped.

"First answer my question," I say. "Then I'll find you a cigarette. You can smoke as much as you want."

He looks ahead and thinks a bit. Is he changing his mind? Is he not going to confess? My increasing doubt ends with Tonguç's weak voice saying, "It was Meryem Abla."

I hear what he says well enough, but I have to solidify his defeat.

"Who?"

"Meryem Abla," he says, lowering his handcuffed hands into his lap. "The woman was Meryem Abla. And she's the one who said let's go over to Bingöllü's venue. Because she loved Yusuf Abi like crazy. She shot Bingöllü to take revenge for Yusuf. Neither Meryem Abla nor I are PKK. We have nothing to do with Kurds. You understand, Chief? We have nothing to do with separatists."

"If you tell it like it is, I'll understand. Who pulled the trigger?"

He's about to tell me the truth as I guessed it. I am so close, but then I make one mistake. I rush it and ask, "It was Meryem, wasn't it? Henna Meryem. She did it, didn't she?"

Even my accusing Henna Meryem is enough to frighten him. He looks away. Yes, he's going to lie.

"It wasn't her. I pulled the trigger."

"You're lying," I firmly rebuke. "Meryem shot Bingöllü."

"No, I did."

"Tonguç, quit lying to me. We both know very well it's Meryem who did this."

He hunkers right down into his chair. Like a slug, his stocky body struggles to retreat into the protection comprised of the merciless rules of the underground. I know it; he's not going to talk anymore. No matter how much I pressure him, I'll get no results. But I still ask.

"All right. Let's say you pulled the trigger. Explain to me, how did it happen?"

He stares at me with the meaningless gaze of a man who has been dispossessed of his honor.

"First a cigarette," he says. "You promised."

From the envelope I remove his own cigarette packet and hand it to him. He pulls one out with shaky hands. I also light it, again with his own black Zippo. Hungrily, passionately, he takes a deep drag, as if it's the remedy to all his problems and will fix all his troubles. He holds the smoke inside him for a bit and then lets it out. As the gray cloud spirals up into the middle of the room, he begins to explain, "After Nazareth closed, we came to Beyoğlu. Meryem Abla and me. There was no one else with us."

"Why did you come to Beyoğlu?"

"Meryem said she wanted to talk to Bingöllü. And I said okay. So anyhow, we came to Beyoğlu. As we were walking from Taksim to Bingöllü's bar, I asked her if he was the one who killed Yusuf. 'Who else would it be, Tonguç?' is what she said. 'Does anyone else come to mind?'

"No one did, so I told her, 'No, but how would Bingöllü have the guts to do it?'

"She said she'd felt the same way at first, but that she was mistaken. Bingöllü did have the guts. She said, 'Before my father died, he used to say that times have changed, and I wouldn't understand. He said someone pops a couple pills or takes a couple puffs of weed, then finds a bit of riffraff like himself to butcher us, and again I didn't understand. They ambushed my father and shot him,' she said, but she still didn't understand. But when Yusuf died she understood what her father wanted to say. 'It's the era of men who are worthless pieces of trash, Tonguç,' she said. 'The era of devious, treacherous people who shoot you in the back. If you look at their heights, postures and mustaches you would think they were men, but their era is one of fickle minds and hearts. The lions are dead now, Tonguç. It's the time of the jackals.'

"When Meryem Abla said that, it got to me. 'If that jackal Bingöllü was the one who did this, then it's our duty to bring his era to an end,' I told her. 'It may be the era of the jackal but the lions aren't extinct yet,' I told her.

"We walked to Nane Street where Bingöllü's bar is. The weather had got really cold but the snow hadn't started yet. When we got close to the bar, I took out my gun just in case. I loaded it and stuck it in my coat pocket."

"What did Meryem do?" I say, interrupting him.

He takes his time answering. After another drag on his cigarette, he says, "Meryem Abla saw me put the gun in my pocket but she didn't say anything. What could she say? Anyhow, we went into Bingöllü's street. The street had got pretty empty and the bars were closing one by one. When the bar and cafe lights go out, the street gets dark. It was two o'clock in the morning. As we walked up the street, I looked, Bingöllü and the bodyguard with him, I mean the man who was wounded in the incident, were coming towards us. At first Meryem didn't see them. 'Abla,' I said. 'Your guys are right there.' As Meryem looked up at them, Bingöllü also saw us. The distance between us was maybe twenty paces. Bingöllü suddenly panicked. He turned and said something to the man. The man looked at us and then reached for his waist. Now was not the time to hesitate. I pushed Meryem Abla aside and pulled my gun. Before he pulled the trigger, I did. The guy went down with one bullet. I turned to Bingöllü. I couldn't exactly see him in the dark but it seemed like his hand was going to his hip. I fired again. Then I emptied the remaining bullets into him."

Tonguç takes refuge in his cigarette again. I let him be, to smoke to his heart's content. Getting no new question from me, he says, "And that's all, Chief. That's how it happened. We have no connection to PKK or Kurds. I did this for Meryem Abla. Her deceased father helped our family a lot. He was a second father to me. And his daughter is my big sister. Bingöllü took away a man Meryem loved more than life, and I took away his life. And that's all there is to it."

He seems to have regained the confidence he lost. He says Meryem instigated it but his explanation is unclear. He'll deny this statement at the prosecutor's anyhow. And at court he'll say he spoke under duress. If Ferhat identified Meryem, especially if he saw her fire, then that's another story. To find out, we'll have to wait for Ali.

My silence makes Tonguç uncomfortable.

"Yes, Chief. If you have other questions, I'll answer them too."

"What you mean to say is, you'll make up some other lies if I want."

"What lies, Chief? I told you letter for letter everything that took place."

"Tonguç," I say, looking him in the eye.

"Don't you believe me? I swear I'm telling the truth."

"Tonguç, I've been putting people like you away since before you were in this world. So don't tell me you are telling the truth. There is some truth to what you say, but you didn't tell the truth. If a woman like Henna Meryem wants revenge on Bingöllü, she wouldn't leave it to men like you. Maybe you shot Ferhat. Maybe Bingöllü also fell to the ground in that turmoil, I don't know. But I am dead certain that you did not fire the bullet that killed Bingöllü. Meryem fired that. And in all likelihood, she went right up to Bingöllü and looked him in the eye as she did it."

He lifts his handcuffed hands and scratches his nose. There's an impudent smile on his face.

"That's quite a scenario you are writing, Chief."

He sees I'm not smiling and collects himself.

"I'm sorry, sir... I meant no disrespect."

I feel like telling him the whole speech from the ground up was disrespectful, but I change my mind.

"Where is Meryem now?"

Yes, Tonguç's round face gets confused again. The fact that I'm going to speak with her about him, that he'd given Meryem's name, that he'd partially sung, as they say, brought him back to reality. He doesn't know what to tell me.

"You aren't going to say you don't know where she is, are you? You were just together a few hours ago."

"I guess she went home, Chief. I mean I don't know exactly where she is but she must have gone home. Where else would she go?"

I take out my notebook and pluck a pen from Muammer's pen box.

"Where is this house?"

I wait there with pen in hand for a bit. There's not a peep from Tonguç.

"Where is this house?" I repeat. "Don't say you don't know the address."

"No, I know the address... Etiler, in the neighborhood of Ulus."

When I've finished writing the address, Tonguç looks at me with imploring eyes.

"Chief, I've told you everything. You're going to help me, aren't you?"

"I believe that you aren't PKK. I'm not going to give you to the counterterrorism unit. As to the other subject, don't rely on me, Tonguç. If you had told me the truth I would have helped you, but you lied."

"Chief, please," he calls out from behind me. I ignore him, but as I go towards the door to call the blond officer to take him to a holding cell, I still feel the weight of Tonguç's desperate stare on my back.

Chapter 10
An ancient pain as old as civilization.

Ali comes in after Tonguç's interrogation. As I hold a brief assessment with my assistant, Muammer does us another favor, bringing us the file of Bingöllü Kadir, whose form rests in the morgue, in an icebox colder than this winter morning. He had the file at hand of course, but on the subject of letting us read it, we think he's just made that decision. At any rate, what's important is that we read it. So with Ali and Muammer, we do just that.

Bingöllü Kadir's file tells a typical informant's story. He came into the world the third child of a poor and congested village family. He lived in a hole-in-the-wall with his mother, father and eight siblings. The five years spent at the village primary school, then the crops to be collected from the arid field, the shepherding of four or five sheep and goats, then seasonal labor. And then the arrival of the pro-PKK teacher in the village. The friendship that blossomed between Kadir and the teacher. The conversations at the teacher's house that lasted throughout the winter nights. Subjects he'd never before heard in his life, but which could open doors to a new world for him, make him an entirely different person. Discussions that explained poverty, loneliness and isolation, turning oppression into anger, making sure he felt pride rather than shame for his origins. And that is how he came to join the PKK at age sixteen. But he doesn't immediately head into the mountains. First he provides the organization information on the gendarmerie station near the village. Because Kadir is on good terms with the gendarmerie. In fact, he gets on well with the whole village. If the gendarmerie needed anything from the village, the dark-skinned, light-footed youth would get if for them in no time. That's why the soldiers loved him. That's why Kadir could come and go from the station with ease. And he gives the organization an hour-by-hour account of life in the station: how many soldiers there are, how much ammunition, when the guards relax, when they are alert, where in the station is vulnerable to attack... He reports it all to the organization in great detail. In the light of this information, the PKK attacks the station one night at dinner time. Four soldiers are killed, one of which is a lieutenant, and another seven are injured. Aware that they will suspect him, Kadir resolves to join the mountain cadre. Maybe it is what the organization wants. First, he gets guerrilla training in a camp in Northern Iraq. Not just weapons training, but how to hide in the mountains, how to fight, how to stay alive, he learns it all. As soon as he's back in Turkey, he takes part in some much-extolled actions. Raids on the station, ambushes, attacks on gendarmerie patrol, laying mines on the roads, blowing up cars with remote control... The list goes on and on. But Kadir's mountain adventure doesn't last long. In his second year of actions within Turkish borders, he is wounded and captured. Eleven friends in the same group are killed; he's the only one alive. They put him in the military hospital, where he stays for one month. Then there's the interrogation... And two days later he's back in the hospital. The excuse is that his wounds haven't completely healed. This time he stays in for a week. Then another interrogation. In the second interrogation, Kadir goes in as a faithful PKK militant and comes out three days later as an enemy of the PKK. "I've finally understood the error of my ways," he says in his statement. "The PKK has deceived us for years. They made us enemies of our government, our country and our flag." To show he's sincere, he puts a hand on a flag and a Quran, and swears his allegiance to the government. He stays true to that oath, and after the long bloody period of clashes, when the PKK is defeated, instead of returning to his village he comes to Istanbul. In the best way he knows how, I mean, with a gun and brute force, to earn a living. And not neglecting to use the opportunities that being a PKK informant brings. And this, in short, is this midnight conclusion to Bingöllü Kadir's story. It's not an unfamiliar one to me. A painful story, full of fear and regret, that begins in the struggle against injustice and gains momentum through anger and violence. The story of hundreds of young men from the Southeast. It's not only their story, but all of ours. It's an anger, regret, shame and pain which belong to us all. Pain that we don't know where, how and when will end. An ancient pain as old as civilization.

Ali closes Bingöllü Kadir's file and says, "Ferhat's statement confirms what is written here, Chief. Kadir had no connection to Assyrianism or Christianity. Their villages have been Muslim for hundreds of years."

"Is Ferhat a relative of Kadir's?" Muammer asks.

"They were cousins. They're all from the same village. And their religious beliefs are strong. There were sheiks, and those sheiks influenced their attitude towards the PKK."

"I wasn't really that suspicious of Kadir from the start anyhow," I say, pulling my coat on.

"Where are you going?" says Muammer. "Sit down; let's have breakfast."

"Let's go, Muammer. It's getting exasperating here."

"Exasperating? Man, you've been here two hours and you can't take anymore. What about us? I've been on duty exactly twelve hours!"

"You'll wait it out, Muammer. Not many days left here till retirement. Like the dervish said, "He who guards the lodge eats the soup."

We ignore Muammer's grumbling behind us and take our leave. And here we are in Beyoğlu's deserted streets. From somewhere comes the call to prayer. It's still dark out but the snow has stopped. Trying not to slip, we walk on the melting snow, the abrasive voice of the muezzin in our ears. I really don't like this wetness.

"Shall we have some soup, Ali?" I say.

His face sours, but I know he'll come to the soup shop because I want him to. Why do our tastes never coincide with this kid?

"I changed my mind," I say. "Soup will be too heavy right now. That bakery on the corner is open, the one opposite the coffee shop. Let's get some *poğaça* from there, or *börek*."

His eyes shine.

"And we can have our tea at Dolmabahçe, Chief."

By Dolmabahçe, he means the small snack bar on the waterfront between the Dolmabahçe Palace and Mosque. It's calm at this hour.

"Nice idea," I say. "Come on. Let's go."

Istanbul wakes gently like the waters of the slowly melting snow. Savoring the still empty streets, we make our way down to Dolmabahçe. We're in my trusty old Renault, but Ali is driving. The smell of the *poğaça* and cheese *börek* has spread inside. I feel hungry. Maybe Ali is too, but he doesn't show it. He is driving, while at the same time explaining what he did last night after leaving me.

"You know how I was supposed to meet that waitress last night, Chief? I killed time wandering around the bars and cafes in Ortaköy."

"So you waited there until one o'clock."

"I did, Chief. At close to one, I went to the cafe on the corner and sat at a table with a view of Nazareth's door. I ordered a coffee and started to watch the door. Before long, I saw Henna Meryem and Tonguç leave the bar in a rush. For a moment I thought about following them, then I changed my mind, afraid I would miss the waitress. I wish I'd gone; maybe I could have prevented Bingöllü getting shot."

"Or got yourself shot," I immediately goaded him.

"Well in any case, I didn't go. And ten minutes later our girl came out. I paid up and left. The girl was waiting in front of the bar. I was just about to go over when this punk rocker with dyed orange hair appeared. He had a leather jacket, an earring like a horseshoe and chains hanging all over him. At first I thought he was harassing her but I looked and the girl showed no such indication. Even in that cold, she didn't balk at putting her arms around him and kissing the guy. And what a kiss. The kind they call French, you know. I stopped in my tracks. Now I can't go over to her. She's obviously giving me the slip. If I stop her, tell her I just have five minutes of questions, I'll scare her. Meanwhile the punk will make some snide comment and I'll have to give him a beating. I realized it wasn't meant to be, so I gave up. I couldn't help thinking, if you were going to do that you could at least have left the bar earlier so I wouldn't have let the boss lady get away. But there was nothing to be done. I was annoyed; I didn't want to go home, either. I came to Beyoğlu. As I entered Istiklal Avenue, there was gunfire. At first, I ignored it. These things happen in Beyoğlu, I thought, but then when I got to Vakko, I saw the crowd in Nane Street. I remembered that Bingöllü hung out somewhere around there. I pictured Meryem and Tonguç rushing from the bar. It suddenly sank in. I dived into the crowd. When I got to the crime scene, I saw two men, one of them already dead, the other unconscious. Just then the mobile team burst onto the scene. I showed my ID and asked who the victims were, and they didn't raise any difficulties. The dead one was Bingöllü. After that I went to the station and explained the situation to Chief Inspector Muammer. While we were talking, Tonguç came in. He placed his gun on the desk and gave himself up. You know the rest."

"So what does this injured guy Ferhat say?"

"He's not aware of anything, Chief. He doesn't even know who shot him. They were walking down the street and Bingöllü told him, 'Watch out.' When he looked ahead, he saw a man and woman coming towards them in the dark. The man's hand was in his coat pocket. And before he could pull his own gun, the man pulled his out and opened fire. He was shot and he fell down. When he opened his eyes, he was in the hospital. He couldn't even recognize Meryem in the darkness. When I mentioned her, he was shocked. 'We had no beefs with her. There was one little issue but we solved it,' he said. I asked him if he knew Yusuf. He said he'd only ever seen him on the night he fought with Bingöllü. 'Yusuf really clobbered you. Why didn't you think of taking revenge?' I asked him. 'Kadir Abi warned us Yusuf isn't a man to be messed with. So we didn't mess with him. But Yusuf showed no mercy for Kadir Abi, or for me. The moment he saw us, he opened fire.'

"When Ferhat said that, I realized he thought it was Yusuf who'd shot them. But to make sure, I asked him. 'Was it Yusuf who shot you?'

" 'Who else would it be? Of course it was him,' he said. He had a huge grudge with Yusuf."

Ali's account confirmed my thinking.

"You mean he didn't know Yusuf is dead?" I asked.

"He didn't know, Chief. Would he have said that if he had?"

"He wasn't lying, right? He was aboveboard?"

"He was aboveboard, Chief" says Ali. "I mean, he looked that way. It's hard to be sure but he seemed sincere."

And so the picture in my head is completed. But I don't want to discuss this with Ali. We are already at the Dolmabahçe traffic lights, anyhow. They are red, and we stop. In front of us is the magnificent Dolmabahçe Mosque. The lights turn green and we cross over towards the mosque. Ali parks the car next to the snack counter. A young waiter sees us park and comes out from behind the counter, approaching us. We ask for two large cups of tea. I'm so hungry I start eating, not waiting for the tea. Ali joins me without any reluctance. There are two other vehicles on the waterfront. One is a Mercedes. We can't see who is inside because of the steam on the windows, but it is most likely some fat cat and his mistress. The other is an Opel with Izmir plates and a pharmaceutical company logo. The right front window is open, and occasionally a woman's hand with red nail polish flicks cigarette ash outside. It appears our friend in the driver's seat has set out on his debauchery in the company car. Our tea arrives before I get to my second *poğaça*, or Ali to his *börek*.

As we finish our breakfast and have our last tea, I notice a shy blush spreading over the snowy rooftops of the houses on the opposite shore. I turn my gaze to the sky. Beams of light filter through giant snow clouds resembling bales of cotton.

The sunlight is turning the color of the sea from milky white to a calm blue. It's so beautiful that I can't help commenting.

"Look how lovely, Ali... The messes we're dealing with while nature is creating this."

Ali, sipping his tea, doesn't grasp my meaning.

"What did you say, Chief?"

"The view, I'm saying. Isn't is beautiful?"

Ali looks out like he's seeing it for the first time. It's plain he isn't as affected as I am.

"Chief," he says. "You remember last year the corps took us to America for fifteen days? You had to be there; you should have seen New York."

Now what can I say to this kid?

"There's no need, Ali. Real love accepts no comparisons. I'm sure New York is also great but I love the city of Istanbul. Like the poet said, 'Many brilliant cities can be seen throughout the world, yet you are the creator of enchanting beauties...'"

Ali listens with interest to Yahya Kemal's lines but he doesn't understand a thing. "That's true, Chief," he mumbles, so as not to be rude.

I can't take my eyes off the sea.

"Chief," Ali says.

"Yes, Ali?"

"Chief, this Bingöllü, seeing as how he's not Yusuf's killer, the real killer..."

"Wait, Ali," I say. "Forget about murder and murderers right now... Let's just soak up this view a bit."

Chapter 11
Justice sits somewhere between the law and our conscience.

When I enter his room, I find Director Cengiz in front of the window. His back is turned and he's puffing on a cigarette, looking out the window. He knows I've come in - the secretary just buzzed him, - but he watches out the window without changing his position. He's pensive; there's something weighing on his mind.

"The snow melted really fast, didn't it, Nevzat?" he suddenly says. "Just a dirty slush left behind, and that'll be dried up by noon."

"It's normal. The first snow... My father used to compare Istanbul's first snow to fickle crushes, passing quick as a wink, leaving no trace on the heart or emotions."

"Nice analogy," he says, turning round. "What did your father do?"

"He was a teacher. Literature."

"Good vocation," he says, coming towards me. "If I weren't police, I'd want to be a teacher."

Cengiz limps a bit when he sets his right foot down. A gift from the conflict in the Southeast. He worked with counterterrorism for a long time.

"Have a seat, Nevzat," he says, indicating the chair in front of the desk. I go over and sit down. He doesn't go to his desk though. He takes another puff on the cigarette and, after putting it out in the metal ashtray on the coffee table, chooses to sit in the chair opposite mine as if he were the same rank.

"Tell me, how do you take your coffee?"

"Without sugar..."

He picks up the phone and orders two sugarless Turkish coffees. After putting the receiver down, he continues. "What happened with last night's murder?" There is no curiosity in his face or his voice.

"It's complicated. Another murder has been committed with ties to the same incident." Even this new information isn't sufficient to arouse his interest. And anyhow I can't explain anymore. "We're working on it. It'll take some time but I am hopeful we'll solve it."

"When the reports and the records are clear, I'll take a look too."

"As you wish, sir," I say.

He smiles, sincerely, like an old friend.

"No need to say 'sir'. When you think about it, you have seniority. I spoke with Director Sabri on the phone today. It seems you were classmates; you went to Vefa High School together. I didn't know that."

The Sabri he was talking about, our director general, had studied at the same high school. He was such a wimp, we had nicknamed him "Bumbling Sabri". Nobody ever thought he would be police. But we were all wrong. After law school, as if joining the force weren't enough, he even became our supervisor. Still, he is a good man. Even if politically calculating, he has his own kind of integrity. To tell the truth, he's always protected me when I've quarreled with our superiors.

"Director Sabri," Cengiz continues, "speaks well of you. 'If things hadn't gone awry,' he said, 'It would have been Nevzat in my place.' "

"Nice of him, but he's just being polite. Whenever this subject comes up, the other superintendents and directors don't say 'If things hadn't gone awry,' but rather, 'If he hadn't been so pig-headed.' "

Cengiz bursts out laughing.

"You don't mince words, Nevzat. That's what I like about you. But Director Sabri is right. This is not your place; you should have been higher up. So you don't need to call me 'sir' or anything when we're alone. If there are personnel around, that's a different story, of course. We have to address each other by procedure out of respect for the institution."

"I understand, thanks."

He watches me with the same cordial smile on his face.

"Do you believe in laws, Nevzat?"

Now what was this man getting at?

"You mean that laws ensure justice?"

"Let's say that. Do you believe that laws ensure justice?"

"I know that law and justice are two separate things. That even if laws exist to uphold justice, most of the time they don't succeed. Or rather, every day I learn through experience that it's not like that. Because there is no perfect law. Maybe that's why laws keep changing. Maybe they'll always change. I suppose justice sits somewhere between the law and our conscience. That's why laws alone are not enough to ensure justice. But in order to ensure justice, we have no other recourse but to believe in the law."

"True," he chimes in. "Because if everyone defines guilt, criminality and punishment however they want, it would be anarchy. We'd be swimming in criminality. As you say, justice cannot be served solely through law. The law is a fuzzy and flexible thing that can be bent however you like. Just like science, yes, science... And while we're at it, think about criminal science. These days we say we all need to use these methods to fight criminality. Which is fine but, criminalistic method, I mean even when we use science, we can't avoid reaching false conclusions. Let me tell you about an incident that comes to mind.

"Years ago I was serving in Kayseri. There was an interesting murder case there. A fifteen-year-old boy stabbed a sixty-year-old woman to death. I personally questioned the boy. He was still under the effects of the incident and he couldn't really speak. Anyhow, we calmed him down. He said the woman was their neighbor and from time to time he'd help her with her shopping. The day of the incident, the woman asked the boy to pick her up some bread. As always, he did what she requested. When he brought it, she invited him in. The boy saw no harm in this and accepted the invite, but when he went inside the woman started to grope him. The boy wanted to leave, but the woman pulled out a bread knife and wouldn't let him. 'You are going to be with me,' she started to threaten. The boy resisted, he tried to take the knife off her and during the struggle his left shoulder was wounded. The boy, in pain and losing control, grabbed the knife from the woman and started stabbing away. He killed her.

"We examined the scene, went over it with a fine-tooth comb using methods of criminology. We checked if the boy had slept with the woman, who the murder weapon belonged to, whether the boy's wound was self-inflicted, and whether the victim had ever molested anybody else. We learned that she was a bit of a floozy and that she'd previously had a relationship with the son of the corner grocer. As for the boy, we found out his record was squeaky clean, and that he was much loved. It turned out what he said came pretty close to the truth. Which is what I'd thought. But there was a middle-aged police officer named Tahsin on the force who said the boy was lying. 'Did you notice his eyes while he was speaking? He was supposedly looking at you, but he was seeing something else. The kid's not in earnest. I don't think things happened the way he says they did.' So I asked Tahsin, 'How did it happen then?' He couldn't explain. Tahsin's was just intuition.

In any case, the boy ultimately got off with self-defense.

"Six years went by and I was assigned to Mardin. It was the time of terrorism; there was no sleep, and you were always on your feet, operation after operation. One night we were having a meal on the mountainside and we spread out some old newspapers. A news item caught my eye. Or rather a photograph. A young man of about twenty years. Something seemed familiar. I read the story in order to jog my memory. It said that the individual in the photo had called the neighbor's eight-year-old daughter to his house and, after raping her, he'd murdered her. As I read the news I recognized the man in the photo. It was the murder suspect from Kayseri. Had Tahsin been right all along? If he was, we'd made a big mistake, even having used science and the law. Whether out of remorse or a desire to know, I kept the incident in my head for months. While I was on leave once, I dropped by Kayseri. I have friends at the station. I asked them about the incident but they couldn't exactly remember. I didn't think twice about checking the court files. The boy's lawyer, leaning on a psychological evaluation, had said, 'Years ago, my client suffered a sexual assault while he was not yet of age. He was compelled to kill the person who was molesting him. This is a huge trauma for a child so young. The psychological state of my client broke down as a result of this trauma, and he was unable to use his mental faculties. It is for this reason that he needs hospital treatment, rather than incarceration.'

"In the end the court, at the defense's request, sent our killer to a hospital. After that I don't know. Whether he improved and got reintegrated into society or was plotting to rape and murder another neighbor's daughter is unclear. If the latter was true, it means Tahsin was right. If we had taken his opinion into account, that girl would be alive today. But we'd disregarded Tahsin's intuition. It's why in our profession, I trust people first and foremost. Science and law are indispensable, of course, but above all we need people with the same perspective who we can completely trust."

While he carries on, excited at having the floor, there's a knock on the door. "Come in!" Cengiz sternly shouts out, annoyed that his story is interrupted.

An officer with a tray of coffee appears at the door. Seeing the coffee, he calms down and leans back. It's obvious he doesn't want to talk in front of the officer. As he sets our coffees down on a side table, I try to figure out just why Cengiz has explained all this to me. What is he getting at? Does he think we aren't collaborating enough? After a speech like this, is he going to say I'm not in tune with them anymore?

It's possible. If that's how he feels, are they going to have me retire, or will they prefer to give me another try after this warning? When the officer leaves, Cengiz doesn't immediately start up again. He gets a fresh cigarette, then reaches out and takes a sip of his coffee. I just watch him. As he places his coffee back on the table, he says, "You are wondering why I'm telling you all this."

"I suppose it's to do with our working together..."

"Yes, that's right. Two years ago, we met up in this room. You remember, right?"

"Of course I remember."

"Then you'll remember what we talked about. You were supposed to retire, but I asked you if you wanted to stay and you said you did. Without giving it much thought, you stayed. And that's a good thing. We've had some successes, but..."

As he speaks, I say to myself, all right, this is as far as it goes. He thinks the time has come for me to quit. Who doesn't think that? Look, isn't Evgenia also saying I should quit my job and marry her? She didn't exactly tell me to quit; she just asked why I didn't marry her. But doesn't it all amount to the same thing? And to be honest, I was tired now too. It was beyond time to pass the baton to younger men. Fine, then why did it leave such a bad taste in my mouth? Why was it bothering me?

"We've solved a good many complex murders together," Cengiz continues. "Or rather, you and your team have."

As I wait for him to say, *Thank you for your service but we need new blood*, he says, "But our work is not done yet. I think the police force needs someone in Istanbul with your experience. Experienced people are not easily reared. The ones we do bring up don't know the people of the city they work in. You know this city, these people, neighborhoods, streets... the soul of this city, I mean. That's why I'm talking to you. In the days ahead, the police force is expecting new regulations and task distribution. I'd like you to keep your post. But I don't want to be unfair to you. You think you are tired and all. So this time I'm going to ask. What do you say to staying on with us a few more years?"

My discomfort disappears in a heartbeat and all the night's exhaustion seems to just fly away. I worry that Cengiz will see my enthusiasm, my delight. Instead of answering straight away, I reach out to my coffee cup and take a small sip. After the coffee I had last night, this is dishwater, but who cares? My heart is beating like a child's on the way to an amusement park. It's not like this happiness doesn't scare me deep down as well; this job will end, if not today then a few years later, and I'll retire. I have to prepare myself for that conclusion. But you see how I am. Most of the time, when things come at me, when murders become unbearable, when I face evil in its purest form, I feel like dropping everyone and everything and running away. It's genuinely what I want. But when it comes to my leaving the profession, this is how it goes; I freeze up, and I feel this fear, this sorrow. Maybe not everyone in the police force is like me. Maybe I can't give up the job straight away because there is no other job I can do. Our vocation is not an easy one. I know a lot of other people who have retired and gone on their way, or like Tubby Muammer, whose retirement can't come soon enough for him. I guess there is something wrong with me. Cengiz notes my continued silence and concern spreads across his long, thin face. "You aren't going to tell me this is as far as it goes for you, are you?" he says, placing his cigarette on the ashtray.

I'm not going to say that, but I'd do well not to advertise my delight either. Also, it's the perfect time to assert that for a while now I haven't agreed with something I've sensed in Cengiz's behavior. Otherwise this "yes" could be construed as my approval of his every opinion.

"No, I won't throw in the towel. I will happily keep the post..."

Cengiz sees me pause. "But..." he says, waiting for an explanation.

"But only under the condition it's kept within the bounds of professionalism... Here's what I mean, Cengiz. Two years ago, we formed a team at homicide. Me, Ali and Zeynep. And as you say, we were a success. I don't have any grievances with this team. I am completely happy with both Ali and Zeynep. And I've had no problems with you either. But in truth, no supervisor or manager is falling over backwards to work with me. It is blatantly clear that I am out of favor. Knowing this, you've still accepted working with me. What's more, you've always treated me with tolerance, and I should thank you for that. But as far as I understand, your tenure is on the agenda. You know, you said new regulations and task distribution are expected. Actually, that's what your words mean." I ask the same question with my eyes. "Am I wrong?"

He smiles, reaches out and takes his cigarette from the ashtray, and before settling it between his lips, answers, "You aren't wrong. I'm not going to hide it from you."

"Seeing as we're both being open with each other, I want you to know this. You know me now. I don't have my eye on management or directorship. I like the job I'm doing now. If I'm going to stay, this should be what I do. I don't embrace approaches like, 'We are a team and we need to look out for each other.' Solving murders, catching criminals, I mean team fieldwork, sure. But politics inside the police force, acting as bedfellows, being someone or other's man and that business, I'm sorry, but I'm not in. Throughout my professional life, I've kept out of those things, and I'll keep out of them from now on too."

Cengiz takes one deep puff after the next as he listens to me. Perhaps he's going to say, 'Enough already. I'm in no mood to put up with your capriciousness. If you don't want this, we'll pack you in.' But Cengiz does nothing of the sort. Once the smoke around his face has thinned, I make out a gleam of admiration in his eye. I realize he appreciates my attitude, but he doesn't want it to be forgotten that he's the one in charge here. So that's why he also doesn't hesitate to reproach me.

"Come on, Nevzat. Has anybody ever asked for anything like that from you? My only aim is for you to stay on the job. And I don't like insider politics or clique forming either."

I don't let him continue.

"Then there's no problem. I'm on the job. Sorry I spoke to you this way but I had to get it out in the open."

"No need to apologize, Nevzat. I'm happy you're staying." Then he adds, insinuatingly, "But if there is a promotion, you wouldn't turn it down, I suppose?"

I take a sip of my coffee, which has completely cooled. "It depends on the promotion," I say jokingly, in response to his insinuating tone. "If it's to the directorship of a large province, why should I object?"

Chapter 12
The sword has gone into action and Yusuf was murdered.

I leave Cengiz with his plans for promotion, appointment politics and several other trivial matters and return to my room, lit by a shy winter sun. A few minutes after I ease into the comfortable arms of my dirty upholstered chair, the cloth chafed from wear and tear, Zeynep and Ali also trickle in. I guess they'd been waiting all this time for me to come out of Cengiz's room.

Zeynep wears a gray suit and black shirt. Her face is lightly made up. She's collected her chestnut hair onto the back of her head, and her brown almond eyes, under thin lashes, complement her wheatish complexion. The only thing conflicting her elegancy is the file she clasps. Apparently, she didn't just while away her time last night either.

Zeynep is the daughter of a family of Bulgarian immigrants who came to Turkey twenty-three years ago. Her father, Veli, is the hardest-working man I've ever met. As soon as he arrived from Bulgaria, he started at a factory and didn't retire until two years ago. Even then he didn't stop working, and now he is a taxi driver. It's how he put Zeynep and her two younger siblings through school.

One day I asked Zeynep's father, "Where does this penchant for hard work come from, Veli?"

"From socialism, where else, Chief." he said. "Now you're going to get angry with me but I'll tell you the truth. Socialism taught us to work, to be disciplined and honest."

"But your socialism has toppled," I said.

"The administrators were bad eggs, Chief... like in Turkey," he said, silencing me. "Corrupt men overran the party and the government. The nation was being ruled by thieves. And they opened up a race issue. Separated people into Bulgarians, Turks and Pomaks. If there'd been a little freedom, if people had had a little breathing room, socialism wouldn't have failed."

Hearing her father speak like this had made Zeynep uncomfortable. Yet the man was saying everything he felt with utmost sincerity. I don't know how right he was but Veli Bey had gained my admiration with his hard work, discipline and honesty, as had his daughter. I don't recall Zeynep ever leaving any job I assigned her half-finished. She is beyond reproach. Ali, for example, is careless, disorganized. It's not just Ali, I'm not that organized myself. But Zeynep, no matter how much she has on her plate, she tidies it up and puts it in order. If Ali is my brawn, Zeynep is my brain. Look, even now she is planted in front of me with the enthusiasm of a high school girl who's completed her homework, while our nutjob Ali has itchy feet, as usual.

"Sit down, kids," I say, indicating the chairs.

Zeynep sits in the chair near the right corner of the desk, the files still in her lap. Ali chooses to stay standing.

"Has Ali brought you up to date?" I ask.

"He has," says Zeynep. In her voice is the tension of having missed something important. "I wish you had called me too."

"CSI dealt with the situation. I couldn't catch up with them myself. You'll get the information from them now... What did you do? Did you manage to find out anything of consequence?"

She doesn't speak straight away. First, she places the files on my desk.

"The autopsy hasn't been performed yet, Chief. But yesterday I had an opportunity to look at the livor mortis on the back of the body. The body hadn't been moved. Yusuf was murdered on the sofa where we found him. The cause of death appears to be stab wounds."

"Any fingerprints on the knife handle?" I ask. "Or on the Bible?"

"None on the knife; either the murderer wiped it off or he used gloves. There was an abundance of the victim's fingerprints on the Bible. Yusuf must have looked at the book frequently. There are several prints on the door and around the house, but we need to weed out who they belong to. From the results we have so far, I can say the murderer hasn't left any clues behind. After you left last night, I spoke with the building custodian and the neighbors. It seems they didn't see anyone suspicious. In fact, they said they didn't see Yusuf either. Perhaps the victim never left the house."

"That verse in the Bible," I say. "The one that's underlined..."

Without waiting for me to clarify, Ali recites the line by heart.

"Awake, O sword, against my shepherd, and against the man that is my fellow."

This time, Zeynep smiles.

"Bravo, Ali! You got every word."

Ali throws his head back and mumbles in a spoiled voice, "Don't take this as a brag, but I've got a strong memory."

Zeynep's smile turns into a teasing expression.

"The memory is strong but the processor is slow. When the processor is slow, like an old man, what good is a big hard disk?" I don't quite get her, she's using computer lingo, but it's evident from Ali's pouty face that Zeynep's words have hit their mark. They'll squabble for hours if I let them.

"Guys, how about we set aside this discussion of memory and processors and return to our work?"

The two pull themselves together immediately.

"Yes, Chief." Zeynep launches into her explanation. "That line has been underlined in the victim's blood. Analysis says so."

"So the murderer has a message," Ali mutters. His tired eyes are wide open with interest. "Awake, O sword, against my shepherd, and against the man that is my fellow," he says, repeating the line. "I wonder what it means."

"It brings to mind a betrayal," I say. "Maybe the betrayal of someone he once worked with, maybe a friend or family member. And this betrayal won't go unpunished. What else could 'Awake, O sword' mean?"

"And the sword has gone into action," says Ali, supporting my idea. "The sword has gone into action and Yusuf was murdered. I mean it's Yusuf who is dubbed a 'shepherd' or a 'fellow'."

Zeynep pulls a paper from out of the files.

"The words are from the Bible, from the book of Zechariah."

Ali is puzzled. Despairingly, he says, "Who on earth is Zechariah? I'm hearing the name for the first time."

"How would you know, Ali?" I say. "These are religious topics."

"But it didn't faze you, so I guess you know, Chief?"

"I've heard the name Zechariah. Not because I'm interested in religion, but because Father Dimitri explained it. Zechariah was an eminent prophet."

"Eminent, huh?" he says softly. Wow. I never would have pegged Ali this affected by religion. So even the biggest crackpots among us have a need to believe. I guess this is the shortest, easiest path to finding meaning in life; religion, that is. Maybe it is something to do with our security. Ali lost his parents at a young age and he found a way to ensure his safety in this world by becoming a cop, but what about after death? How would he ensure his security in those dark times a poet once described as "the endless night of repose"? Well, only religion provides that answer. If you do good, it's heaven; do evil, and it's hell. Simple enough for even the most ignorant to understand. And as effective as it is simple. Maybe that's why religion is an institution mankind has always felt a need for.

"As it happens, I believe in God," says Ali. It seems he's troubled in himself, as though forgetting we are in a murder investigation. Just yesterday he was over the moon that we'd come across such a compelling murder. "When we were in the dormitory, a few of us kids even went to prayers," he continues to explain. "The principal supported us. We learned the rituals of worship and prayers and such. But I've forgotten it all now. If you ask me how many prophets I know of, I wouldn't even be able to list them properly. I'd say the Prophet Muhammad, the prophets Moses and Jesus... and that one who was going to sacrifice his son, so God sent him a goat."

"Abraham?"

"Yeah, that's him. I'd say Abraham too. I swear I don't know any other prophets."

"So take a look at the Torah then," says Zeynep, cutting into the discussion. Apparently, she doesn't find Ali's fixation with religion very meaningful. "The lives of the prophets you don't know are in there." She turns to me. "Chief, I've written down the whole passage the underlined line is from. I can read it if you'd like."

"Great," I said. "Maybe it'll provide some insight."

Ali sets his eyes on Zeynep, preparing to give her his attention.

" 'Awake, O sword, against my shepherd, and against the man that is my fellow, saith the Lord of hosts: smite the shepherd, and the sheep shall be scattered: and I will turn mine hand upon the little ones. And it shall come to pass, that in all the land, saith the Lord, two parts therein shall be cut off and die; but the third shall be left therein. And I will bring the third part through the fire, and will refine them as silver is refined, and will try them as gold is tried: they shall call on my name, and I will hear them...' "

Zeynep finishes reading and Ali asks, "It's Zechariah who wrote that?"

"Yes," Zeynep affirms. "But the words aren't his; they're God's. He attests that God had him write them, to intimidate people, and purge them of their sins and transgressions."

"God must have been pretty angry at those shepherds," Ali comments. "I wouldn't want to be in their shoes."

This religion thing is dumbing Ali down, for sure. Otherwise he wouldn't sound so gormless. He has such an innocent look on his face that I hesitate to offer my own interpretation, but Zeynep puts hers forth without batting an eye.

"Shepherds are just a symbol, Ali. He's not talking about real shepherds. Shepherds represent ungodly kings and corrupt leaders who have lost their way. And the flock is their people."

"Whoever they are, dear," says Ali, filling in the gap, "shepherd or king, they really infuriated God."

"Like Yusuf infuriated our murderer." They both look me in the face. "What do you say; was Yusuf a sinner like the people Zechariah was warning? Then again, those who knew him said he wasn't like that but..."

For a moment Zeynep doesn't understand who we are talking about, because she's never met Tonguç and Meryem.

"Those who knew him? Who are they?"

"Tonguç, who claims responsibility for Bingöllü's murder, and Meryem, who loves Yusuf so much she'd risk being a murderer for his sake."

"What about the people in the apartment building. What do they say, Zeynep?"

It's Ali who asks, so he is finally freed from the mysterious labyrinths of religion his mind takes such strange pleasure in wandering.

"They didn't have anything bad to say either. The custodian's wife, the neighbors, everyone was happy with Yusuf. They say he was quiet and kept to himself."

Ali scratches his head and grumbles. "Either the man was misrepresenting himself or else the murderer is wrong about him."

"Either way," I say, "the result remains the same. We've got a murderer to catch. Yes, Zeynep, what else did we find?"

"This writing, Chief... the two words written in the margin of the Bible. They were also written in Yusuf's blood."

I envision the words, as Zeynep clarifies.

"I'm talking about 'Mor Gabriel'."

"No need to remind us, Zeynep," Ali answers back. "We're not senile just yet."

I have to intervene.

"So who was this man? Have we found out?"

"We haven't fully researched it yet, Chief," Zeynep explains. "Most likely he's an Assyrian saint. Because in the Syriac language, the word 'Mor' is used for saints."

"What were the characters like? Şefik said the letters were very neat, that a template may have been used."

"He's right. It was written with a template. In the rubbish bin, we found a plastic template and a fountain pen dipped in blood. There are no fingerprints on them."

"I'd have been surprised if there were," I mutter. "The murderer is working meticulously. But the Mor Gabriel thing is significant. We can determine which affiliation the victim belongs to."

"We'll ask that expert," Ali cuts in. "I'm talking about that Caner guy with the glasses. He said he knew everything about Christianity."

He seems quite eager to talk to Caner. He didn't like him at all yesterday. I'm sure he's going to get off topic and ask him a bunch of silly questions about Christianity. But speaking with Caner really could benefit us.

"Good idea, Ali. Let's get him over here tomorrow. I have some things to ask him about Meryem, anyhow." I turn back to Zeynep. "So what is this Assyrianism? Is it a sect, a people, or a tribe or what?"

Zeynep seems reluctant to give false information; she opens one of the papers she's taken notes on. As she looks it over, Ali gives up on standing and settles into a chair. It's not easy; he didn't sleep a wink all night. He's young but there's a limit to his endurance.

"Assyrians, or Syriacs, are a people, Chief," Zeynep starts to explain after consulting her notes. "Their homeland is accepted as Mesopotamia. Some call them Aramaeans. It's said that their roots go all the way back to Noah's son, Shem. After the Great Flood, the prophet Noah divided the world between his three sons. He gave his son Shem a big piece of land where the Syriacs live today. And Shem left an area of this land to his son Aram. This is why they called themselves Aramaean. The Aramaeans were pagans. Only when some of them chose to become Christians thanks to the efforts of Saint Peter, one of Jesus's apostles, did they begin to use the name Syriac, in order to differentiate themselves from the idolater Aramaeans. According to some sources, the root of the name 'Syriac' dates back to the Aramaic king Sürrüs, who founded the city of Antioch between 1400 and 1500 BC."

Ali is getting confused. "That last notion seems a bit silly to me," he admits. "If these men are living in Antioch, what did they care about Mardin?"

"What did they care? Of course they cared. Mardin is another of the cities they lived in. They lived in other cities too, like Diyarbakır, Elazığ, Urfa, Adıyaman, Malatya, Gaziantep, Kahramanmaraş and Adana. They migrated from Antioch years ago. There are hardly any Assyrians left in Antioch now. Not just in Antioch; the majority of Assyrians abandoned where they lived because of terrorism and other reasons. Today in Anatolia, the bulk of Assyrians only continue to live in Mardin and nearby. But even there the numbers are low. There are only around fifteen thousand Assyrians in total left in Turkey. Most of them live in Istanbul. Can you imagine? Only fifteen thousand."

"Minus one," says Ali. "Did you forget? They lost another one yesterday. Yusuf of Midyat is also dead."

No, he isn't making light of it. He's just stating the matter simply. If, out of a population once expressed as in the millions, only fifteen thousand Assyrians remained in this country, every death really did carry great significance for the future of this people.

"What about crime?" I say. "I mean a crime that stands out among the Assyrians... I don't know, smuggling or drugs or something..."

Zeynep feels the need to look at her notes again. Ali takes the opportunity to speculate.

"I think I heard something. Was it gold smuggling, or historical artifacts? Something like that. There was even a murder in the Grand Bazaar..."

Zeynep raises her head from her notes and explains, "I don't know about that, but it is a fact that Assyrians stand out in the jewelry business. They are very skilled in the working of silver and gold, and have even recently got into the diamond sector. But they aren't a people who have a tendency towards crime. When we look back in history, we see they were peaceful. Before the Republic, there was an attempted rebellion provoked by English missionaries. The Ottoman government used Kurdish men to bloodily quash that uprising. They as good as wiped out one branch of the Assyrians, called Nestorians."

"This Malik," I say, looking at Ali. "Both Caner and Meryem said the man is Christian."

He remembers right away.

"The antique dealer... He has a shop in the Grand Bazaar."

"Yes, that's him. Let's test that brilliant memory of yours. Did either Caner or Meryem mention he was Assyrian while they were talking about him?"

Ali's forehead wrinkles but his eyes are empty.

"No, Chief. They only mentioned he was Christian. Meryem hinted that he's a bit cuckoo or whatever, but nobody said he was Assyrian."

"Maybe they didn't say it because they weren't asked," says Zeynep. "He's got a shop in the Grand Bazaar, he's Christian... I suppose he could very well be Assyrian."

"Well, we'll find out. I'm going to pay the man a visit today."

Ali gets a look of disappointment on his face.

"By yourself, Chief?"

"You are going to follow Meryem, Ali, and I am going to talk to Malik. Oh, and Zeynep, before I forget, we have to inform Yusuf's family of his death. You take care of that."

"All right, Chief. Is there an address?"

"We don't have an address, and we don't know who they are. It's going to be a bit of a bother but you can reach them through the Midyat Registry Office. Ask for help from the Mardin Police Station if necessary."

"Don't worry. I'll take care of it, Chief."

"Good. Let's get back to Yusuf. Did you find anything else at his house?"

"There's an account opened at İş Bank. We found his bankbook. We'll look into it today. And we'll ask about the phone records today too."

"That's good. We need to know who else Yusuf was talking to. The bank account is also valuable. Let's see what he bought from whom, and who he paid out to."

Zeynep takes out a binder paper with handwriting on it that's been placed in a clear plastic evidence bag.

"And finally, there's this, Chief. A letter. We found it under the sofa where the body was lying."

I take the letter together with the bag so as not to mar the fingerprints, but it's hard to read through the plastic. I hand it back to Zeynep.

"You read it. Let's all learn together what it says."

"Dear brother," Zeynep begins.

How are you? Are you okay? I hope you are. As for me, I'm getting better every day. I've started to accept what happened to me. And accepting it gives me comfort. But from what I understand from your letter, you are not very comforted. Your letter is full of rebellion; I was the same in the days I first came to the hospital. But then I understood this is my fate and I took refuge in God. Now I am reading his holy book. Reading his words gives me peace. Believe me, even my pain has started to ease. You read it too, it's the only way you'll find any peace of mind. Rebelling, cursing and getting angry at the world is no solution. This is our fate, and what's more, we chose it. Accept what has happened to you, and I promise you will be comforted.

You wrote that you want to come to the hospital, but that wouldn't be right, nor is it necessary. Timuçin never leaves me alone, thank goodness. Whatever needs doing, he does it. You take care of yourself, that's enough. If nothing else, I want to know you're okay.

Timuçin said you have a bit of a money problem. Don't go doing anything crazy. And don't flash your gun at anyone. I'll be coming into some money soon and I'll send it to you. Timuçin says he'll arrange something. You are angry with him, but that's wrong. Timuçin has always been a big brother to us, and has always wanted what's best for us. If we'd done what he said, none of this would have happened. He's more experienced than we are, and smarter. You'd do well to listen to him.

Actually, I really miss you too. It's been a while, but it won't be much longer. They'll discharge me soon, and then you'll come home and we'll meet freely and make up for lost time. Your sister-in-law Şükran will make some of the moussaka you love.

May Allah's mercy and grace be upon you.

Your brother,

Fatih

Zeynep finishes reading the letter and her beautiful eyes look at us with a questioning gleam. As always, the first question comes from Ali.

"Is it clear who the letter was written to?"

"No," says Zeynep, shaking her head. "Whoever wrote it didn't address the person by name.

"But he didn't have any qualms writing his own name," Ali opined. "Is that a coincidence? Or did he find it unsuitable to disclose the name of the person it was written to? Look, he says, 'Don't come to the hospital.' He's obviously wary... And then there's this trust thing. He was saying not to trust anyone, wasn't he? From this, we can say he went out of his way not to write the man's name."

Zeynep doesn't care much for this conclusion.

"So?"

"So, the man it was written to may be a criminal or a fugitive. And the one who wrote it, plus that other guy Timuçin, are the man's accomplices. Or at least accessories."

"That's logical," says Zeynep, "but what we really need to know is whether this letter was written to Yusuf."

"I'd say it was," Ali says confidently. "If you ask me why, first of all, it was found in his house under his bed. Secondly, yesterday Meryem talked about how Yusuf had a friend named Timuçin." He's looking at me. "Then again, this guy Fatih who wrote the letter was never mentioned, but maybe Meryem doesn't even know him."

"I could agree with every word of that," says Zeynep, "because we also found numerous fingerprints of Yusuf's on the letter. But you're skipping one important detail. She points at the last line of the letter. "The sentence 'May Allah's mercy and grace be upon you.' That sentence doesn't sound very Christian. It's a sentence a Muslim would write."

I'm listening to them intently. They've set their needless squabbling aside and put their finger on an important point that's piqued my thoughts too.

"All right, let's say that's so..." says Ali. "The man who wrote the letter, I mean Fatih, is Muslim." He smiles to himself. "Anyhow, I doubt there's any Christian named Fatih. But this doesn't prevent him from using traditional Muslim niceties when he writes to his Christian friend. I mean, Yusuf and Fatih are friends, but one is Muslim and the other Christian. Why not?" He turns to me for a moment. "For example, the Chief is Muslim but his closest..." He's having difficulty finding the word. "His best friend Evgenia is Christian." He looks at me as though to check if he's made a faux pas. "Isn't that right, Chief?" he asks, to remedy the situation.

I don't take offense.

"That's right, Ali," I say. "I agree with you. This letter was most likely written to Yusuf. Still, we aren't sure." I point towards Zeynep. We need a little more proof to convince her. So I suggest we wrap up this constructive debate and get to work. You find Henna Meryem and bring her here and I'll go talk to Malik.

Chapter 13
Vengeance is mine; I will repay, saith the Lord.

I've left my trusty Renault in the parking lot in the square, so I enter the Grand Bazaar by the Beyazıt Gate. As I go in, I look to see if it's still there. Yes, Abdülhamid II's tughra, his calligraphic monogram, is still there, as is the Ottoman writing under it. "Allah loves the merchants." My late father-in-law Fehti Bey pointed it out to me. And he's the one who told me what it meant. He knew the Ottoman language well and would calculate his finances in it. He was an artist, but I suppose he wasn't successful, and that's why he was doing restoration and repairs on old paintings. His shop was on the left, in the middle of Perdahçılar Street as you go in through the Beyazit Gate. I'd come over a few times with my wife, and once with my daughter. When he saw us, he jumped straight up. Indifferent to his age, he would fuss about getting us tea, coffee or *gazoz*. After he died, they sold the shop. He was a good man; may he rest in peace. He had explained to me how the Grand Bazaar's first *bedestan*, or covered market, had been built by Sultan Mehmet the Conqueror. The ruler, who turned Hagia Sophia Church into a mosque, later decided that for a source of income he would build the *bedestan*, which in turn became this massive bazaar. Fethi Bey gave me a lot of other information about the bazaar but I've forgotten most of it; this is all that stuck. Whenever I come to the Grand Bazaar, I remember the warm smile of the mild-mannered Istanbul gentleman who was father to my wife Güzide and grandfather to my daughter Aysun.

The warmth of the Grand Bazaar feels good after the cold outside. I pass between the shiny shop windows full of colorful objects and go down inside. Malik's shop is in the Sandal Bedestan on the far side of the bazaar. There used to be public auction halls at the Sandal Bedestan. I'd even joined an auction once in order to find a missing necklace which had been an important piece of evidence in a homicide investigation.

Malik's antique shop is called Orontes. I don't know what it means; it must be a Latin or Greek name. I find the shop by the address, but there's no sign for Orantes above it. Still, I go in. There's a narrow entrance, and the interior is the same, stretching back inside like a train wagon. From within comes a deep hymnal melody. It reminds me of Nazareth Bar, even though it's not the same music. Two silver-framed mirrors have been placed on opposite walls to make the dimly lit shop appear larger. The images of the goods exhibited in the shop are in the mirror: from busts to old perfume bottles, Persian silk carpets to Indian stoles, silver candlesticks to oil lamps made from hammered iron... There are handwoven coverlets, French consoles, old money, copper trays, snuffboxes and wooden wall clocks, everything you could possibly look for. A stout, swarthy young man greets me. With an artificial smile meant for customers on his thick lips, he asks, "Hello, can I help you find something?"

"Is this Orantes?" I ask.

"Orontes, not Orantes," he immediately corrects. That would have been enough, but as if I've asked, he explains, "It's the old name for the Asi River. Yes, this is Orontes."

So that he'll realize the old and new names of the rivers don't interest me, I say, "I wanted to speak with Malik Bey."

The young man looks me over. He must have decided that, having pronounced the Orontes wrong, I didn't possess the qualities necessary to see Malik Bey. "I can help you," he says.

There's no point in dragging this out. I show my ID. "Chief Inspector Nevzat. I need to see Malik Bey straight away."

A cloud of uneasiness passes over the dark youth's face.

"Why do you want to see my dad? There's nothing wrong, is there?"

"What's your name?"

"Zekeriya..."

I suppose Ali would get goosebumps if he heard this.

"Nothing to worry about, Zekeriya. The issue is not to do with him. I just want to ask him a couple questions, is all."

My words don't allay Zekeriya's doubts.

"Is it about Yusuf Abi's murder?"

"Who told you Yusuf Abi was murdered?"

He thinks about not answering.

"Did Caner call?" I say, and he surrenders.

"Yes, Caner Abi called. Last night."

"Did Yusuf Abi come here often?"

This Zekeriya is not a stupid kid; he averts his eyes and just says, "Yes, he did."

"Well, when was he last here?"

"I don't know," he says, fidgeting in his place. He's afraid of making a wrong move. "Let me tell my dad you're here. It's best if you talk with him. He knows better."

He walks through the shop. I follow him, uninvited. At the end of the narrow corridor, we come to a wooden double door with various motifs and figures carved into it, as if it's one of the antique items for sale. He turns to me with an imploring look in his eyes and says, "If you'll wait a moment, I'll tell my father you're here."

"All right. I'll wait."

Zekeriya opens the right wing of the door and goes in. The door closes in my face again, and in this way I can make out the figures on it better. There's a picture of a man on both wings. On closer inspection, I see that the one on the left is Jesus. His face is in profile; there's a halo around his head and his long hair falls down to his shoulders. The palm of his right hand is stretched out in front of him facing downward. The person on the right wing is kneeling. He has a wide, balding forehead and a beard adorns his thin face. The man must be a saint because he also has a halo. He has the appearance of asking Jesus for forgiveness; you can read the regret, pain and sorrow in his face. The carver is really worthy of admiration; even if the lines are a bit crude, he manages to successfully depict the details in the wood.

The door suddenly opens and Jesus's hand is pointing inside the room for me. Where Jesus is pointing, the other man I'd just seen in the wood relief appears in the flesh.

"Welcome, sir. How can I be of help?"

No, I'm not joking. The spitting image of the man on the door stands right in front of me, addressing me. I quickly shake off my surprise and ask, although I am already certain of it, "Malik Bey?"

"Yes. Please, come in. We can talk more comfortably here."

I approach the door. He politely steps aside and ushers me in. He's not tall, but he's built. His skin is pale, as with someone who hasn't seen the sun in days. His grizzled beard lends his slim face an air of respect. There's neither tension nor excitement in his eyes. You know those types who are at peace with themselves, as well as everybody and everything? He's one of those. As we go in, I point out the picture on the door.

"Is this you?"

He looks at him lovingly, like at an old friend.

"His name is Paul. Saint Paul."

I've heard of Saint Paul. Father Dimitri would speak of him with reverence, the man who was accepted as a saint although he was not an apostle. Someone important enough to have his missionary work and thoughts on Christianity included in the Bible.

"Are you related? To Paul, I mean?" I realize the absurdity of the words as soon as they leave my mouth. We're talking about two people who lived almost two thousand years apart. Malik just looks at me without changing his calm expression and leaves it at that. "I mean, you look so similar," I say, trying to recover.

"It's so nice that you've noticed. Thanks for your interest."

I haven't got an answer to my question but I shouldn't insist or I'll look foolish. I go in. The room smells lovely, like linden flowers. I see the boiling kettle on a plugged-in electric stove and understand where the smell is coming from. In contrast to the bedlam of the shop, Malik's room is stripped-down, without the slightest clutter. It is illuminated in a soft, unobtrusive light. There's an old carpet on the floor, a small table, immediately behind which is a picture of Jesus, three chairs upholstered in black leather, and a small bookcase with thick books bound in black, red and green cloth. Malik points me towards the chair in front of the bookcase.

"Have a seat." Before I do, he turns to his son, still on foot. "Zekeriya, son, could you leave us for a bit?" His eyes slide over to me. "I suppose Nevzat Bey would prefer to speak alone."

"Yes," I say, "that would be better."

As Zekeriya leaves, Malik opens the cupboard under the bookcase. He places two glasses and a sugar bowl on a small tray, and then as he straightens up, says, "You'll have some linden tea, won't you, Nevzat Bey?"

"I will, thanks."

He places the tray on the table.

"We'll have to wait a bit," he says apologetically. "It hasn't steeped yet."

As he sits on the chair behind the table, his nose wrinkles up in pain. His hands go down, I suppose to his lap.

"My knees," he explains then. "When the weather gets cold, they start to ache. That's old age for you."

"You don't look so old."

I'm not saying that to flatter him. He really does look fit.

"Thank you, but I am. This body of mine passed sixty a while ago... but don't think that makes me sad. I trust neither this world..." He indicates himself, "nor this body. These are temporary. Even though God created this world and this body, this is not the real world or real life. That is why I gladly welcome even the wear and tear, because your body's frailty is in fact a divine message. A message that says: Don't believe this body, don't be a slave to its desires, look deeper, more inward. Try to see that, because that never gets old."

Malik speaks with an accent, but has an impressive tone of voice. The man would make a good priest. What surprises me is that he's calm despite his news of Yusuf's death. Without any ado, I get to the point.

"I guess you heard about Yusuf?"

His pale face is shadowed in sadness.

"May God forgive him his trespasses. He was a good man, Yusuf. I liked him."

"Who do you think could have killed him? Did he have any enemies?"

"You would have to ask Meryem Hanım," he said, without losing an ounce of his composure. "Last night when I heard the news, I called her to offer my condolences. She said she knew who killed him."

"Who? Did you ask?"

"I didn't. I'm not curious about it. Whatever dress evil wears, no matter who does wrong, this doesn't change the fact that evil is the devil's artifice. As for the devil, there's nothing to be curious about. That's why I didn't ask. But I did speak to Meryem Hanım. She was in pain. She was angry and she wanted revenge. I reminded her of God's words: 'Thou shalt not kill!' I said. I told her, 'Dearly beloved, avenge not yourselves, but rather give place unto wrath: for it is written, vengeance is mine; I will repay, saith the Lord.' I told her, 'Be not overcome by evil, but overcome evil with good.' "***1

As I understand it, Malik is unaware Bingöllü has died. He must not have spoken with Meryem after last night.

"So was Meryem Hanım convinced?" I ask.

He opens his arms hopelessly.

"I don't know. I hope so. Or blood will be spilled."

He's interrupted by the sizzle of drops falling onto the electric burner from the kettle. He slowly gets up.

"Our linden tea is ready," he says, picking up the kettle and filling two glasses with the honey-colored liquid. He holds out the tray and adds, "Sugar, lemon..."

"Just sugar, thank you. It doesn't need lemon."

With a small pinch, he tosses one sugar lump into my glass.

"Thank you."

As I reach for my glass, he warns, "Careful. It's hot."

A pleasant aroma rises from the glass of linden as I pick it up and place it within easier reach. "How did you meet Yusuf?"

Malik, occupied with his glass, answers without looking up.

"He came here. We had business, that's how I know Yusuf. Then we became friends.

"He was Christian, wasn't he, Yusuf?"

Before answering, he stirs the linden for the sugar to dissolve.

"Look, Nevzat Bey," he then says. "I don't ask people about their beliefs. It's not good to ask someone if they are Christian. It's not nice to ask if they are Muslim, either. I'll tell people my thoughts and my beliefs, but I won't ask anyone are you this or that. To tell the truth, there was a time when I also wasn't a believer. I was a sinner, for that matter. Ten years ago, I realized I was leading a false life. I started to change."

He was digressing. I put the question another way.

"Was Yusuf also a Christian, as his identity card states?"

Malik is in no hurry.

"Real faith cannot be written on an identity card, Nevzat Bey. Real faith is in our heart. Real faith is our very soul."

"So Yusuf's faith wasn't strong?"

He shakes his head measuredly.

"That's not what I meant. Yusuf also believed in God, but not like I do. His interest in matters of religion increased this last year."

"Why this year?"

He sips his tea and lets out an audible sigh, a contented look on his face.

"It's just right." He nods towards my glass. "Don't let it get cold."

I also take a sip. It's delicious. As I set my glass down, Malik explains, "He was continually seeing a saint in his dreams. For the past year, the same saint kept appearing to him."

I recall the saint whose name is written in the book at Yusuf's house.

"Mor Gabriel?"

For a moment the composure on Malik's face seems it'll break, but this doesn't last long. He wears the same smiling, at peace with the world expression again.

"What difference does it make? It's not the name that's important, or even that he is a saint necessarily. It's what the saint said that's important."

"What did he say?"

"He said to choose Christ the Savior's path. He told him to liberate himself from the bondage of this body and this world and embrace love. Because this world is finite, and this body is sinful and tainted. Only love is pure and immortal. And it is this love that will lead us to real salvation."

Malik has begun to explicitly preach. He'll probably lay out the whole Bible if I let him.

"This saint must have affected Yusuf a lot," I say, trying to get back on topic. "What was he like, this saint?"

He looks at me as if to ask why I don't understand, but it isn't an expression of anger; his eyes reflect the helplessness arising from not being able to explain on his own merit.

"I don't know what he was like. And to be honest, I'm not interested. God can call to us in different forms. What's important is not the appearance, not the voice, it's what the voice says."

"Was it after these dreams that Yusuf decided to be religious?"

"Not immediately. He mostly just tried to understand. He started to ask me questions."

"Why you? Yusuf was also Christian, so why didn't he consult the people from his own church?"

"I don't know. And truthfully, I didn't ask him. I suppose he wanted to talk to someone he trusted. I guess he was afraid to talk to someone who had never had doubts, even if it was a clergyman. That's right; he had doubts. And he asked about those, too."

Malik's rock-solid composure, his logical answers to every question, are starting to get to me. I take another sip of the linden tea and say, "So then, did you manage to quash his doubts?"

"In part. In part, because faith can't just be grasped with logic alone. For someone setting off on a journey into the universe of beliefs, logic is a bad blueprint. You have to develop your insight in order to believe. There are truths that you cannot perceive with your five senses. Yusuf didn't understand that. He was searching for the truth with only his logic, his senses. He thought the only way to reach the truth was to see, hear, feel, taste and smell. The path he used was erroneous. The truth can never be reached with those faculties. I tried to explain this..."

"I guess your explanation wasn't enough. Yusuf consulted others, as well. I'm talking about Caner. They were also discussing Christianity."

Malik wears that docile expression again.

"I introduced those two. Caner is from my hometown. We're both from Antioch. Caner is a well-versed kid, especially on the subject of Christianity. His uncle was a priest at the Antioch Catholic Church. He sent him to the Vatican. Caner spent three years studying theology."

Now this is interesting. Caner never mentioned it to us.

"So Caner is Christian too?"

"No. He has no faith. He calls himself agnostic. If you ask me, he denies God outright, but he's a good kid. I still have hopes for him."

"You said his uncle is a priest, so Caner's family is Christian?"

"That's where it's a bit complicated. His father was a Nusayri..." I'm thinking Caner's surname must be 'Nusayri' or something, but I can't be sure. Malik continues. "I mean, he's an Arab Alawite. Nusayrism is a common belief in the Antioch region. My family is that way, too."

I'm confused.

"Just a minute... You are also Nus..."

"Nusayri," he completes the word I can't say. "Yes, my family is Nusayri."

I start to doubt myself, whether I've misunderstood.

"Alawite. You mean, Muslim," I mumble.

"Yes. My family was Muslim. I chose to be Christian. Or more accurately, I understood I was Christian."

"You understood..." I say bewilderedly.

He raises his conjoined eyebrows.

"Through a striking ordeal," he says emphatically.

"Have you been having dreams like Yusuf too?"

He gets an offended look on his face.

"I'm sorry," I say. "It's not my intention to mock you. The subject is so far beyond me, I am just trying to understand."

He sees that I am sincere and says, "Mine was a more jarring experience than Yusuf's." He picks up his tea glass again. My hand automatically goes to mine. Before bringing his glass to his lip, Malik adds, "An experience of the sort explained by the carving on the door." He drinks. I hold my position without drinking. My gaze goes to the door. I just now realize there's the same relief on the inside. Saint Paul kneeling, asking forgiveness from Jesus. This conversation is getting more interesting by the minute. I wonder if I too am finally getting swept up in the excitement. No, I have to stay calm. At least as calm as this man sitting across from me.

I take a sip of my linden and say, "If it's no problem, I'd love to hear about your experience."

His reaction comes completely unexpected. "No," he says, shaking his head resolutely. "Please don't ask that of me. I'm not entitled to recount it."

Malik's words whip up my curiosity more. I don't know how beneficial it will be to the investigation but I'm aching to hear what he underwent. I point to the engraving of Paul. "I've heard the name Paul, but I have no idea what he went through. I suppose you'll have no qualms telling me about that."

Malik's smile is full of insinuation.

"You're a very clever man, Nevzat Bey," he says. "I wouldn't want to be one of the criminals you're hunting down. As to your question, of course I'll explain. Actually, you can find your answer in any Bible. In the section called the 'Acts of the Apostles', which Saint Luke wrote." He thinks a moment, then says, "What Saint Paul experienced was extraordinary." He seems to be living the moment himself. I see his composure fail him in a real sense for the first time. A strange gleam appears in his eyes and the muscles in his face tense up. "An experience on the road to Damascus..." he starts again. "Saul, that is Paul, was going to Damascus..."

I give in to my curiosity and interrupt.

"Who is Saul? Are we talking about the same person as Paul?"

"The same. Saint Paul was both a Jew and a Roman citizen. Saul is a Hebrew name with religious roots, whereas Paul is a name the Romans were wont to use. Soundwise, the two are similar. It should be read as Paul, as the world knows it, rather than the Turkish Pavlus. And the Hebrew name is Saul. They sound the same, right?"

"Yes, similar..."

"Did you know Saint Paul was from Tarsus?"

"No, I didn't know that. So he lived in Anatolia..."

"That's right. In Anatolia. He lived in the lands I was born in."

It's not what he says so much as his eerie tone of voice that gives me goosebumps. Does this man believe himself Paul incarnate? Perhaps it's to chase this thought from my mind that my lips automatically intone, "But a long time ago..."

"A very long time ago," he agrees. Neither the creepy tone to his voice disappears, nor the strange gleam in his eye. I watch as his face grows paler and, with a deep shudder, his beard quivers slightly.

"He was going to Damascus," Malik continues. "In those days Paul was an enemy to Jesus. He had received some letters from the high priest of the Jews. He was to take the letters to Damascus, arresting all those who walked in the way of Christ, women and men alike, and bring them to Jerusalem. Because Saul had not yet seen the truth. His eyes were still veiled with an invisible cloth of darkness. Saul set off on his Damascus journey with this purpose. But as he neared Damascus, a light suddenly appeared from the sky. As Saul looked at it in wonder, the light encompassed him. Saul was captivated by the light and fell to the ground. He heard a voice. The guttural voice of a wounded gazelle, and therewith the enraged voice of a young lion.

" 'Saul, Saul, why are you persecuting me?'***2

"Saul was in a daze, but eventually gathered his courage. 'Who are you, Lord?' he asked.

" 'I am Jesus, whom you are persecuting,' is the response he got.

"Not knowing what to do, Saul trembled in fear where he lay. The voice from the sky roared again. 'Arise and go into the city. You will be told what must be done.'

"Those with Saul were also incredulous. They had heard the voice as well. Saul managed to get to his feet, but he was blind. His companions hooked arms with him and lead him to Damascus. For three days, in Damascus, he neither saw, nor ate or drank.

"There was a man called Ananias in Damascus. Christ appeared to him and said, 'Ananias! Arise, go to the house of Judas and inquire of Saul of Tarsus. He is praying now, that his eyes may see again. Go and help him.'

"Ananias answered, "Lord, I have heard of all the bad things this man did against your holy people in Jerusalem. And what's more, this man has received authority from the high priests to arrest those people known to be devoted to you.'

"The Lord answered without hesitation. 'Go,' he said. 'Because that man is an instrument chosen to bear testimony to my name before gentiles, kings and the children of Israel. I will show all the suffering he'll endure for my name's sake.'

"With that, Ananias rose and went to that house. He put his hands on Saul's eyes and said, 'Saul, my brother, the Lord Jesus, who met you on the road, has sent me to fill you with the Holy Spirit and restore your sight.'

"At that moment, scales like those from a fish fell from Saul's eyes. He could see again. He got up and was baptized, and after eating, regained his strength.***[3]

"And that is how Saul, Paul of Tarsus that is, started down God's path, spreading the gospel, an ambassador for Jesus Christ."

Malik's voice begins to tremble as his words come to an end, and I notice his eyes moisten. He turns his face away from me and, putting his hand in his pocket, pulls out a cloth handkerchief. He's going to wipe away the tears he's trying to conceal.

"Malik Bey, are you okay?" I ask.

"I'm fine, I'm fine. Every time I tell this story, it's as if I'm reliving it. It's such a powerful emotion that it throws a person for a loop."

"I'm sorry. If I'd known, I wouldn't have asked you to tell me."

"No need to apologize," he says, putting the handkerchief back into his pocket. "Even just reliving that moment is a wonderful experience..."

Well, this man definitely thinks he is Paul. How can this be? The poor guy has lost his mind, I guess. He believes so strongly in what he says, it has even affected me.

"I suppose yours was a similar experience," I say, trying my luck a second time. "It must be wonderful too."

He gives a determined shake of the head.

"Please, Nevzat Bey. I don't want to talk about this matter."

It's time to set the civility aside.

"Look, Malik Bey, I respect your wishes. But I'm not here as your friend or an enthusiast. I'm investigating a murder. A brutal one at that. You should have some understanding, too."

"I do understand you, Nevzat Bey. But what does this murder have to do with Christianity?"

"Yusuf was murdered with a knife with a cruciform handle. There was an open Bible next to him. And a verse from that Bible had been underlined in blood. Yusuf's blood."

Nothing remains of Malik's steady repose or his self-assured smile. His face tightens in horror.

"A cross? A Bible?"

"Yes. A cross, a Bible, and Yusuf's blood. So you think this murder has nothing to do with Christianity?"

He's frozen, staring at my face.

"You know Yusuf," I say. "Perhaps you also know the people around him. A Christian cult, or somebody else who wants him dead. It could be someone he disagrees with over religion, or someone he's argued with..."

He shakes his head and the horror in his eyes gives way to apprehension.

"No," he says. "No, Nevzat Bey. There is no such cult, nor any such person. Who would want to do something like this? This... this is the devil's work."

"There were two words written in the margin of the Bible," I say, to help try and jog his memory. "Two words written in Yusuf's blood. The name of an Assyrian saint: Mor Gabriel."

The blood drains from Malik's face. I interpret it as his having some knowledge of the saint. But he doesn't offer an explanation. I have no other choice but to keep insisting.

"This Mor Gabriel, could he be the saint Yusuf said he saw in his dreams?"

"Yes, it's him," says Malik, averting his eyes again. "But I don't know much about him. You'd be better off talking to an authority on the subject."

I'm sure Malik is hiding something from me but I'm in no position to prove that right now. There's no point in badgering him. As I'm ready to ask him if he knows of anyone, the phone on the table rings. The phone ringing puts Malik at ease a bit. He apologizes and picks up the receiver.

"Hello... Oh, is this Meryem Hanım?"

Malik's unsettled gaze wanders my face. It's Henna Meryem! So then Ali hasn't got to her yet.

"How are you doing?" Malik continues. "Yes, I've been agonizing over it since I heard too... That's right, Meryem Hanım. Let's call it fate... It's all God's will." Malik's gaze is stuck on me. "You aren't going to do anything wrong, are you, Meryem Hanım?" He's saying this in front of me intentionally, so I'll see he has nothing to do with this business. "Is that right? You want to talk? I'm in the shop... You? What, in Yusuf's house? I'm afraid I can't make it today. I have a meeting in a little while... Would tomorrow be possible? No, tomorrow, for certain... All right... I'll be expecting you here tomorrow. Again, I'm so sorry for your loss."

Malik never mentioned me. In fact, this is also a message. Look, I'm always on the side of the law, is what he means. Or is there some other reason? I wonder if he suspects Meryem.

"Meryem Hanım," he states, after hanging up. "She sounds better. Like her anger has subsided. People adapt to everything."

She hasn't adapted. She just feels good because she has taken revenge for her lover. I don't enlighten Malik on this. He'll just say that since Yusuf's killer Bingöllü is dead, there's no problem anymore, and then wheedle his way out of this business.

"Why did she call?" I ask.

"She didn't say. She just said she wanted to talk. Maybe she's going to ask what kind of funeral ceremony is required."

He's lying again; I'd bet money on it. But it won't be too long till we find out what he's hiding.

Chapter 14
A Muslim prayer after a Christian death.

As I come out of the Grand Bazaar, I see that daylight has disappeared. Like yesterday, big, ashen clouds have covered the sky again. It's a bit colder. I suppose the snow will start again. I button the front of my coat up tightly, then take my phone from my pocket and dial Ali. The poor guy is still chasing after Meryem.

"We couldn't find her, Chief," he says, his voice agitated. "We checked her home but she's not there. I'm hanging out near the bar, waiting."

"There's no need, Ali. Henna Meryem is at Yusuf's house. Let's meet there in half an hour. Don't go in till I get there."

"Got it, Chief."

His voice is flat because he hasn't completed his mission.

As I merge into the crowd in Beyazit Square, I am thinking about what Malik said, or rather what he didn't say. Has the man really lost his mind, or is he acting? He didn't seem to be acting at all. Although he doesn't openly say so, he believes he is Saint Paul. Look, he was even hesitant to explain his ordeal.

He's not entitled to, so he says. But who would entitle him? God or Jesus Christ, who else? Mind you, according to Malik's beliefs, both of them lead to the same door: God and Jesus are the same divine being. In fact, Malik fits our killer's profile. He's crazy enough to not balk at murdering for Christianity. If he believes he is someone who lived nearly two thousand years ago, why not get it into his head to up and kill Yusuf one night? But would a person committing this type of murder hide their identity? Murders committed in the name of religion function as punishment, to make a point, and that's why a murderer demands the motive of the act is known by all. He'd want everyone to acknowledge him, his bravery and devotion. Moreover, in this type of crime, the killer believes he will find true justice, not in court, but in the realm of God. So it isn't important that earthly courts put him on trial or punish him. What's important is divine judgment, divine justice. But if Malik thinks his mission is not yet completed, if there is still unfinished divine business, and even more, if this divine business manifests in serial murder? In that case, he would do anything he could to stay hidden. It's a great sin not to bring a divine mission to fruition or leave it half-finished. It is falling into guilt in the realm of God. On the flip side, Malik really doesn't look the type to commit murder. If you ask me what the murdering type looks like, I don't actually think I could give a convincing answer, but once I've spoken with a suspect I can tell how susceptible to committing murder he or she is. Allowing for fallibility, of course. I'll admit that I've been mistaken in my presumptions a few times.

All this is running through my mind until I get into my car. I start the engine and, as I'm adjusting the rear-view mirror, I suddenly meet my own eyes. I see a funny twitch in my distracted pupils, a spark that I haven't seen in years, leftover from the first days of my profession. What's that about, I wonder? While I am teasing Ali, could this case also be affecting me? That's silly; I am just doing my job. Although the eyes in the mirror disagree... And so, what if I am affected? Where's the harm in my feeling excitement again? Maybe I should be pleased, because this shows I have changed... and started to forget. My wife, my daughter, sacrificing them to an unsolved assassination... Last night, when Evgenia asked me why I don't marry her, no matter that I averted my eyes and made light of it, a voice inside me whispered, *really, why don't I marry her?* Is this all the fidelity I have in me? Is this how long the pain of losing loved ones lasts? Before I've even found their killer... I look into my eyes in the mirror again. The gleam I've just seen there is gone. I feel an odd sense of relief. After my uneasily fidgeting conscience has ruthlessly smothered the curiosity growing inside me, I go back to my customary, cold levelheadedness. Yet as my car pulls into the avenue, I can't stop looking at my watch to avoid being late for Ali.

The street Yusuf lived on is remarkably calm. The Vatican Consulate gets my attention. Looking at the walls of the building, like a sheltered fort isolated from the rest of the world, I wonder whether it is coincidence that Yusuf's house is on the same street. My thoughts are interrupted by my phone ringing. It's Zeynep.

"I just got out of the autopsy, Chief," she says excitedly. "I noticed an important detail."

"What's that? Was Yusuf not murdered with a knife?"

"No, he was. Two stabs to the heart. If the first didn't kill him, the second one did. That's not what I was going to say, Chief. Wasn't Yusuf Christian?"

"It's written on his ID card, and everyone who knows him says he is."

"But the man is circumcised..."

"How's that?"

"He simply is, Chief. Yusuf is circumcised." Her voice gets embarrassed. "I saw it with my own eyes."

"That's strange."

"And that mark that looks like a strawberry on the victim's right wrist," says Zeynep, changing the subject. "It's not a tattoo. It's a birthmark."

"Okay, Zeynep," I say. "Thanks for letting me know. I'm on my way to talk to Meryem. Let's ask her too, see how she'll explain this. Oh, and Zeynep, can you look into this guy Malik? Has he got a record or anything? Let's see what the man's about."

I get to the apartment and find Ali waiting for me. He's parked in front of the building so as not to miss Meryem if she comes out. When he sees me, he gets out of the car. He's pouting, still making an issue out of not having found Meryem himself. I stop my car in front of his. Ali has a buzzing radio in his hand. "Turn that thing down," I tell Ali as I get out. "I don't want them to understand who we are till they see us in front of them."

"Yes, sir." He turns off the radio and follows me in silence. As we enter through the apartment's big double door, he asks, "Is Meryem alone?"

"I don't know, Ali. Even if she isn't, I doubt they'll resist us. The woman got her revenge. Why would she unnecessarily clash with the police?"

"Even so..."

"You're right," I say. "We'd better be on the alert all the same."

As we go through the door, we pull out our guns and load them. We cock the hammers and place them where they're easily reached. This time when we go up, we opt for the stairs instead of the antique elevator. Ali goes up quickly with the strength of his youth. I'm trying not to fall behind but to be honest I'm breathless before I've reached the third floor. Ali wants to get to Meryem as fast as possible, and he's taking the stairs by two, unaware of my condition. I try to keep up, thinking I wish we'd taken the lift. As I reach the third floor, I hear a noise from inside. A person's voice, gripping and melodious. I can't hear exactly what it's saying but it has to be a folk song or a ballad. Ali notices the voice as well. He's stopped five steps up and is looking at me. "What's that?" he asks when I reach him.

"Sounds like someone singing."

"Not a song though, Chief. More like a hymn."

We need to get closer to understand. I catch my breath and we start up the stairs again. Ali is in front, as always. The voice gets clearer with every step. Ali is right, it's not a folk song. It's a hymn, or rather, a prayer. When we get to the top floor, we start to make out the words. Not the meaning of the words, but what language they're in. Yes, it's Arabic. Although

149

we don't know their meanings, we know the words by heart having heard them probably hundreds of times since childhood, and we understand it's a prayer from the Quran. Most likely, it's a prayer read after a death.

What's strange is that the prayer, being read by the captivating voice of some imam, is coming from the victim's house. A Muslim prayer after a Christian death. Ali and I exchange glances outside the door. There's no sense in waiting any longer. I ring three times in succession, but the sound of the bell doesn't disrupt the prayer. Just as I wonder if they aren't going to open up, I hear the sound of the lock. From the cracked door, the long face of the other bouncer from last night at Nazareth appears. What was his name again? Ali's magnificent memory kicks in, and he remembers immediately.

"Hello, Tayyar," he says derisively. "You having a memorial service?"

Tayyar swallows before answering. "Reading a prayer, for Yusuf Abi..."

Ali pushes on the door and says, "That's no good, Tayyar. Why weren't we invited?"

I walk through the door, which Ali has pushed wide open. Tayyar steps aside helplessly.

"Sir," he says, to save the situation. "There's prayer going on inside... Let me tell Meryem you're here, if you'd like."

I also adopt Ali's sarcastic tone.

"So let them pray, Tayyar. Nothing wrong with that. We're all Muslims, alhamdulillah, aren't we?"

Tayyar starts inside again. Ali grabs his shoulder.

"Where to, Tayyar? Turn and face this wall. Let's pat you down."

Tayyar gets an indecisive look in his eye. Ali immediately pulls his gun.

"I told you to lean against the wall. Has the anguish of Yusuf's death made you deaf?" He raises his voice. "Come on!"

Tayyar turns to face the wall and raises his hands. Ali starts to search him. A 35mm Beretta comes out of Tayyar's waistband, and three magazines.

"Shame on you, Tayyar. Bringing a gun to a funeral ceremony."

Tayyar holds his tongue.

"There's a license for this thing, right, Tayyar?"

"Yes," says Tayyar, though his voice is feeble.

Ali buries the barrel of his gun into Tayyar's side.

"What's that? I couldn't hear you."

"Yes, there is. I said there is, Inspector."

"That's good, Tayyar. Otherwise I would have fed you the bullets from these magazines one by one."

Once we've taken some weight off Tayyar, we follow him towards the living room. I see Meryem there first, sitting in a chair in front of a window, eyes closed and palms open, her red hair hidden under a black headscarf. The chair next to hers is parceled out to Caner, a bored look on his face like he wants it over so he can go; he has no interest in this prayer or ritual. The lead actor of this ceremony, an imam who has opened a Quran on the table where the bible had been yesterday, carries on reading, wagging his head with its skullcap faintly from side to side. He's so engrossed in what he's doing that he doesn't even realize we've come in. We've taken a couple steps in when Caner sees us. When he does, the boredom in his face immediately gives way to worry. He whispers to Meryem, "The police are here."

Meryem is in no hurry. She slowly opens her eyes and looks at us. There's not a hint of surprise in her eyes. It's as if she was expecting us. Without a word, she gestures towards some empty chairs, inviting us to sit. For a moment I can't decide what to do. Ali is no different. He's watching me for a sign on how to proceed. The imam comes to our aide; he turns his palms up and starts into his final words. I know this not because I know the prayer, but rather from the emphasis he puts on the words. The imam notices us when he finally invites those in the room to recite the *Fatiha*. He understands straight away that something isn't right. He doesn't stop the prayer but he looks from us to Meryem with surprise. Meryem signals for him to keep going. His voice gets anxious and he rushes through the words. Looks like he knows plenty about Meryem. Finally, he completes the prayer and runs his palms down his face. If Ali and I weren't stopped in the living room behind Tayyar, he might have read some more prayers for the dead man and completed the ceremony with some other words, but our presence is making him uneasy.

"God rest his soul," he says, closing the Quran. He carefully folds his skullcap and stands up.

"God rest his soul," I say too, before turning to Meryem. "Why don't you send the imam on his way and we can get back to worldly affairs."

My suggestion pleases the imam most of all. His right hand strokes his thin moustache as he looks at her. Meryem's eyes are on me.

"Welcome, Nevzat Bey," she says. "The timing of your visit is a bit off, but in any case, welcome."

"You're right, Meryem Hanım. We are a bit ill-timed, but untimely murders lead to untimely visits, whatever you do."

She knows well what I'm talking about, but despite that, doesn't care one whit. While the blood drains from Caner's face, Meryem says to Tayyar with utmost calm, "Show the imam to the door."

Tayyar's vacillating eyes are on Ali.

"What's with that look, Tayyar?" says Ali, resuming his sarcasm. "I need a good deed too. Come on; let's show the imam out together. Then we can carry on the conversation from where we left off."

The imam, plainly relieved, approaches Meryem. He squeezes her hand and says, "Again, I am sorry for your loss, Meryem Hanım, my girl. "May he rest in peace."

Meryem maintains her solemnity.

"Amen. Thank you, Hoca Efendi. It was nice.

As Ali, Tayyar and the imam are leaving the living room together, I go over to the chair opposite Meryem's.

"I don't understand," I say. "Isn't reciting a Muslim prayer for a Christian meaningless?"

Meryem doesn't get offended.

"Christian, Muslim, it doesn't matter. A prayer is a prayer. Don't we all believe in the same god?"

"That's true, but there's another truth as well. The god we all believe in says not to kill. He never permits one of his subjects to take the life of another..." I lean forward in my chair and look into her eyes. "Isn't that right?"

Meryem holds my gaze. She seems so fearless, like she's given up on the world, that quite frankly I'm startled. It occurs to me she might reach over to the end table on her right where her purse is, take her gun out and empty it on me, but I keep talking.

"I guess you are relaxed now, Meryem Hanım?"

"Why would I be relaxed."

"You understand very well what I mean."

"Are you talking about Bingöllü?"

"Who else?"

Meryem doesn't bat an eye. She just says, "Tonguç shot Bingöllü. He turned himself in last night."

"How do you know?'"

"Because I was with him." She gives me a serious look. "Come on, Nevzat Bey. You know all this. Tonguç told you everything that happened."

"Yes, he did. He also said that you put him up to it."

A smile of disbelief appears on her pale lips.

"And that's not all," I say, trying to get her dander up. "You yourself shot at Bingöllü, at close range, no less."

She leans back, the smile still on her lips.

"You're grasping at straws, Nevzat Bey. I know what Tonguç told you. I heard it from his lawyer. Things didn't happen the way you say they did. Yes, it's true we went to see Bingöllü Kadir together."

I interrupt. "Why were you going to see Bingöllü?"

"To ask about Yusuf's murderer, of course."

"So, you were going to ask him if he killed Yusuf?"

"Yes, that too. But as we were going to the bar, we ran into Bingöllü and his man. And they saw us. Bingöllü's man put his hand to his midriff and pulled out a gun, after which Tonguç fired, to protect himself. Seeing his man hit, Bingöllü pulled his gun too. And Tonguç shot him also. That's all there was to it. Tonguç has already explained all this to you."

"But that's not the reality," I say, shaking my head. My voice is taut, almost angry. What's with me? I should be making Meryem angry, instead she is getting to me. "The reality is, you killed Bingöllü. It's true you ran into them on the street. It's true Bingöllü's man Ferhat went for his waist out of reflex when he saw you two. But he never intended to shoot. You did intend to, however. You were out to kill Bingöllü. This is why when we came to Nazareth last night, you didn't mention Bingöllü at all. Because you wanted to take your own revenge. You were obliged to as Henna Meryem, daughter of Burnt Fehmi. If you hadn't shot Bingöllü, you would have been erased from this underworld where you already have difficulty keeping afloat as a woman. Sure, Tonguç shot Ferhat, that's also true, but then you took the gun. And you killed Bingöllü. The laws of the underground didn't change here either, the ways of the underworld came into effect and Tonguç took the fall for the murder."

Meryem unwraps her black scarf. She gently shakes her head, freeing the red hair that has earned her the nickname Henna Meryem.

"Why would Tonguç do that?" she asks. "Why would he go to prison for someone else?"

"As payment for the favors you did him and his family. But not only as payment, doubtless Tonguç also thought this murder would land him a good career. Who knows? Maybe in the future he could even take your place. This is why he happily took the blame for a murder he didn't commit. It's the best solution for you, too. Even though police say Tonguç did it, the underworld would know you were the one who pulled the trigger, so there'd be no stain on your reputation. And that's what happened. I'm sure right now there's no one left in your world that hasn't heard about this murder."

"Did Bingöllü kill Yusuf Abi?" It's Caner who asks the question. He looks with surprise from me to Meryem. He answers as if trying to explain events himself. "And then Tonguç killed Bingöllü?" His hazel eyes, behind glasses, slide with reproach to Meryem. "Why don't I know about this?"

The answer comes not from Meryem, but from Ali, as he comes back into the room with Tayyar.

"Are you from the underworld? We thought you were a highbrow intellectual."

Caner doesn't even get angry at the "highbrow" comment, he just tries with all sincerity to clarify the situation.

"I just wanted to say I never heard about it. I have nothing to do with the underworld. I mean, yet another person was killed after Yusuf Abi." He shoots a look at Meryem again. "Nobody told me."

Meryem doesn't pay him any attention. She's busy folding up the scarf she's removed. But the young man persists.

"Was it really Bingöllü who killed Yusuf Abi?"

Meryem gently raises her head and looks at Caner.

"You'll ask Nevzat Bey that, not me. He represents the law here."

Caner's gaze is turned towards me, a deep curiosity in his eyes. Before explaining, I lean back, as Meryem has.

"You are an educated guy, Caner, you would know," I say. "There are two kinds of people in this world. Those who believe what they see, and those who seek the truth, not satisfied with what they see. The second kind, those not satisfied with what they hear and see, continuously search for new evidence to find the truth. Even at the expense of bringing down their own beliefs, their own ideas and their own worlds. Even if it's horrific, they try to find the veiled truth of events.

"When it comes to the first type who believe what they see, they look at life, at situations, and search for evidence to confirm what they already believe, rather than looking at reality. From their experiences, they tease out facts that corroborate the ideas in their heads. Because believing any other way will bring down their beliefs, their thought processes, their worlds. They can't bear to have their worlds destroyed. Despite all those shows of bravery, they actually harbor a big fear. And it's this fear that guides them. Because they are afraid, they make mistakes. Just like Meryem did when she killed Bingöllü Kadir."

While Caner hangs on my every word, Meryem looks as if to say, what nonsense is this man spouting? Ali and Tayyar aren't much different from Meryem. Ali may maintain his belief that his Chief Inspector Nevzat never talks nonsense, but Tayyar's blankly gawking eyes show he hasn't understood a thing I've said. I turn to Meryem and, raising my voice, continue to explain.

"Bingöllü didn't kill Yusuf. That murder was too complex a plan for someone like Bingöllü to design. Bingöllü was a poor, pathetic man trying to eke out a living through pilfering. If he'd wanted to kill Yusuf, he'd have done it his own way. I mean, in plain sight, and most likely in your old bar. Because that's what the code dictates. That's right, the code. This is a very important concept for you. You also killed Bingöllü because of this code. Sorry, and maybe I'm going too far, but if you ask me, your love for Yusuf was waning. Just look, you hadn't seen each other in days. Maybe you'd have broken it off with him if he hadn't died. But unfortunately, Yusuf died before you split up. And the code requires you to kill his murderer even if you don't love him anymore, because the underworld knows you as sweethearts. Yes... Don't look at me like you don't give a damn. You know what I'm saying is right. Bingöllü's death has more to do with your reputation than the love you felt for Yusuf. But Bingöllü wasn't Yusuf's murderer. You murdered Bingöllü for nothing. And you sent poor Tonguç to prison for nothing, too."

Meryem's full attention is on me, trying to figure out if I am telling the truth or if it is a trap. She sets her scarf down on the side table and asks, "If Bingöllü didn't kill Yusuf, then who did?"

I smile and look at Caner.

And that's how quickly they jump to conclusions. If he didn't do it, the other guy did. They want to find out right away and take that one out too. Like I said before, it is what the code dictates. But life is not so simple. And murder is not nearly so simple. In even a seemingly cut-and-dried homicide, you can find dozens of intertwined motives, never mind a homicide as sophisticated as Yusuf's.

I look over at Meryem again.

"No, Meryem Hanım. We don't know who killed him yet. But I can guarantee you it wasn't Bingöllü."

She blinks skeptically.

"You killed the wrong man, Meryem Hanım. You'll understand that soon enough."

While Meryem's black eyes stay anchored to my face, Caner mumbles in amazement, "Wow. To think all this happened last night!"

"What's up, Caner Efendi? Are you sad?" says Ali.

With the middle finger of his right hand, Caner pushes up the glasses that have slipped down his nose. "Why would I be sad?"

"Why else? Because you couldn't go on the rat safari in Beyoğlu with Meryem Hanım."

"Of course not. There is no such thing. I just wanted to say I wasn't aware of what happened."

"Nevzat Bey," says Meryem. Her voice is emotional; she's dropped her air of indifference. I'm expecting her to say she'll help me but she says, "You're wrong. I wasn't going to leave Yusuf. I loved him. This is not a matter of any code. I haven't been so sad over a death since my father's." She averts her moist, black eyes. "You say Bingöllü didn't kill him but you have no evidence, nor any witnesses. Why should I believe you? Besides, Yusuf didn't have any other enemies besides Bingöllü."

"Not that you know of," I interrupt. "Tell me, Meryem Hanım. How well did you know Yusuf?"

"I knew him..."

"Don't deny it. You said yourself that you didn't. Apart from Caner and Malik, what other friends did he introduce you to? You mention a guy named Timuçin, but you never even saw the man's face. You say Yusuf was a Christian but the man was circumcised." I watch Caner. "Well, Caner? Can a Christian be circumcised?"

The young man is completely taken aback.

"What? How?"

"I'm asking if there is such a thing as a circumcised Christian?"

"No," he says. "Although, in the initial years of Christianity, those who were originally Jewish but later believed in Jesus were circumcised. Because they were all Jewish. Jesus himself was circumcised. In fact, this became the subject of an important debate at the start of Christianity. Saint Paul, who spread Christianity in the region of Antioch, maintained that circumcision wasn't necessary, but the Christians in Jerusalem wanted to continue the practice which existed in Judaism. In the end, what Saint Paul said held sway, and the practice of circumcision was done away with."

"They did it for health reasons," Meryem interjects. Her face is red; it must embarrass her to discuss this. "I asked as well. He had the procedure as a child."

That answers our question, so long as Yusuf didn't lie to Meryem.

"This Malik," I say. "What was his relationship with Yusuf?"

"I guess they had some business deals. Malik has become really religious these last years, though, so they ended up just being friends."

"Did they like each other?"

"They did," said Caner, answering the question. "Yusuf said he felt at peace around Malik."

I picture Malik. Not as a suspect, but as someone with a serene face, who has shed the weight of the world and his own body. I almost see a halo on his head. I chase away the image with my own words.

"Malik is from the same place as you, isn't he, Caner?"

"Yes, he's also from Antioch. In fact, he's from a Muslim family. He became a Christian later on."

There is so much about Malik I want to learn from Caner, but I don't want to talk in front of Meryem.

"Meryem Hanım," I say, turning back to her. "There's something else. This guy called Timuçin. He could tell us a lot about Yusuf. How can we find him? Is there a phone number, an address... anything..."

"I don't know, Nevzat Bey. I don't know a thing."

"And you?" says Ali to Caner. "You don't know Timuçin either?"

"I've heard his name. They spoke on the phone a few times around me. But I never saw him. And I don't know who he is. One time I asked. He evaded the subject, saying it was just a friend."

"Okay, so have you heard of anyone called Fatih?" I ask them both this time. "We found a letter here in this house. We think it was written to Yusuf. Someone by the name of

Fatih wrote it. The man was in hospital for a while; he must have been sick or something. Did Yusuf ever mention someone like that?"

Caner shakes his head. "Yusuf Abi didn't really like to talk about his friends. Not about his friends, and not about his family." He looks at Meryem. "He never talked about his family to me. Did he ever tell you about them?"

"No, he didn't tell me either. I guess he has relatives in Mardin, but I never met any of them."

"We'll meet them soon enough," says Ali. "I suppose they'll come to the funeral."

"Yusuf didn't really like his relatives. It's fine if they don't come. I'm taking care of the arrangements, in any case."

"But," says Caner, his broad forehead wrinkling up, "Yusuf Abi should have a Christian ceremony."

"We'll do what needs doing," Meryem says, brushing him off.

"I'm afraid that's impossible," I say.

She reels as if she's been slapped.

"Why is that?"

"We have to take you into custody. Because in Tonguç's statement last night, he named you an accessory. You aren't hiding that you were at the scene anyhow. The prosecution will decide whether you're arrested or not. Even if they let you go, you have no relation to the victim. I mean, they won't hand the body over to you. Only a relative can claim that. You'll need to get permission from his relatives for the funeral."

"I'll get it if I need to, but we'll talk about that later. Right now I need to call my lawyer."

While Meryem phones her attorney, Caner misinterprets what I've said and asks, "Chief Inspector, are you taking me in, too?"

"Don't worry, Caner. We aren't going to arrest you, although if it's not a problem, I would like you to come to the station with us. There are a couple things I'd like to discuss with you."

Chapter 15
I am Jesus, whom you are persecuting.

It is snowing again by the time we get to the central station; we walk in through the dense whiteness, like heavy fog, that suddenly presses down. Meryem's lawyer Sıtkı is waiting at the door, bag in hand. As soon as he sees his client, he starts yammering. What right do we have taking the honorable Meryem Hanım into custody; have we got any evidence, any witnesses? I shake off the snow without a peep. Before heading for my room with Caner, I hand the short chunky lawyer his honorable client, and Tayyar, trying to appear brave although his eyes are growing with fear, over to Ali. Ali doesn't object; he loves this kind of messy business. Now he's going to squabble with the lawyer, taunt Tayyar, harangue Meryem as he takes her statement, ...

Going up in the lift, Caner brushes the snow from his shoulders as if he's just noticed it. The worry in his eyes has given way to curiosity, and after he's cleaned the snow, he looks at the sign that indicates which police unit is found on which floor.

"Is this your first time to the central station?" I ask him.

"Yes... I've been to a police station a few times, but it's my first time here."

"Not so pleasant, is it?"

He looks at me wondering whether to tell the truth or be polite.

"Don't hold back..."

"It's not as cozy as home," he says, smiling. "Thank God I'm only your guest."

When we get to my room, I understand from the feeling of foreignness in his gaze as it wanders the furnishings that he hasn't found the coziness of home here either, and I try to make him comfortable.

"Sit wherever you'd like... Are you hungry? Shall I get us something to eat?"

"No, thank you," he says, settling into the nearest armchair. "I've eaten. I don't need tea or coffee, either."

It seems he's warmed to me, because most people who come for an inquiry sit in the furthest chair from the desk.

"All right then. I'm going to be straight with you, Caner."

He plants his hazel eyes on me, wanting to understand.

"I was in Malik's shop today. He had some interesting things to say."

A sweet smile spreads on Caner's bright face.

"That's true. Malik Amca is an interesting man."

"He said some interesting things about you too. Especially about your uncle."

His smile freezes, he tenses up and leans forward ever so slightly.

"Your uncle was a priest in the Catholic Church..."

"What about it, Chief Inspector?"

"He sent you to Italy, to study theology... In order to learn Christianity, that is."

Caner shrugs as though it's not important.

"That's true..."

"You never told us about that."

"It never came up. I don't know; I guess I didn't find it relevant. And you never asked. I can explain if you'd like."

I lean back in my chair.

"Yes, I would. Explain away."

"Okay, I will. I told you I am Arab. My mother and father were Arab, both from Antioch. My mother was Christian and my father was Nusayri, Arab Alawite, that is. They met in high school, and it was love at first sight. It didn't matter at all that they were different religions. My father didn't ask my mother to convert, nor did my mother ask him to. For them, the only thing that mattered was love. But not everyone shared their feelings, least of all the head priest of Antioch's Catholic Church, my uncle Daniel. When my father completed the Education Institute and asked to marry my mother, my uncle was against it. He couldn't accept his only sister Elizabeth marrying a Muslim man. 'This marriage is not going to happen,' he said. My grandmother and grandfather had died years before, so it was his word in the house. My mother really loved her big brother, but this time she didn't listen to him. At the risk of being ostracized, she married my father. No one from my mother's family attended the wedding, and that made her really sad. Years later, they explained Uncle Daniel to me. He was sorry for what he'd done. Maybe he took me in as penance for his regret. He sent me to Italy and saw that I got a good education."

"But a religious education," I point out.

"That's right. A Christian education."

"What did your father say to that?"

A slight wave of sadness washes over his face.

"My mother and father died when I was little. Together..."

This was a response I hadn't expected.

"I'm sorry..." I say. "Was it a traffic accident?"

A pained smile appears on Caner's lips.

"Something like that... An act of terrorism. They were shot up in a car in Istanbul."

As my eyes stick on his face in surprise, he continues to explain.

"In the period before the military coup. The country was a blood bath. In those days my father was employed at a school in Kadıköy. He got a reputation as a communist there. Later I learned that he was just a social democrat. I have a vague memory that my father's car was a clunker: a Murat 124. One morning my parents got into the car to go shopping, with no idea what was going to happen, but some people had set up an ambush at the edge of the neighborhood and were waiting for them. Just as my parents were leaving the neighborhood, they sprayed my dad's car with bullets. My father died on the scene and my mother in hospital." The bitter smile stays on his lips as he glances over. "You would know about those days better than I do, Chief. Every day, several people would die. Well, my mom and dad were killed in that chaos."

Caner recounts the event calmly as if he is over it, but I doubt it is that easy.

"It must be really hard for you. How old were you then?"

"Nine or so. It was hard, I guess. I don't remember so well. My uncle didn't abandon me. He picked me up and took me straight to Antioch. Enrolled me in a school there. Whatever I asked for, he delivered. And after high school, he sent me to Rome."

"And it was you who asked him to send you to Italy? I mean, for this Christian education?"

He thinks a bit before answering.

"No, I didn't ask for that, but I didn't object to it either. Anyhow, I'd already learned a lot about Christianity from being with my uncle. And what I'd learned didn't strike me as so wrong. I loved Jesus. He was a good man; he was for peace, on the side of love and the poor. As a matter of fact, I still love him. Just like I love Moses and Muhammad... They were all good men in their own time."

"So then your views changed in Italy," I say.

He stares into space as though he's reliving his days there.

"That's right... I was into my third year. I met a girl named Alessandra from the University of Rome. The girl took an interest in Arabic. She was studying art history and interested in Islamic philosophy. I suppose she wanted to be friends in order to learn Arabic from me. But anyhow... She told me about Tommaso d'Aquino. This Saint Thomas of Aquinas is a very important man for Christians. He was one of the men who had brought about a reformation in Christianity which Islam somehow never managed to do. When I learned his views, I got confused. Because Thomas Aquinas was inspired in certain matters by Ibn Rüşd, known to the West as Averroes. I mean, an Islamic philosopher. It was thanks to Ibni Rüşd, whose books Thomas Aquinas read, that he rediscovered Aristotle. Yes, it is a marvel but, rather than a western philosopher, it was Ibni Rüşd who brought such an important philosopher as Aristotle to light again. At that time, the West was living some of its darkest days in the Middle Ages. Christianity had settled over Europe like a black fog. The church had accused the Antique Greek philosophers of Paganism, declaring them, along with all their thoughts based on reason, as enemies."

I understand part of what Caner is saying, and I've heard the name Aristotle, for instance. I knew about the darkness of the Middle Ages, but I knew nothing of Thomas of Aquino or Ibn Rüşd. It's clear Caner is talking about some lofty issues, but in the midst of a murder investigation, it all just seems like trivia.

"Sorry, Chief. These are some weighty subjects," he breaks off, noticing my bored expression. "Too academic. It's natural it doesn't interest you. I can sum it up this way: When I learned that Islamic philosophers influenced and shaped a devout Christian like Thomas Aquinas, I was confused. Add to that my being the son of an Alawite father, and I began to distance myself from the longhaired, wide-eyed, innocent-faced Jesus. I turned towards the books of Islamic philosophers. After that came the others, and the next thing I know, I'm agnostic." He starts to smile to himself. "Not to over-emphasize this agnosticism. All right, in those days we were into religious philosophy and whatnot, but what really got me disoriented were Alessandra's green eyes, shining like two huge emeralds in her dark skin. After all, I was learning all this because of Alessandra. I was debating it all with her. And this debate soon moved from the university canteen to Alessandra's house."

I begin to smile too. This Caner is an affable guy, hardly one of those know-it-all intellectual types who think they are something special.

"What did your uncle say to this?"

"It was my uncle that worried me most those days, anyhow. I wondered what he was going to say. When I went back to Antioch for summer holidays, I gave it to him straight, without mincing words. I already had an interest in painting and sculpture. I told him I wanted to study art history, not theology anymore. My uncle wasn't angry in the least. He just asked, 'You're in love, aren't you?' I didn't know what to say; I turned three shades of red. My uncle had never married; he'd devoted his body, along with his soul, to the ideals of Jesus. What could I do with a man like that? To say I had fallen for Alessandra's green eyes, her long legs, would come off as frivolous. I was expecting him to scold me, to belittle me even, to tell me to go confess my sins immediately, but he didn't do that. He put a hand on my shoulder and explained.

"God's tests never end. You are being sorely tested in the way our father Adam was. As you know, Adam didn't pass that test. He was expelled from paradise together with our mother Eve. But this is how humankind started off on its big adventure. If Adam hadn't eaten the forbidden fruit, there wouldn't be a you or a me. There wouldn't be a thing called sin. Father Adam and Mother Eve would still be traversing paradise, with no grasp of either paradise or themselves. Because they ate that forbidden fruit, they became independent of God, and they sinned. Put another way, they created sin. And it's because of that sin that the lord Jesus came to earth to save us. It's because of that sin that we walk the path of Jesus Christ, and that you as a young man face a test at every step. With that first sin, your body's desires and your soul's desires separated. So don't be ashamed. This battle between your body's and your soul's desires will go on till the end. Right up until the words of Jesus Christ come to fruition, until your soul is free of the prison of your body and you find true freedom.'

"Yes, Chief, that's what my uncle Daniel said. Actually, I understood just what he meant. But the joy I felt made what he said go in one ear and out the other. My uncle wasn't going to get involved. It meant I was free, I could go to the school of my choice, work on paintings and sculpture and be closer to Alessandra. And I was, right up until Alessandra left me for a goateed American professor of Islamic philosophy."

There's no grudge in his voice and no dejection, just the acknowledgement of defeat.

"Didn't your thoughts change once Alessandra left you?"

"As to Christianity? No, they didn't. Once logic and thought enter the equation, your preferences don't easily change, Chief. After reading so much, becoming aware of so much, you don't just think, well then, the girl I love left me so I may as well go back to Jesus. Besides that, Alessandra left, but other girls came in her place. As life goes on, you realize love is also just a temporary emotion."

We both chuckle.

"And your father's religion never appealed to you?" I ask then.

"Nusayrism? No, it never did. The questions in my head weren't just about Christianity, they were about all religions. I mean, about God."

"But Malik still has hope for you," I say, to bring the subject round to the antique dealer. "He believes you'll be born again one day."

He smiles until his smooth teeth show.

"Yes, Malik has that expectation. But he's wrong. Like other religions, Christianity holds no attraction for me. And anyhow, I've never been a Christian. I've never even been baptized. I tried to learn about Christianity, but well, it never happened. I don't regret it. In fact, although Alessandra dumped me, I owe her my thanks. Malik doesn't want to understand that. Despite being a born-again Christian, he's more stubborn than my uncle Daniel."

"Seriously, what is this Malik's story?"

His face wrinkles up.

"What happened?" I say. "Or don't you want to explain?"

"I will, Chief, but it's a bit of a complicated subject."

"That's fine. I have time."

"I've explained it to so many people. Nobody could understand how a man, who for years had nothing to do with religion, and whose father was Nusayri, suddenly came out and said he's Christian. I was even the one who explained the situation to his son Zekeriya. He couldn't wrap his head around it either."

"I just met Zekeriya. He was in the shop today when I went to talk to Malik. Is he Christian too?"

"No, Zekeriya didn't leave his mother's faith. His mother, on her deathbed, made him swear never to take on his father's religion. The poor woman could never understand why her husband suddenly changed. And anyhow, when Malik became Christian, he ended his relationship with his wife. He left his house and bought another one in Kumkapı."

"So why did Malik change?"

"Now Chief, this situation is directly related to Nusayri culture. Or more precisely, the Nusayri thought process. You know I told you Nusayris are Arab Alawites? Well, this belief system is quite different from the Alevism of Anatolia. Their only common ground is their idea on the Prophet Muhammad's nephew, Ali. Oh, and that politically both sides lie more to the left. Anatolian Alevism is a mix of Turkish Shamanism, certain doctrines of antique Greek philosophy, and lastly Ali's judicious system of thought. Nusayrism essentially rises from Ali's ideas. The roots of Nusayrism go back to the developmental stage of Islam. In that time, like many places in the world, Muslim soldiers organized incursions into Egypt in order to spread the faith. They made Muslims out of the priests of Egypt, who had been keeping faith in polytheism as they had for thousands of years. Yet it wasn't as easy to change the religion of the people as they'd thought it would be. And the people who did change their religion couldn't just drop all their old beliefs and embrace the new faiths. Even if they adopt a new religion, they drag their old beliefs along with them. They try to assimilate the old faiths into the new within themselves. There's a Jesus mosaic in Hagia Sophia that's a great example of this. Before Christianity, Apollo was the god of light in the polytheistic religious culture of Anatolia. It was said that he lit the world. Today, if you look at the mosaic above the door of Hagia Sophia, you'll see that Jesus holds a Bible in his left hand. On the Bible is written, 'I am the light of the world'. You see, the old religions, the old beliefs, don't just vanish into thin air. They meld with the new ones in a cultural exchange and come out as another form of faith."

Caner's explanation really does arouse curiosity, but what it has to do with our subject, that I don't fully understand. Yet I continue to listen patiently to him.

"I think Nusayrism is one of the cultures that can be combined with new beliefs while carrying within it the old. There is no belief in reincarnation within Islam, and yet in the region of Antioch, where Nusayris live, nearly all people believe in it. The belief in reincarnation is so prevalent that in every family there will be one person who can tell you of such an experience."

The fog in my head is beginning to clear. Malik's family is Nusayri, so that means Malik thinks he was Saint Paul in a previous life. Was it from the gleam in my eye or the tautness of my face, Caner senses what I'm thinking and confirms. "Yes, what happened to Malik was exactly that."

Yet it shouldn't be this simple.

"Okay," I blurt out, "but how did this come about? I mean, how did Malik understand he used to be Paul?"

Caner's pleasant face takes on a serious expression.

"In a pretty appropriate setting, actually. On the road to Damascus..."

"At the place where Paul saw Jesus," I mumble.

"It's hard to know if it was the very same spot, but it was on the way to Damascus."

"Why was he going to Damascus?"

"To purchase a handwritten Bible."

"Illicit business..."

"Just so. Malik's past is not so clean, up until he decided he was Paul. But anyhow, let's get to the Damascus trip. They were going along the highway and stopped for a rest after quite a long journey. Malik said he felt restless and wanted to take a little walk, and that's when he saw the light. And under the light, a man who looked just like him. But the clothes the man wore looked like something from thousands of years earlier. Malik stopped and began watching his likeness in amazement. The man was staring into the surrounding light, oblivious to Malik. The light was so bright, so strong, the poor man collapsed to the ground. Malik watched the man fall, and at the same time heard a voice. A voice angry as a lion's and deep as a wounded gazelle's...

" 'And he fell to the earth, and heard a voice saying unto him, Saul, Saul, why persecutest thou me?

And he said, Who art thou, Lord? And the Lord said, I am Jesus whom thou persecutest: it is hard for thee to kick against the pricks.

And he trembling and astonished said, Lord, what wilt thou have me to do? And the Lord said unto him, Arise, and go into the city, and it shall be told thee what thou must do.'***1

"Malik remembered that he'd lived this moment before. And as soon as he remembered, everything went black. When he opened his eyes, he found himself in the restaurant where they'd stopped for a break, his traveling companions trying to revive him. He told his friends what had happened to him. 'You didn't hear anything, didn't see anything?' he asked. But he was the only one to witness the event. And from that day, Malik began to dig into the past. His research brought him to some interesting conclusions. Like Paul, he'd been born in Tarsus and they'd migrated to Antioch later. His father, just like Paul's, was a tentmaker. When he learned this, he was quite convinced he'd been Paul in a previous life. He avoided people and retreated into some kind of seclusion, trying to shed his present knowledge and remember his past. The past he remembered was Paul's life. But he couldn't quite deduce what had taken place, and so he consulted the Bible. In the Bible, he read the Acts of the Apostles and Paul's letter to the Romans. As he read, he remembered better, and became more certain that in his past he'd come into the world as Paul. From that day on, Malik became a fervent Christian. Other Christians, however, never took him seriously. Even my Uncle Daniel - and they were close friends - said he was just feeling remorse for his past crimes, that he'd fancied himself Paul after getting sunstroke on the way to Damascus and having some kind of catharsis. His Nusayri relatives didn't believe him, despite reincarnation being a part of life, because Malik had chosen Christianity. But Malik didn't pay the Christians or the Nusayris any attention anyhow. He believed he was Paul incarnate."

Caner, having finished his story, looked at me as if to say that was that, Malik's whole road to Damascus experience.

"And you? Do you believe Malik?"

He answers without hesitation.

"I don't think Malik is lying. He's not a fraud. He may really have seen what he says. But I don't believe what he saw was real. Or more to the point, there's no reason for me to believe it. Most probably it's like what my uncle Daniel said. Malik got sunstroke. In any case, he'd passed out. We know he was going to Damascus to pick up a handwritten Bible. So he was trafficking the Holy Book. That's both illegal and a sin. Despite the dollar signs in his eyes, Malik may have felt some kind of fear underneath it all. If we add to that his belief in the possibility of reincarnation, we can explain why he would consider himself to be Paul. Though ultimately, this explanation is no more than conjecture. It's impossible to know with any certainty what the reality is."

He's right, but my reasoning is simpler; simple and backed by evidence. That's why Daniel's assumption seems more plausible to me.

Caner, seeing me keep silent, asks, "Why is it so important that Malik is a Christian, Chief?" There's a mix of suspicion and curiosity on his face. "Let's not forget my interest in Christianity too. Seeing as how you asked so much, my having studied Christianity at one time must somehow enter into it. Why is all this important? What has Christianity got to do with Yusuf's murder?"

"A lot. Yusuf was murdered with a knife that had a cross for a handle. And also, there was an open Bible in the room where the body was found. Some of the verses had been underlined in Yusuf's blood. And in the margin of the book, also written in Yusuf's blood, were the words 'Mor Gabriel'."

"Mor Gabriel?" he asks. His voice is laden with fear and bewilderment. "Are you sure? It said Mor Gabriel?"

"That's what it said."

"Is the book here? I'd like to see it."

"It's here. We'll send for it, but first let's talk about this Mor Gabriel a bit. Who is this man?"

Before starting, his concerned eyes stay on my face for a spell, although he isn't seeing me. Maybe he's trying to collect his words, or maybe he's searching for an explanation.

"Mor Gabriel is a saint," he finally says. "An Assyrian saint. He's an important man, and it's said he performed miracles. There's even a monastery named after him."

"Is he living in that monastery?"

A smile spreads compulsively across Caner's lips.

"Living, Chief? Mor Gabriel's been dead about one thousand four hundred years now."

I'm not sure what to say to that. Before my eyes, I see the script written in blood in the margin of the book, and I feel my my hair standing on end. I chase the strange thoughts away and ask, "Did he die a natural death?"

"He did. And not only that, he lived to be seventy-four, quite a long life for those times."

"So what were the miracles he performed?"

He tries to remember.

"There was one related to healing the sick. Oh, and for years his body never decomposed."

"How do they know that?"

"There's a legend told about him in the Mor Gabriel Monastery. Hundreds of years after he'd died, some people stole his corpse. The priests of the monastery weren't aware of it. But the next morning, they found all the body snatchers dead outside the monastery, and beside them, the corpse of Mor Gabriel. They looked and saw the body was as fresh as the day he'd died."

As he explains this, Caner also gets a wave of excitement. His face is taut and his voice gets hoarser.

"Do you believe all this?"

"I don't." He averts his eyes. "I don't believe it but..." he says, looking me in the face again, "I'll admit I got a bit confused when Yusuf Abi told me about a dream he kept having."

"What was the dream?"

"In fact, I'm not sure whether it was a dream or a hallucination." He hesitates for a moment. "As you've concluded, Yusuf Abi smoked cannabis."

"How do you know we concluded that?"

"Meryem Abla told me. You asked her. Isn't that right?"

"Yes, I guess Meryem was smoking too." He confirms it by staying silent. "And you? Do you smoke?"

He gets an innocent look on his face, the charm of a child waiting to be forgiven for the small crime he's committed.

"I won't lie to you, Chief. I smoke too, but not always. You know, if I'm in that environment and I'm craving it. And not so much that I lose control. If everyone else is smoking, I will too…"

"Did you smoke with Yusuf?"

"I did, but only to a certain point. I know when to stop. Yusuf Abi's problem was he didn't know when to quit. Once he started, he'd smoke till he was comatose, or till he passed out. It's like there was something bad he was trying to forget, and he was smoking in desperation as if the marijuana would help. That's why maybe the events he explained to me as a dream were a figment of his imagination, under the influence of the cannabis." He shuts up a bit, as if he himself is now seeing that figment. "It's a strange vision though," he tries to explain. "He'd get this smell that burned his nose first. A familiar smell. Reminding him of a monastery that had stayed closed up for hundreds of years. Oil lamps, crumbling stone, wasting marble, rotting wood, worn pages and moldering corpses. Yes, corpses… That's how Yusuf Abi explained. But it hadn't scared him; he would just look around. And then he'd see a moving black form. Shapeless and vague… A jet-black silhouette. He would smile at the form and the words 'Mor Gabriel' would spill out of his mouth. He didn't choose to say the words, they came out spontaneously. As he said them, the form would slowly draw closer. And as it drew closer, it assumed the shape of a human body. A bearded person dressed in black. That person came up to him and whispered in his ear, 'Do you know me?' And Yusuf would mumble, 'Mor Gabriel.' As the words fell from his mouth, he'd hear music. Deep, ceremonial music. It was a passionate repetitive murmuring in the Syriac language, read by someone as if in raptures. At the same time, he'd notice a cross. A silver cross. And as he tried to understand whether the man carried it in his hand or in his chest, he'd see a flash splitting the void. He'd feel a pain, and when the light flashed again, the pain would disappear. Relief spread through his body and the voice moved away, the colors in the room faded, and finally that black spot disappeared. And just as soon as the spot had disappeared, Yusuf Abi would wake up."

"He saw the flash of light twice?" I asked.

"Yes, twice. He said so. Why do you ask?"

"Because there were two knife stabs to Yusuf's body."

He narrows his hazel eyes and tries to make sense of it.

"Think about it," I say. "A raised knife thrusts quickly down, and that is the flash that divides the air in two."

"I suppose you're right, Chief. But it's the cross at the hilt of the knife that freaks me out. Because Yusuf Abi clearly said he saw a cross in his dream."

He is practically whispering as he says this.

"What, you mean Yusuf foresaw his own death?"

"I don't know, Chief," he says, his eyes worried and restless. "I really don't know what to say. What do you think?"

"What can I think? Most likely, the killer is one of the people Yusuf told his dream to."

Although it's not what I was getting at, Caner assumes I'm accusing him. He pulls away from the table and leans back in his chair.

"Then your job's not hard," he says, his voice bitter. "I doubt Yusuf Abi told his dream to too many people."

"I doubt it, too. Apart from you, he probably told Meryem, maybe this elusive Timuçin, and Fatih... And of course, Malik."

I watch him as I name Malik. Let's see what he'll say.

"He did tell Malik," he says naively. "I was with them. And he told Meryem Abla, although I don't know about Timuçin or Fatih."

"Because you don't know them," I say, my gaze heaped with insinuation. "Isn't that right?"

"I don't, Chief. I told you before..."

I intend to press Caner a bit more, but then the phone on my desk starts to ring. I look at it. It's Zeynep calling.

Chapter 16
A Book of Aramaic text on antelope hide.

Zeynep's voice on the phone is excited. She speaks quickly, with the eagerness given by what she's learned.

"I've turned up some interesting information, Chief. I'd like to report it if you're available."

"Really? What did you find out?"

"Should I explain over the phone?"

It's better than doing it in front of Caner.

"Yes, I'm listening."

"Yusuf's account received a one hundred-thousand-dollar transfer. And it was Malik Karakuş who made it."

"Is it clear what it was sent for?"

"No, Chief. There's no description. However, Yusuf and Malik definitely had a monetary connection between them. And Malik is not remotely clean. His file is pretty bulky. Smuggling of everything from guns to historical artifacts. Whatever you're looking for, it's there."

"Has he committed any crimes in the last couple years?"

"No, none recently, but I found the hundred-thousand-dollar payment interesting."

Zeynep's right. My gaze goes to Caner, who sits calmly minding his own business, his eyes on the locked hands on his knees. I wonder if he knows about this hundred thousand dollars. If he knew, he'd have told me. Wouldn't he? Well, we'll find out.

"So what else do we have, Zeynep?" I ask.

"There is one other notable finding. Yusuf's cell phone records. He made frequent calls to Meryem, Caner, Malik and the police station."

Well this is a genuine surprise.

"The station? Are you sure?"

"Absolutely, and many times..."

"Do we know who he was calling?"

"Unfortunately not. There's just the central switchboard."

That's bad. It will be hard to find out who it was.

"I understand, Zeynep," I say. "Thanks." As I'm about to hang up, something occurs to me. "This Bible we found at the crime scene, can you bring it to me? I have an expert on Christianity here with me. Let's have him take a look."

"As you wish, Chief."

"My friends came across some interesting facts," I say, hanging up and giving Caner an accusatory look. "Something you didn't tell us about."

He squirms nervously.

"What facts, Inspector?"

In place of an answer, I sternly ask, "What were Yusuf and Malik up to? I'm warning you, Caner. Don't lie to me."

He goes pale and swallows before answering.

"No lies," I reiterate. "Don't forget. You are still a suspect."

"Believe me, I have nothing to do with it, Inspector," he says, his white face turning red. "I was just consulted."

"Consulted about what?"

"A purportedly valuable handwritten manuscript. A book written in Aramaic on antelope hide."

"A Bible?"

"Not exactly a Bible. The Diatessaron."

"What does that mean?"

"Actually, it's a musical term. 'A harmony of four', it means. What Christians accept as the Gospel today is made up of four separate books: Matthew, Mark, Luke and John. The Diatessaron was written by an Assyrian named Tatian, utilizing fragments from these four texts. A handwritten copy of this manuscript was found during the 1933 excavation at Salihiye. The original text is thought to have been written in 170 A.D."

"Where did Yusuf find the copy he has? Shouldn't it belong to his church?"

"I agree with you that it should belong to the church, but Yusuf Abi says he inherited it from his family."

"How is it that Yusuf comes to inherit church property?"

Caner looks away.

"Why don't you call it what it is? Yusuf was smuggling antique artifacts..."

Caner goes quiet with the shame of being caught red-handed.

"Isn't that right, Caner? Why don't you speak up?"

"I don't know, Inspector. I just acted as a consultant."

"You mean you abetted a crime."

"No, Inspector, I didn't abet anyone. I didn't even know whether the Diatessaron Yusuf Abi brought over was valuable or not."

"But Malik knew for sure," I say, "because he sent Yusuf a hundred thousand dollars."

"A hundred thousand dollars?" he says, curling his lip. "If that work is authentic, a hundred thousand dollars is a trifling sum."

"Maybe he was meant to pay the balance later... Or maybe he killed Yusuf so as not to pay it."

"Malik Amca?" he says. He's sounds flummoxed. "I don't think so, Inspector. Malik Amca would never kill anyone."

For a moment I visualize Malik, his face at peace with the world and himself, but we've seen our fair share of angel-faced killers before.

"Why? Because he fancies himself Saint Paul?" I argue. "The man has an exhaustive record. Maybe the Paul thing is a lie he has crafted as a cover."

He disagrees.

"No, Inspector. Malik believes what he says. You don't know him so..."

"Well that much is true," I say, interrupting. "I don't know you or Malik. Maybe you are in this together."

The blood seems to drain from his face.

"What are you saying, Inspector?" He can't finish his words because the door opens and Cengiz comes in. As soon as he does, he says, "This murder..." but then he sees there's a stranger in the room and changes course. "Could you come to my room? Let's have a chat, Nevzat. And you should hurry, because I have to go out."

Caner has a curious expression as he looks first at Cengiz and then at me.

"Yes, sir. Right away," I say.

As Cengiz is leaving, Zeynep appears at the door. She is clutching the Bible we found at Yusuf's.

"Come in, Zeynep. This is our specialist," I add, indicating Caner. Have him take a look at the book. You stay with him. I'll pop into Director Cengiz's room and then we can all sit down and evaluate it together."

The flicker in Zeynep's brown eyes shows she has grasped my meaning. Reassured, I head for Cengiz's room.

I find Cengiz waiting for me in front of the window, just as he was this morning. He's smoking again, but this time he's not looking out the window but at me. The clothes he is wearing are different too; he's put on a dark blue suit. I guess he'll be meeting some officials. He always keeps a spare suit in his room. In our profession, after a certain rank you have to heed protocol, it's one of the first prerequisites to advancement. His navy-blue cashmere coat is not on its hanger, but on the back of the chair. Meaning he's really in a hurry.

"Come in, Nevzat," he says. His voice is tense, distracted. "This Syriac murder... It's always on the news. Apparently that encounter in Beyoğlu is connected to it. Why don't I know about it?"

"I told you this morning..."

He tries to remember.

"You're right. You did," he says, then, "So many incidents it's hard to keep them straight. So what is this Syriac murder?" He continues, not giving me a chance to answer. "I'll go to lunch from here. The internal affairs minister will be there, our director general, the governor, everyone. They're going to ask about the situation. Director Sabri has already rung twice. The dead guy is Christian so, you know, they're worried that Europe, and the Church, will put pressure on us."

This bothers me.

"Who said the victim was Christian?" I ask.

"Wasn't he? All the TV channels are talking about that."

"Yes, the man was Christian, but who leaked that to the press, that's what I want to know."

Cengiz glowers at me as if to say, how should I know.

"Must have been one of yours. Who else could it be?"

"None of us would disclose that; neither Ali or Zeynep talk to the press. Someone from CSI must have a big mouth."

"Şefik?"

"I doubt it. It must be one of his men."

"Anyhow, there's always a leak. What is this thing?"

I stand there and explain. He listens attentively. As he hears the details, he starts to relax.

"It's good that Henna Meryem is in custody," he says, sighing contentedly. "We have two of her men in custody too. That makes three suspects we've got. And you say one of them confessed..." He hastily presses his half-smoked cigarette into the ashtray and continues. "Bingöllü Kadir killed Yusuf, and Meryem incited the suspect Tonguç to shoot him. So, the case is nearly solved. The murders have nothing to do with Christianity. If you get a move on, you could even hold a press conference tomorrow. For that matter, maybe the governor would like to make the announcement." Satisfied with the situation, he starts towards his coat, dragging his right foot with its slightly perceptible limp. "Nice job, Nevzat. You've outdone yourself."

"I wish that were true."

Cengiz's arm, reaching for his coat, stops in mid-air. He turns quickly to me. With deep concern in his light brown eyes, he says, "What do you mean, you wish that were true?"

"I don't think Bingöllü killed Yusuf. There's something else to this. We've accessed new information and it looks like it could be antique smuggling. There's this antique dealer. Malik. Suspicion is gathering on him."

Cengiz is not happy; the agitation in his eyes spreads across his entire face. It would have been great, giving the good news to his superiors tonight. I've taken the wind out of his sails. And now for the really bad news.

"And Yusuf called the station numerous times."

He winces and the eyes beneath his bushy eyebrows narrow.

"Which station?" Without giving me a chance to answer, he mutters, "This one?"

"This one... But we don't know who he talked to. He called the switchboard operator and they connected him to whoever he asked for."

"Can't you determine who it was?"

"We can't. Thousands of calls come through central..."

"I wonder who it was."

"Maybe he had a contact. Or maybe he was getting death threats and he called an officer he knew to ask for protection."

"That's possible. Let's ask around, whether someone among us knew Yusuf."

"They'll deny it if they do. Yusuf seems like a bad egg."

"We'd better look into it anyhow." Cengiz appears better now. He's recovered.

"Listen, Nevzat, let's do this. Let's give the press this Tonguç, say that he admitted to killing the man. We won't announce that Yusuf's killer is Bingöllü Kadir but we'll state that Tonguç killed him because he thought he was. That way we can keep the press from sniffing. And you can smoothly carry on the investigation. What do you say?"

Bravo, Cengiz, it occurs to me to say. With this political shrewdness you'll soon be the director general, and the governor, even run for interior affairs minister and run the country. But of course I don't say it.

"All right. Agreed. However, you'd better not call a press conference, because it's not clear what this thing is going to churn up."

He puts a hand on my shoulder and his cigarette breath hits my face.

"Don't worry, Nevzat," he says, skillfully winking his right eye. "We won't hold a press conference. But everyone will think this business is completely resolved. And if there is still a murderer at large, he will think so too. That will work to your advantage, won't it?"

"Very much so, thank you."

"Ha, by the way, Director Sabri wants to see you." He steals a glance at me. "If you want to come..." His tongue says this, but his eyes are saying it's better if I don't. "To tonight's dinner, I mean. Director Sabri invited you too."

"No thanks, Cengiz. Let me put this business in order. But tell him I said hello. He should be my guest one evening. We could go to Agora Meyhane in Balat. You're invited too, of course."

"Okay, I'll tell him," he says, going for his coat again. "But this time around he has no time, I guess. You know, the ministers and such are here."

"Whenever you want. The offer's always valid."

"Thanks, Nevzat. I should go to this dinner and put our superiors at ease now. You go back to your investigation." He takes his coat. I beat him to the door. As I'm about to walk out he calls out from behind me. "Oh, and Nevzat. Keep this investigation as quiet as possible, will you? Don't let the press get on our back again."

"I'll do what I can," I say, leaving his room.

Chapter 17
It's not Jesus who founded Christianity, it's Paul of Tarsus.

Walking up the calm corridor, lit with white fluorescents, I'm thinking it's good Sabri didn't directly call to invite me. It would have been hard to turn him down, and I'd have had to attend the gathering. The minister of internal affairs, the governor... The insincere conversations, the little lies told to ingratiate with superiors, the veiled payoffs... And dinner. No one would get any pleasure from what they ate or drank. But thinking about food, I get hungry. I haven't had a bite in my mouth since morning. I should wrap up this business with Caner and eat something.

Nearing my room, I hear the discussion from the half open door. It's not hard to pick out Caner's voice.

"It's not Jesus who founded Christianity, it's Paul of Tarsus," he says.

I'm hearing this claim for the first time. To tell the truth, it piques my interest, so I pick up my pace.

"Jesus was Jewish, and he said his mission was to correct the degeneracy of his religion."

"Jesus Christ was Jewish?" asks a surprised male voice. It belongs to none other than our Ali, ignorant of Christianity and of Judaism. So then, he's finished his business with Meryem. I go in as Caner's about to explain. He's sitting in the chair where I left him, with Zeynep opposite him and next to her, Ali. Our two young officers have their eyes on the scholar, but the moment they've noticed me they jump to their feet. Only Caner stays put.

I turn to Ali as if I haven't overheard their conversation.

"What's the situation downstairs?"

"There's no problem, Chief. They're being processed and tomorrow they'll appear before the prosecutor."

"Good," I say, going over to my place. I see the Bible on the table. It's open to the page with the verse underlined in Yusuf's blood. I nod towards the book and ask, "What did you do? Have you taken a look, Caner?"

Caner leans forward and looks at the two words written in blood again.

"Yes, I looked, Inspector."

"So these highlighted spots, do the lines have any special meaning?"

He pulls the book to him and starts reading out loud.

" 'Awake, O sword, against my shepherd, and against the man that is my fellow.' It isn't enough. He repeats the line and continues reading.

" 'Awake, O sword, against my shepherd, and against the man that is my fellow, saith the Lord of hosts: smite the shepherd, and the sheep shall be scattered: and I will turn mine hand upon the little ones. And it shall come to pass, that in all the land, saith the Lord, two parts therein shall be cut off and die; but the third shall be left therein. And I will bring the third part through the fire, and will refine them as silver is refined, and will try them as gold is tried: they shall call on my name, and I will hear them...' "

As his eyes wander the lines, he shakes his head no. "I don't think the words have any special meaning. The prophet Zechariah said or wrote them. They are a reminder of God's wrath, to purge people of their sins and transgressions. It intimidates those who do evil with holy laws, a common method in the Torah. Judaism accepts mankind as essentially evil, and the best way to fix people is to apply holy law."

"Did Jesus feel the same?"

The question comes from Zeynep. Apparently our clever girl is as affected as Ali by this chat about Christianity.

"No, Jesus had another view. Jesus recommended love and forgiveness in place of punishment."

Although Ali hasn't lost interest in the subject, he must not be too amused by Zeynep's attention to Caner, because he directly switches to that snippy attitude he always gets.

"You said Jesus didn't come along for another religion, but to correct the degeneracy of Judaism. How is it that someone trying to bring Judaism back to its old form gives up on the fundamental understanding of the religion? If your own religion regards man as sinful, wouldn't Jesus have to think the same?"

The question is sensible enough, but Caner easily explains, as if his words hold no contradiction.

"Jesus represented the savior they'd been waiting hundreds of years for. The Jewish clergy were completely corrupt. The holy city of Jerusalem was under the Roman Empire's occupation, and what's worse, the Jewish clergy were living in harmony with their Roman occupiers. The great temple of the Jews was on the side of the Roman garrison. The people had given up hope on the clergy and were waiting for a messiah to save them. And Jesus was that messiah. No doubt, it didn't happen all at once; he didn't even believe it himself in the beginning. But the process managed to convince both him and others. It was a grueling struggle. There was constant conflict. The conservative clergymen known as Pharisees were against Jesus. And Jesus waged an intellectual battle with them. A kind of ideological war. Throughout this war, Jesus adopted a different kind of language from conservative Jews. A language that uplifted, rather than instilling fear in people. A language that promoted forgiveness, love and peace over punishment."

"But they crucified him," Zeynep intones. Her voice is sad, like she's asking why they'd done it.

"That's so," Caner agrees. "They crucified the man who said, 'Turn the other cheek.' But if he hadn't died on the cross, there would be no Christianity today."

"Nonsense!" Ali cuts in. "If Jesus hadn't died on the cross, Christianity would never have been born? Wasn't Jesus sent by God?"

Caner looks at Ali before answering. It isn't a belittling look but rather one that says, I understand you, but you also don't have any knowledge on the subject. How can I explain? The troubled look of a man made helpless by knowing. It seems he'll take a step back and end this discussion, but after taking a deep breath, he says, "If you look at it from a religious perspective, that's right. Jesus was sent by God. Mind you, the views on this subject among the religions vary a lot. Judaism accepts Jesus as neither a prophet nor God, but as to Christianity, Jesus is not merely a prophet, but God himself. According to Islam, Jesus is only a prophet. But he didn't die on a cross. In his place, Allah brought the betrayer Judas to the cross, giving the traitor the appearance of Jesus in order to trick his enemies. As for Jesus, Allah brought him to his side. Because Allah is not so cruel that he would allow his prophets to die."

After this commentary, he looks round to see if there are any objections. Ali still hasn't digested all he's heard, so he holds his tongue. When there are no raised eyebrows, Caner spreads his hands and continues.

"That's how religions see it. It's a matter of faith. There's nothing to argue with. There's the idea that they are to be believed, cohered to, and amalgamated with. The idea itself is God or Allah. The mentality in a belief system embraces, serves to embrace, only this."

Ali thinks he's finally found a weak spot in Caner's argument. "What," he gibes, "are you saying believers are feeble-minded?"

Anyone who didn't know better would think Ali was religious. Up until this incident, I can't recall a single word to do with religion leaving his mouth. Now, all of a sudden, he's the defender of every religion on the face of the earth. Ah, love, what power you wield! With no clue as to why this inspector is attacking him like this, Caner tries to elucidate. I put an end to the meaningless dispute, saying, "This is all neither here nor there. The person who concerns us in this case is Paul..."

The shadow of a problem he can't grasp falls across Caner's eyes.

"While I was coming into the room, you were saying how it was Paul who founded Christianity, not Jesus. I'm hearing this for the first time. Is there such a theory? Or did you come up with that?"

"The idea was around before me. But at the same time, it was the subject of one of my assignments in university."

"Tell us a little about this Saint Paul."

My request leads to Caner hanging his handsome face. It's clear he doesn't know how to explain or where to begin. If the people with him were knowledgeable on the subject of Christianity, it'd make things easier, but how does he explain the details of the matter to these cops now?

"It's complicated," he says, trying to be as gentle as possible. "I mean, how much do you know about Christianity?"

"Don't underestimate us, Caner Bey," says Zeynep. She's not reproachful at all. She has grasped the young man's uneasiness and is trying to reassure him. In doing so, she also aims to destroy the common image of police Caner has in his head. "We're open to learning. In fact, we have to do our jobs scientifically too. We learn something new every incident we come across. Three months ago, we dealt with a case in a university where a quantum physicist murdered his colleague as the result of a rivalry. The case obliged us to learn about quantum physics, the basic theory, at least. So don't worry that we won't understand the history of Christianity. We will."

The tension in Ali's dark eyes gives way to a spark of tenderness. This rebuke of Zeynep's has pleased him. To myself, I say, *Nice job, Zeynep.*

"No," Caner says, squirming. "That's not what I meant, I mean..."

"Come on, Caner. Drop the politeness and start explaining," I say. "My blood sugar is beginning to fall from hunger, so tell us and then let's go get a bite."

"All right," says Caner, reconciling himself to his fate. "Okay then..."

But this 'okay then' comes out a bit loaded.

"Just a minute," I say, compelled to cut in again. "Don't go making some convoluted speech just because Zeynep says we've learned quantum physics. However it is you would tell your students, tell us the same way."

"All right, Inspector," he says, smiling. "I'll tell it simple." But he still can't manage to start. "Actually..," he says, "actually, in order to understand the situation, we have to compare the historical Jesus to Paul."

Ali doesn't let him continue.

"What do you mean by historical Jesus? How many Jesuses are there?"

"There are two. The first was born to a mother, like all people. The Jesus who like us, ate, dressed, lived and in the end died. We call that the historical Jesus, while the other is the Jesus who came to earth on a sacred mission, and having completed it, became God. So the historical Jesus, as far as is known, was not so cultured. He'd got a religious education with some Jewish clergymen and that's all. Anyhow, it wasn't his deep wisdom that impressed people, but his simple, naive behavior, his loving heart and the miracles he performed. As he called on people to love, the creed he referred to was a Jewish creed. He wanted everyone to obey the law and to abide by the Ten Commandments." He reaches for the Bible and turns the pages with fingers deft from habit, stopping somewhere near the end.

"Here, in the Book of Mark, it explains what Jesus did when he entered the Great Temple of the Jews in Jerusalem. '... and Jesus went into the temple, and began to cast out them that sold and bought in the temple, and overthrew the tables of the moneychangers, and the seats of them that sold doves; And would not suffer that any man should carry any vessel through the temple. And he taught, saying unto them, Is it not written, My house shall be called of all nations the house of prayer? but ye have made it a den of thieves.'***1 Because as a Jew that temple was his, and Jesus wanted to clean it out. He saw himself not as a Christian, but a Jew, plain and simple."

"Jesus was not the first to use the word 'Christian' either; that was his antagonists. In the Bible, in the section called Acts, it's written that King Herod Agrippa, while arguing with Paul, teasingly said, 'Almost thou persuadest me to be a Christian.'***2

"The term 'Christian' was widely used in the era after Jesus by Antioch's Jews and the people against Jesus. I mean, Jesus never said, 'I've brought you a religion called Christianity.' And anyhow Jesus wouldn't have accepted any mediator between God and man. Whereas Christianity states that it is possible to reach God through a messiah. And with that being the case, it is impossible to call Jesus Christian."

"Give me a break," Ali protests. "You're practically saying Jesus has nothing to do with Christianity."

"Isn't that possible? The Crucifixion is the most important event to inspire Paul. It was based on Jesus's crucifixion that Paul created a systematic religion, that is, Christianity."

Like Ali, I can't be sure of the truth of these words.

"You mean Jesus was just a figure for Christianity?"

He wags his index finger to emphasize the importance of what he says, and answers.

"A significant figure. The cross carries a deeper meaning than two planks nailed together. I'm talking about the four elements life is made up of: earth, air, fire and water. The four tips of the cross symbolize those elements, or life. And Paul set forth from these symbols. Life, which the crucifix represents, and right in the middle of this life, a man who carried the pain of his human brothers and sisters on his back: Jesus."

Zeynep has planted her eyes on Caner, and listens intently, admiringly even. As her interest increases, so Ali's jealousy grows.

"That's ridiculous," he bellows. "Why would Jesus put up with this suffering?"

"To save mankind. As I said before, according to the Torah, people are sinners. Let's remember the story of Adam. Adam and Eve ate a fruit that wasn't meant to be eaten, and were expelled from heaven. But this exile made the children of Adam wise, and they continued to do evil. This is why God created the flood. He punished with death everyone except the prophet Noah and his sons, but people still didn't take the correct path. Allah sent prophets to the world to fix humanity, but humankind's selfishness, cruelty, deception and destruction never diminished. Finally, he sent the Ten Commandments by way of Moses. This was a very stern warning. Allah, in order to intimidate the human race, sent tablets engraved with fire. Thus, divine law and divine punishment came into effect. And yet mankind still did things their own way. Well, that is the point in history when Jesus came onto the scene. He addressed the Jewish community under Roman occupation, and spoke of love, tolerance and forgiveness. His purity, good intentions and power to heal influenced people. Jesus was a kind of revolutionary, a kind of good Samaritan, and most importantly, was accepted as the much waited for Messiah.

"Paul took this figure and made him the axis of the religion he created. He appealed to people this way: Jesus was crucified and died for you. He was a martyr, a sacrifice necessary for God to forgive people. He was a savior, a savior who rescued people from the heavy burdens of divine law and facilitated godly love. He was an emancipator, liberating mankind from the prisons of their physical desires and calling them to live in the eternal world of the soul."

He looks us each in the face one by one as though to weigh the effect of his words.

Ali is unmoved; in fact he even brashly states, "What you're saying makes no sense at all to me." He points at the Bible and continues. "Four books, all those prophets, and everything they say is empty, only what you say is true." His annoyance grows as he speaks. He doesn't really know exactly what he's saying himself, but as he talks he becomes more resentful towards Caner. He's honing his jealousy with his own words. "I think you are bullshitting, Caner Efendi. Where did that man you call Paul get this information? If it weren't for Christ the Messiah, would there even be such a man? And you have the nerve to defame Jesus."

Caner listens to Ali with a patronizing look in his eye.

"Did you say Christ the Messiah?" he then says.

The remark had got my attention too. Why has Ali referred to Jesus this way? Before giving Ali a chance to answer, Caner asks another question.

"Are you Christian, Inspector?"

I don't know the answer to this question either. I've never asked him. But he's also never asked me; he knows I'm Muslim. And I know he is Muslim. Unless he's converted? No, he certainly would have told me. As this passes through my mind, Ali leans forward in his chair, his eyes locked on Caner, rage in his face on the brink of bursting. "What's it to you?" he spits.

Caner graciously yields.

"Please don't take it the wrong way. I'm not questioning anyone. It just interests me that you say Christ the Messiah. Although it comes up in the Quran as Jesus the Messiah, in daily life, Muslims generally call him the Prophet Jesus."

Ali glowers.

"I swear it was just curiosity, Inspector," says Caner. "Really though, you aren't Christian, are you?"

"Christian Shmistian," Ali snaps back. "You don't need to be Christian to defend the Prophet Jesus." He's giving him such a hard look, I think it's good that I'm here. If I weren't he'd have already popped him in the face. "And we are the ones who ask the questions here. Not you, you got that?"

Caner turns to me, the mischievous expression still on his face.

"I thought I was here to help you. If I'd known I was being interrogated..."

"Friends, you're off topic again," I say, trying to get back on track. It disappoints Ali that I've referred to Caner as a friend along with him. But what can I do? We're in no position to beat on Caner to make him talk. "This Paul," I say, turning to Caner, "you say he's the one who founded Christianity. If that's the case, it's no joke, the man has established a massive religion. Where did all this knowledge come from?"

"Yes, that is the question that needs asking," says Caner. With this attitude, he makes Ali a bit angrier still. But Ali holds his tongue. He must be upset at my reaction, as he chooses to sit back, his arms crossed over his chest. "Paul was already a cultured man, Chief Inspector," Caner continues. "He was not only a Roman citizen, but also a Jew. Yet he was living among people who embraced paganism. Tarsus at that time was an important cultural center. It had some eminent schools of philosophy. This is how Paul learned not only Greek philosophy, but also those secret religions of Tarsus and Syria and, as a Jew, add Judaism into the mix. According to one hypothesis, his family sent him to Jerusalem, enabling him to receive a religious education from the Pharisees. Most importantly, whether you call it Hermeticism or Gnosticism, Paul believed in arcane knowledge."

Hermeticism, Gnosticism, arcane knowledge... Caner sees from our questioning gazes that the three of us know nothing of this subject, and he expounds.

"Hermetics and Gnostics perceive and interpret the world differently. According to them, there are two worlds: first the world we perceive with our five senses, and second the one we can't perceive with our senses, but can only intuit. Put another way, the secret world that we divine, that we see with our heart's eye. The visible world is limited to material objects and is worthless. The secret world is limitless and valuable. While the material world is sinful and finite, the secret world is pure and infinite. In the material world, seeing God is impossible, but in the secret world, God is with you, inside of you. Yet not everyone can see the secret world. You must free yourself from physical impulses, set aside your analytical rules and move towards your intuitive perception. Only those with keen intuitive perception and profound cognitive abilities can pass through the door to this world. This thinking is so deep, you have to be free of not just the weight of your body, but the weight of your rational mind. And this is the culture which nurtured Paul. Paul's Christianity project rises from this conception. By shaking off the boundaries and desires of the human body and attaining the everlastingness and exalted desires of the soul. That is meeting, or perhaps becoming one with, God. When Paul talks about Jesus becoming God by means of his crucifixion, this is actually what he's talking about. This doesn't just apply to Christian thought; the roots go back to Ancient Egypt and Greece, the Temple of Zoroastrianism in Iran, Brahmanism and Cabbalism. It includes *tasavvuf*, our Islamic mysticism, also known as Sufism. To be one with Allah, to identify with him and become a piece of him, means being Allah himself. *'Enel Hak'* as Mansur Al-Hallaj puts it. 'I am God'.

With these words, he starts flipping through the Bible. "I'd like to read you another passage. In the section called Paul's Epistles, in the letter he wrote to Corinthians, Paul says this. 'Howbeit that was not first which is spiritual, but that which is natural; and afterward that which is spiritual. The first man is of the earth, earthly; the second man is the Lord from heaven. As is the earth, such are they also that are earthly: and as is the heavenly, such are they also that are heavenly. And as we have borne the image of the earthly, we shall also bear the image of the heavenly. Now this I say, brethren, that flesh and blood cannot inherit the kingdom of God; neither doth corruption inherit incorruption.' "***3

He turns back to us and enthusiastically continues.

"Here is where a comparison between Adam and Jesus is made. Adam came first, and is sinful. Jesus is the second, who came from the heavens, and is holy. Paul represented the material world with earth and the holy one with sky. Paul would say that, just as Jesus showed us, if people choose the path of love, throwing off the prisons of their bodies, they can reach the heavens."

It's plain this guy is knowledgeable on the subject and is addressing some important issues, but I don't understand exactly what he's getting at. Not to mention, I'm getting hungrier by the minute. My head is spinning a bit and I have difficulty following Caner's commentary. "So...?" I say, trying to wind things up.

"So this, Chief Inspector. Paul is the man who created Christianity. More importantly, like I said before, nothing on the face of the planet is entirely new. Every new thought, every new faith, carries within it the ones preceding it."

Ali can't help jumping in again.

"Who else besides you says this?" He can't stop; he keeps on in anger. "Brother, you say there is no proof that the Prophet Jesus ever lived. Is there any documentation showing that Paul is the man who created Christianity?"

Caner retreats to that aggravating calmness again and points to the Bible.

"Here is the evidence. Christianity has two crucial saints. One is Peter, who was also Jesus's apostle and one of Jesus's closest companions. Jesus complimented him, saying he would build his church upon him. The second is Paul, who was an enemy to Jesus while Jesus lived. Paul earned the rank of saint through his thoughts and missionary deeds. If the ideas he held weren't as important as I've said, would the fathers of the church have allowed him such a distinction? If you take a look at the Bible, you'll see that the most detailed information on the Christian faith was given in Paul's doctrine... If Paul weren't that important, would what he wrote have been included in the Bible?"

I had to ask the question really niggling at me, otherwise not only would Ali not shut up, but Caner would never abort his running commentary.

"This Paul of Tarsus," I say, "was doing missionary work. He visited a lot of countries to perform his sacred duty. During these trips, did he ever kill anyone?"

Caner gets a look of surprise.

"Saint Paul?"

"Yes. It can't be an easy thing to do missionary work among pagans, and especially not to carry out these activities within the borders of a Roman Empire that is not yet Christian. He must have encountered a thousand and one problems. Couldn't Paul possibly have killed someone while trying to protect himself? I mean, was there any event like that?"

He objects without even feeling the need to think it over.

"No. I doubt it. There is no such text or narrative that points to such an incident. You're right; it was hard to be a missionary back then. Paul escaped death many times. But he's not believed to have killed anyone. Because Paul was someone who lived in harmony with holy law. At the same time, he respected worldly laws, I mean, the laws of the Roman Empire. I doubt he killed anyone. Why do you ask that, Inspector?"

"Malik," is all I say.

Caner immediately grasps my meaning.

"Oh... You want to know whether Malik Amca committed a murder in imitation of Paul."

I confirm with silence.

"You're mistaken, Inspector. Like I said before, Malik Amca couldn't kill anyone. But if it'll put your mind at rest, I'll repeat, Saint Paul never killed anyone either. On the contrary, he saved several people from death. He healed them. At least it's written as such. Nevertheless, the ruthless emperor Nero didn't show Paul the same mercy Paul showed others. After an inquiry and a lengthy detention, he executed Paul, chopping off his head."

Caner has an accusatory expression on his face as though we were responsible for Paul's death. The interesting thing is, neither I, nor Zeynep nor Ali, make a sound. We just sit there as if Saint Paul's decapitated head has fallen into our midst.

Chapter 18
Mor Gabriel wants something from me.

The next morning when I wake up, Caner's words are echoing in my head. "Malik Amca couldn't kill anyone." How can he be so sure? I sit up in bed. Outside, there is sun. The weather has finally cleared. My eyes slide over to the alarm clock. What? Half past ten? I look again to make sure my eyes aren't deceiving me. It's true; it's half past ten. Have I slept that long? Well, it's not easy, two days' exhaustion.

When we had finished with Caner last night at the station, I dropped by Tekirdağ Arif's restaurant. It's small, but it has the best food in Balat. There's not the coziness of home, but the meals are delicious enough to keep me from yearning for those of my late wife, no offense to her. Arif's restaurant is right on the corner of a street opening onto the shore, a five-minute walk from my humble abode. It's here that I usually have my dinner when I come home early. I still haven't got used to eating all alone in an empty house. I'm thankful to Arif, who values me and rolls out the red carpet. I never feel a stranger there. And so it was last night, when he met me at the door. I had lentil soup to start, followed by Tekirdağ meatballs and *cacık*. After the meal, I felt sluggish. We'd gone around town hungry during the day, and fatigued from the night before. It isn't easy, getting out of a warm bed in the best part of sleep to head to the Beyoğlu Police Station. I must admit I'm not so young anymore. In that state, neither the frothy Turkish coffee Arif made with his own hands nor the icy Golden Horn weather hitting my face all the way home was enough to wake me up. I fell into bed in the early hours of the night.

But now it is time to get up. I rise quickly from the bed and a splash of cold water brings me round. I shave and get dressed. I have my coffee in Tevfik's Kıraathanesi. Tevfik is careful to call it a *kıraathane*, or coffeehouse, but really it's a gambling den. Once I've finished my coffee, I've completely thrown off my drowsiness. My first order of business is to go to the Grand Bazaar to talk to Malik. But Malik isn't in the shop, and his son Zekeriya says his father is at home and won't be in today.

I ask where the house is but Zekeriya is cautious; he phones his father before giving me the address. On hearing my name, Malik says, "Tell him to come on over. I'll expect him." In view of his father's response, Zekeriya has to explain.

"I'm sorry, Inspector, but he's my elder. I couldn't have given out the address without asking."

"Not important, Zekeriya," I say. "You did the right thing."

Malik's house isn't far from the bazaar. He lives alone in a two-story detached house in Kumkapı. Getting down there with a car is a problem; the streets are very narrow and you get stuck between cars. Worse yet is not being able to find a place to park. I have no choice but to ask someone, and he points me to the only parking lot here. I surrender my trusty Renault to an attendant whose right hand is cut off at the wrist and after a few minutes' walk, I get to the old man's house. As he opens the door and sees me, a relaxed smile spreads across Malik's face.

"Welcome, Nevzat Bey. Nice to see you."

In truth, I was expecting him to be a bit out of sorts, but he wasn't like that at all. Perhaps Caner had mentioned our chat last night. Not perhaps, he must have done. Malik is comfortable with this because he knows what he's going to say.

As I enter the hall, I have the impression of being at a church rather than a house. It's not just the depictions of Jesus hanging on the wall. It's the dominant reds and blues of the stained-glass windows, the light seeping inside through the shadows, that strange effect that spreads from the furnishings and brings on bouts of reticence... Everything I see, smell and touch in this half-light of the hallway leads me to feel this way. I remember that recurring dream of Yusuf's. Although I'd heard it from Caner, I see every detail in front of my eyes as though it were my dream. So much so that I even seem to hear Yusuf whispering, 'Mor Gabriel'. Of course I am wrong; it's Malik speaking.

"Let's go in," he says, showing the way to a room on the ground floor. I see the open door of another room as we walk past. I peer inside inquisitively; it's stuffed to the gills with antiques. I feel like I am seeing a duplicate of Orontes, Malik's shop in the Grand Bazaar.

"Storage room?" I ask, briefly stopping. My actual intention is to determine whether the handwritten manuscript, the Diatessaron Caner spoke of, is in there.

"No, it's not storage. The things there have special meaning for me. Would you like to see?"

"Very much."

So we change our path and go towards the room full of antiques. There are gold, silver and iron-plated crucifixes, candlesticks, censers both bulbous and slim swinging from chains, ceremonial robes with crosses embroidered in silver thread, icons in the likeness of Jesus and Mary, a big purple curtain depicting The Last Supper in tinsel, a small marble tub for baptizing babies and a Bible case made of silver. I look over the case, as if I'd recognize the Diatessaron if it were inside. But no, the case is empty.

"I can't store our holy book like an antique item," Malik explains, thinking I'm looking for a Bible. "That would be irreverent. The Bible is in my office."

Meaning we'll search for the Diatessaron there, too. It's as this is occurring to me that I notice the sword. It's just below a small tapestry on the wall depicting Jesus holding a lamb in his lap. It's in a brown scabbard and I can only see the hilt. Malik thinks I'm looking at the tapestry.

"Silk," he says. "A friend of mine from Iran had it woven for me."

"It's beautiful... What about that sword underneath it?"

Malik turns pale.

"That's a very important relic," he says. "From an event that happened sixty-seven years after the death of Jesus Christ."

As you can guess, my curiosity is returning in force.

"Something to do with Jesus?"

"Every event on the planet is to do with Jesus, Nevzat Bey," he says, smiling. "We cannot shake a single leaf without God's knowledge and consent." Freezing for a bit like that with a smile on his face, he then takes up explaining again. "This is the sword of a Roman headsman..." His voice is shrill, as if there's pressure in his throat and he's having a hard time talking. "It's a specially crafted sword, for execution... No doubt there are thousands like it, but this one is unique. It's with this sword that Paul's head was struck off." His face twists up as though he's recalling a horrific memory; a deep pain appears in his eyes. Yet he reaches out and takes the sword from the wall, as if challenging his own feelings, paying no heed to the pain he's suffering.

"Yes, this is it. The sword that cut off Paul's head."

He holds it out to me.

"Would you like to take a look?"

I have mixed feelings. On the one hand, I would like to look it over, but on the other I feel dread, a timidity that I myself don't know the reason for. In the end, I overcome my nerves and take it. It's considerably heavy. I hesitate again. I can't remove it from its sheath straight away. I feel like I'll encounter Paul's dried blood if I do. But since I have taken it in hand, there is no turning back. I slowly slide it from the scabbard. It looks nothing like the swords we're used to seeing in films of Roman soldiers. It's broader, perhaps a bit longer, and I suppose its edges are sharper. It's obviously well preserved; it gleams.

"I found it in Lebanon," says Malik as I examine it. "In the house of a collector."

I'm happy the subject has come to this. The transition to the Diatessaron will be easy, but first I have to voice a suspicion I have about the sword.

"Are you certain that this is the sword that killed Paul? It's in such good condition, no one will believe it's from two thousand years ago."

Malik doesn't hesitate.

"I'm sure. I know the man who sold it very well. He would never lie. But more importantly, the moment I saw it, I felt that it was the weapon that killed Paul."

"You felt..." I say. My voice unavoidably comes out as insinuating. How does a person today *feel* a sword was used in an execution two thousand years ago? Malik notices the slight mockery in my voice.

"It's hard to believe, isn't it? But consider this. Haven't you ever been around suspects, and despite not yet having any evidence or witnesses, said to yourself, 'Ha! This is the murderer!' "

"It's happened a lot."

"So, hasn't a man you said that about ever turned out to be guilty?"

"They have, but not every time. What matters more is that no court could ever judge a person a murderer by trusting in my feelings. Forget about court, even I don't deem a man guilty without witnesses or evidence, even if I'm a hundred percent sure he's a murderer. Hunches are not enough in my line of work, Malik Bey. It may not be a deep, mysterious method that boggles the mind, but I prefer to use reason and science to find criminals."

Again, I can't help the innuendo in my voice. But Malik isn't bothered.

"You're right. Your job is connected to this world. This world's business should be solved with this world's methods, but don't underestimate your feelings and perceptions. Your perceptions can take you to a truth your reasoning will never discover."

This time I smile.

"I'm a simple cop, so that much is beyond me. But I have no prejudices either. I mean, if you'll tell me what you felt the moment you saw the sword, I will be a good listener."

"What are you doing, Nevzat Bey? How can a person explain a feeling they have? Especially when it's intuition-related?"

"Well, I don't find it too difficult. Let me ask this way: What was your reaction the first moment you saw it? Astonishment, pain, grief, hate, fear?"

"All that and more..."

It's time to put an end to this game.

"Malik Bey, do you consider yourself to be Paul?" I directly ask. An expression full of secrecy appears on his elderly face, before he gently answers, "Let's go to my room if you'd like. We can talk more comfortably there."

It would be rude to persist, so I go along with his suggestion. With me in front and him behind, we go through to the hall that resembles a church again. As we walk, I see another door which, to reach, you descend five or six stone steps. Over the door is a large cross. Malik sees me looking at it and stops to explain.

"That door opens onto a chapel. A very old one. Inside is the grave of a monk named Yithzak who is said to have lived in the time of the Emperor Constantine."

"Yithzak? Isn't that a Jewish name?"

"It was to begin with. Just like Saint Paul. But anyhow, Yithzak was a very influential man, despite being Jewish. He was very close to the emperor. His real job was as a slave trader, but to curry favor with the emperor, he also brought beautiful, strong thoroughbred horses from the four corners of the world. The emperor paid back the favor by showing him priority in the slave trade. One night, Yithzak saw the Lord Jesus, wearing slave clothes, in a dream. Yithzak wanted to touch him, but he burned his hands on an extraordinary light spreading from Christ's body. 'Leave the slaves be, Yithzak,' Jesus said. 'They belong not to you, but to God.'

" 'But the emperor...' Yithzak started to say.

" 'The emperor also belongs to God. Both the emperor's sovereignty and your wealth are temporary. Both of you are nothing but two wretched souls who have lost their way. Leave the slaves be and come to the path of God. Do not be afraid of the emperor. He will also choose God's path eventually.'

"Yithzak woke to a pain in his hand. He looked and saw that the hand he touched Christ with in his dream was indeed burned. At that moment, Yithzak became Christian. He freed the slaves, gave his possessions away to the poor, and devoted himself to Christ's path. And the Emperor Constantinus also chose Christ's path, although he hid it till the last moment for political reasons. Before his last breath, he was baptized, and in that way died a Christian. When the time came, Yithzak died as well. They buried him here. The slaves he freed, the Christians, didn't abandon Yithzak after his death, but turned his grave into a meeting place for calling out to God."

Malik's story doesn't surprise me in the least. That's how Istanbul is. Every neighborhood, every street, every house, in fact every room, opens to a miracle, a legend, a dream.

"I'm not going to hide it from you," Malik continues. "I bought this place mostly for the chapel. To be close to God's house."

"And you opened up a door to God's house, too."

"There is only one door that opens into God's house, and that is a person's heart. I wasn't the one to have the door put in, the house's previous owner Kosta Efendi did that. May he rest in peace. He was a faithful Christian. He did the maintenance to the chapel himself. And now I am doing it. There are some good kids in the neighborhood; they help me. We keep the chapel open for worship twenty-four hours a day. Muslims, Christians, Jews, it doesn't matter. Anyone who wants can come and pray here. I like that there's a door here. Sometimes, especially at night, when the memory of my past sins makes it hard for me to sleep, I go down into the chapel and pray. It gives me great comfort."

To be frank, a door in my house that opens onto the grave of a monk who lived hundreds of years ago wouldn't give me comfort. But Malik must need places like this, stories like these, in order to feel like he's Paul. I watch the man from the corner of my eye. He is standing bolt upright by my side. Does he really believe he is Paul? Or is this identity a cover for illegal activities? Let's see how he'll explain this handwritten document business. As we start towards the other room again, I ask, "Do you know why I'm here?"

"I don't. Just Caner called in the evening, saying my name was mentioned in the investigation."

"So Caner rang you. It's weird; Caner doesn't agree with your thoughts at all. Despite that, he really likes you, and helps you every chance he gets."

"I like him too. As a matter of fact, we are like two opposite sides of a medallion. I'm sure Caner told you I am gnostic."

"Not you, but he said Paul was influenced by Gnostics and the secret religious orders."

"In any case, he calls himself agnostic, doesn't he? These words are Greek, 'gnosi' means knowledge, 'gnostic' those who know, and 'agnostic' those who don't. So we are both different perspectives of the same root meaning."

"I don't know about that. If I must say so, I'm not really interested in religious philosophy. In this situation, it's your conduct that interests me more."

"What conduct?"

"Your speaking with Caner. He calls you, tells you your name came up in an inquiry, and yet you aren't alarmed, and don't even ask how your name came up."

"Why should I ask that? I didn't commit a crime. And I'm prepared to answer all your questions."

"So you say, but just now I asked you if you consider yourself to be Paul and you didn't answer."

He smiles and shakes his head.

"I'll answer you with an experience Jesus had... We're still standing. Let's go into my room first. After you."

He opens the door and shows me in. The room smells deliciously of tea. This room, like the one in his shop, is simply furnished. The only difference is the bigger library. Our manuscript could be among these books.

"You can sit here," he says, indicating the chair to the right. "It's really comfortable."

As I sit down, Malik passes behind the wooden table. A plate of biscuits, two glasses and a sugar dish sit ready and waiting on a tray on the table. Next to the table, a teapot bubbles away on an electric burner.

"That's laziness. I brought the hotplate in here. I boil my tea and my linden and drink it here. It's hard to go all the way to the kitchen. Well, let me answer your question first and then we can have our tea.

"I'll recite a passage from the Gospel of Matthew for you. The Pharisees, the enemies of Jesus, came to him one day... 'Master, we know that thou art true, and teachest the way of God in truth, neither carest thou for any man: for thou regardest not the person of men. Tell us therefore, What thinkest thou? Is it lawful to give tribute unto Caesar, or not?'

"But Jesus perceived their wickedness, and said, 'Why tempt ye me, ye hypocrites? Shew me the tribute money.'

"And they brought unto him a penny. And he saith unto them, 'Whose is this image and superscription?'

"They say unto him, 'Caesar's.' Then saith he unto them, 'Render therefore unto Caesar the things which are Caesar's; and unto God the things that are God's.'***1

"I don't know if I've explained myself, Nevzat Bey. Whether I am Saint Paul or not is a divine issue. Giving my opinion on it would be a sin. But in an investigation conducted by the government that rules this world I live in, I leave myself at the mercy of the law. I'm ready to answer any question related to the investigation. But..." Without losing the polite smile, he lifts his right hand gently into the air. "But after I've filled our glasses."

As Malik gets up to take the teapot, I look over the books in the library. Some are Turkish and others Arabic, perhaps there's Syriac, too.

"Do you know Syriac?" I ask.

"Very little, but Caner knows it well."

"He told me. You used him as a specialist when buying some handwritten texts."

"Yes, he came in very handy. But that was before; I don't really buy that kind of manuscript anymore."

Apparently, Caner had mentioned telling me about the Diatessaron. He doesn't want to be labeled an informant, and rightly so. That's good. At least I'll be able to catch the man off guard. As Malik is filling the first glass with tea, I say, "That's not what we heard." He seems unconcerned. He moves to the other glass. "Yusuf sold you a handwritten text." Malik is still silent, as if he isn't hearing what I'm saying. He calmly fills the glass.

"Diatessaron, that's the name of the book," I continue with a similar calmness. "It means 'harmony of four'. But it's talking about four books of the Bible, not music."

"I know," he says, keeping his composure. "A text made up of Matthew, Mark, Luke and John."

He puts the kettle back onto the hotplate, then turns to me.

"One sugar, right? I think you took one yesterday."

"You remember correctly. One is enough, thanks."

He sets my sugar lump next to my glass and then reaches for his own tea and takes a sip. He slowly closes his eyes.

"Mmm. It's good." He opens his eyes. "I get this by combining four different teas. Just like the Diatessaron..." He nods towards my glass. "Try it, Nevzat Bey. Let's see if you like it."

I take a sip.

"It's nice," I say.

"Nice." He takes another sip, and then as he sets his glass down, asks, as though mentioning some trivial subject, "Was it Meryem Hanım that told you about the Diatessaron?"

I take my time, sipping at my tea once more. As I put my glass down, I return to the actual subject. "Meryem Hanım or someone else; what does it matter? The important thing is that you purchased an antique book that should be the property of the church."

"You think I'm an artifacts smuggler..."

I gaze fixedly and leave it at that.

"I am sure you've looked into my history. After reading all that, I would have thought the same. But it's not what you think."

"You paid Yusuf precisely one hundred thousand dollars..."

"You're right. I did."

"For what?"

"For us to deliver the Diatessaron to the monastery to which it belongs."

What was this guy talking about?

"Yes, I got the Diatessaron from Yusuf. Then I sent it to where it belongs, that is, the Mor Gabriel Monastery."

He sees the suspicion on my face isn't letting up and reaches for a black telephone book on the right-hand corner of the desk. He opens it and shows me a number.

"This is the number for the Mor Gabriel Monastery." He pushes the telephone on the table over to me. "Call this number and ask them about the Diatessaron." He notices my hesitancy and insists. "Please, Nevzat Bey, go on and call it."

My hands reach out for the phone and I dial the number. After it rings for quite a while, it's picked up.

"Mor Gabriel Monastery," says an elderly voice in Turkish with an accent. "Who are you calling for?"

"I wanted to talk to whoever's in charge..."

"Yes. This is Father Şamun."

"Hello, Father. This is Chief Inspector Nevzat calling from Istanbul."

"Yes, Nevzat Bey," says Father Şamun, making his voice presentable. "How can I help you?"

"I'd like to talk to you about a book in your monastery. An artifact called the Diatessaron. Do you still have that book?"

The old man's voice gets younger.

"It was stolen years ago. But thank goodness, our book has come back to us, Nevzat Bey."

"So who stole it?"

"We don't know, but one morning when we got up for prayers, we found the Diatessaron on the front pew in the church."

"You didn't see who put it there?"

"We didn't, and it doesn't matter. Our book came back to us."

"Weren't you curious who had put it there?"

"No, we weren't." There's a brief silence. "Actually, we know who put it there."

"Who?"

"Mor Gabriel, who else? Yes, Mor Gabriel brought back the Diatessaron."

"Mor Gabriel? The saint who died hundreds of years ago?"

"The very one, Inspector," says Father Şamun. "Mor Gabriel is the protector of our monastery. His miracles never cease."

"Are you sure the book left for you is the real Diatessaron?"

"We are sure. We know every line, every letter of that book. It is most definitely our Diatessaron."

"All right then. That's all. Thank you, Father Şamun."

"Thank you for taking an interest. If you ever happen to come our way, please visit our monastery. You can be our guest."

As we hang up, I set my questioning eyes on Malik.

"Why didn't you hand over the book in person?"

"To protect Yusuf."

"So he wouldn't be judged a thief?"

"Yes, and anyhow Yusuf is not a thief. He bought the manuscript from someone else. But that is also a crime. More importantly, it's a great sin."

"Did Yusuf give the book to you after he realized what he'd done was a sin?"

"We could say that. But first, Mor Gabriel had to warn Yusuf. Yusuf started to see Mor Gabriel in his dreams. Mor Gabriel asked Yusuf for what belonged to him. When he came to me he was in a panic. He explained his dream. My eyes were swimming while listening to him. A grown man like me, crying my eyes out."

"Why?"

"Because I was confronting new evidence of God's omnipotence," he answers excitedly.

His enthusiasm dampens when he sees my blank stare.

"You don't understand, do you, Nevzat Bey? Yusuf didn't understand in the beginning either. But I explained it to him. I said, 'Don't you see, Yusuf? God is calling you to be redeemed. It's time for you to unburden your sins. This is why he sent Mor Gabriel to you.'

"Yusuf looked at me in fear. 'That's not why Mor Gabriel came,' he said. 'Mor Gabriel wants something from me.'

"I didn't understand what he was talking about because I didn't know about the Diatessaron yet.

" 'I have something that belongs to Mor Gabriel,' he said. 'A handwritten book. The Diatessaron. I bought it from a sinner. He'd stolen it from a monastery. Mor Gabriel wants this stolen book.'

" 'You've committed a huge sin, Yusuf,' I told him. 'But atonement is possible. Return the book and beg forgiveness.'

"He shook his head in despair and said he couldn't do that. 'Meryem and I opened Nazareth Bar together,' he said. 'She went into serious debt. I promised her I would come up with the money. I have to sell the Diatessaron.'

"I asked him how much his debts were and he told me up to two hundred thousand dollars. He was in a tight spot and I needed to help him. I told him, 'I can't cover it all but I'll give you a hundred thousand and you'll find the rest...'

"He looked unsure. He still couldn't wrap his head around the gravity of his situation. It was hard for him not to keep his promise to the woman he loved.

"I told him he had no other choice. 'Your sin is great. You are holding a book stolen from God, and if you don't surrender it and ask forgiveness, Mor Gabriel will take the Diatessaron back with his own hands. Hurling you into the deepest corner of hell, besides.'

"He said he needed to talk to Meryem. That he had to convince her first. 'All right, all right,' I said, 'but don't forget you can't wangle your way out of this business. You cannot escape God.'

"Yusuf left and for three days there was no word from him. At the end of the third day, he came to me with the Diatessaron. He was in a miserable state, like he hadn't slept in days. 'Here's the book, Malik Abi,' he said. 'You were right; I have to give it back. I never should have taken it. That's greed for you.'

"I asked him what Meryem had to say about it. He looked at me with those wide eyes with the purple rings under them and said, 'She doesn't understand me; she's not even aware what's happening. Her mind is on Nazareth Bar. I can't sleep at night, Malik Bey. Whenever I close my eyes, Mor Gabriel's there in front of me. I drink but it doesn't help. I smoke weed, take pills, nothing works. That apparition just somehow won't leave me alone. Get me out of this nightmare, Malik Bey. This book... I don't know how you'll do it but get me out of this thing before I get into trouble. You'll have my undying gratitude.'

" 'All right, Yusuf,' I told him. 'If you are really looking for absolution, I'll save your skin.'

" 'The hundred thousand dollars,' he said, shamefaced. 'That too...' I told him not to worry, that I would pay it, and that perhaps we could pacify Meryem Hanım that way."

"How could you trust Yusuf?" I ask Malik. "How could you be sure he wasn't conning you?"

"Yusuf wouldn't do something like that. But still, I played it safe. I showed the Diatessaron to Caner. Mind you, Caner couldn't be completely certain whether the manuscript was original. So I didn't settle for that, but asked other experts for their opinions. Two separate specialists maintained it was an original. So I paid Yusuf a hundred thousand dollars and took the Diatessaron. And later on, I left it at the Mor Gabriel Monastery."

"What did Meryem say to this business?"

"At first, she didn't believe it. She told Yusuf that I had tricked him. Yusuf brought her to me. I told Meryem Hanım to go to the Mor Gabriel Monastery. I said the Diatessaron was there, under God's protection. She still didn't believe me but she said she would send a man to check. I didn't hear from her again. I suppose when she heard the manuscript was at the monastery, she gave up pestering me. But she also ended her relationship with Yusuf."

So that was what drove a wedge between Meryem and Yusuf. How had the woman hidden it from us? Could Meryem be Yusuf's killer? When she fell on hard times and couldn't pay...

"The hundred thousand dollars," I cut in. "Did Yusuf keep the money or..."

"He gave it to Meryem. Not a single cent went into Yusuf's pocket."

In that case, there was no reason for Meryem to kill Yusuf. As far as we know, of course.

"Your tea, Nevzat Bey," he says. "Don't let it get cold."

It is starting to bug me that Malik is still worried about the tea.

"So it gets cold," I say. "It doesn't matter. Since we are speaking openly, Malik Bey, go on and tell me. Who killed Yusuf?"

He takes my words as a threat. It's not what I intended. "Believe me, we need your help," I correct. "This is a tough case. We say we've found a clue but then our enthusiasm is curbed because it doesn't take us anywhere. Tell us your opinion. Who do you think... Who could have done this?"

"I don't know, Nevzat Bey. Yusuf was a tightlipped guy. He didn't like to talk much."

He averts his eyes. I'm sure he's hiding something.

"Look," I say, leaning towards him. "I believe everything you've said so far. I didn't even feel the need to bring you to the station. But if you are keeping something from me..."

Malik's reaction comes unexpected.

"Please don't talk to me this way, Nevzat Bey. I appeal to you, let's not allow the congenial relationship between us to sour. If you think I am guilty, do what you must. Rest assured I won't get angry. It is your duty. But do not raise your voice or threaten me please, because that's not nice. This kind of behavior doesn't just hurt me. I'm sorry, but it also demeans you. Whereas you are not that kind of person."

It occurs to me to ask him how he knows what kind of person I am, but I tell myself to stay calm.

"I know you, Nevzat Bey," Malik continues. "I don't know your family background or your home life. And we've only met twice. But you've given me plenty of information on yourself. I couldn't believe it when you told me you were a police officer, do you know that? You are nothing like the police I've met."

"Have you met a lot of police?" I ask flatly.

"A lot. You know, I was a sinner too, once."

I'm in no mood to deal with this guy's character analysis.

"Anyhow, let's drop all this," I say. "The thief... I mean the man who initially stole the Diatessaron from the monastery."

"The man Yusuf bought it from?"

"Yes, him. Who was that man? Where did he live?"

"I don't know who he was, but he's dead."

"Dead?"

"It was the man's fate that scared Yusuf in the first place. God forgive his transgressions, the man died at a very young age."

"How do you know that?

"Yusuf told me. I didn't want to leave any open doors behind me when I took the Diatessaron from him. So I asked him, "What will happen if this thief is caught one day and gives your name?"

" 'He won't,' Yusuf said. 'Because he's dead. Mor Gabriel punished him in a very severe way. He died in a cave, of asphyxiation.' "

Chapter 19
Let's remove our saint from his grave.

Maybe we should take Malik into the station and interrogate him thoroughly too. At the very least, we need to notify the Illegal Trafficking Department about this Diatessaron matter. But I don't do either. Although it is normal procedure, something prevents me, whether it's the talks I've had with Malik and his respectful attitude, or that the subject is religion. Anyway, even though my suspicions haven't completely disappeared, I leave him at home and return to the station.

First, I want to stop by the lab and speak with Zeynep. But Zeynep isn't alone; she has Caner with her. Yes, the Caner we hosted last night, whose name is still on the list of suspects. What's going on? Is Ali right to be jealous? Zeynep is having our guest inspect some material under a microscope and therefore they don't notice me come in. The noise of the closing door alerts them. When Zeynep sees me, she quickly pulls herself together. I guess this girl really does have a thing for Caner. If so, Ali has his work cut out for him. Suddenly seeing me there also makes Caner uneasy.

"Hello, Chief Inspector," he says, beating Zeynep to it.

"Hello, Caner. You must really like it here."

"He's brought some books on Assyrianism, Chief," our girl explains in his place.

The pink spreading through her cheeks makes her even prettier. I feel like a father who has caught his daughter in an inappropriate situation with her sweetheart. The feeling is unsettling.

"Chief," says Zeynep, "Evgenia Hanım called for you."

And Evgenia has been the subject of their gossip.

"Why didn't she phone my cell?"

"She did, but she couldn't reach you. It's important; she wants you to call."

Has Zeynep got a mischievous look on her face or does it just seem that way to me? To change the subject, I affect my utmost formality and ask, "Where is Ali?"

"He went to forensics, Chief. Yusuf's little brother has arrived from Mardin. He took him to the coroner's to identify him. It's been a while; he'll be here soon."

I think to myself, they'd better not run into Caner.

"Good. I'd like to see Yusuf's brother too when he arrives, but first I need to talk to you. When you're finished..."

Caner understands from my cool attitude that he isn't wanted here. "I was off to the faculty building anyhow," he says, getting up. "You do your thing."

I don't tell him not to go. In fact, I act like I haven't heard him.

"I'll wait for you in my office, Zeynep," I say. On my way out, I turn to the young man and say, "See you later," so as not to be rude.

"See you, Inspector," he says. I think he's offended. Let him be; I don't care. They have no right to hurt Ali. If they want to meet up, let them do it outside. Then I get angry with myself for thinking this way. Is it right for me to take Ali's side against Zeynep? Is Zeynep absolutely obliged to like Ali? She isn't, but... For whatever reason, I can't help getting angry at them.

Just as I'd feared, I bump into Ali in the corridor. Next to him stands a short, dark, thin young man, who I take to be Yusuf's brother. He wears an old coat and there's deep fatigue in his bony face. He must have come from Mardin by bus.

"Chief, I was looking for you..." says Ali hastily. "This is Yusuf's brother." He stops and scratches his head as if there's some complicated situation he can't explain. "Not this Yusuf, but..."

What was he on about? Yusuf's brother's dark eyes are anxious. I smile and extend a hand.

"Hello, I'm Chief Inspector Nevzat."

He squeezes the extended hand awkwardly.

"Hello..."

"What's your name?"

"Gabriel."

Gabriel? I suppose there's no connection to Mor Gabriel. But he's definitely connected to Yusuf. Ali's talking about something else, I guess.

"Have you identified the body?"

Ali shakes his head and looks at Gabriel. The young man is nervous; he's chewing his lip. He's going to explain but for the shyness.

"Is the body your brother's?" I directly ask.

"That person..." he says, swallowing. "That person is not my big brother Yusuf."

"What?"

"That's what I was trying to tell you, Chief," Ali blurts out. "We couldn't identify the body."

"Just a minute..." I turn to Gabriel. "Is Yusuf Akdağ not your brother?"

He hangs his head as if he's done something wrong.

"Yusuf Akdağ is my brother. But that corpse is not him."

"A resemblance of names?"

"No, it's not that. There's some mistake here. The identity card Inspector Ali showed me is my big brother's. But the photograph on it isn't his. The body isn't one of ours. That corpse in the morgue is not my brother Yusuf."

We need to sit down for this.

"Come on. Let's go to my room and carry on the conversation there."

"Zeynep," Ali reminds me. "We should let her know too."

I quickly brush over the subject.

"She's coming. I spoke to her..."

But before I can even finish my sentence, Caner and Zeynep come out, laughing. As soon as he sees them, Ali's face changes.

"I summoned him," I lie. "I asked him to bring some books on Assyrianism."

They come over to us; Caner's smile is unfeigned.

"Hello, Inspector."

"Hi…" Ali halfheartedly answers.

You could cut the tension in the air with a knife. It's not possible Zeynep hasn't noticed, but she ignores it.

"What happened? Did you identify the body, Ali?"

Ali doesn't want to talk around Caner and neither do I.

"We were going to my office. Gabriel has something to explain to us."

"And I should get back to my school now," says Caner. "Good luck to you all."

Zeynep is the only one to answer him.

"You too. Thanks for the books."

As Caner moves away, I wonder if Zeynep is doing this to make Ali jealous. To make him jealous and set things in motion. Maybe she's bored with the uncertainty of the relationship too, and saying from now on whatever happens, happens. Well, we'll find out. The four of us continue along the corridor.

"You are Assyrian, right, Gabriel?" I ask as we walk.

The blood seems to drain from Gabriel's long bony face.

"Yes, we are," he says obsequiously. "We're Syriac."

I place a friendly hand on his shoulder.

"Great. In that case, you can give us some information on Syriacs."

He relaxes a bit but he's still shy.

"I will, Inspector. You ask, and I'll tell you." He speaks with an accent. But not a Kurdish accent.

We go into my room and I show him to the seat Caner sat in last night. He sits down on the edge. Zeynep asks the first question.

"Does your name come from Mor Gabriel?"

"That's right. They gave it me so I'd be a good man like Mor Gabriel." He watches our faces. "Mor Gabriel is our diviner. He's a great saint. The guardian of our monastery. Our monastery is also called Mor Gabriel. Mor Şamuel and Mor Şamun Monastery... Kartmin Monastery... Deyrul Umur Monastery..."

Our impatient Ali is confused.

"So which one is it? Make up your mind already."

"All of them. Our monastery has four names. But we call it Mor Gabriel Monastery. Mor Gabriel." He crosses himself, then continues.

"He's like Jesus Christ. He performs miracles. Heals the sick, punishes the evil, and helps people. He is a venerable saint. That's why my father named me Gabriel. So I'd be saintly, like him. But my big brother Yusuf was a better man. More devout than I am. Albeit a bit peculiar. The villagers thought he was mad, but he wasn't. My brother was a shepherd. He'd talk to everyone and everything. The walnut tree at the entrance to the village, the cloud in the sky, a snake among the boulders, the sheep he herded... Whatever creatures there were, he'd talk to them all. And they would talk to Yusuf Abi. Yusuf Abi would say to them, 'How are you? Are you well?' And they would answer him, 'We're fine.' Plenty of creatures understood and listened to Yusuf Abi. It was only our village folk that didn't understand him. The villagers would say, 'This Yusuf Abi of yours is crazy. Who talks to trees and bugs?' I'd get embarrassed but my father didn't pay it any mind. He would tell me not to listen to them. 'Your brother is chosen. He will be a seer, although the time is not yet ripe. When the time comes, Mor Gabriel will appear to him and your brother Yusuf will become a true diviner.'

"And then the time did come, and Yusuf disappeared. He left his donkey and his sheep on the mountainside and vanished into thin air. Everyone wondered where he had gone. Only my father wasn't curious. My mother, and relatives, we were all sad. Only my father wasn't. 'It's good tidings,' he said. 'My son went over to Mor Gabriel.' Then one night he saw my brother Yusuf in a dream. He woke us all up in the middle of the night. He said, 'My son is with Mor Gabriel. He will appear before Jesus Christ. Then he will come down to earth and join us sinners. He will save us.'

"Then my father waited. A year passed, and he waited, but my brother didn't come. Two years passed, he waited, but my brother didn't come. Three years passed and my father died, but still my brother never came. In the fourth year, my mother died, but still no sign of him. This is the fifth year, and still my brother hasn't returned. When you said you'd found him, that he was dead, it scared me. I said, was my father wrong? Isn't my brother with Mor Gabriel? But when I got here and saw that the dead man isn't Yusuf Abi, I was so happy. Not that the man is dead, God forbid, but that it wasn't Yusuf. It means my brother is with Mor Gabriel."

As Gabriel explains all this, I don't know what to think. All I know is that despite living in the same country, and having served in Urfa, a place not so far from his village, I am a foreigner to him. But this lack of familiarity doesn't come from my finding his stories strange. I could hear similar stories or similar beliefs in a Muslim village if I replaced his saint with a Muslim one. I guess what surprises me is that there is so much Christian thought in us, and it is so much a part of us, without my having known about it. Perhaps it wouldn't seem strange if a Greek acquaintance in Istanbul, Dimitri Amca for example, were to explain this. Because once upon a time Istanbul was Rome's eastern capital. But being suddenly confronted with this archaic culture in the Southeast baffles me. Now is not the time to fall into confusion, however; there's a murder I need to solve. The outcome of this investigation eludes me - and not just that; everything I learn, every statement I take baffles me more. Malik, Caner, Timuçin, Fatih, maybe someone else... from these people, I'm trying to find the real murderer. But after what Gabriel's explained, I understand I have a missing person to find too: the real Yusuf Akdağ.

"Listen here, Gabriel," I say. Feeling the weight of my gaze on his face, he shrinks back again. "This is a very important case. Somebody has killed that man you saw. We don't know who did it. All we had was the man's identity. And now you are telling us it's bogus."

"It's an imposter, Inspector. What I said is not a lie."

"I know, Gabriel. I believe you. But here's what I don't understand: What is your brother Yusuf's identification doing on him?"

Gabriel's eyes open wide with desperation.

"I don't know, Inspector. Maybe that man came across Yusuf's papers somewhere. Because we couldn't find anything of Yusuf's on the mountain. His shirt, his trousers, shoes, whatever he had on him disappeared altogether."

"You mean you've never seen this guy."

"I haven't, Inspector."

"The date of Yusuf Abi's disappearance... What year, which month, what day? Can you remember?"

Gabriel answers without hesitation.

"Five years ago, on 31 August. That's the day Yusuf vanished."

Even Ali, seething with jealousy, is surprised by Gabriel's remembering so clearly. Forgetting his own emotions, he asks, "How do you remember the exact day like that?"

"Because 31 August is the Mor Gabriel memorial day. Or more precisely, a memorial for the day of the dismemberment of his right hand."

"Dismemberment of his right hand?" says Zeynep, grimacing.

"Yes, our priests explained. After Mor Gabriel died, a plague hit the region. People began to break, falling like stalkless grains. Nothing the doctors did worked. One of the priests said, 'Mor Gabriel performed miracles. Come on, let's remove our saint from his grave.' And so they exhumed him. They saw that his body had not decomposed at all. They leaned him up against a wall of the church so he wouldn't fall. The next day they went and looked at him, and Mor Gabriel was standing upright. And that is when everyone began to recover. The outbreak of plague rolled away like fog. After that, the priests came to a decision: 'If there is ever a plague again, we won't disturb Mor Gabriel. For this, we can cut off his right hand. Because every part of Mor Gabriel is sacred. Every piece of his body heals.' From that day forward, every 31 August there is a ceremony for the dismemberment of his hand. And well, Yusuf disappeared on that day of the ceremony, five years ago."

"Did Gabriel have any enemies or adversaries?" I say.

"No, none. We're not a threat to anyone. And no one meddles with us."

He suddenly gets shy again, but his face demonstrates his eagerness to talk.

"Yes, what were you going to say?" I encourage him.

"Six years ago, four 'village guard' families came to our village. Some of our relatives had emigrated to France. They were afraid of terrorism. After they emigrated, that's when the 'village guards' came. They settled into the homes of the people who had left. We didn't say anything. If the government is doing it, it's right, we said. But these guards wanted to expand their territory. They started to divide up our vineyards and our gardens by force. We made complaints against them. And they slandered us, calling us PKK. Later on, there was a captain, a good guy called Rüstem. He came and he saw the reality. He told the families, 'Cool it. Don't mess with these people.' And from then on no one messed with us."

Like always, Ali goes off half-cocked.

"How's your relationship with the PKK?"

He means, could your big brother have joined the PKK? It's a fair question, in fact, because in that area a lot of people join the illegal organization and go up into the mountains. And we know there are Turks, Assyrians and Armenians among them.

Gabriel is getting upset. Ali sees him struggling and, softening his question, asks, "I mean, did the PKK badger you? Did they come to you? Your brother was a shepherd and he spent his time in the mountains. Maybe they talked to him. Pressured him to join them. They used to kidnap people around there."

"No, the PKK never kidnapped Yusuf Abi," Gabriel finally says. "If the PKK had kidnapped him, he would have come back... We have no love for the PKK. My aunt's son Aziz died because of them. Suffocated on smoke in a cave."

When I hear how he died, I immediately think of the painful end of the thief who stole the Diatessaron. 'He suffocated to death in a cave,' Malik had explained. Could the thief be Gabriel's cousin?

"Tell me about the incident. How did your cousin suffocate in the cave?"

"It was written in the papers. Six people died in that cave."

"How did the six people die?"

"A Police Special Operation Team took them to the cave. They accused them of being PKK and asked them where the PKK were hiding. Because the Special Team had fallen into an ambush. Two police had died and one was injured. The team followed some PKK, but they lost their trail. The team went and knocked on the door of the Mor Gabriel Monastery. They asked them if the PKK members were there. A priest came out and told them, 'There is no PKK here. We don't like them and we don't let them in. Come in and look if you'd like.'

" 'We aren't going to do that,' they said. 'But if the PKK are here, hand them over.'

" 'Those men are not here,' the priest assured them.

" 'All right, we believe you,' they said.

"But they didn't leave. They lay in wait outside the monastery. After evening prayers, when the villagers came out, they cut them off. They pulled the young ones aside. There were six of them. My cousin Aziz was one of them. They took the six youth to the cave. That cave is bad news. Years earlier, when the Mongols came, Timurlenk also burnt some villagers alive there. The Special Team took them to that same place.

"They accused them of being PKK. The six people all told them they weren't. 'Then tell us where the PKK are,' they said. And they answered that they didn't know.

"They kept them in the cave for one day and they beat them. The following evening, they brought our cousin Aziz home. He told my aunt, 'Mom, don't be afraid. I'm going to give the commissioner something and he'll let me go.'

"Aziz took a wrapped bundle from the house. His mother didn't know what it was. Aziz gave it to the inspector but the inspector didn't release him. That night, they asked the six again, 'Where are the PKK?' and they said they didn't know.

"Then they herded the six of them inside and lit the cave on fire. And that's how the six of them died of smoke inhalation. After that the Special Team left but then some European priests came to visit the monastery. They found out about the incident, that people had been killed there. And that's when the reporters and the TV channels showed up. They filmed the cave for television and interviewed some locals. They asked my aunt about it too. After that, the government opened a court case against this Special Team. But before it could go to court, we heard that the inspector who had come to my aunt's house was murdered. The PKK had caught him and thrown him into a thresher. It ripped his body to shreds. And then the case was dropped. The court said, 'The inspector gave the order and now he is dead. The other officers are not at fault.'

It's now coming out why Gabriel is having such a hard time talking about this situation. The poor guy is struggling to tell policemen that their fellow officer has committed a murder. Getting no adverse reaction from us, he calms down.

"What is this thresher you're talking about?" asks Zeynep.

"A machine that grinds the harvested crops. It has a wide mouth. You put the grains in there. Inside there are some blades, and the machine chops it all up."

"Dirty bastards," Ali growls. His face looks horrified as he pictures his colleague getting torn up in the thresher. "Bastards. What a brutal way to kill a man."

I'm confounded. Zeynep stares at Gabriel, deep in thought. I suppose she feels no different from me.

"Aziz. What did he give the inspector?" I ask. "Did your aunt see it?"

"She didn't. The thing he took, it was wrapped up in a cloth."

"What business was Aziz in?"

"He was a peasant. He worked on the land, like us."

"Did he attend the Mor Gabriel Monastery?"

"He did. Aziz was on duty there. He recited prayers beautifully and would join the services. But then later on, when his father died, he went back to the land. He couldn't make it to the monastery much."

I guess we've found who stole the Diatessaron.

"While Aziz was still alive, a book was stolen..." Ali and Zeynep, more than Gabriel, are surprised by what I've said. I couldn't manage to bring up the subject with them. "Have you heard anything like that?"

"I heard. There used to be a big library and a lot of books at the monastery. Very valuable books. Books written by saints and soothsayers. They all burned, or were stolen or plundered. Most recently, a very valuable book was lifted. The priests gathered the villagers together.

" 'A book has been stolen from here,' he said. 'This book is not ours. It belongs to Mor Gabriel. If the book doesn't come back, Mor Gabriel will go and get it himself. And he will send whoever stole it to hell. That person will burn forever.'

"Nobody returned the book. But before I left for Istanbul, I heard the book was back at the monastery. The priests were delighted, and they said a prayer. 'Thanks be to Jesus Christ, our protector Mor Gabriel has returned our book.' We were all thrilled that it had come back.' "

"That incident," says Zeynep, furrowing her shapely eyebrows, "the fire in the cave, when did it happen?"

Gabriel can't immediately answer.

"Before my brother Yusuf went missing. Maybe two months, or maybe three months before. It was spring. The crops were coming into leaf."

Apparently Zeynep is stuck on the same point I am and wants to learn the details.

"So this commissioner who died in the thresher. Was his head, his face chopped up?"

"It was. The man was a ball of meat. Where his hands or his legs were was anybody's guess. The skin on his head was peeled off; it was indistinguishable."

"Sons-of-bitches," Ali curses again.

"How did they know it was the inspector?" I ask Gabriel.

"His clothes were there. They took his weapons but left his I.D."

"Did you ever see this inspector?"

"When he was alive?"

"Yes... Did you see him, talk to him?"

"I didn't talk to him. But I saw him once, from far away. Later, I went to the field where he was killed. Our cross-eyed Melki's field. That's where the thresher was. The field was totally red. It was watered in blood. Can that much blood come out of one human?' cross-eyed Melki asked."

"Bastards," Ali mumbles. Zeynep, with the excitement of catching an important clue, tries to complete the picture in her head.

"Would you recognize the inspector if you saw him?"

"No, I wouldn't. I just saw him the once, in front of the local church. He was getting out of a Jeep. I was scared and I didn't look. I kept my head bowed as he passed by me. But Yusuf Abi used to talk to him. Yusuf Abi wasn't afraid of anyone."

"Do you know his name?" Zeynep continued.

"The villagers called him Inspector Yavuz. Everyone was terrified at the mention of his name, God forgive him."

Even though I knew the answer, I couldn't help but ask this question. "Look, Gabriel, you can tell us everything, okay? If you know of an officer who has committed a crime, you can tell us that too. There's nothing to be afraid of. Now this is very important. I want you to think hard before answering. His big eyes open wide. "Did you get a good look at the body you went to identify today?"

"I did..."

"You weren't afraid, were you?"

"No, I wasn't."

"That body, could it be Inspector Yavuz?"

His big eyes grow still and his chin gently drops.

"The body..." he says. It's like he's talking to himself. "The man who took my brother Yusuf's I.D... No... No, it isn't Inspector Yavuz. I don't think it is."

Chapter 20
Those who drank the wine were believed to have acquired immortality.

Although Gabriel says it doesn't, it appears Yusuf's abduction has something to do with Inspector Yavuz. What exactly that is, however, I don't yet know. If Gabriel's cousin Aziz stole the Diatessaron, if Yavuz, who took the Diatessaron from Aziz, hadn't died in the thresher, this upped the possibility that it was the shepherd Yusuf who had died there, and this corpse in the morgue is probably Inspector Yavuz's. I think Zeynep has the same idea. As for Ali, as he stopped swearing at the PKK towards the end of the interrogation, I guess he was confused too. To understand that, we'd have to wait for Ali to get back from downstairs, where he was about to take Gabriel's formal statement.

"I think Şefik's going to turn out to be right," says Zeynep. "Yusuf's..." She immediately corrects herself. "Whatever his name is, when we found the body in the apartment in Elmadağ, if you'll remember, Şefik said, 'It's the darndest thing...' " She's prefacing in order to clarify her thoughts. Unlike Ali, this girl can never jump straight into a subject. "This inspector by the name of Yavuz."

"I was going to say the same, Zeynep. Let's look into this colleague of ours. Talk to his family and friends. Find out not just about Inspector Yavuz, but who the six people that suffocated in the cave are and what the situation was. Also, what happened to the real Yusuf Akdağ, we need to know that too..."

Zeynep records my remarks in the notebook in front of her. What can I say? She's organized. When she's finished jotting it down, I say, "Oh, and don't mention this inquiry to anyone, Zeynep."

She stares, uncomprehending.

"Whatever you dig up, I want to hear it first. This ban includes Ali and Director Cengiz, as well."

Zeynep looks uneasy.

"Director Cengiz came to me this morning, Chief. He'd looked into your room and couldn't find you, so he asked me. I told him you weren't here. He was cross because he wanted to talk to you."

"Never mind. I'll go over now."

"Don't bother, Chief. He left. He was going to do the rounds with some managers and the interior minister and said it would be difficult to make it back. He said it'll have to wait till tomorrow, and that he'll ring you if necessary. He asked me how the investigation was going and I told him what I knew."

She looks sheepish, like she's made a mistake.

"Should I not have told him?"

"No, you did well. Just from now on, whatever you find out, I'll know first. Don't say anything to anyone before telling me and getting my consent."

"Because of Yusuf's call to the station?"

There's that too, isn't there? But we're in no condition to go on a hunt for moles in the police force.

"It's not about that, Zeynep," I say. "I just don't want things to get all tangled up before learning the real story. That's all."

"I understand, Chief."

"Caner..." I say as Zeynep prepares to get up. The moment she hears the name, Zeynep's face starts to turn red again. "What was he explaining to you?"

"He brought over some books on Assyrianism, Chief. I requested them while you were in Director Cengiz's office yesterday evening. Thankfully, he gathered them up and brought them round."

"I know he brought over books on Assyrianism, Zeynep. You told me that when I came into your room. I asked you what he was telling you."

Zeynep's embarrassment turns into distress.

"About the prophet Jesus, Chief," she says in a whisper.

"We discussed that last night..."

Zeynep can't answer straight away but it doesn't take her long to recover.

"He talked about different aspects this time," she clarifies. She has control of her voice now. "Jesus's resurrection after he dies, and his being God and other things. It's said these rituals are taken from Anatolian religions. And it was Paul who took them. The idea that Jesus became God after he died is a very old tradition in Anatolia and Mesopotamia, which he explained goes all the way back to the Hittites. The Hittites would say of their kings who died, 'He's become God.' And the Romans would say of certain emperors 'God's son'. Or else they would proclaim themselves to be God's sons. And people would worship them as gods. The resurrection of Jesus is interpreted differently. This belief comes from certain religious traditions in Tarsus and Antioch. There once was a faith called Mithraism. They would sacrifice bulls in the temples. It was thought that the wine drunk in these rituals represented the blood of the bulls. Those who drank the wine were believed to have acquired immortality. Caner says the rituals of eating the body of Christ, the drinking of his blood, carried on from this tradition. And it was again Paul who brought this tradition into Christianity. That's what he explained to me, Chief. He's a very well-informed kid."

Kid, huh? In a heartbeat, she's turned a grown man into a little boy. That's women for you. The moment they take to someone, they present them to you as the sweetest person in all the world. Doubtless they convince themselves of it first.

"Are you aware, Zeynep, that the man you call a kid is still a suspect?"

The remark extinguishes all the stars in her eyes one by one. Still, with all good intentions she tries to explain.

"That's true, Chief, but we never spoke about the case. He didn't even attempt to imply that he's innocent. He just said we as a society are making a mistake."

"What mistake is that?"

"Despite the huge cultural treasure we are sitting on, our lack of recognition for it. Before the Turkish Republic, there were the Hittite, Eastern Roman and Ottoman Empires on these lands, but it seems we never claim these cultures. Westerners say that civilization began with the Ancient Greeks, but if it weren't for the Sumerians and Hittites, would there be an Ancient Greece? He says we ignore these cultures we live on top of and intertwined with because their races and religions are different from ours. It's the reason he is so concentrated on Paul. 'If it weren't for Paul, an Anatolian man, would there be any modern-day Christianity?' he says. He says we have shunned important peoples like these on the grounds that we are Turk and Muslim, and that we ignore them although we've lived on the same land. In fact, it was Islamic philosophers who rediscovered Greek philosophy. He gave a few examples but I don't remember the names now. He asks, 'Why don't we do this?' If we love our country, we have to look after the cultures we're sitting on. Rumi, who once said, 'Come, whoever you are,' did this, why aren't we following in his footsteps?' "

"That's all well and good, Zeynep. But this is not an institution dealing in Anatolian civilizations, nor are we teachers of philosophical history. We here are trying to solve a murder that is getting increasingly complicated."

Zeynep listens without a word.

"What's more, I don't think you two were just talking over the roots of Christianity. When I came into your office, Caner was over your microscope."

Zeynep swallows and answers, "That wasn't related to the case we are working on, Chief..."

"So then what was it related to?"

"I was explaining that investigation of the textile man's murder we solved with the strands of fiber two months ago. I was showing him the fibers we found from that case."

"Would you open the lab up to someone off the street, Zeynep?"

"I wouldn't. I thought Caner was helping us."

Her head is hung and she's not looking at my face anymore. Have I laid into her too hard? Zeynep and I have always got on. Maybe I'd inadvertently put her in the place of my deceased daughter Aysun. And that's why I look out for her. But I shouldn't drag this on.

"Anyhow, you'll act more mindfully from now on."

"As you wish, sir," she says. It's not a sincere response. She's talking as a subordinate is expected to talk to her superior. I guess she finds me unfair.

"Can I go now?"

She still isn't looking at me. Her voice betrays she is upset. I pretend not to notice.

"Of course. You can go."

She stands up.

"Oh, and Zeynep," I say, as if I weren't the one to just issue her a stark warning, "What happened with Meryem and her men?" They were going to the prosecutor's office today?"

"They arrested Tonguç. Meryem and her other man, I guess his name is Tayyar, he was released."

"May as well say it's what we expected."

"That's true, Chief. It's what we expected."

My unaffected attitude rubs off on her. She may not be smiling, but she isn't averting her eyes anymore.

"Good then. You get back to work," I'm saying, when my telephone rings. After wishing Zeynep luck and sending her off, I pick up. It's Evgenia. Oh dear, I've completely forgotten about her.

"Hi, Nevzat. How are you?"

"Hi Evgenia... I was just going to ring you. I just got in. How are you? What are you up to?"

"I'm fine I guess..."

"What do you mean, I guess?"

"No, I'm fine. I'm fine. I was going to say, shall I come round to your place tonight?"

"My place?"

"Yes. To your house, I mean."

Here we go. Where did this come from all of a sudden? Something is up with Evgenia recently. After why don't you marry me, now it's I'm coming over. She never used to bring up subjects or make requests like this. Actually, what could be more natural than her wanting to come over to my house? She is my best friend in life, and my lover. And she has never set foot inside my door. Because I've never invited her. My wife and daughter are still in that house. The whole place is packed with memories of them. I can't imagine Evgenia together with them. Maybe I should be able to, but I can't.

"My house is freezing," I say. "We won't be comfortable..."

Evgenia doesn't make a peep. There's a deep silence as if there is no one at the other end of the line. Evgenia doesn't like silence, doesn't like breaks in the conversation, and doesn't like giving me the silent treatment. She equates silence with coldness, distance and separation. She always has something nice to say. If she feels offended, she doesn't carry it inside her, she finds the right words to explain, baring her heart to you. Since she is quiet now, it means I've blundered. She must really be upset. I guess today is my breaking women's hearts day. After Zeynep, I've hurt Evgenia. But why? Where did this insensitivity come from? In any case, seeing she's gone quiet, it's up to me to fix it.

"Let's go out somewhere... We've been saying we should for ages. Let's go to the fish restaurant on the Çengelköy Pier. It's sea bass season... I'll leave early if you want..."

I hear Evgenia's deep sigh.

"No, Nevzat," she says. Let's not go to Çengelköy now. Since you can leave early, come to Tatavla. It's calm here. We can talk more comfortably."

"Okay, I'm coming. But there's something up with you. Nothing's wrong, is it?"

"No, don't worry." Her words come out choppy. "Come round and we'll talk. See you soon."

Without even letting me open my mouth, she hangs up. This is also a first in our relationship. No, it must be something serious; Evgenia would never do something like this. Well, we'll find out what it is. Meanwhile, Ali walks in. He's also unhappy. His eyes slide over to the chair Zeynep was sitting in. Zeynep is gone, Ali. If up till now you haven't made an effort and spoken to the girl, this is what happens. Don't get the wrong idea; I actually feel sorry for the boy. But my situation isn't so bright either. Who knows what Evgenia is going to say? With all due respect to Ali, I'm in no state to deal with his affairs of the heart. And anyhow he doesn't ask that of me.

"We took Gabriel's written statement," he says, bottling up his swelling love pangs. "Shall we let him go, Chief?"

"Is he going back to Mardin?"

"No, he's here for a few more days. He has relatives in Feriköy; he's supposed to go to them."

"Get his relatives' address and phone number and send him off."

"Yes, sir."

"Wait, Ali. Sit for a second..." As I reach for the phone, I continue. "Let's research this Inspector Yavuz. You've also noticed the issue seems complicated. Let's ring Nusret at the Intelligence Agency. Have him help us."

Ali doesn't sit. With his usual restlessness, he prefers to stand. Nusret answers on the third ring. "Hello," says a husky voice.

"Hi, Nusret. It's me, Nevzat."

"Wow, Chief Inspector. You're calling us?"

"Why do you say that? Wasn't it me who called last? The day we wet our whistles in Beyoğlu... Remember?"

"Was it?"

"Of course it was. You might be younger than me but your memory is shot."

"Things are so busy, Nevzat. Who can think straight?"

"And you should give up the cigarettes. You're rasping. God forbid you should get cancer."

"I'm quitting, friend. I am, but it never quite happens."

"I stopped by Muammer's the other night. He keeps saying he's going to quit too, yet continues to smoke."

"What can we do, Nevzat? Life is hard. Anyhow, what's your command, tell me that."

"What command, Nusret? I just have a little request; you'll fulfill it."

"Of course, with great pleasure."

"Maybe you've read in the papers. An Assyrian was murdered."

"I heard. That murder in Elmadağ."

"Yes, that's it. There may be some connection to an inspector that was killed five years ago in the region of Midyat. The inspector was killed in a grisly sort of way. They minced the man up in a thresher."

"Yes... I heard something about that. But that wasn't my territory. I don't really remember the situation now."

"The thing I'm asking is if you can find out who this inspector was, if anyone knows him and who he was working with at the time. We're also investigating an individual by the name of Yusuf Akdağ in connection with the same incident."

"Wait a minute; let me write down the name. Yusuf what?"

"Yusuf Akdağ. Now, does this individual's name come up among PKK? He might have been killed. If his name is in any statements, or wanted lists or such..."

Nusret seems perturbed.

"Got it. You want two things from me..."

"If it's not too much trouble."

"It's no bother, but it'll take some time, Nevzat. I'll have to rummage through old files, call a few people..."

I'm not letting him make things difficult.

"Well, I don't want it today. You do your research, make your phone calls, and I'll send Ali over tomorrow morning."

Nusret immediately goes sour.

"Don't you be sending Ali over. What we are doing is already irregular. Don't go getting a third person involved on top of it."

"That third person you're talking about is my most trusted right-hand man. Don't you know Ali? He's sorted out no small number of things for you too."

"Yeah, I know him. That's not the issue. We've got orders from above. Every kind of intel is to be recorded. Where it comes from, why it's wanted and who receives it is to be specified. That's why."

"Don't drag this out, Nusret. Do we do this when you want something?"

"All right, all right. Send the crazy kid over. But first you implicitly forewarn him; he doesn't mention it to anyone."

"Thanks, Nusret," I say. "I won't forget the favor."

He answers in a cheerful, yet meaningful voice.

"Don't mention it, Chief. It's our duty."

"Good on you, Nusret."

As I put down the receiver, I say, "You heard what I said, Ali. Drop by Nusret's tomorrow. He'll give you all the facts he has on the incident. If there's anything missing, breathe down his neck and don't leave till you've got it. He bellyaches a lot but he's a good guy. He'll give you whatever you ask for."

"Don't worry. I'll take care of it tomorrow. Now, with your leave, I'll go down to Gabriel."

"All right, Ali. I'm out of here soon, too. We'll see you tomorrow."

Chapter 21
She cries silently to herself, Evgenia. Just as she said, alone even while crying.

When I get to the street Tatavla is on, I see that the sky has gone crimson. The large clouds that curtain the sun turn from white to red, from red to black. The street is slowly moving from an ash-colored luminosity towards darkness. In front of Tatavla is a white van. Chef Ihsan has taken two waiters and they are unloading crates of vegetables and boxes of *rakı* and wine. Evening preparations.

"Good luck with that," I say.

When they see me, they immediately pull aside and let me past.

"Thanks, Chief," says Ihsan. "And welcome."

I leave them behind me and go inside. The interior is in half-light and the stove is still blazing. The glow emanating from the mouth of the stove illuminates Evgenia, sitting at a small table in front of a window looking on to the garden. Evgenia is alone at the table. She's dressed in black and deep in thought. Has someone died? No, she would have told me straight away. She's so self-absorbed that she doesn't even notice me come in.

"Hello, Evgenia," I say.

"Oh, Nevzat," she says, startled. "It's you. You scared me."

"Come on, darling, since when have you been scared of me?'

"I've never been scared of you," she murmurs, falling into my arms. "I thought you were someone else."

She hugs me tight. Has she hugged me like this before? She doesn't appear upset, so I guess I'd fretted over nothing. I breathe in the scent of lavender from the hair that falls on to my shoulders.

"You smell so lovely today."

"Same smell as always," she says, disentangling herself from me. "Are you just noticing?"

There's a distance in her green eyes unfamiliar to me.

"No, sweetheart. Of course not. But sometimes a person is more sensitive to smells. Aren't you ever that way?"

"Come on. Forget this now and let's sit at the table."

As I sit, she reaches towards the switch on the wall and turns on the lights.

There's a banquet on the table again. White cheese, calamari, aubergine salad, salted mackerel, samphire, stuffed mussels, whatever you have in mind, it's there. I sit down, smiling. No, I've wrongly accused Evgenia. Everything is fine. I pick up the carafe and lean towards Evgenia's glass but she covers it with her hand.

"Thanks," she says, "but I'm not drinking tonight."

My optimism quickly disappears. Evgenia never lets me drink alone. There's definitely something wrong. Just like her silence on the phone, this is a first. To be honest, I feel a bit let down. If I don't drink either, it'll be weird. I fill my glass. In order to possibly entice her, I joke about it.

"It smells heavenly. Are you sure you don't want some?"

"Don't push, Nevzat. I won't drink tonight."

I stop pushing and raise my glass. "To you," I say.

She doesn't even deign to smile. A sedate "Bon appetite," falls from her lips, is all.

The mood at the table is spoiled. I set my glass down. My hand doesn't reach for any of the *mezes*.

"Eat," she says. "Chef Recai made it for you."

"Thanks, but I'm not hungry."

I suppose she's understood I've gone off.

"You can't drink without *meze*."

I take a smidgen of white cheese with the tip of my fork for appearance sake.

"Look, I'm eating."

"Eat; it'll do you good."

She's finally smiling, as if all's well. But it's not. The joy that always gives Evgenia's skin vitality and adds a glimmer to her eyes is not on her face. Evgenia has lost her gaiety. All this smiling, hugging, and attempted warmth is just a pretense. It's not a situation I am used to. It doesn't suit Evgenia at all. I know very well how to hide my emotions while I'm talking to people, it's part of my job, but I can't do that to her right now.

"What's going on, Evgenia?" I directly ask. "There's something up with you."

She grasps that I want to talk straight, without holding back, and answers without hesitating.

"I'm going, Nevzat."

Her words are clear enough, but I don't understand.

"Where are you going?"

"To Greece..."

"What is it? Did you get some bad news?"

"From Greece?" She's watching me with a wry smile on her lips. "No."

"So you're going on a trip. For Christmas?"

She shakes her head.

"We don't go to Greece for Christmas, Nevzat. They come here."

"Why?" I ask innocently.

"Because Greece has a longer holiday than the one here... No, Nevzat. I'm not going for Christmas. I'm going for good. To stay there..."

Is she serious or just being funny, I'm trying to figure it out.

"I am very serious. I want to live in Greece from now on."

She's not joking. She's really leaving.

"What do you mean?" I ask, perplexed. "Where did this come from all of a sudden?"

"It's not all of a sudden," she explains calmly and confidently. "I've been thinking about it for a while."

"You never told me!"

She looks into my face as if my words have stung her. I see her nostrils flare and her eyes fill but she doesn't cry.

"It was never the right time," she says, glossing it over. "I'm telling you now."

"After you made up your mind..."

"After I made up my mind..." She takes a deep breath. "My dear departed father would say, 'Always make your decisions on your own, daughter.' You can't walk all the way relying on others. One time I didn't follow his advice. You know what happened to me in Urfa. But I got smart. Smart enough at least to listen to my father." She gets a loving expression on her face. "Seriously, you told me once too. Don't you remember? In those days when I kept calling you. You said, 'You'll never learn.' When I didn't understand and asked, you said, 'You barely even knew Murat and you went off all starry-eyed to Urfa. And now you choose to be friends with someone, I mean me, who you've seen maybe three, four times at best.' You were right. I was the mistaken one; I always think of life together with others. That's not right. Lovers, friends, family... can only go so far. The sole truth is our solitude." Her expression says, I understand you, I forgive you, but you should understand me too. "Isn't that right, Nevzat? Aren't we all alone?"

I have no reply; my head is all mixed-up.

"What's more, Nevzat my dear, I am alone in every sense of the word. All my relatives have migrated to Greece. I am the only one who stayed. You know my uncle Hristo passed away last year. I'm his only heir. There's another *meyhane*, bigger than this, in Crete. And that *meyhane* is also named Tatavla. It was left in the hands of strangers. I'm saying I'll go and run the place. What other recourse have I got? Our business is *meyhanes*; it's what we do."

A heavy sadness washes over me. All the initiative, courage and anger brought about by my initial indignation are melting away and I'm tongue-tied. I should tell her outright not to go, that I am here. But instead I say, "What's going to happen to this place? Are you going to leave the restaurant your father built from the ground up to someone else?"

"If it had been up to my father, we'd have gone to Greece the year I came back from Urfa. He stayed here on my account. While he was dying he told me, 'Go to Greece, my girl. Don't stay here by yourself. Uncle Hristo will look after you like his own daughter.'

"But I didn't go. I mean, I didn't listen to my dad for a second time. Now I'm going to fulfill his wish. And I won't have to keep an eye behind me. There's Recai, and Chef Ihsan... People we've worked with for years. They've put every bit as much effort into Tatavla as I have. They have rights here too."

"What do they say about your leaving?"

"They tell me not to go. It's strange, Nevzat; they are very sincere, you know? Even though if I go, the place will be left to them and they'll be the owners of a *meyhane*. But they're not thinking that. They genuinely don't want me to leave. It seems humanity is not dead. There are people who want me to stay, so for a time I almost even reconsidered it."

Perhaps she's not saying it to hurt me but her words are harsh.

"What kind of talk is that, Evgenia?" I say. "Are they the only ones who don't want you to go?"

She stares, as though surprised.

"Is there someone else?" A veneer of callousness settles onto her face. "Who is that, Nevzat? I don't know of anyone. Do you? Who is it?"

"Don't, Evgenia. You're breaking my heart."

She leans forward in her chair towards me. Her green eyes are narrowed, like two sharp knives.

"Really, Nevzat. Am I really breaking your heart? Are you really sad that I'm leaving?"

"What kind of question is that? Of course I'm sad. Do you doubt that?"

She leans back again and looks calmly into my eyes.

"I don't doubt it, Nevzat dear. Of course you will be sad. It's not easy, losing a friend you can have a few drinks with when you feel down. A woman you climb into bed with some nights... Don't misunderstand me. I don't regret a moment I've spent with you. Every minute was wonderful. But frankly speaking, you never... You never, in any real sense... Whatever this real sense means... You understand. You never in any real sense loved me..." She shakes her head despairingly. "You've never loved me, Nevzat." The green in her eyes is breaking up, rippling. "You have your own world, Nevzat. A world that is enough for you, consecrated with your dead and your memories. You are afraid that I will break the sanctity and purity of that world. You didn't accept me into your world, Nevzat... Never... You've never accepted me..." Tears begin to strain down through the tips of her long lashes. She ignores them and continues.

"I don't know what was in your head. Maybe you didn't find me worthy. Maybe you took me lightly, a tainted woman... I don't know; maybe I'm being unfair to you. I don't know because you've never really talked to me about this. You've always been a man who smiles down at me, dealing with your own problems, so sure of yourself. You've never showed me your wounds, given me a glimpse of your pain, let me see your weaknesses or told me your problems. Because you didn't value me. Whereas I loved you together with your mourning, Nevzat. With your pain, with your longing for your wife and daughter. I regarded them as my own deaths. Even if not like you did, I loved them in my own way..."

Evgenia can't hold back anymore and she starts to weep. I sit there not knowing what to do. She cries silently to herself. Just as she said, alone even while crying. When she's calmed a bit, she reaches out and takes a napkin from the holder and wipes her nose, dries her eyes. I stay silent.

"I really loved you, Nevzat," she says, sniffling, "more than I've ever loved anyone. Maybe that is why I am so angry with you. I'm speaking out of anger. Don't take it too hard. You'll forget everything once I've gone..."

She believes what she's saying, is so sure of her words, that I begin to accuse myself too. So I don't know how to answer. But the more I think about it, I see that Evgenia is not so right. And this realization gives me the strength to speak. Still, my first words spill out not as a result of this willpower, but practically of their own accord.

"You know I won't forget you." An unconvinced expression in those wet, green eyes. "Yes, most of what you say is true. I couldn't be a good boyfriend, and maybe I'm not even a good friend. Nevertheless, aren't you being a bit unfair, Evgenia? You knew very well what kind of man I was. You've seen me on my lowest days. I'm a man handicapped at love. They've cauterized that side of me. I'm not trying to make excuses. And I'm not saying this so you'll forgive me. I'm saying it because it's the truth. I'm so sorry that I've hurt you. I am at least as sad as you are right this moment. But I never promised you a dazzling relationship. It's not that I didn't want to, but I couldn't. You are right. I still live with my wife and daughter. Even though they are dead, I couldn't expel them from my life. But I never saw you as tainted, or light, or lacking in value. The most important thing in my life right now is you."

A sarcastic little smile spills from her lips.

"I know. You told me the other night. I'm one of the ties that bind you to life. Otherwise, life wouldn't be beautiful for you."

"Don't be so brutal, Evgenia. I've told you what's inside me. Everything I said was the truth..."

Suddenly, she's the Evgenia I know again. She gazes at me in desperation, with love, sorrow and compassion.

"I know it's the truth, Nevzat. That is why I am leaving this place. You say I'm one of the ties that bind you to life. Maybe it's just selfishness but I want to be that life in and of itself. Because for me, that life itself is you."

Her eyes tear up again. She covers her face with her right palm to hide her crying. I reach for the left hand forgotten on the table. I touch her fingers gently and she doesn't pull her hand away, but she doesn't respond to my touch either. She just weeps noiselessly.

"Let's talk, Evgenia," I say. "Let's sit and talk. I don't know if I can change, but for you I will try. I don't want you to go,

Evgenia. You are very important to me. And I want to change; you should help me... You'll say I didn't let you but from now on it'll be different. I promise you I will try... Together..."

Just then my cell phone rings. I ignore it.

"Together we can try again. I mean, if you want. Let's go back to my place from here if you want. But the house really is cold. I still haven't solved the natural gas installation..."

My phone continues to ring while I talk. Since it's so insistent, there must be some important development. Or maybe it's someone random. Evgenia pulls her hand back, and as she reaches for the napkin holder again, says, "Answer it."

In fact, the words relieve me, although I pretend otherwise.

"Never mind. Let it ring."

Wiping her eyes, she says, "Come on, Nevzat. I know you want to answer it."

"I'm answering because you want me to," I say, taking my phone out of my pocket. Ali's name appears on the screen. *If it's something insignificant, you are in big trouble, Ali*, I say to myself as I pick up.

"Hello?"

"Hi, Chief..." His voice is excited.

"Yes, Ali. What is it?"

My gaze is on Evgenia as I say this. "Sorry if I'm disturbing you, Chief. Something big has happened. I thought you'd want to know."

"What is it?"

My eyes are still on the woman I love.

"Malik has been murdered, Chief."

"Malik?"

I just spoke with the man today! I picture Malik's peaceful face, so confident in himself and the world.

"How? How was he killed?"

"Just like Paul. Decapitated."

"Decapitated?"

"That's right. With the sword in his house..."

The broad Roman sword that Malik had shown me.

"But there's a nice development," he says with continued enthusiasm. "We caught the perpetrator."

This news surprises me more than Malik's death. "You caught the murderer?"

"Yes, Chief. We did. Well, not us. Malik's two friends caught him. Neighborhood kids..."

"So is it someone we know?" I ask impatiently. "The murderer, I mean. Is it one of the suspects?"

"Yes," says Ali. The voice that says yes is full of spite but at the same time cheerful. "Yes, the killer is Caner, Chief."

"Caner?" It's not as if I'd completely ruled him out from the start, but I feel a strange disquiet nonetheless. "Are you sure? Caner?"

"We're sure, Chief. They found him standing over Malik. He'd broken down the door of the chapel and entered. The two young neighborhood kids caught him as he tried to run away. When you get here you'll see too."

"Okay, I'll try to make it."

Ali is dumbstruck.

"You mean we shouldn't expect you?"

"All right, Ali. I'll call you back. See you."

As I hang up, my gaze shifts to Evgenia again. She is still watching despairingly, with love, sorrow and compassion.

"Something unbelievable, Evgenia. A man who thought he was Saint Paul incarnate, he's been murdered. Decapitated, just like Saint Paul... And with the actual sword that cut off Saint Paul's head."

Evgenia's face scrunches up and that's all. The story of the decapitated man doesn't affect her too much.

"You have to go, don't you?" she asks.

"If you don't want me to..."

"No," she says. "No, Nevzat. You have to go - but finish your rakı first." She smiles. A bitter, pained smile. "If you don't finish it, the rakı in your glass will cry after you." That same stern look comes and settles onto her face again. "Finish your rakı and then go, because the dead are waiting for you, Nevzat. It's not right to keep the dead waiting."

There is such decisiveness in her bearing, her gaze and voice, that whatever I say will fall on deaf ears. I know Evgenia will definitely go now.

Chapter 22
And the beast was taken, and with him the false prophet..."

I'm going from Kurtuluş to Kumkapı, where Malik's house is. The pain, the sorrow inside me, strange feelings and strange thoughts... The woman I love is leaving me and we may never see each other again. I'm losing yet another valuable person. Perhaps the most beautiful relationship of my life is ending. I may be losing the only thing that gives meaning to my life. I am sad, very sad. But this sadness can't prevent my mind shifting to the murders. I guess Evgenia is right to leave me. I am incorrigible. Death entices me more than life. Death is more appealing. Not death, but murder. I smile to myself. Evgenia is closer to life than I am. Not life, but love. I suppose what solving murders is to me, that's what love is to her. If I said that, she would be enraged, asking how I could equate love with murder. However, neither of us loves the ordinary: Evgenia tries to make life extraordinary with love, and I solve murders... It's not normal, of course, but it's real. My reality. And I can say this with ease, murder keeps death from being ordinary as much as it keeps life from being ordinary.

Isn't that so? If Malik had died of natural causes, his friends and relatives would be sad, then call it providence and forget about him. But now, along with sadness they will feel anger, as well as a deep curiosity. They'll wonder who killed him. They'll put their minds to it and make attempts, even if amateurish, to find the killer. It doesn't matter if they find him or not, but it's sure to bring excitement to their lives. And what excitement! To solve a murder, to find the truth, to catch the killer. And solving homicides has other rewards that are good for the human soul, like ensuring justice. But only if the real criminal, the real killer is found. Because usually the truth is quite different from appearances. Just as in Malik's murder. I've been thinking about this since Ali phoned and said, "It seems the killer is Caner, Chief." It may be this misgiving that pulls me out of the sadness of losing Evgenia. It doesn't seem at all logical that Caner has murdered Malik. Yes, I know there are big differences of opinion between Caner and Malik, especially on the subject of Christianity. But the young man doesn't look like someone who would commit murder on account of that. And as if performing a religious ritual, no less, with the sword that killed Paul... No, this doesn't seem possible. Someone he loves like Malik, besides... when there is no problem between them. I wonder, was there a problem? I suppose one of them would have said if there were. Malik had not the slightest gripe against Caner. On the contrary, he took every opportunity to say he loved him and even kept repeating how he'd win him back to Christianity. No, Caner committing this murder is pointless. Really pointless... Unless maybe there were some other facts we didn't know about that they hid from us. "Actually, we're like two sides of the same medallion." Didn't Malik say that today? Maybe he was talking about a common belief that united the two or, I don't know, an illegal organization or a cult. What could they have in common? Nusayrism... Yes, weren't they both Arab Alawites? Their roots were. But one was a non-believer, the other obsessed with Christianity. Did either of them have any Nusayrism left in them? Maybe a secret religion we've never caught wind of... A secret doctrine. Caner was talking about esoteric religions, wasn't he? Yes, arcane religions... They had been more common around Adana, Antioch and the vicinity of Syria. But that was long, long ago. Could the mystic religions still persist? But why not? Around Antioch, they allegedly still believe in reincarnation. If Malik can think he is Paul, then plenty of people may still believe in the old mystic faiths. These thoughts keep gnawing at my mind until I reach Kumkapı.

The street where Malik's house is located is jammed with people. The entire neighborhood has amassed here. Malik's house is cordoned off by our men. The glow reflected from the flashing lights of the police cars falls over the crowd, whipped up in outrage. As they hoot and holler and yap noisily amongst themselves, I try to cut through and get to the house. A young officer in uniform is about to stop me at the police tape, but I show him my identification and pass under it.

As soon as I've stepped through the door, a smell that wasn't here this morning, the sharp odor of blood that has lost its freshness, fills my nasal passages. My eyes adjust to the light inside, and I make out Malik's headless body in a darkening pool of blood. Someone stands in the way, blocking my view of the corpse.

"Hello, Chief."

It's our Şefik, the tension of encountering such a complicated case reflected in his face.

"Hi, Şefik," I say. "How is it going?"

"Well, the situation is getting increasingly interesting." He points to the inner door that opens onto the chapel. "Our boys are hard at work, and Zeynep's there too."

Seriously, I wonder how Zeynep is faring. I squint and look in the direction Şefik is pointing. I see Zeynep leaning over Malik's headless trunk, studying the body in the pool of blood. She is so caught up in her work; it's hard to imagine what she's thinking and feeling.

"Where's Ali?" I ask Şefik.

"He took the suspect to the local station. The crowd has gone nuts; they were going to lynch the man. Ali barely got him out of here."

"He didn't mention that on the phone. When did all this happen?"

"A little while ago. But there is some background. Two youths caught the suspect in the chapel. I suppose he was trying to escape. They immediately jumped on him, but the suspect broke away. The people who were drawn to the noise of the fight grabbed him again. They gave him a good beating, and just then two officers who were passing by stepped in. They took the suspect and put him inside the house, then gave word to the station. By the time we got here, the crowd had grown considerably. They were screaming and shouting; they wanted us to turn the suspect over to them. Turns out the whole neighborhood, Muslim, Greek and Armenian alike, believes the chapel is auspicious. Everyone comes and makes wishes to this saint named Yithzak. When they heard someone was murdered in the chapel, they naturally went crazy."

"Malik was killed inside the chapel? Ali said the murder took place inside the house."

Şefik points at the lifeless body and says, "They cut the man's head off here, right at those steps there. The decapitated head dropped onto the chapel floor."

"Was the door open?"

"Yes, it was. Or more accurately, the suspect broke down the door from inside the chapel and entered."

Why would Caner break down the door? And what business did he have in the chapel anyhow? If he'd wanted to see Malik, he would have rung the house doorbell and his elderly friend would have welcomed him in. There was something fishy to this incident. I approach the body lying on the floor. Şefik follows. I'm a few steps away when Zeynep notices me. She straightens up; her plastic gloves are covered in blood. Although she's seen her share of murders, she's grimacing.

"It's shocking," she explains. "He laid the victim down on the floor... brought the head over the stairwell, and then chopped it a few times with the sword. It's not a clean cut. There are several blows to the neck. But the sword is quite sharp, and in the end he succeeded."

My gaze shifts to the sword at Malik's feet, its shiny surface spotted with blood. In my wrist, I again feel the weight of the sharp metal I held just this morning. I immediately chase the memory from my mind.

"Did the victim put up a fight?" I ask Zeynep. "Isn't there any sign of a struggle?"

"There is." She points out an icon of Mary and the child Jesus at the bottom of the wall to the left. "The victim defended himself. That's when the icon must have fallen. But I don't think he put up too much of a fight. You know, the victim wasn't so young. I didn't find any wounds or blows to his hands."

"Can't say the same for the suspect," Şefik cuts in. "They really roughed him up."

Zeynep's voice comes out almost too weak to hear.

"That's true. The crowd was on the verge of killing him."

The poor girl, should she feel sorry for Caner or embarrassed that she'd got close to a suspect? "Any other clues or evidence?" I ask, to save her a bit from this state of mind.

Zeynep begins to explain with enthusiasm.

"We found a dark blue filament under the fingernail of the middle finger of the victim's right hand. We're looking into whether it belongs to the killer or the victim's own clothes. I can tell you for sure after the lab work."

"Have you looked upstairs? Could it have been a thief or something?"

"I did look upstairs," says Zeynep. "Everything is very orderly. I don't think the perpetrator even went up there. It could be a robbery; it's difficult to know. There's so much stuff in the house. But we called the victim's son Zekeriya and he'll be here soon. He'll understand if there's something missing."

Şefik offers clarification.

"It's hard to work in this house. There are too many fingerprints."

"Don't be surprised," I say, "if you come across mine somewhere, especially on the sword handle."

Şefik's face distorts.

"Stop looking as if you've seen the devil, Şefik. You can assume I didn't kill the man. I was in the house this morning, is all. I talked to poor Malik. I handled the sword that killed him."

"You handled it? Why?"

"The man insisted. Never mind that now, Şefik. What, are you suspecting me?"

"Don't be silly, Chief. I just got a little surprised when you said that about your fingerprints."

The CSI officer is bent over the stairs, looking for footprints, hairs, any clues that give the perpetrator away. I'm looking over his back at the chapel door, which is wide open. Where the lock is, the wood is splintered. A bloody, ball-like object on the floor of the chapel grabs my attention. I immediately look away. It's Malik's head.

"And there's a Bible, Chief," says Zeynep. "Yes, some of the lines of this book are also underlined in the victim's blood."

"Where? Can I see it?"

We all go over to the room Malik hosted me in this morning. Where the tea tray had been, I see a Bible opened up just like the one in the imposter Yusuf's house. It doesn't take me long to pick out one of the lines underlined in blood on the opened page. I take out my glasses and try to read it.

"And the beast was taken, and with him the false prophet..."***1

Before raising my head from the book, I ask, "Is it from the prophet Zachariah again?"

"No, Chief. It's from Revelation, written by John and added to the end of the Bible." Zeynep moves closer to the book. "Also, the lines here are not straight at all. If you remember, in the book in Yusuf's house, the sentences were underlined as if with a ruler." She points to the margin on the right side of the book. "There's another difference. There's no Mor Gabriel written here."

"So what," Şefik puts in. "How important is that?"

Zeynep is sure of her assumption and answers resolutely, "Very. These signs are like the killer's signature. So he performed the ritual of drawing a line under the verse in the victim's blood, but this time he chose another chapter. A chapter that has no relation to the one before. Let's say there is an explanation for this, but why is there no Mor Gabriel?"

"Maybe he couldn't find time," Şefik explains. "The two young guys caught him in the act."

Şefik could be right, but thereıs no sense in dragging this argument out right now. I have more important things to talk to Zeynep about.

"We'll find out, Şefik," I say. "Let's not rush it. Let's get all this evidence together and then we'll decide."

Şefik doesnıt push the subject, but he has no intention of leaving the room either. I have no other recourse but to openly tell him, "Could you excuse us, Şefik? We need to talk about another case so..."

Şefik isnıt pleased with the request, but he complies. As heıs about to go out, I remember what Cengiz had to say about the news leaked to the press.

"Şefik, just a minute. In this Assyrian murder case, the news came out in the press about the victim's being Christian."

Şefik pales.

"Is that so? I didn't know that, Chief."

"I wasn't aware of it either. Director Cengiz told me."

"I wonder who leaked it?'

I think he knows who that is.

"Well it didn't come from us, so it must have been one of your men."

"No, Chief, where did you get that from?'

"This is some friendly advice, Şefik. Warn your men they should keep their lips sealed. Otherwise you'll be left holding the bag."

"All right, Chief," he says. "If it's one of us, I'll pull their ear."

Then without even waiting for what I'm going to say, he struts out.

"Guilty yet cocksure," says Zeynep. "I saw that curly-haired guy of his Namık talking to a reporter."

"I know, Zeynep. In the end Şefik will figure out where he went wrong. I hope he does so before it's too late and he gets into trouble. Anyhow, let's get back to work. When did you get here? What did you see when you arrived? Tell us."

"I came with Ali. When we arrived, there was a bigger, angrier, crowd than the one outside now. They were kicking up a fuss, demanding Caner be handed over to them. Ali made an announcement. He called for backup."

"Where was Caner at this point?"

"He was inside, in the room across there..."

"In the room with the antiques..."

"Yes, this big room over here. There were two uniformed officers with him."

"How was Caner's condition?"

"He was bad. His glasses were broken and he had blood all over his face."

"Could he speak?"

"Yes, he could. He was happy to see us. 'It's a good thing you are here,' he said. 'They're making a big mistake.'

"I didn't know what to say but Ali didn't believe him. 'Man, you were caught red-handed but you are still denying it?' he said.

"Caner started to beg. He said he didn't kill Malik Amca. That he was just trying to get in. Ali told him, 'Enough. Everything is as clear as day; you slaughtered the man like a sheep.'

"Caner realized he couldn't convince Ali and he turned to me. 'I didn't do it, Zeynep Hanım,' he said. 'Believe me, I didn't.'

" 'So who did?' Ali said. 'Who killed this man? The chapel demons?'

"Caner looked indecisive. I thought he knew the killer. That he was going to tell us now, but he didn't. He asked for you."

"For me?"

"Yes, Chief. For you. 'Isn't Chief Inspector Nevzat coming?' he said.

"Ali didn't say much but just snapped, 'Don't get ahead of yourself. The game's up, and you can't fool anyone anymore.' Caner was persistent. He asked again if you were coming. I answered even though I knew it would make Ali angry. He was in such a pathetic state; I felt sorry for him. I told him you'd be here in half an hour.

"Just then the crowd outside started to raise a ruckus again. They wanted Caner. Some people even threw stones at the house. Because of that, we decided to remove him from the premises. We dressed Caner in a bulletproof vest and police uniform and put a cap on his head. Ali, the two officers and Caner went out. However, the crowd recognized Caner. They all furiously attacked together. Ali and the officers barely managed to protect him. The poor guy was punched and kicked a few times. Ali also took his share of punches. I got really scared something would happen to him. I nearly pulled my weapon and dove into the crowd as well. Ali did what I was thinking. He fired three shots into the air to disperse the crowd. The crowd settled down straight away. Ali took advantage of it, quickly throwing Caner into the squad car and taking him to the station."

"Nothing happened to Ali, did it?"

"Thankfully, no. He got a few punches to the back but he managed to bust a few people's jaws himself. He didn't look bad when he got into the squad car. He even winked at me from the window."

"The dog," I muttered fondly. "He loves brawling."

In fact, I'm tickled by Zeynep's concern for Ali. No, this girl loves Ali, but what kind of love it is, I don't know.

"The two people who caught Caner, where are they?"

"They went to the police station, Chief."

"Good... I had better get over there too. Have you got a lot to do?"

Her smooth forehead wrinkles up with the tension of some unresolved problem.

"I saw blood spatters on the stair railings going up to the second floor. It's not possible the severed head sprayed blood up there. It's the wrong direction. Maybe it's the perpetrator's blood. I'll get some samples. I'm here a while longer, Chief."

As we speak, there's shouting from outside again. I hate these lyncher types. Alone, they are each as timid as a mouse, but when they all come together, they throw their weight around like lions.

"Where's the man in charge of the teams out there?" I ask as I leave the room. "Let's tell them to disperse this riffraff."

Chapter 23
Malik Amca's severed head...

I leave the angry mob with my fellow men in uniform trying to disperse it from in front of Malik's house, and I go into the police station a few streets beyond. As soon as I step inside, Ali's voice rings in my ears.

"And you're going to be tough guys. The man beat the two of you black and blue. If our officer hadn't got there, God knows he would have put you in hospital."

He must be speaking with the two witnesses. I rush down the wide corridor, illuminated by the red light spreading from the ugly chandelier, and go into the room the noise is coming from. A clean-shaven young inspector sits at the table, listening to Ali with great pleasure. There are a total of five people apart from the young inspector, the two black-eyed witnesses, two police officers and Ali, who is completely caught up in the exchange. They all hold half-filled glasses of tea. Caner is nowhere to be seen; he must be in a cell. The young inspector is the first to notice me, and he respectfully jumps straight up.

"Chief Inspector Nevzat. Welcome."

So he knows me. With the inspector's words, Ali collects himself. The two officers stand, and so the others are obliged to stand at attention too. I don't relish this business at all.

"Have a seat, friends."

As the others sit back down, the young inspector keeps up the courtesy and points to the armchair he's got up from.

"No, sir, you come sit here."

With no other resort, I go to the head of the table. Before sitting on one of the chairs, the young officer asks, "What'll you have to drink, Chief, tea or coffee?"

"Thanks, nothing for me. Let's get down to work."

This "let's get down to work," also means enough of this prattle. Without insisting, the young inspector moves over to a chair beside the witness with the blackened left eye.

Apparently, these two boys had really taken a beating. Did Caner do this by himself? He doesn't look the type. Ali sees me looking at the witnesses and explains, "These are our friends who caught the suspect." One is fat, the other thin as a toothpick, and as he looks at them he can barely contain his laughter. "Really, whether they caught Caner or Caner caught them is hard to tell."

"Why do you say that, Inspector?" the one like a toothpick objects, "The upshot is, we caught the man."

Ali continues to tease.

"That's not what I heard. It's the neighborhood that did that."

Caner's ending up a suspect must have really put Ali in high spirits, but it's beginning to strike a sour note. I don't let him drag it out.

"Let's hear your side of the story," I say to the witnesses. "Tell us, how did things transpire?"

The one like a toothpick knocks back his tea in one go and then answers.

"Malik Amca hired us to keep an eye on the chapel."

"You mean he was paying you?"

"He was... but we would have done it if he hadn't paid. The chapel was in bad shape before Malik Amca came. People would go and make wishes, but nobody did the cleaning or repairs. Some nights glue-sniffers or winos would sleep

251

there. Malik Amca came along and took on the job. He took charge of cleaning, maintenance and security in the chapel. And we started to help him...."

"Now, the place you are guarding is a chapel. A small church, I mean. Are you Christian too?"

"Christian, Inspector? We're Muslims, praise Allah. But after all, our Lord Jesus is also one of Allah's prophets. And Saint Yithzak, who rests in the chapel, is also a holy man. Muslim, Christian, Jew, it doesn't matter. He's a saint to us all..."

"Okay then, but ultimately Malik is a Christian. Didn't he ever try to convert you?"

"No, Chief. Malik Amca has respect for everyone's religion. And anyhow, what are we, children? If he had tried to do that . . ."

"He gave me a Bible," the fat one said, refuting his friend. "A hefty book... starting all the way back from Adam. I was reading it and our father saw it at home. He got angry and so I gave it back. Malik asked me, 'Didn't you like it?' I told him I did but that the book was not for us. He didn't push the subject, the poor guy."

"May he rest in peace; he was a very good man," says the skinny one, taking the floor again. "He wasn't a Muslim but everybody in the neighborhood loved him. Even the grumpy imam from our mosque got on with him. Anyhow... This evening we..." He nods towards his friend. "We were passing by the chapel with Faruk here and we heard noises."

Faruk corrects him as if reminding him of an important detail.

"No, we didn't hear a noise. First we saw that the door of the chapel was open." Faruk turns to me. "When I saw the door was open, Chief, I told Alper, 'I think there's someone inside. I hope it's not glue-sniffers ...' "

"No, man. You're remembering wrong. No, Chief, we heard the noise first. After that we went over to the chapel. That's when we noticed the door was open."

"What kind of noise?"

Alper answers.

"Like someone was ramming the door with their shoulder. Then we heard a crack. As you'll guess, it was the sound of the door breaking. We thought the sniffers were inside tearing the place up. We went straight in. We looked and there was a man standing in front of the door that opens into Malik Amca's house. And the door was broken. When we shouted at him, 'What are you doing?' the man panicked. He started coming towards us, aiming to escape. I jumped right on him. But the guy was prepared; he dodged and punched me in the eye. It's really heavy, that bastard's hand. I was knocked to the ground. Faruk opened his arms up like a goalie and tried to block the guy from getting out. What did the man do but put his trust in God and punch Faruk in the stomach too. Faruk sat down on his backside..."

"The guy caught us off guard, Inspector," Faruk says, taking over. "But of course I didn't give up. Just as he was going through the door, I grabbed him by his left pant leg. He's a tough nut; he started kicking me with his right foot. Thankfully, Alper came to my rescue."

"Yes, Inspector, as soon as I recovered, I picked up a chair and swung it at him. But the guy is as nimble as a cat and he slipped aside. The chair missed its target and it came down on Faruk's head."

"Yeah, it landed on my head, and that sure did hurt. But I still didn't let go of the guy's leg. Anyhow, he lost his balance and fell to the floor. And that's when Alper jumped on him."

"I jumped on him but when he pulled back, I fell on to the ground too, and I hit my head on the protruding door."

"Meanwhile, I was trying to grab the guy's other leg. The man is sharp. As I was trying to grab his leg, he caught my lapse and kicked me squarely in the chin, so hard I saw stars. I was out like a light."

"When Faruk passed out, I got really pissed off, Inspector. I grabbed the leg Faruk had let go of and started to bite like there's no tomorrow. The guy is shouting his head off on the one hand, trying to kick me with his free foot on the other. Durmuş Abi, the corner coffeehouse's owner, had raced over towards the clamor, and then the waiters, the shoe sellers, and the whole neighborhood swarmed around us. That's how we caught him. The neighborhood heard Malik Amca had been murdered, and they flew into a rage and wanted to lynch the man." At this point, he gestures towards the two uniformed police. "These nice policemen rescued the man from the mob. And that's about the gist of it, Inspector."

"I see," I say. "Now, think hard about what I'm going to ask, and answer accordingly. All right?"

They both nod in agreement.

"When you first saw the suspect, I mean when you first went into the chapel, what exactly was he doing?"

"He was just standing at the door looking inside," Alper is saying, though his friend doesn't concur.

"You're wrong; he wasn't looking in. He was staring at Malik Amca's head."

Before the other one can object, I ask, "Where was Malik's head? Could you see it clearly?"

"I saw it," says Faruk. "I saw it and I shuddered. It's not easy; it makes a person feel funny. So I hung back a bit. Malik's head was all bloody and his eyes and face were unrecognizable. It was sitting at the killer's feet like a deflated ball. And the man was just standing there, staring at it."

"Was he holding a sword?"

"No, we didn't see a sword or anything..."

Faruk's friend backed him up.

"There wasn't one, Inspector. If there had been, he would have hacked us up too."

"So what state was the man in exactly? I mean, was he shocked, or angry, or nervous?"

"He was in shock. Like he didn't know what to do. Anyhow, when he saw us, he panicked.

"Was there any blood on his hands or clothes?"

"Well, I got blood on *my* hands," Faruk says. "Because I was holding onto the man's leg. The bottoms of his shoes were in the blood. Was there any blood on his hands or clothes? With all the commotion, I didn't notice."

"I think there was," says Alper, "but I noticed it after the fight. Maybe it was the guy's own blood. Because he really took a beating from the locals."

"Anything else get your attention?"

"No," they both say. "That's it, Inspector."

I turn back to Ali, taking his last sip of tea.

"Good, then let's talk to Caner. See what he has to say."

"Shall we bring the suspect here, Chief?" the young inspector cuts in before Ali can.

"If you have another room it'd be better."

"The one opposite is empty."

"Great, let's move over there."

The young inspector sends one of the uniformed officers to the holding cell to bring Caner back. Our two witness friends are bored now. Faruk's pleading eyes stare into my face.

"Can we go now?"

"Let our colleagues take down your statement, and then..."

"We'll take care of it, Chief," says the young inspector. I like this kid; he's not only well-mannered but seems to know his job.

As I go into the other room, Ali follows me uninvited.

"How are you, Ali?" I say. "I guess they roughed you up too..."

"I'm fine, Chief. You can't hurt someone who's been around the block as much as me."

This kid was never going to grow up! And I have had it with sermonizing.

The small room is filled with steel filing cabinets. It must be a storeroom. In front of the wall is a wooden desk. As I move to the chair behind it, I ask, "What do you think, Ali? Is Caner really the murderer?"

"Who else would it be, Chief?" He looks at me with disappointment, surprised by my uncertainty. "The man was caught at the crime scene. Trying to run away, no less..."

"He may have got scared, panicked."

"A man who is scared or panicked asks for help. Why would he run away? And what was he looking for there anyway? If you remember, when he left the station, he told us he was going to the university. He lied to us. He came to Malik's house. I already suspected that highbrow from the start. Okay, so he's well read, and cultured and whatnot, but there's a devilishness in his face, a cunning."

He gives me a dubious look.

"Or do you think he's innocent?"

Before Ali can even finish his sentence, Caner comes limping in. His hair is disheveled, there are no glasses on his face, his brow is swollen and his right eye is nearly closed. The other eye is completely bloodshot. There's a deep gash on his nose, his lower lip is split and his sweater and coat are covered in blood. I feel bad for him. I'll admit I wasn't expecting this much; they'd beaten him to a pulp. He sets his open bloodshot eye on my face and says, "You finally made it, Chief Inspector. I've been waiting for you for hours."

"Come on over, Caner. Come, have a seat."

"No, Chief. Now is not the time to sit. We need to talk right away. They're making a big mistake. I didn't kill Malik..."

"Sit, Caner," Ali barks. Seeing my empathy for Caner is making him angry. "When you are told to sit, you'll sit."

Caner turns his open eye fearfully on Ali.

"All right. I'm sitting.

He grimaces as he settles into his chair. He must be in serious pain.

"Look," he says, turning to me. "I didn't kill Malik. Why would I?"

Ali immediately snaps back.

"The same reason you killed Yusuf."

Caner ignores him.

"Chief Inspector, I need to speak with you. It's imperative..." He is whispering as if divulging a secret. "I know the truth."

Now what does he mean by that?

"Good, so tell me then. What are you waiting for?"

He gestures towards Ali and the other officer.

"We should talk alone."

Is he putting me on?

"Please, Chief." He starts to shake. He's lost a fair bit of blood and he looks drained. "What I have to explain is very important."

I say to the police officer, "You can go."

"Yes, sir."

When he's gone, I explain pointedly, "Ali is in this business with me. "Whatever you mean to tell me, he has a right to hear too."

"But..."

"No buts. You'll either explain it with Ali here or you'll keep it to yourself."

With his one eye, he looks from Ali to me.

"All right. I trust both of your impartiality and your honor."

Ali can't hold back.

"What the hell do you think you are saying? We don't need your trust!"

"Wait, Ali. Just stay cool," I say, to calm him down. "Let's hear him out."

Caner looks dolefully at Ali.

"I don't understand why you are so hostile towards me. What have I ever done to you?"

Ali waves his right hand in the air.

"I'm not hostile to anyone. If I was, would I have snatched you out of that crowd? I just want to see justice done."

"Thank you so very much for rescuing me. And what I want is no different."

Ali doesn't understand. He gives him a look as if to say, how so?

"I want justice served just like you do. I hope both of you will stay true to this desire till the end."

Is this guy going to keep sidestepping?

"Come on, Caner. Say what you're going to say."

"I'm explaining, Chief..." He must be in pain when he opens his mouth because his face contorts, although he keeps talking. "You know I told you I was going to the faculty building. But on my way, Malik Amca called. He told me you'd paid him a visit. 'Come round if you have time,' he said. To be honest, I was curious to hear what you'd talked about. This murder investigation is a strange thing. It consumes people. You know we've been mulling it over, discussing it for a few days now, and I guess I've started to see myself as one of you..."

"Cops don't come from killers," says Ali. "You'd best just stay a highbrow."

Caner ignores the gibe again. Anyhow, he has no choice.

"I accepted Malik Amca's invite, despite having things to do at the college. He met me with boundless hospitality, as always."

"Hold on," I say, interrupting. "You mean you were with Malik before he was murdered."

"Yes, Inspector. I was with Malik Amca an hour before he was killed. We had lunch together." For a moment his eyes are far away. "Malik was a great cook. He learned in prison. He made spinach with minced meat. While we were eating, he explained what all you talked about. This Diatessaron thing. I was so pleased that he'd handed the book over to the Mor Gabriel Monastery. And I also appreciated that you'd been understanding and not taken him into custody.

" 'Who do you think might have killed Yusuf Abi?' I asked him. His face grew deeply concerned and, after thinking a bit, he said he didn't know. 'I think you do, Malik Amca,' I said. Then he said he hoped he was wrong, and that's when I was sure he knew something. I asked him why he said that, and he said, 'Because if it's like I think, then we're in a bad way'.

"I was worried but my curiosity got the better of me. I asked him what he meant. He said, 'Never mind, Caner. It's best you don't know.' Then he looked at his watch and said, 'Forgive me, but I have to ask you to leave. An old friend is coming round. Someone important.'

"As soon as he said he had to ask me to leave, I understood he was talking about a subject related to the murder. And when he said an old friend was coming, I thought that person could be involved in the murder. Then I got this crazy idea. I decided to lie low on the corner and find out who this houseguest was. I got up without objecting. I said goodbye to Malik and went out. But I didn't leave the street. I went into the coffeehouse on the corner. From the window looking onto the street, I could easily see Malik's door. I had just finished drinking my tea when I saw a man in a navy-blue coat coming across the street. It seemed like I knew him from somewhere but I couldn't quite place it. If he hadn't knocked on Malik's door, I wouldn't have made much of it. But the man stopped in front of Malik's house. He looked around and then knocked. Where had I seen this man before? I focused all my attention and tried to remember. Meanwhile, Malik opened the door, and as the guy went in, it came to me." Ali and I are watching his face intently. "I saw him with you, Chief Inspector."

What kind of game is this one playing?

"With me?"

"Yes, in your office..."

"Nice one, Caner," Ali taunts. "Maybe you'll find some idiot who'll fall for that..."

"I'm not making it up. I swear on my honor that I'm telling the truth."

As I mull over who he could have seen in my room, I remember that Yusuf had called the central station. Could the person Caner was talking about be the same one Yusuf had phoned? I can't bear it so I ask, "Who is it you saw in my room?"

"Don't you remember? He came in while we were talking yesterday. He called you into his office. I think it's your boss..."

"Cengiz..." The name spills spontaneously from my mouth. This kid is off his nut. "Are you talking about Cengiz?"

"I don't know his name. But that was the man in the navy-blue coat I saw going into Malik's today."

As I recall with surprise Cengiz putting on his navy-blue jacket, Ali bawls, "Why are we listening to this guy? He's looking us straight in the eye and lying. If you had made me go out, I am sure it would have been me he said he saw instead of Director Cengiz..."

Caner's single open eye stares at me as if appealing for help.

"I am not lying, Inspector. I'm putting myself at the mercy of your conscience. That is the man I saw."

The truth of the matter is Ali is as confused as I am. Maybe this is why he is thinking aloud, trying to tone down the impact of Caner's words.

"He heard that Yusuf called the station. Well now he's ad-libbing..."

"I know nothing about Yusuf calling the station."

True enough, so long as Zeynep didn't tell him. If she did, we'd find out. But more importantly, why would Caner lie like this? If you're going to slander someone, why would you choose such an influential man as Cengiz? That's not a wise move. In other respects, what relationship could there be between Cengiz and Malik?

"Maybe you should ask Zekeriya," Caner says, as if reading my mind. "Malik Amca said an old friend was coming. This old friend may know Zekeriya as well..."

"Sure he knows him, my dear. Director Cengiz has nothing better to do, so he just hobnobs with the ex-cons..."

Ali says this, but his voice doesn't hold the same conviction anymore. He's starting to think like me. He also knows Caner stands to gain nothing from a lie like this. Still, he can't stomach accusations against a colleague, a superior officer.

"That's ridiculous, Caner," I say. "Maybe whoever you saw just looked like Director Cengiz to you. You only just got a glance of him in my room. Isn't that right?"

"You're right, it was only a glance, but I have a very strong memory. I never forget a face."

"This is a very serious thing, Caner. You're toying with a police officer's fate."

"He killed Malik Amca. He's a murderer."

"What a confident pitch," Ali protests. "To hear him, you'd think it was true."

"It is true, Inspector Ali. Believe me, what I'm saying is real. I wouldn't say it if I weren't sure. And what do you have to lose by checking it out? Ask Zekeriya. Find out where Director Cengiz was at the time of the murder. You'll see I'm right. That is, if you want to catch the actual killer. If you really want to uphold justice."

Ali rudely interrupts again.

"Quit the comments on justice already, and tell us what you were looking for in the chapel."

It's the right question. Perhaps the most crucial thing we've been waiting for since the start of Caner's speech. He answers without hesitation.

"I sat in the coffeehouse for two hours. If you don't believe me, you can ask the coffee guy. I had to drink four teas in a row. But Cengiz somehow wasn't coming out."

"Do not call that man Cengiz," Ali warns.

"But it was him..." Ali's stern glare is effective. "All right, if you don't want me to use Cengiz's name, I won't use it. When the man didn't come out, I got nervous. A voice inside me was saying something bad was going on inside the house. It occurred to me to call Malik's house phone. I dialed the number on my cell. He didn't pick up. I got really anxious. I remembered the door connecting the chapel to Malik's house. I could go into the chapel and listen from the door. I paid the bill and left. I went into the chapel. There was no one inside. I went over to the door to Malik's house and listened in. It was quiet. At that moment I noticed my foot was in something liquid. I looked and it was blood. At first I cringed back, then in a panic I pounded on the door. In the meantime, I heard some noises inside. I started kicking, but saw that it wasn't working, so I put all my strength into it and finally managed to bust the door. But the door still wasn't opening. There was something stuck behind it, so then I yanked the busted door towards me. When I did that, this round thing like a ball rolled down between my legs. I looked down and all my hair stood on end. It was Malik Amca's severed head. I froze, and at exactly that moment the chapel door opened and two people came in. I thought they were Cengiz's... I mean the man who killed Malik's friends. I panicked and wanted to run for it... And that's all there was to it."

Chapter 24
Whoever touched that book has been killed.

Once we've sent Caner to the holding cells, neither Ali nor I can speak for a while. My mind has already automatically created a file on Cengiz and started to silently flip its pages. I recall the conversation we had last night. It seemed hectic. But then he had said he was in a hurry to try to make it to this official dinner. Allegedly he'd needed to expound on the murders of Yusuf and Bingöllü to his superiors. Whether it was really necessary or that was just what he told me is hard to say. Why would he do that? To get information on the incident. Or to see what I knew. Perhaps his higher-ups hadn't even asked him about the murder. It would be easy enough to find out if I called Sabri. He'd probably be happy I called, and I'm sure he would hear me out, but wouldn't that be unfair to Cengiz? What point was there in putting his name among the suspects out of the blue? Caner could be lying. Or maybe mistaken. He says his memory is strong but how can he be so sure it's the same person when he only saw him for one second? What he's saying isn't very consistent. And we don't even know Caner. Is it right to suspect a director we love and trust, relying on the word of someone we don't know? But what if Caner isn't wrong? If his words reflect the truth? No, we can't just turn a deaf ear, saying he is slandering our director. But first we need a solid investigation. I hope it turns out Caner is wrong and I won't have to accuse Cengiz, but if I have to do it, I'll need to have more than just Caner's word. At least I should find answers to these three questions: First, who is it that the Yusuf imposter called at the station? Second, who is the Yusuf imposter really, and what happened to the shepherd whose identity he took? And third, did Cengiz and Malik know each other?

"This Inspector Yavuz who died in the thresher," I ask, turning to Ali. "Did you manage to look into that?"

"Sorry, what did you say, Chief?"

Apparently, like mine, Ali's head was full of possibilities, conjecture and thoughts that didn't quite connect.

"The file on Inspector Yavuz," I reiterate.

"I didn't get a chance, Chief. We got news of Malik's murder after I'd sent Gabriel away. We came here right away. And you know, we're meeting with Chief Inspector Nusret tomorrow."

"It may be too late by tomorrow, Ali. This file on Inspector Yavuz is urgent. I'd like you to deal with this business as soon as you return to the station."

Ali doesn't exactly get my meaning.

"Tonight?"

"Tonight. From this point on it's a race against time. Get on your computer, or go down to the police station archives, but whatever you do, bring me a conclusion by morning."

Ali is unaware what I'm thinking and rightfully asks, "Sorry, Chief, why is Inspector Yavuz's file so important?"

I don't have the time or inclination to explain it to him. But if he knows my thoughts, perhaps he'll do better research, so I explain.

"If we take a look at all that has happened, Ali, we see that at the center of the murders is this stolen book, the Diatessaron. You heard what Gabriel said. The packet his cousin Aziz gave Inspector Yavuz was most likely the Diatessaron."

A gleam passes through Ali's narrowed eyes.

"If this is true," says Ali excitedly, "whoever touched that book has been killed. Gabriel's cousin Aziz, Inspector Yavuz, the phony Yusuf, Malik the antique seller... Maybe there is something in that book."

Ali is carried away by the mystery again.

"There's nothing in the book, Ali. What book can choke people in a cave, throw them into a thresher, stab someone twice in the heart or cut off a head with a sword? The Diatessaron is merely a book made up of parts of the four Gospels. There's nothing in that book but it's also a fact that the murders revolve around it. That's why we have to find the first person, I mean Inspector Yavuz, who took the book from Aziz."

Ali okays me with the decisiveness of having grasped my meaning, "All right, Chief, don't you worry. I'll be on it as soon as I get to the station. I'll have my report to you in a few hours."

"Make me proud, Ali. Get this thing solved swiftly."

"I can stop by Chief Inspector Nusret's first if you want. Although he did say to come tomorrow..."

"Never mind Nusret. You go straight to the station and start researching immediately."

"What about Caner?"

"You haven't got time. Let the guys here deal with him. Have them take him to the hospital first for the doctors to look him over, then have them bring him to the central station. Keep an eye on him; I don't want anything to happen to him."

"Yes, sir." As he's getting up, he suddenly stops. "What do you say, Chief? Could Director Cengiz..."

"Too early to tell, Ali," I say, cutting him off. "What I want from you is for you to conduct this research as secretly as possible. We need secrecy in order to prove Cengiz innocent and to learn the truth. You understand, right?"

"I understand, Chief."

"So then, back to work."

While Ali goes off to speak to the officers inside, I leave the local station without saying goodbye. I call Zeynep as

I'm walking to Malik's house. Zeynep answers on exactly the sixth ring.

"Sorry, Chief. I was getting blood samples."

"Not important, Zeynep. Has Malik's son Zekeriya arrived yet?"

"He has. He's waiting for you."

"How is he?"

"Not great, but he could be worse. Thankfully we sent the body to the morgue before he came. He didn't see his father in that state."

"Good. Don't let him go, whatever you do."

"I won't, Chief. The poor guy can't move a muscle anyhow. He collapsed into a chair and is just sitting there."

"I'm coming, too. I won't be ten minutes."

But I don't go straight there. There are two stop-offs I need to make first. First the parking lot; Caner said the man who entered Malik's house was coming from that direction. If he has a car, he must have left it in the lot, because it's impossible to find a space in this neighborhood. In fact, I could sort this question out when I go get my car, but my curiosity is making me antsy and I want to find out what happened straight away.

The lot attendant, the man with his right hand cut off from the wrist, is sitting in his little room watching a soap opera on his TV. He's so involved in the show that he doesn't notice me.

"Hello," I say.

When he sees me, he's annoyed by the hassle he'll have, but he attempts to stand anyhow.

"Are you taking your car?"

"No, no. Don't get up. I just want to ask you something. This afternoon, has a smoke-colored Nissan been here?"

I don't know why, but it rubs him the wrong way.

"Why do you ask?" he says roughly. I'm in no mood for his vagaries so I show him my ID.

"Chief Inspector Nevzat! Now, answer the question and make it quick."

He jumps straight up.

"So sorry, Inspector. I didn't know; that's cluelessness for you..."

"Okay, okay. Give me my answer. Was there a smoke-colored Nissan here early evening?"

As you can guess, the Nissan is our Cengiz's. I don't remember the plate number so I can't tell him.

Still, our one-handed parking attendant remembers. And without any ambiguity, at that. He says he remembers all the plate numbers of cars that have come to the garage.

"34 ASZ 214..." he says, reading off the number in one breath. "Yes, Inspector. The car was here. As you said, in the afternoon. It was here for about two hours. Then the guy came and picked it up. Tall, clean-shaven, a bit younger than you. He was wearing a dark blue coat."

He was describing Cengiz to a tee. Apparently, Caner was telling the truth. At least it was true he had seen Cengiz around here. He could have made up a lie after seeing him, fine, but what had Cengiz been doing here? Who could say; maybe he'd come to see a friend, maybe he has a relative living nearby... There's no rule saying everyone who comes to this area is going to Malik's house. Despite my trying to justify it, I was becoming more convinced that Caner was telling the truth. But I shouldn't be. Hoping to come into some facts proving Cengiz's innocence, I head for the coffeehouse next to Malik's place.

The street has emptied, as if the crowd has suddenly melted away. Apart from two officers chatting under the still blinking lights of the squad car in front of the house, there's no one to be seen. As I enter the coffeehouse, I understand where everyone's gone. The people from the street have filled the place. They aren't shouting anymore; they've calmed down a bit. But at some tables, the conversation about the murder continues. I overhear it as I walk past, someone saying, "The guy they caught wasn't a Turk. Didn't you see him? He's blonde. There is no Turk like that. Look I'm telling you, there's some missionary activity to this business."

"What missionary activity, Kazim Abi?" the other cuts in. "The man looks exactly the thieving type. His face is like a girl's. Nobody would suspect him. He heard somewhere that

Malik Amca is an antique seller. He broke into his house and when Malik came on to him, he killed the poor man."

Someone else jumps into the discussion.

"That sounds good, but why would a robber cut the man's head off? No, friend, this is mafia-related. In any event, Malik used to be a bit of a bad seed. Ziya from the Grand Bazaar came over here recently. You remember him, that old jeweler from Kadırga. 'Don't go thinking Malik is as clean as he looks,' is what he said. 'Smuggling, arms trading and drug deals, the man has done it all.' "

I leave them to their speculation and head for the stove. This time I take out my ID and show it to the man at the stove before he asks. He was one of the first to hear the noise in the chapel and come to Alper and Faruk's aid.

"That's true, Inspector," he says. "The blonde kid sat at the window for two hours. I noticed him because he's not from the neighborhood, but a customer is a customer and so long as he drinks his tea and pays up, there's no problem. How should we know the man is a murderer? He stood up from here and killed Malik Amca, the bastard. If I had known..."

"Did you see anyone coming or going from the house at that time?"

"Malik Amca's house? No, I didn't see anyone."

"So would you have seen it if someone had come or gone?"

He looks out from inside the coffeehouse.

"I couldn't have seen from here, but while I was handing out tea to people, maybe... But no one grabbed my attention, Inspector."

I'm still trying to protect my hopes that Cengiz could be innocent, despite a second witness confirming Caner's testimony. This time I head for Malik's house, with the hope that Zekeriya will say something to invalidate Caner's claims. I say hello to the officers next to the squad car and go in. It's gone calm inside too; Şefik's team has left and Zeynep is still in the hall, placing the evidence bags into a bigger case.

"How's it going, Zeynep? Have you finished?"

Her tired face lights up with a sweet smile.

"Good thanks, Chief. This part here is finished. I was going to the central station; I have to work in the lab."

"Good. I sent Ali to the station too. He's working on this Inspector Yavuz's file."

Zeynep looks flustered.

"I couldn't get to that, Chief. Everything developed so quickly..."

I put a hand on her shoulder.

"I know, Zeynep. But we have to solve this business now. Caner told us some interesting things. Ali will explain. Don't stray from the station tonight. I'm coming too. If Ali asks for your help, drop what you are doing and help him. That work takes priority. I suppose the twist of the murders lies with this Commander Yavuz. If we can figure that out, we'll crack this thing. Do you understand, Zeynep? Tonight is critical."

"I understand, Chief."

"Good then, if you are done here, don't waste any time getting over to Ali."

She closes the cover of the case she's placed the evidence bags in.

"I'm on my way, Chief..."

"By the way, where is Zekeriya?"

She points towards Malik's workroom.

"He's waiting for you in there."

In Malik's room, Zekeriya is plunked down, crushed, in the chair his father was sitting on this morning. Deep sorrow, shock and fear on his face. When he sees me come in, he neither tries to stand nor can even budge. He just stares at me with eyes that resemble his father's, as if appealing for help.

"I'm sorry for your loss, Zekeriya..."

"Thank you."

His eyes fill up.

"How did this thing happen, Inspector? Just this morning you two..."

"Yes, Zekeriya. We just spoke this morning. He didn't mention any danger to me. If I had known, we would have protected him."

"He wasn't in any danger, Inspector..." A few drops seep from his eyes. "He didn't have any enemies. I mean, as far as we knew."

He wipes his eyes with his hand, trying to pull himself together.

"I heard a suspect was caught."

"Yes, there is someone. Actually, someone you know."

"Someone I know?"

"Caner."

"What? Caner Abi? No, there's some mistake, Inspector. Why would Caner Abi want to kill my dad? The two of them loved each other. No, there's definitely some mistake."

"There's nothing certain yet, anyhow. We're investigating," I say, planting my gaze on Zekeriya. "Oh, and by the way, Director Cengiz extends his condolences." He stares into my face like he doesn't understand. "Director Cengiz, I'm saying. I guess he's an old friend of your father's. I think he knows you too."

The scattered look in his eyes is gathering into focus.

"Cengiz Amca?" he says, proving Caner right once again. "He always came to the rescue whenever we were in trouble. But this time..."

He starts to sniffle and cry quietly. My mind is on Cengiz. So Caner was telling the truth. Assuming that's true, it must be Cengiz that the Yusuf imposter called at the station. But why would Cengiz kill Malik? The twist comes back round to the book again: the Diatessaron. Cengiz must have got tangled up in this business with the antique book. As I mull this over, Zekeriya tries to dry his tears and says, "Sorry, Inspector. When I think about it... This thing happened so suddenly...."

"It did, Zekeriya. But you know, we have to keep going. Now is the time to catch the man who did it. He has to pay for what he did. As Director Cengiz put it, 'The murderer can go seven layers underground, but we will find him. Your father goes way back with our director, doesn't he?"

"Way back... I wasn't even born when my dad met Cengiz Amca, that's how long. I don't think he was even police in those days."

"Interesting. I wonder where they met."

"He used to come to our shop. I think he did business with my dad. After that, Cengiz Amca went to study. He became a policeman and served in Anatolia. When he came back to

Istanbul, he found my dad again. He's a good man, Cengiz Amca. If we had any trouble, he'd be the first to rush to help."

"So did Cengiz know Yusuf? I mean, did they ever come to the shop together?"

Zekeriya finds the question odd.

"Why are you asking that, Inspector? What would Yusuf Abi have to do with Cengiz Amca?"

"I just asked. Yusuf was also your dad's old friend, so maybe they knew each other."

"No, I don't think Cengiz Amca knew Yusuf. They are two totally different people. Cengiz Amca has integrity."

"And Yusuf? Did he not have integrity?"

"It's not good to speak ill of the dead, but Yusuf Abi was a real good-for-nothing. He never kept his word. He borrowed a bunch of money from us and didn't pay it back. Then he went and found that woman. I'm talking about Meryem. You'd know better, the woman is mafia. She was into a lot of nasty business. Cengiz Amca wouldn't even let people like that near him."

We need to wrap up this Cengiz thing, or Zekeriya might call him and then we'd really be rocking the boat.

"So do you think there could be some connection between Yusuf's murderers and your father's?" I say, pulling Zekeriya's attention to another point.

"I don't want to wrongly accuse anyone, Inspector, but I wouldn't put anything past that woman Meryem. We already had a disagreement between us. Yusuf Abi wanted to sell us a book. Like a Bible. We even consulted with Caner to see if it was real or fake. He couldn't tell. And my father changed his mind about buying it."

Meaning Malik didn't tell his son what went on. It's not easy; how would he explain the hundred thousand dollars he sent to Yusuf? Zekeriya might have really kicked up a fuss.

"I didn't want that book anyhow," he continued. "Meryem called my dad about it a few times. I guess she talked pretty tough. My father didn't tell me, but I could see from how angry he got while he talked to her."

"Why didn't your father tell you?"

"He didn't want me involved, Inspector. There was some dirty business in the past. Maybe you know too. Smuggling of antique artifacts and gun sales and such. My father regretted getting mixed up in it. His biggest wish was for me to be a man who did honorable business. I asked him about the book a few times. 'We took care of that matter,' he said. But I didn't believe him. Most likely he said that so I wouldn't get into trouble."

"You're saying Meryem did this?"

"Meryem or her men. That woman is smart, Inspector. Why hold a burning coal in your hand if you have tongs?"

I pay no regard to Zekeriya's words. At the moment it isn't Istanbul's sole female mafia boss who is implicated in this investigation, it's my director. But I have to placate Zekeriya.

"Don't worry. If Meryem is the one who did this, she won't get away from us. By the way, were you able to walk round the house? Is there anything stolen or removed?"

Zekeriya shakes his head.

"I couldn't look anywhere. My head is so mixed-up, Inspector. I might not even notice if they stole the coat off my back right now. I'll pull myself together... Don't know how I'm supposed to do that but... Then I can inventory the stuff."

"All right. If anything grabs your attention, let me know. Director Cengiz is extremely busy, but don't worry, I'm looking after the situation for him."

Chapter 25
Some writings are written, not to be read, but to not be read.

Once we've left Malik's house, I think about what I need to do. This is a race against the clock. Cengiz will hear he's been accused soon enough. Even if we don't tell him, this accusation will come out in Caner's statement. When that moment comes, I'll have to choose sides. Cengiz will expect me to be by his side, and in fact will openly demand it of me. If I don't have enough evidence by the time he has this talk with me, Cengiz will use every connection he has, resort to every trick in the book, to find a way to get out of this. The only way to stop him, and the only way to not be an instrument for his dirty work, is to come up with some evidence that shows he's guilty. If he is indeed guilty, of course. Yes, despite all the evidence against him, Cengiz may not be guilty. Just because he was in Malik's house, that doesn't mean he's a killer. I've experienced so many murder cases that I've learned not to accuse anyone of being a killer until I know for certain. No, I'm not just saying that because Cengiz is a colleague. I'd have felt the same no matter who it was. On the other hand, the findings I have clearly show another actuality, that Cengiz is somehow involved in this. What's more, compared to Caner, the possibility of Cengiz being a murderer is much higher. The bad thing is that despite the much higher possibility of his innocence, Caner is the one seen as a suspect. Unless there's an honest investigation, it will take nothing at all for Caner to spend his youth within four walls. That's why I have to get on to it.

Before taking my key from the one-handed man at the parking garage and unlocking my trusty Renault's door, I dial Nusret from Intelligence.

"Hello Nusret! It's Nevzat."

"Nevzat! What's up, you too impatient to wait till morning?"

"No, I couldn't, Nusret. There've been some important developments. We've run up against a really dirty situation. I need some urgent information."

He understands from my tone of voice that it's no laughing matter.

"Same subject as this morning's?"

"Yep, same subject. But there's another individual that needs investigating."

He takes a deep breath.

"One of ours again?"

"One of ours. My director, Cengiz. Cengiz Koçan."

"What! Cengiz Koçan? We're going to investigate Cengiz Koçan? Are you mad, Nevzat? What the hell are you doing?"

"I'm not doing anything, Nusret. The one who's doing it has already done it. I'm trying not to sink into the filth. If I don't fight back against it, I'll be buried up to my nose in it."

A brief silence...

"Okay, come over then," he says tensely. "But look, don't bring anyone with you. I don't want to hear about Ali or anyone. Come alone. I'll look over these files until you get here."

"Thanks, Nusret. I'm coming alone."

"I'm going to get myself into a very sticky situation one day thanks to you, but let's see when that is."

I don't pay his bleating any mind. I've known Nusret for a long time, he's the best in his field and he'll collect everything he has on Yavuz and Cengiz and hand it over to me. But Nusret is more than just a competent intelligence gatherer. More importantly, he's a man who has managed to keep his integrity, at least up till now. I say up till now because one of the most dangerous places in our profession is the field of intelligence. Crucial facts are gathered not just on the average citizen, but also politicians, businessmen, journalists and even police chiefs. They have information at hand that could in a single moment either make you rich or send you to your grave. It takes willpower to possess control like this and not yield to temptation. What we are doing right now is not by the book either, mind you, but if I were to employ in-house procedure, I might not ever access this information. The cumbersome nature of the rules would be an obstacle and I'd never be able to learn the truth.

I take my car from the garage and descend Kumkapı's narrow streets to the coast. On the coastal road, traffic is a mess. I'm trying to advance in spurts. As I approach Yenikapı, my phone rings. Ali? No, I see Cengiz's name on the screen. Oh dear. I hope he doesn't say he's at the station and ask me to come down for a chat. If I don't answer? But no, I can't do that. Best not to raise the man's suspicions for no reason. Maybe he's just calling to put out the feelers, to find out what I know.

"Hello," I say, finally picking up.

"Nevzat, hi. It's me, Cengiz."

"Hi, Cengiz."

"It took you a while to answer. Are you busy?"

"No, I'm not. I'm in the car. I had to pull over, that took some time."

"Nevzat, I heard over the radio. This Assyrian murder... Another person was killed again I guess."

"Yes, you know I mentioned Malik, the antique dealer?"

I suddenly recall that, sure enough, I was the one who had told him about Malik. I even told him suspicion was gathering on him. I mean in some way, I was the one who sent Cengiz to Malik. If Cengiz is the one who killed Malik, then he didn't want others, especially me, to find out what he knew. I wonder what it was Malik was hiding from me.

"You still there?" says Cengiz, bringing me back round.

"You already heard over the radio, Malik's been murdered."

I don't offer more, and he can't take it and asks, "Apparently there is a suspect?"

He wants relief. I give him what he wants.

"This faculty member, Caner... You know, the one in my room yesterday. You saw him too. The blonde, baby-faced young man."

"Yesterday? Oh, that's right. He was with you when I came to call you to my office. That was the perpetrator?"

"It would seem so. Two witnesses caught him at the entrance to his house. The victim's severed head was right at his feet. The neighborhood almost lynched him. Our guys barely got him away from them."

My explanation is somehow not enough for Cengiz.

"What does the individual you caught say? Does he accept the blame?"

"Of course not, Cengiz. He said he didn't do it. That he just came to see Malik. But we kept at it. Ali, Zeynep and the whole crew are collecting evidence to put him away."

"That's great, Nevzat. I told you before, let's wrap this up before the journalists spread it around. Those people view everything with a jaundiced eye, anyhow. While the interior minister and chief of police are on-hand..."

"Really, what is Sabri up to?"

"Director General Sabri," he says, emphasizing the word 'general', "Director General Sabri is good. We were together all day. We just split up. I dropped him at the police lodgings."

Amazing how he lies. Let's see what he would say in front of our one-handed lot attendant tomorrow.

"He asked about you again," Cengiz continues. "I extended your invitation. 'Once these ministers are gone, we'll definitely do it,' he said. He says hello. 'Take good care of Nevzat,' he said. 'He's our good luck charm.' "

Good luck charm, was it? In school it was 'Aman Vermez Avni', 'Uncompromising Avni' like the book, and now I am a good luck charm? What do I expect; that's Bumbling Sabri for you. People do resemble their nicknames. I don't say this to Cengiz, of course.

"Thanks," I say. I may need him tomorrow when things get heated, so I try a tiny bit of intimidation. "He loves me, Sabri. In school we were inseparable."

"It seems so," Cengiz says, participating in my lie. "Apparently, you had a real nice group at school. And the two of you were like blood brothers."

I don't know if it's Sabri who made up this story, or Cengiz? What blood brothers? Sabri was so shy, he'd never mix with a gang like that. Everyone made fun of him. I was the only one who didn't. Maybe he's inflating my behavior. But calling us blood brothers would be an overstatement. Well for now, a little inflation couldn't hurt.

"That's true. Like blood brothers."

"That's really nice for you, Nevzat. Such a decent person as your blood brother."

Things are going well, so our beloved director is in high spirits and he'll get a good night's sleep. Then again, how you can murder someone and get a good night's sleep; that I'll never understand. Well, let him sleep away. If he gets suspicious or nervous and comes down to the station, we'll be in big trouble. Still Cengiz doesn't appear nervous in the least.

"Good night, Nevzat, my friend."

So in the end I am 'Nevzat, my friend'. Yet I can't say, *Good night, Cengiz, my friend*. It's too much.

"Good night. See you tomorrow."

By the time I've hung up, I have no doubts at all that Cengiz is in on this. I want to get over to Nusret as soon as possible and get some facts to untangle this knot, but the evening traffic in my beloved Istanbul won't allow it. I'm dragging along the road for nothing short of an hour. As I approach Nusret's building, my phone rings again. It's Nusret, and I assume he's going to ask what's taking me so long. But that's not what he says.

"Nevzat, I got the information you asked for. But don't come here. Ring me when you are close and I'll come down. I was going out to eat anyhow. I'll pass the printouts to you and go to the restaurant from there."

His voice is tense, nervous. Has someone been caught? I doubt it. Nusret wasn't born yesterday; he could steal the eyeliner from a camel's eye and nobody would be the wiser. Maybe he'd read the data, come across some anomaly and that's why he's sweating.

"All right, Nusret," I say. "I'm pretty close now anyhow. Come straight down if you'd like. I'll wait for you at the corner of the upper street. Where that liquor shop is. The one we got the rakı and white cheese from on the way to your house that night."

"Fincancı Büfe. Great. It's deserted at this hour..."

No, he's definitely panicking. I wonder what he's found. Well, we'll find out soon enough. I turn my car into a side street. Fincancı Büfe is at the end of the street. There's no point in squeezing my car in front of the snack bar. I don't want to stick out like a sore thumb under its light. I start to laugh. As if we are being followed. I guess paranoia is contagious; just look how Nusret's uneasiness has passed to me. Even so, I park my car twenty meters back from the snack bar, turn off my lights and wait. The car is stuffy and my head hurts a bit. I open the window a crack. This is no picnic; things have accelerated so suddenly. And I'd downed a double rakı on an empty stomach at Evgenia's. I wonder what Evgenia has done. Although it's been at most a few hours since I left her, it feels like it's been days. As soon as Evgenia comes to mind, I can't avoid the stinging sensation inside me. She could be packing her things up right now. I didn't even think to ask her when she was leaving. Maybe I should take her to the airport. Sheesh, Nevzat, do you still not understand? Evgenia is not going on a tourist trip. The woman is leaving you. She is going to Greece to get away from you. Still, I should offer. What perfect timing, taking your girlfriend to the airport smack in the middle of this chaos. And if the plane is delayed, you'll sit and wait with Evgenia for hours... In the meantime, Director Cengiz can slyly lay his plan, nicely do away with both you and this intellectual highbrow. No, it won't be that easy, but in any case, I don't know when Evgenia is going.

My mind is still on Evgenia when I notice Nusret coming up quickly on the snack bar. He gets there and doesn't see me, so he looks back and forth anxiously. I flash my headlights. All right, he's spotted me and is coming my way. I start the car while glancing around to see if anyone is following Nusret. There's not a soul around, save two rowdy tomcats in front of an apartment building, squabbling over rubbish, unable to share. I did say paranoia is contagious. Nusret hurriedly gets into my car. Without saying hello, he hands me the yellow envelope he's taken out from under his coat.

"Take it, Nevzat. Everything you want is here."

His voice is nervous, like his movements. I take the envelope and place it in my lap.

"Thanks, Nusret. I don't know how to repay this favor."

"By not getting me involved. From this minute forward, do not call me about this business, Nevzat. That's the biggest favor you can do me."

He's really scared, this guy. Before I've asked, he continues.

"If you ask me, you shouldn't mess with this thing either. Cengiz is a powerful man, Nevzat. It will be difficult for them to sacrifice him. In the meantime, you'll be used up."

"What's going on, Nusret? What's all this fear, this panic?"

"It's nothing. I'm just speaking as a friend."

I search his face to try to understand.

"Come on. Let's not stay here," he says, gesturing towards the road. "Move your car. Once you are out on the street you can let me out at the Adana kebab place on the left. And we'll say goodbye."

I do as he says, I move the car, but when I get to the end of the street I'm compelled to ask, "You read the contents of the envelope, right?"

He flinches as though I've touched him with a hot poker.

"No, Nevzat. Why would I read it? Where do you get that idea? I didn't read anything."

"How do you know what's in it if you didn't read it?"

He points to the file in my lap.

"I don't need to read the papers in that envelope to smell the stink emanating from them. You'd do best not to read them either, in all honesty."

I try to make light.

"They put so much effort into writing it, wouldn't it be a shame not to read it?"

"No, it wouldn't, Nevzat. Some writings are written not to be read, but to not be read. Those writings are cursed. They'll get people in trouble."

Nusret's words remind me of the Diatessaron. But this is not the place to mention it, and anyhow even if I did explain, who is listening? It's best to keep joking.

"I swear, Nusret, say what you want, but you have read this file. You've read it and this Inspector Yavuz's death has shaken you."

"No, I didn't read it. Not Inspector Yavuz's story, and not Cengiz Koçan's. I don't know anything. And don't you tell me, please. I don't want to hear. You asked for my help as an old friend, and I broke the rules and helped you; that's all. I haven't got the slightest clue about the file you asked for, and I don't want one. Well, here we are at my kebab place. Let me out here, *abi*."

As I pull the car over, he continues.

"I wish you had stayed out of this, Nevzat. Take my advice and sneak out while you can."

"It'd be hard now, Nusret. If I try to sneak away, they won't let me."

The door opens and he turns to me before getting out.

"I know you are in a tough spot, but sorry, there's nothing else I can do."

"Don't worry, Nusret. You've done enough."

He reaches out and shakes my hand.

"You're a good man, Nevzat. Too good for this job. Take care of yourself."

I smile and answer him with the proverb Ali said to me a few hours ago.

"Don't worry. A bitter eggplant seldom gets frostbitten."

He doesn't believe it but smiles anyhow.

"Fine then. God help you."

Chapter 26
We are up against a huge conspiracy.

The envelope I took from Nusret is sitting here in my lap. I'm impatient to learn its contents. I consider pulling my faithful old car over and looking inside, but I change my mind when the headlights from a car behind me reflect off my rearview mirror. Not because I am being followed so much as that I could be followed. Nusret doesn't spook easily. If the contents of the file scared him that badly, this thing may be more dangerous than I'd supposed. It isn't wise to look at a critical file like this in the middle of the street. Best to read it at the station, with Ali and Zeynep. Or should I not involve them? Am I putting the kids at risk? It is too late. They are involved, and in danger, whether I want them to be or not. If I don't inform them properly, Cengiz will mislead them, getting my two most trusted officers on his side and bringing them into the fold. Yes, this is war. A war that will be lost by whoever doesn't act smart, or stay alert, or think meticulously. My only advantage is that Cengiz doesn't know what I know. So I am one step ahead of him. The moment I lose this advantage, I lose the war. And Ali and Zeynep will lose with me. That's why I should share everything I know with them, and straight away. I shift gears and step on the gas.

Zeynep is in the lab, and I find Ali at his computer. I call them both into my room. Ali comes in first, computer printouts in hand. With a questioning look in his eyes, he says, "Chief, we have an interesting situation. I found this: The PKK really did kill an inspector in a thresher five years ago in Midyat. But the man's name wasn't Yavuz, it was Selim. Selim Uludere. I guess our Gabriel doesn't remember correctly."

"I doubt he misremembers, Ali." I show him the yellow envelope on the table. "I suppose the answers to our questions are in here. It won't be long till everything is revealed."

There's a childish expression on his face, a little boy's mix of admiration and surprise.

"Where did you get that? From Nusret?"

"It has nothing to do with Nusret, Ali. The birds brought it... Ask no questions, hear no lies. What have you got?"

"A case was opened on this Selim Uludere. But I got this info from the newspaper archives. Why the case was opened wasn't stated too clearly. There are incidents of torture, maltreatment of the villagers, and fatalities. It's quite complicated..."

Ali goes quiet as Zeynep comes into the room. Are these two still on the outs? No, they've smiled at each other. Good, I'm happy they've made up.

"Come on in, Zeynep. Did you uncover anything?"

Standing, she explains, "I've identified the filament under the victim's fingernail, Chief."

"Cashmere?"

"How did you know?"

I point to the empty chair.

"Have a seat. You'll learn soon too."

Zeynep sets her curiosity aside and sits down. Surprisingly, Ali, who always prefers to stay standing, quietly settles into the chair opposite Zeynep's. We are all aware now that we are up against extraordinary circumstances.

"Did you tell Zeynep what we heard?"

"About Director Cengiz? Yes, I told her, Chief."

Zeynep doesn't believe it. She's shaking her head.

"Director Cengiz wouldn't do such a thing," she says, with her usual prudence. But sometimes prudence can mislead a person. "No, Chief," she adds. "Caner must have seen it wrong."

"He didn't see it wrong, Zeynep." My gaze combs both their faces." Caner is right. The witnesses I talked to confirm his statement. The parking garage attendant has identified Cengiz's car. The owner of the coffeehouse confirmed that Caner was sitting there for two hours. And most importantly, Zekeriya said that Cengiz is a family friend."

Yes, now it is Zeynep's turn to be surprised.

"What? Director Cengiz was Malik's friend?"

"That's right, Zeynep. And let me make another prediction: The filament you found under Malik's fingernail is from that navy-blue cashmere coat of Cengiz's. If you examine his armchair, you'll find some the same threads there. I am certain of this, but what I'm not certain of is why Cengiz did all this." I smack the envelope on the table with my hand. "I suppose it is written in here."

"You haven't read it, Chief?" Ali asks.

"I haven't, Ali. I didn't get the chance, and also I prefer to read it together. The three of us have intertwined fates right now. Tomorrow all hell's going to break loose here, and I want all three of us to grasp the truth correctly. I trust your judgement. And I could be wrong; each of us can be wrong individually, but it would be hard for the three of us all to be wrong at the same time. That's why I wanted to read the file together, in order to interpret it together." I hold the envelope out to Zeynep. "Yes, Zeynep, can you read this out loud?"

As Zeynep recovers from her shock and reaches for the envelope, Ali gets up without my saying to and closes the door. We're ready to listen now. Zeynep glances over the papers she's taken out.

"It's marked 'highly classified', Chief..."

"Never mind that, Zeynep. You read what's inside..."

"Errors in the fight against terrorism... The region as a whole has seen major damage by way of impulsive lashing out and undisciplined behavior in the fight against the terrorist organization. The bulk of these impulsive approaches have been seen to come from our outstanding members who are not hesitant to go into hot clashes with the terrorist organization. The nature and difficulty of the fight most often incites these servicemen to abandon discipline." Zeynep looks up from the paper. "Does this have any pertinence to our subject, Chief?"

She's right. She's holding at least fifty pages of computer printouts here. I wonder which section concerns us.

"Give it here," I say, pulling the papers in front of me. I flip through them. On the third page, under a heading reading "EXAMPLES", these lines grab my attention. "In the province of Mardin, in the rural area of the county of Midyat, two police officers were martyred and one heavily wounded in a skirmish." I scan the lines quickly. The name of Inspector Selim Uludere jumps out at me.

"What's the name of the officer killed in the thresher?"

"Yavuz," says Zeynep.

"No, Zeynep. We were wrong about that. The man's name was Selim Uludere," Ali corrects her.

"All right then, we've found the section that interests us," I say. Before handing the file back to Zeynep, I go to the back page to find the name in my head. And a photograph that will shock us all pops out. I freeze for a moment. Ali and Zeynep notice I've stumbled onto something relevant, and they lean over my table to look with curiosity at the photo. It's Ali who reacts first.

"Isn't that the Yusuf imposter?"

"That's him all right," Zeynep confirms. "But 'Selim Uludere' is written underneath."

As they talk this over, I squint and read the name on the bottom line of the page.

"Chief Inspector Cengiz Koçan... Yes, our beloved director is here too."

I turn the page, this time Cengiz's photo appears in front of us. It's from five years ago but it's not so different from his present state. From within his uniform, he looks into our faces with great confidence.

"Selin Uludere's superior officer, Cengiz Koçan. I can't believe it," says Ali. "The man knew Selim, too. He never told us..."

Doing this in bits and pieces isn't going to work.

"Zeynep," I say, handing the papers back to her. "Take this and read us the part that concerns us."

Zeynep pulls the papers in front of her and sits back down. Ali also settles back into his chair. I rest my chin in my right palm and wait to hear more surprising facts. Zeynep doesn't make us wait long. She pushes back the hair that's fallen into her face and says, "I guess the facts that concern us are here, Chief. '...twenty kilometers from Midyat, in close proximity to the Mor Gabriel Monastery, close contact to a group of PKK terrorists was established. Two police officers were killed and one inspector badly wounded in the ensuing clash. The PKK terrorists, under cover of darkness, escaped towards the Mor Gabriel Monastery. Selim Uludere, who commanded the police team, pursued the group of terrorists after sending the two fallen officers and his critically injured friend Mehmet Uncu to the hospital. However, they failed to pick up the PKK's trail. Inspector Selim Uludere subsequently made for the Mor Gabriel Monastery and asked monastery authorities for the PKK terrorists. He received a negative response from the monastery's authorities but did not settle for it and, positioning himself near the monastery, continued to stake it out. After two hours, the monastery door opened and a group of people came out. Inspector Selim Uludere, convinced there were terrorists among these people, detained six suspects from the group. Since no appropriate indoor space for questioning could be found in the vicinity, he took the suspects to a nearby cave, where they denied the charges against them and declared they had never seen the PKK. However, the following day, the six suspects were discovered inside the cave dead from smoke inhalation. With the news of the deaths came public outrage in the region, and due to the presence of the foreign press who had come to visit the Mor Gabriel Monastery, the incident suddenly made it to the global agenda. Inspector Selim Uludere, when asked for his defense during the inquiry, stated that they had released the six suspects before leaving the cave themselves. Inspector Uludere said that it was most likely members of the PKK that they had been skirmishing with who had killed the six individuals. Inspector Selim Uludere's assertions were supported by his superior, Chief Inspector Cengiz Koçan. However, because the incident had resonated in the national and international arenas, inspectors were sent to the site, and as a result of the ensuing investigation and enquiry, a discrepancy was determined in the statement provided by Inspector Selim Uludere. Hereupon, an investigation into Inspector Selim Uludere and his superior Chief Inspector Cengiz Koçan was opened. Nevertheless, neither Selim Uludere nor Cengiz Koçan was suspended, and they were allowed to continue their duties in the region. After a period of approximately three months, preparations concerning the incident were completed, and with the court date was approaching, Inspector Selim Uludere was kidnapped by PKK terrorists and brutally slaughtered in a threshing machine. After the death of Inspector Selim Uludere, the court dropped the case, and the charges against Chief Inspector Cengiz Koçan were also lifted. As was seen in this case, some of our police force members' petulant and emotional outbursts in the fight against terrorism cast a shadow over not only our organization but also over its reputation at home and abroad...' "

"All right, Zeynep. It's clear now; that'll suffice."

Ali disagrees.

"This Inspector Mehmet Uncu, what happened to him? Does it say, Zeynep?"

Apparently, there's some point niggling at him. Zeynep flips quickly through the pages.

"Yes, here it is. 'Mehmet Uncu, while critically injured in the incident, is now in a stable condition, although he remains paralyzed due to a bullet having shattered his spine. Mehmet Uncu has retired from the police force with a physical disability.' "

Ali hits his hand excitedly on the table and proffers, "Those three were friends, Chief."

"Where did you get that idea?" says Zeynep. "The report only mentions that Selim and Mehmet were friends. Couldn't Cengiz just have supported Selim as his superior officer?"

"No, Zeynep. The three of them were friends," Ali repeats. His thoughts are conclusive now; he's sure of what he says. "Do you remember the letter? The letter you found at Yusuf's - I mean, Selim's house? You know, it came out from under the sofa. The letter written by someone named Fatih, talking about Timuçin."

"I remember, but that was Fatih there. There's no mention of Mehmet."

"Don't you get it, Zeynep? They were using aliases. Selim called himself Yavuz. The man is not humble in the slightest; he was inspired by Yavuz Sultan Selim, aka Selim the Grim. But the other friends also had illusions of grandeur. Just look, our Cengiz took the nickname Timuçin, as in Genghis Khan's other name, and as for Mehmet..."

"Fatih," says Zeynep, finishing his sentence. "Fatih Sultan Mehmet, the Conqueror. You're right, Ali. The three were friends. Cengiz kept at his job, and rose to director. Mehmet was confined to a wheelchair when his spine was injured, and Selim faked his death and with someone else's identity..." The conclusion she's reached leaves Zeynep speechless. There's a strange gleam in her eye. This is the moment she solves the problem. Perhaps she's entertained the possibility before but now she is sure. "Yusuf... It was Yusuf who was killed in the thresher. Gabriel's elder brother. They killed that poor shepherd."

"Exactly so, friends," I say, agreeing with their conclusion. Rather than a clarification for them, this may be a speech I'm giving myself in order to complete the picture in my head. "We are up against a vast conspiracy. A conspiracy to cover up the insanity, slaughter, scandal or whatever you want to call it, caused by Selim's rage. I'm talking about this conflict, where Mehmet was gravely injured and two officers martyred on the day of the armed encounter. Selim must have gone crazy. Two of your men die before your eyes and a friend is seriously injured. That's not easy. Selim wants to find the PKK members at any cost, but he can't. He gets even crazier. Rage and a sheer sense of vengeance overcome him. From the crowd leaving the monastery, he takes the young people into custody.

"Maybe if they had given him some information on the PKK he wouldn't have killed them but he doesn't get what he wants. And as he doesn't get it, he decides to kill them all. Right at that moment, Gabriel's cousin Aziz understands they are going to be killed. To escape death, he gets an idea. To give Selim the Diatessaron that was stolen from the monastery months earlier and save his skin. As far as what Gabriel told us, he handed over the manuscript hidden in the barn to Selim, and yet it didn't save him. Because every person who comes out of there alive means a big danger for Selim. Selim takes the Diatessaron, thinking of it as a safety net for any dark days ahead, but doesn't hesitate to send the six youths, Aziz among them, to their deaths. However, things don't go as he'd hoped. The foreign press that comes to the monastery in those days lets the world hear about this massacre. Bad times begin for Selim; not only for him, but for our Director Cengiz, who in those days was a daredevil of a Chief Inspector. But the contents of the report are out in the open and Cengiz doesn't sell out his friend. He defends Selim till the end. Both in front of the press and in the investigation. And he doesn't stop there; together with Selim, he cooks up a plan to save them both. He chooses a lunatic whose disappearance won't cause an uproar as a victim. The scenario is clear, to murder the person in such a way that he is unrecognizable, and then leave Selim's ID and clothes at the scene of the murder. And as you said, Zeynep, the ideal candidate for this is Gabriel's naive brother, the shepherd Yusuf. They set out to implement this scenario before the court convenes. And it's hard to say they failed. Right up until Selim started rocking the boat. It's not possible to know when Selim first stepped out of line."

"Most likely after he met Meryem, Chief," Ali cuts in. "The man is already prone to losing control. She just encouraged him."

I absolutely agree. Women are the soft underbelly of men who live in the underworld. They are the reason most killers or mafia bosses are nabbed or take a bullet in the forehead. A woman is never good for these men. I don't say this though, perhaps because Zeynep is with us.

I just say, "You're right, Ali. For Yusuf... no, I mean Selim, of course... getting into a relationship with Meryem is not at all right for a man in his circumstances. I'm sure Cengiz was really upset about it. Meryem must have aggravated their disagreements."

"Maybe he even divulged his real identity to Meryem," says Ali, wanting to reinforce his claim.

"I doubt it," Zeynep counters. "If that were the case, her thoughts on Bingöllü being the killer would have given her pause. Isn't that right? If Meryem had known the real relationship between Selim and our director, wouldn't she have first blamed Cengiz?"

"It's hard to know that for sure," I say. "But one thing is for certain, Selim had no qualms about selling the Diatessaron he was hiding in order to come up with the money Meryem wanted. And that's when he made his greatest mistake."

Zeynep blinks; I suppose she didn't understand.

"You mean you think Cengiz killed Selim because he wanted to sell the Diatessaron?"

"In my opinion, he probably always thought of being free of Selim. Selim was like a monkey on his back. The only dark spot on a brilliant career. If he could get rid of Selim, there would be no obstacle left for his rise to the top."

This time the question comes from Ali.

"Then why did he kill Malik?"

"I'm not certain, but I suppose because of the Diatessaron again. Probably Cengiz got wind that Malik wanted to buy it. Selim must have told Malik what happened. Or Cengiz thought he did. What's more, Malik knew about Cengiz's history. I mean, in order for our beloved director to completely dispose of his dirty laundry, the antique dealer had to die too." I go quiet and look into both their faces. "Otherwise, why kill Malik?"

"Yes," Ali echoes. "Why kill Malik?"

"He wanted to give the situation an air of mysticism," says Zeynep, adding her two cents. "The dagger with the cruciform handle, Malik's head decapitated just like Paul's, the lines of the Bible underlined in blood... All of it meant to mislead us."

Ali's young forehead creases.

"And that dream Selim had?" he asks.

When no explanation comes from Zeynep, I put forth my own premise.

"Despite everything, Selim must be a believer. And Malik was continuously whispering in his ear, 'You've sinned. You shouldn't have touched this book.' After meeting Meryem, under the influence of the hash he was addicted to, he starts to have hallucinations. In moments when he's out of his mind, the guilt he feels manifests itself in visions of visits from Mor Gabriel. No doubt he told the dreams to Cengiz. Our beloved director must have taken a cue from those dreams to supply mystical significance to the killings."

"And this Mehmet?" Ali reminds us. "The man in the wheelchair. If Cengiz wants to get rid of his corrupt past, would he leave him alive?"

Neither Zeynep nor I are as bothered as he is.

"Maybe Mehmet isn't aware of anything," I say. "For instance, he may not know the shepherd Yusuf was killed and that Selim took on his identity. He just knew six youths were killed, asphyxiated in a cave. And he saw that as a necessity of war. I mean, he would blame neither Cengiz nor Selim for it."

"But what'll happen when he hears about Selim's death?" Ali rightly asks. "How will Cengiz explain that to him?"

"Maybe he'll say the PKK did it... He'll say Selim was killed in order to take revenge for the six people who choked to death in that cave. That way, the case will be closed for good."

In truth, my explanation falls short for me too, although Ali doesn't object further. Still it's best to leave no stone unturned.

"You could be right too, Ali," I say, taking a step back. "Let's check out this Mehmet first chance we get tomorrow."

"All right, Chief."

"Zeynep, there are some other things you'll need to do beforehand. First, compare the sample threads from Cengiz's coat to those taken from under Malik's fingernails. Go into Cengiz's room now if you need to."

"I can't, Chief. Director Cengiz locks his room when he leaves. We'd have to break his door down or get a spare key from someone. If we did that, they'd inform him."

"All right, we need a bit more time. The coat business can wait till tomorrow. But let's get Gabriel over here. We need to take a DNA sample, to compare it to the fake Selim Uludere once we've exhumed the body there."

"Right away, Chief." Ali jumps in with all his energy. "I have the address and phone number of his relatives in Feriköy on me. I'll go pick Gabriel up."

"That'd be great. Tomorrow things will get messy here. Let's do everything we can manage tonight. Get Caner's official statement, and we have to bring in this parking lot attendant. His statement is crucial. We should have all that on hand as soon as possible. And I'll talk to Sabri. If I can't convince him, all our efforts will be in vain."

Chapter 27
We solved it for tonight, but our work in this city never ends.

I'm at the wheel of my car again, back on the streets. The roads are emptier now. I'm advancing on Rumeli Hisarı from Beşiktaş. Droplets are falling onto the windshield. Looks like it's starting to rain. I open the window a crack. The car is filled with clean, damp air. I take a deep breath. My headache has let up; I suppose the *döner* sandwich chased by the aspirin I had before leaving did me good. But the real reason is that Sabri has accepted my request to meet. I was worried he'd put me off, purporting to be busy, and I must admit he reacted more warmly than I expected.

"Let's meet right now, Nevzat," he'd said. "I'm at the police lodgment sitting with friends. Come on over."

Let's see what he'll say when he hears what I tell him about Cengiz. It's not a very pleasant situation. Think about it; one of your directors turns out to be a murderer. An operation is being conducted within the police force. What boss would want that? It's not like I want this either... Cengiz has never done me the slightest wrong. But while such a reality exists, how can I stay silent? Sabri can't either. He shouldn't. I have very strong evidence. But still, nothing is for certain. It's hard to know who is mixed up with whom and whose man is whose within the police force. I hope Cengiz and Sabri are not in the same group. Then again, Sabri is not one to get mixed up in this kind of duplicitous business. He's always taken care not to cross the line. He would never jeopardize himself. The police force's ordinary manager plays straight by the book. And that's good; it's exactly why he has to arrest Cengiz. Men like Cengiz sully the police force's reputation. Isn't it time to clean this kind of man out?

I pull the car into the police lodging's parking lot and walk over to the restaurant area. It's crowded inside; nearly all the tables are full.

Sabri should be sitting at a place with a view. I scan the tables near the window that look out at the sea. I'm not wrong. At a table of eight people, I see Sabri's large head balanced on his slim neck, which always gives me cause for wonder. As I aim for his table, I get a real surprise; a real and very bad surprise: Cengiz is sitting right opposite Sabri. Didn't the man tell me he was going home? No, he didn't say that. He said, "I dropped Sabri at the police lodgments." So that means he came here himself after that. I wonder if Sabri called him after I rang him. Why would he do that? Crassness, maybe? I don't think so. Sabri wouldn't do such a thing. Maybe Cengiz found out we were investigating him. But how could he? If that were the case, he would have immediately called me. I shouldn't panic over nothing. Cengiz could be here entirely by coincidence. He's seen me now too. His face gets tense. Even from a distance I can see him pale. Look at the dubious expression in his eyes. I smile like nothing has happened, and even bow slightly in greeting. My attitude confuses him and he answers my salutation by smiling back. Sabri sees Cengiz greeting someone and turns around, standing up as soon as he's seen me.

"Oh, Nevzat! You made it!"

To be clear, this isn't the reception I expected from Sabri. He never used to act so chummy with people. Not that he didn't, but he couldn't. It wasn't in his nature. Apparently he'd got over his aloofness. Being senior management must have developed his confidence. And a good thing, too. At this moment I really need his support, understanding and courage.

"Hi, Director," I say, giving him a hug. "You were so insistent that I came, and here I am."

Thankfully Sabri didn't give away my lie. He doesn't ask, "What do you mean insistent? You called me and asked to come over." He gives me a friendly pat on the shoulder.

"Good for you, Nevzat! Come, have a seat next to me."

When Sabri says this, Yalçın from the traffic department, who is sitting on his left, immediately cedes his place to me.

"I'm imposing, Director Yalçın," I say.

"Sit, Nevzat, sit." He points out a police chief I don't know, sitting at the head of the eight-person table.

"I was already planning to move over next to Salih."

As I sit down in the relinquished chair, I meet Cengiz's gaze. He's been watching me since I arrived.

"Hello, Director," I say, to allay his skepticism. "How have you been?"

"Good, Nevzat. Good. I was surprised to see you here."

I think to myself, your real surprise will come later.

"I changed my mind at the last minute." I turn and look at Sabri. "I wanted to come see my old friend."

Sabri gives me a warm grin. But Cengiz smells a rat and he won't let it alone.

"You must have finished your business quickly," he says.

"We solved it for tonight, but our work in this city never ends."

"Wouldn't I know it," Sabri interjects. "I worked exactly five years in public order. Not an uneventful day went by. I got worn out." He gives me an affectionate look. "Are you seeing our friends from school, Nevzat?"

"I haven't seen anyone."

"Those were the days. Cengiz, Nevzat's nickname used to be Aman Vermez Avni. He'd always read detective novels. Mayk Hammer, Sherlock Holmes and Cingöz Recai. Our history teacher, Deaf Süleyman, caught him with a copy of

Ebüssüreyya Sami's *The Adventures of Uncompromising Avni* one day. From that day forward, he was called by the name..."

It wouldn't be right to call Sabri 'Bumbling Sabri' with Cengiz sitting in front of me like a dragon. After signaling the waiter to look after me, Sabri continues. "Cengiz mentioned this Agora Meyhane. I hope we can go once things have relaxed a bit."

Seeing the conversation turn to our friendship, Cengiz's suspicious gaze, while not completely disappearing, does seem to wane. Yet he still doesn't understand why I'm here. I don't believe for a moment that he's bought my explanation. He has to find out, and for that he'll need to call someone. He does exactly as I suspected. After filling my rakı glass and toasting, he excuses himself to go smoke a cigarette. Sabri doesn't allow cigarettes at the table. As soon as Cengiz moves away, I turn to my school friend.

"Sabri, we have an urgent matter."

At first he doesn't understand. He looks blankly at me with eyes blurry from *rakı*. I don't have time to wait for him to compute.

"It's big, Sabri," I reiterate. "It's do or die. The honor of the whole police force is at stake, not just mine or yours."

He starts to frown. He finally grasps the gravity of the situation.

"What are you saying, Nevzat? What are you talking about?"

I lean in to his ear. "Let's go inside, Sabri," I whisper. "What I have to say is serious."

He looks at the empty seat opposite him.

"Cengiz..."

"He in particular should not hear."

The bleariness in his eyes vanishes. However many glasses he's already had, the effect of the *rakı* is wiped out in one moment.

"These latest murders... There are dirty circumstances, Sabri. Filthy. You need to know."

He still isn't sure what to do.

"If we don't step this up, you'll be the one to pay," I say.

To which he replies, "All right then, let's go inside."

I'm certain he's is cursing me internally, wondering what I got him into this time. But who cares?

We leave the restaurant and go into the cafe on the left. There's no one inside. We sit at a table in the corner. A young waiter approaches, but I send him away with a wave of the hand. Everything comes out to Sabri in one breath. He's listening with his mouth literally hanging open.

"That's bad," he says. "Very bad."

"Yes, it's very bad, but unfortunately it's all true."

Knowing what answer he'll get, he still asks, "Are you sure? Cengiz is an invaluable officer. A lot of people in the police force love him. Let's not go accusing him out of nowhere."

Actually, he means let's not get ourselves in trouble out of nowhere. I don't let him waver.

"I like Cengiz, too. Or I did... I thought he was a good police, and a good director. But the man is a murderer. You know me, Sabri. I don't just make things up. There are nine bodies, one a police officer, in his wake."

"Nine bodies? Who are they?"

"I told you, Sabri... The six youths who suffocated in the cave, the shepherd Yusuf, former Inspector Selim Uludere and Malik the antique dealer. Like a massacre. And what's more, six of them are Syriacs. Christians, I mean."

His eyes grow wide with consternation.

"Christians?"

"Yes, Christians. Exactly the subject Europeans and Americans have an appetite for. They are already on the lookout for some shortcoming to pin on Turkey."

Poor Sabri. He doesn't know what to say. It's not enough I've made his night miserable, I'm persistently continuing to drag his mood down.

"So far they haven't noticed, but that won't last forever. The Syriacs emigrating from Turkey are forming powerful lobbies abroad. One of those lobbies will step in sooner or later. We have to sort this thing out before they do. We should solve this so these guys don't get the upper hand. If we don't cut off the gangrened finger, the rot will spread through our body. There'll be a reckoning for the entire force, you and me included."

In desperation he asks, almost beseeches, "Well what do you want me to do?"

I want you to allow me to arrest Cengiz. We have to detain him. Whatever we do for a suspect in his position, we have to employ the same procedures for Cengiz."

He bows his head and starts thinking. No, there will be no order to detain from this man. He's a director now, but he hasn't got over his tendency to bumble along.

"Let's not do this, Nevzat." There's a soft look in his eye appealing for understanding. "Okay, you lead an investigation. Get witness statements, gather evidence... Let's turn it all over to the prosecutor's office. If he's guilty, let the prosecutor make the decision to arrest. For those accusing us of having an internal operation, we'll just tell them the judge has made his decision and that's that."

"Good, but Sabri, he's our superior. What if he uses his influence to intimidate witnesses, or tries to tamper with evidence?"

At precisely that moment, Cengiz's voice interjects, "What are you doing, Nevzat?"

Yes, he finally knows. Meaning it's time to put our cards on the table. I slowly turn my head. Cengiz is in the doorway of the cafe, coming briskly towards us, dragging his right leg. Just in case, I keep my hand on the Smith Wesson at my waist as I answer his question.

"My job," I say calmly. "Solving unsolved murders."

"Bullshit!" he says, spraying saliva. "You aren't doing your job. You're setting me up." He turns to Sabri. "Director, this guy... Excuse me for speaking this way but this guy... This guy is spinning something behind my back."

Sabri again acts in a way I don't expect.

"First calm down, Cengiz," he chides. "What kind of entrance is that, as if you are on the attack? Are we your enemies?"

"No, of course not. Not enemies, but Nevzat is ensnaring me..."

"I'm doing no such thing. I was conducting a homicide investigation and you turned up."

"What the hell are you talking about?" he starts to shout again.

"Stop yelling, Cengiz," Sabri warns him. "We can both hear you. Come sit over here. Whatever your problem is, tell us calmly."

Cengiz does as he's told, pulling a chair out and sitting down opposite us. But he can't manage to calm down.

"This Nevzat wants to implicate me in this Syriac homicide, Director..."

"Why would I do that, Cengiz? I've never had any beefs with you."

"How should I know why you are doing it? Maybe you have your eye on my position..."

Sabri answers for me.

"Come on, Cengiz, don't do this. Have you forgotten? Nevzat was going to retire but you convinced him not to."

"I wish I hadn't. So when you get a taste for power..."

"You're being ridiculous," I say. I continue to stare into his eyes. "You gave the game away, Cengiz. You have no hope of escape. If I were in your place, I'd confess what I'd done. In that way we may be able to help you."

"What is it I did?"

"Don't deny it, Cengiz. I know everything you've done going back five years, since Midyat."

The vein in Cengiz's forehead starts to pulse. It must not only surprise him but also anger him that I've been able to get hold of so much information so quickly.

"Don't you talk about Midyat and the Southeast. I lost my friends to martyrdom there. I left there with a crippled leg. It's not something a stuck-up city cop like you can understand. Only true patriots understand this."

"Quit regaling us with the stories of heroics, Cengiz. I also served in the Southeast," I say, keeping my cool.

"Leave the Southeast out of this. That's not our subject," says Sabri.

I immediately jump on the remark.

"Director Sabri is right. Let's talk about Istanbul first and then we'll get back to the Southeast. You were spotted going into Malik's house today, Cengiz. At the exact time of the homicide..."

He knits his bushy black eyebrows.

"That's a lie!" he shouts. "You are lying."

"You know that I'm not. You told me you were with Director Sabri in the afternoon." I turn back to my school friend. "Is that true? Was he with you?"

"Um, no," says Sabri. "Didn't you leave me around two o'clock saying you were going to the station, Cengiz?"

"I left, and I went there. I was at the station."

"You are digging yourself in deeper, Cengiz. Don't deny it. We have very strong evidence. We turned up some threads from your cashmere coat under Malik's fingernails."

My every word comes out as a punch to his face, but he's every bit as experienced as I am in an interrogation so he recovers quickly.

"Because I am the only one in this whole huge city of Istanbul with a navy-blue cashmere coat."

"I spoke with Zekeriya, Cengiz. He says you were a friend of his father's."

"Yes, you tricked the kid." He turns to Sabri as though he's caught an oversight of mine. "He lied to the kid, Director. I just talked to him on the phone. Nevzat told the kid 'Director Cengiz sends his condolences, seems he was an old friend of yours,' although I said nothing of the sort. How should the kid know any better? He played along."

Sabri is confused, yet he asks the right question.

"Played along with what?"

"Nevzat directly told Zekeriya that I'd sent him, to offer condolences... Do you understand, Director? I mean, he's deceiving Zekeriya in order to accuse me."

"You're blowing hot air," I say, interrupting him. "Did you or did you not know Malik?"

"I knew him."

"Then why didn't you say so when I was talking about him?"

"You never talked about Malik to me..."

He's so desperate that he doesn't hesitate to openly lie anymore. This is a war where every kind of hit goes.

"Actually, you are the one who is lying, Cengiz," I say. "I never thought you'd go so low."

"Watch your tongue!"

The vein in his forehead pulses again and with a snap decision, his hand goes to his waist. I am just watching. Forget about moving my hand, I just stare without even blinking.

"Go on, Cengiz," I say, daring him. "You know, it's a custom. You reach for your gun, you pull it."

For a moment, there's a pregnant pause at the table.

"What are you two doing?" Sabri says, grabbing the hand Cengiz has reached for his gun with. "You going to shoot each other?"

Cengiz comes to his senses and takes his hand from his waist.

"Look, Director. This guy pushes people over the edge."

I lean back and continue to goad him.

"It's a shame, Cengiz, a real shame. You're losing control. Whereas when you committed the murders, you really kept your cool."

Cengiz is foaming at the mouth.

"I didn't commit any murders. Do you understand? I didn't kill anyone."

"Eye witnesses say otherwise..."

"Director," Cengiz says turning to Sabri. "Please, say something to this guy. Shut him up. Or else there's going to be an accident."

Sabri, in order to defuse the situation, says in an authoritarian tone of voice, "All right, Nevzat. Back off. You say you have witnesses and evidence, so bring them in and let's see. Look, Cengiz says he's innocent. I'm sure he has witnesses and evidence too. He can also bring them in. Right now, there is no sense in you two flinging accusations and insults at each other here. There's obviously some mistake. We'll sit down tomorrow and get to the bottom of it. I'll come over at nine in the morning. You can both lay out what you have and the truth will come out. You'll shake hands and continue your duties from where you left off." He touches Cengiz's arm amicably. "And don't get so angry at Nevzat. I doubt he has it in for you personally. He's doing his job. But it's clear he has been wrongly informed."

"That could be, Director. If he had asked me at the start, there'd be no problem. I'm furious he got up to something behind my back. I'm his boss. Shouldn't he share what he learns with me first? Especially if someone is accusing me, doesn't he need to ask me first?"

"You're right…" He turns to look at me. In truth, he understands the situation perfectly but is choosing to play along. "But I can't blame Nevzat either. Maybe he got carried away with the investigation." I can't handle Sabri's hypocritical remarks anymore.

"I did not get carried away with the investigation. I would never accuse anyone without witnesses and solid evidence. Particularly my own director. Do I have 'stupid' written on my forehead? You think I'd inform on my own director on a subject I'm not sure about? And that he's committed murder, besides? You think I'm that big an idiot? No, Sabri. I think you are making a big mistake. If you do not arrest this man immediately, this very moment, you won't see him, not tomorrow nor any other time. If he saunters out of here, you'll be hard pressed to ever find him again."

"Come on," says Sabri. "You're starting to take things too far, Nevzat. Tomorrow, I said. Tomorrow morning we will sit down together and work this thing out. And we'll have calmed down by then too."

Chapter 28
Smite the shepherd, and the sheep shall be scattered.

Cengiz is sure of himself and still playing the innocent man; even if he's deeply worried, he continues to sit opposite Sabri as if there is no rush and life is flowing along its normal path. He takes one sip of *rakı* after another, trying not to meet my eyes. He can sip away. I have no time for playing games. I, for one, am in a hurry. I am afraid Cengiz will act faster than I can in seizing the case, intimidate Caner and the parking lot attendant, try to get them to change their statements, and tamper with the evidence. This is why, at the risk of Cengiz influencing Sabri, before even an hour has passed since our altercation, I ask their leave and get up. As might be guessed, Sabri is not as affable as when we first met up. He doesn't even ask me to stay on a bit longer. He just says, "See you tomorrow, Nevzat," and leaves it at that.

The man is right! He's sitting having a nice meal, chatting with his subordinates, and I come along spoiling his evening and stirring up trouble. Trouble that will bring the entire police force to its feet. Anyhow, this is Sabri's problem now. As soon as I've left the Police Lodgments, I rush to the central station. I find Zeynep in the lab taking a DNA swab of Gabriel's mouth. As for Ali, he's busy jotting down the one-handed parking attendant's statement. Good for them; they haven't wasted a moment. I go downstairs to the holding cells. One of the three rooms is full of illegal immigrants from Pakistan, another, suspects detained for disruption of public order. They've put Caner in a room to himself. He's lying on one of the benches; there's a blanket on him. This must be Zeynep's doing. As soon as he notices me, he tries to sit up, although he's in so much pain that he only manages to do so with great difficulty. His face seems a touch more swollen but his open eye shines with hope.

"Hello, Chief."

His voice is in expectation that he'll hear some good news.

"How are you, Caner?" I ask.

"Better. They gave me some pain relievers at the hospital. This board is a little hard is all, and I'm sore all over."

"Have them give you another blanket and you can spread it underneath you."

The hope in his open eye instantly goes dark.

"Am I staying here tonight?"

"It looks that way, Caner. But don't worry. Our business with you will be wrapped up tomorrow."

"They already took my statement."

"The prosecutor may want to take it as well."

"What if I go home now and tomorrow..."

"Not possible, Caner. We can't let you go. There are eye witnesses who say you are a murderer."

"But I'm innocent."

"Even if we knew that to be true, we couldn't let you go. Unfortunately, you are our guest for the night. Besides, it's better for you to stay here. I don't think outside is safe." Caner's one good eye looks into my face with distress. "There's nothing to be afraid of," I say to reconcile him. "We are here until morning. Try to sleep. Tomorrow after we go to the prosecutor's office. Everything will be clear."

As I'm about to leave, he says, "Chief..." He has the meek voice of someone appealing for help. "Chief, you understand that I'm innocent, don't you?"

"We understand, Caner. Come on. You try and get some sleep now."

In fact, I could take him upstairs to my room, but I want to do things by the book. If an inquiry is filed against me, little missteps like that would stick out like a sore thumb to the administration. As I leave the holding cells, I give the on-duty officer a stringent warning.

"If Director Cengiz comes here, you will call me straight away. And he will not know about it. I'm in my room till morning. Understood?"

"Understood," says the young officer. "Don't worry, Chief Inspector."

There's nothing left to do except wait for Cengiz's arrival. But Cengiz doesn't come. I go up to my room and look over the information in the file I got from Nusret again. Zeynep is working on Gabriel's DNA sample and Ali is finishing up the parking attendant's statement. Cengiz doesn't come. Zeynep compares blood taken from Malik's headless body with that found under the stairs in his house and determines that they both belong to the victim. Cengiz still hasn't come. Ali brews us some fresh tea and we send Zeynep home, ignoring her protestations, and Cengiz doesn't come. The night winds down, Ali is passed out sleeping in the chair across from me, I get cold and pull my coat over me, and still no Cengiz. The prim winter sun strikes my window and now I'm starting to nod off too. Ali starts to snore in the deepest part of sleep, but no Cengiz. I get up, wash my face, shave in the sink and Ali wakes up, but Cengiz doesn't come. We have a breakfast of *simit*, cheese and tea. We send breakfast to Caner as well. After breakfast, Ali goes to the house of the inspector Mehmet Uncu, who was left paralyzed in the conflict with the locals near the Mor Gabriel Monastery. There's still no sign of Cengiz. Zeynep arrives, we open Cengiz's room with his secretary's key and take samples of thread from his chair. In the lab, Zeynep compares the threads from the chair to those under Malik's fingernails. She determines they are both from the same fabric. Cengiz doesn't come. It turns nine o'clock and Sabri's car pulls into the station's garden. The directors meet him at the door but Sabri doesn't pay them much attention. When he learns Cengiz hasn't shown up, he comes straight to my room and as we sit across from each other having our coffee; there is still no Cengiz. We both know now that Cengiz has fled. Still, Sabri wants to be sure. He rings him on his cell. The phone is off. But he doesn't give in. He calls in Cengiz's secretary. She doesn't know anything.

"Put me through to his house," he says. "I want to talk to him. Him or his wife or children, whoever you find."

His wife answers the phone. In a very polite manner, Sabri has a brief conversation. Once he's hung up, he explains.

"Cengiz has run away. He told his wife he was on assignment outside Istanbul. The poor woman doesn't know very much. You were right, Nevzat. It seems the man really is guilty."

I assumed he was going to be embarrassed for not having taken Cengiz into custody last night and apologize to me, but instead, an expression of relief appears on my old school friend's hungover face.

"It's better this way, Nevzat," he says. "Cengiz dug his own grave. You complete your investigation, give the witnesses and evidence over to the prosecution and let the court deal with him from now on. No one in the police force can denounce us anymore."

I'm about to say fine, but the man slipped through our fingers, when my telephone rings. It's Ali.

"Chief, you'd better come over here."

It's hard for me to collect my head since my mind is on Cengiz.

"Where are you, Ali?"

"At Mehmet Uncu's house, Chief. You know, that cripple dubbed Fatih..."

"That's right. You went over there, didn't you?"

"Yes, I'm here at the man's house..."

Why does he sound so strange?

"Oh, is..."

"Yep, Chief. It really stinks in here. He must have been murdered a few days ago."

"How was he killed?"

"With one of those cruciform-handled knives, just like Selim Uludere. But this time the murderer finished him off with one blow. Another difference is, the victim was crucified."

"Wasn't he in a wheelchair? How could they crucify him?"

"He's still in his wheelchair, but his hands are opened up to either side and nailed onto a board. Half crucified, we could call it."

I'm in no mood for jokes.

"The Bible, the verses underlined in blood, these Christian rituals..." I ask gravely. "Has the perpetrator left us a sign or a message or anything?"

"He has. There's a Bible and a message. And he's left the message twice, besides. The first is the underlined verse in the Bible and the second is written on the TV screen. 'Smite the shepherd, and the sheep shall be scattered ' it says."***[1]

"Isn't that one of the prophet Zechariah's verses?"

"Yes, Chief. It was written in the continuation of the underlined verse from Selim Uludere's house. Zeynep should have a Bible on her. If she can bring it along when she comes, we can check it."

"All right, Ali. Zeynep and I are coming together."

When I've hung up, Sabri asks, "What's happening? Another homicide?"

"Cengiz's other friend. The inspector left paralyzed from his injuries in Midyat. He's been killed too."

The composure in Sabri's eyes is crumbling. He's starting to grasp that this case won't be closed so easily.

"Is this also Cengiz's work?"

"I suppose so. Who else's would it be?"

He takes a deep breath.

"What kind of mess have we got ourselves into? Our solidest man turns out to be a murderer. We're at a loss to know who to trust."

"Ambition makes people do anything, Sabri. Cengiz had set his sights high. The three people killed were individuals who were encumbering him. He got rid of them, solving the problem at its roots."

"A person just doesn't want to believe, Nevzat."

"That's so. I couldn't believe it myself when I first heard."

"Anyhow, let's see what else life will throw our way." A short while later, he stands up. "Okay, Nevzat, this job is on you. From now on you have my support. For heaven's sake, let's take care of this matter as soon as we can. Without the press latching on to it, of course."

For a moment, I feel as if I'm talking to Cengiz. He also felt compelled at the end of every discussion to warn not to let the press hear.

After I've put Sabri in his car and sent him off, I head with Zeynep for Mehmet Uncu's house in Seyrantepe.

It's just as Ali has said. The moment the door opens, we're hit with the stench of a rotting corpse. We cover our faces with our handkerchiefs until we've adapted. Şefik and his team are not around yet. It won't be long; they'll trickle in soon. Ali has acclimatised. He's even made himself an instant coffee in the victim's kitchen. He sees me gaping at the cup he's holding and says, "To wake up. We didn't get a decent sleep last night, you know, Chief. If you want I'll make you some too."

"No, thanks. None for me."

"Me neither," says Zeynep. "How did you get in?"

"Thankfully, the building custodian had a spare key."

This time it's me who asks, "And how did the perpetrator get in?"

"By normal means, Chief. I mean, by ringing the bell. Just as in Selim Uludere's murder, neither the door nor the window was forced. There's no sign of any struggle inside. So the victim must have known his killer."

"Where is the victim?"

"In the living room, Chief." He points to a long, dark corridor. "Come on. This way." As we pass along the corridor, we see a fairly large, messy room. "This is the bedroom, but the man was sleeping in the living room. When his wife left him, he really let himself go. Only Yusuf ever visited him, and Director Cengiz."

"How did you find that out?" asks Zeynep.

"I spoke to the next-door neighbor. Sıdıka Teyze. Very sweet woman. Also a chatterbox. It seems before Mehmet was shot, he had a great marriage. His wife Şükran was crazy in love with him. However, the bullet that shattered his spine didnıt just leave Mehmet crippled. At the same time, it took his manhood. Şükran didnıt appear to care about that. But Mehmet cared. A few months after getting out of the hospital, he started to get aggressive. It seems the poor guy couldnıt accept his circumstances. A while later he became openly paranoid. If Şükran was a little late after sheıd gone to the market or the bazaar, he started to chastise her, saying İWhere have you been? Youıre cheating on me.ı According to Sıdıka next door, Şükran never cheated on Mehmet. But try telling Mehmet that. One night he pulled his gun. He was going to kill her. The poor woman barely got away. When this incident repeated a few times, Şükranıs parents saw this man was going to kill their daughter, and they had Şükran file for divorce. They never sent their daughter back to Mehmet. Some mediators intervened, but Şükran didnıt go back to her husband. İThank God they had no children,ı Sıdıka Teyze says, İtheyıd be destitute, the poor little things.ı When the wife left home, Mehmet totally lost his mind. And that was when Selim made more frequent visits./

"How do you know it was Selim?" I ask.

"In one of the cabinets inside, I found a photo of Selim, Mehmet and our Director Cengiz taken together. Sıdıka Teyze recognized them both as soon as I showed her the photo. It appears Director Cengiz also came here often."

As Ali explains, we come to the door of the living room, where the odor intensifies.

"Wasn't there anyone helping Mehmet?" asks Zeynep.

"He couldn't get along with anyone, Zeynep. They hired several nurses. He fought with all of them." He points to the right side of the living room. "And here's our corpse."

Our former fellow officer's face was the color of limewash. His glassy eyes were locked onto some point to the left. Turning the direction of his gaze, we see a seventy-centimeter-screen TV. The TV is off; on its glass the words Ali read over the telephone are written in red liquid: 'Smite the shepherd, and the sheep shall be scattered.' I turn back to the body. It's sitting in the wheelchair. A knife with a cross for a handle like the one in Selim Uludere's corpse is stuck in the left side of his chest. The left side of his yellow shirt is stained a dark red. His arms are spread to the sides like the wings of a large bird ready to take flight. Dried bloodstains on his palms, pounded into the cabinet behind him with two thick spikes.

Ali indicates the open Bible in the victim's lap.

"And our book is here."

Zeynep leans in and takes a look.

"He's underlined the same line. 'Smite the shepherd, and the sheep shall be scattered.' Most probably it's in the victim's blood. Yes, and here's Mor Gabriel written in the margin of the page."

"As you see, our perpetrator has performed all the rituals," Ali expounds.

Zeynep looks up from the book and looks around.

"It's so dirty in here. I guess the man never left this room."

Ali takes a sip of his coffee and agrees.

"You're right. The man was living here." The wide table displayed a picnic gas canister and uncollected breakfast items. "He cooked his meals here, and he ate here. Then he'd watch TV all day long."

Ali and Zeynep aren't provoking each other anymore. I'm delighted to see them making up after the situation with Caner. But now is not the time for this.

"In the letter we found at Selim's house," I continue, "it was saying some really sensible things. I'd expect its author to be someone more reasonable."

"But when he wrote that letter, he was in the hospital, Chief."

"How do you know that, Zeynep?" Ali asks.

"It said so in the letter. Don't you remember?"

Yes, I suppose it did say that. Seeing Ali's and my uncertainty, she opens her big bag and takes out the Bible and a photocopy of the letter we found at Selim's house.

"I brought a sample of the letter with me. After all, this letter is the only evidence we have on Mehmet."

"Bravo, Zeynep," I say. "Why don't you read it aloud; it'll jog our memory."

She immediately fulfills my request.

How are you? Are you okay? I hope you are. As for me, I'm getting better every day. I've started to accept what happened to me. And accepting it gives me comfort. But from what I understand from your letter, you are not very comforted. Your letter is full of rebellion; I was the same in the days I first came to the hospital. But then I understood this is my fate and I took refuge in God. Now I am reading his holy book. Reading his words gives me peace. Believe me, even my pain has started to ease. You read it too, it's the only way you'll find any peace of mind. Rebelling, cursing and getting angry at the world is no solution. This is our fate, and what's more, we chose it. Accept what has happened to you, and I promise you will be comforted.

You wrote that you want to come to the hospital, but that wouldn't be right, nor is it necessary. Timuçin never leaves me alone, thank goodness. Whatever needs doing, he does it. You take care of yourself, that's enough. If nothing else, I want to know you're okay.

Timuçin said you have a bit of a money problem. Don't go doing anything crazy. And don't flash your gun at anyone. I'll be coming into some money soon and I'll send it to you. Timuçin says he'll arrange something. You are angry with him, but that's wrong. Timuçin has always been a big brother to us, and has always wanted what's best for us. If we'd done what he said, none of this would have happened. He's more experienced than we are, and smarter. You'd do well to listen to him.

Actually, I really miss you too. It's been a while, but it won't be much longer. They'll discharge me soon, and then you'll come home and we'll meet freely and make up for lost time. Your sister-in-law Şükran will make some of the moussaka you love.

May Allah's mercy and grace be upon you.

Your brother,
Fatih

Zeynep finishes reading and clarifies, "As you can see, Mehmet is still in the hospital when he writes this. In fact, he tells Selim not to come there." Zeynep turns to me. "You're right, Chief. He hasn't gone into depression yet. And he still believes he can be happy as a cripple. In the hospital, his hopes still haven't been dashed. Meaning that it was after he left the hospital that he couldn't handle normal life."

As Zeynep relates this, I think about just how many people are in Mehmet's situation. How many policemen, how many soldiers, how many citizens were left lame after fighting battles in the Southeast. How many human dramas are hidden in the invisible face of those conflicts.

"Of the three of them, the craziest must have been Selim."

It was Ali speculating.

"I suppose so, Ali," I say. "They didn't give him the moniker Yavuz for nothing."

Ali gestures towards the corpse with the cup he's holding.

"And this poor guy must be the most wretched. He was the first to be expended, in any event."

While we're speaking, Zeynep folds up the letter and sticks it in the Bible, after which she pulls plastic gloves onto her hands and starts to concern herself with the body. Her job's going to take a while.

"Did you find anything else?" I ask Ali.

"Nothing besides this photo, Chief."

"But as Mehmet wrote a letter to Selim, the other must have written to this one. Didn't you see a letter or a note or anything?"

"I didn't. He must have ripped up the letters to protect Selim."

It made sense. Both Cengiz and Mehmet tried to protect him. They did whatever they could to keep Selim's real identity secret. I understand Cengiz, but why would Mehmet do this? I suppose because they were friends. Because one of the reasons Selim went crazy in the first place was that Mehmet himself had been shot. Maybe that's what he thought. And maybe Mehmet really did love Selim, just as he loved Cengiz. In the letter, he speaks of Cengiz with great respect. Maybe Cengiz was the guy who pulled them together. But look at the quirk of fate; the man killed his two best friends in order to save his own skin. I wonder if he'd felt sorry. I remember the talk he had with me after the event. I was explaining Selim's death and he wasn't even bothered by it. He was so hardened, so unmoved. Maybe he was putting on an act.

"Where's that photograph?"

Ali takes an evidence envelope from his leather jacket. The photo is inside. It's quite an old photo; the paper has yellowed. The three of them are at least twenty years younger. They are wearing civilian clothing, with Cengiz in the middle, Selim to his right and Mehmet to his left. They don't have their arms on each other's shoulders, but look extremely serious: an expression that challenges the world on their faces, the sort seen on faithful militants or fighting men rather than police officers.

"This corpse must be at least four days old," says Zeynep, scattering my thoughts. She's talking on the one hand, while looking under the victim's eyelids on the other. "Although, they do keep the heat up high here, but yes, yes... it must be at least four days old. Mehmet may have already been dead a while by the time we found Selim's body in Elmadağ."

This is an important point.

"How soon can we be sure about this?" I ask.

"I have to run a couple tests. I can tell you tonight."

"Great, Zeynep."

Meanwhile, Ali has opened the Bible Zeynep brought and has found the prophet Zechariah's verse. He reads.

" 'Awake, O sword, against my shepherd, and against the man that is my fellow.' " Ali is looking towards us. "This is the line in the book in Selim's house that was underlined in blood. If I read what Zachariah wrote in the paragraph from the beginning, it goes like this: 'Awake, O sword, against my shepherd, and against the man that is my fellow, saith the Lord of hosts: smite the shepherd, and the sheep shall be scattered.'***1 " He lifts his head from the passage. "He's not talking about this murdered shepherd, is he? I mean Gabriel's brother Yusuf."

Zeynep's gaze wanders briefly from the body to the book in Ali's hand.

"I doubt it," she says. "Why would he be talking about the shepherd? If Cengiz committed these murders to get rid of the dark pages of his past, why would he choose lines that remind people of those events?"

Ali's answer is ready.

"To confuse things. To make people think some Syriacs or a secret Christian cult committed the murders. You remember, even we thought that these murders might have some connection to a secret Christian sect."

"You're right. We considered it," says Zeynep, her eyes sliding back to the victim's pallid skin. "I don't know; in the whole big Bible, he could have found a different paragraph to underline than this one, which evokes the murder of that shepherd."

"Maybe Director Cengiz was opposed to this business," Ali says. "I mean, the killing of the shepherd. He wasn't present while the first six homicides were being committed. After that, when Selim brought up the scenario of killing the shepherd to save himself, Cengiz could have been against it. Maybe Selim threatened him..."

Zeynep doesn't find Ali's hypothesis plausible.

"He also buckled under the threat? No way. Director Cengiz is not a man to be deterred by such empty barking."

"Okay, he's a solid guy, but these are old friends. Maybe Selim had something on him. Maybe he and Mehmet threatened him together. We don't know exactly what went down."

"So what do you think, Zeynep?" I cut in. "You don't think Cengiz committed these murders?"

"That's not exactly what I'm saying, Chief. I'm just searching for answers to the questions in my head. I mean, does it seem logical to you that Cengiz would choose a verse like this?"

"It doesn't seem too ridiculous, per se. Cengiz wants to pin the murders on an imaginary Christian cult. These days, while films about Christians and Romans are all the rage, he knows we are going to reach this conclusion. So, as Ali said, we did conclude exactly that in the beginning."

"So you say Cengiz definitely did this?"

"He definitely had a hand in Malik's murder. When it comes to Selim and this murder, I can't say he is the perpetrator without knowing exactly what happened. Yet this doesn't change the fact that Cengiz is the prime suspect in all three murders."

Chapter 29
This country really is cruel, Chief Inspector.

Towards evening, things begin to fall into place. The prosecution, having examined evidence and heard witnesses, enacts whatever orders we request. The first is permission to compare Gabriel's DNA to that of the corpse resting in Selim Uludere's counterfeit burial site. Let's see if it'll be the poor shepherd who emerges from the grave, as we've predicted. The second and most important is the order to arrest Cengiz. The search of Cengiz's house we conduct this afternoon is the worst part. However delicate we try to be, Cengiz's wife Neslihan Hanım understands something is amiss.

"What's going on, Nevzat Bey?" she asks. "What are you doing here?" Her eyes say she wouldn't expect this from me. "Cengiz loved you and had great respect for you."

"We're conducting an investigation," I say, leaving it at that.

But Neslihan Hanım won't leave it be. She plants her skinny frame in front of me.

"My husband is an honorable police officer..." She continues, paying no mind to her burst of tears. "How many times has he been injured, or had a brush with death?"

"Don't worry, if he's innocent of the crime..." I start to say.

"What crime is that, Nevzat Bey?" she interrupts me. She wipes her tears with the handkerchief wadded in her hand and carries on. "My husband cannot be guilty. Everything he's done, he's done for the state. Is this how the state rewards those who serve it?"

She stares into my face with a determination that even her tears can't soften. I think of Evgenia. Here, this is what I couldn't explain to her. Marrying a cop means being married to their job. It means being married to every pain, every sadness, every predicament they get themselves into. Exactly what this unappeasable woman in front of me is going through right now. Neslihan huffs off, and it's a good thing she does, because I don't have it in me to tell the poor woman her husband is a murderer. Anyhow, just as I'd guessed, we find nothing in the home.

Catching him will be near impossible now. Many of the police he knows will help him, because Cengiz has helped them at one time or another. If luck isn't on our side, or he doesn't turn himself in, it could take us years to apprehend him. Either way, we will start our search today, at least on paper.

On my way back to the central station, I get that feeling of defeat again. Not because we let Cengiz slip away, and not because we found no evidence in his house. In fact, we can count ourselves successful; seven murders committed years ago have come to light, and even if justice isn't served, neither did they get away scot-free. Yet what is the reward in that? The tears of a woman whose husband is gone, oblivious to what has happened. Once, when apparently quite drunk, I'd told Evgenia, "If I had a lot of money, I'd open a flower shop and hand them out free to everyone passing by. If nothing else, my job would make people happy."

She'd stroked my chin with her long, slim fingers. "It wouldn't work, Nevzat," she said. "Handing out flowers isn't enough to make people happy. You have to give them what they need. And that's difficult. Because you can't know who needs what. People usually don't even know what they need themselves. You'd be better off contemplating the worthy aspects of your profession. You catch murderers, protect the rights of victims unjustly killed and ease the pain of their loved ones, if only a little."

And that is what I do, or try to do. While Neslihan is telling me, "My husband cannot be guilty. Whatever he did, he did for the state," I'm trying to conjure up the image of Malik's face, a face at peace with himself and the whole world. I think of the Syriac shepherd who was shredded to death in a thresher. But none of this eases my mind; on the contrary, it sinks me into even greater despair. Maybe Evgenia is right. I should throw in the towel. Maybe I should ring Evgenia immediately, this very moment, and tell her, "Don't go to Greece. Marry me and let's run Tatavla together." This is what goes through my mind, yet I know very well I won't be able to do it. I must admit, I'm used to living this way, and maybe all these troubles, pains and sorrows strangely add meaning to my life. I suppose I get a secret pleasure out of all this, otherwise why stay here? Isn't that so? And I've asked myself so many times - but this is a question to which I've somehow never found an answer.

In the evening, as I'm leaving the station, I see Caner there at the exit. He looks exhausted; his shoulders are slouched and he's dragging his feet. I call after him. He hears my voice and looks back, his eyes full of consternation. When he sees me, he shakes it off.

"Oh, it's you, Chief Inspector? And I thought something else came up."

Has this kid been here all day?

"Are they just now releasing you?"

He tries to smile but it's difficult with his lips bloated up like inner tubes.

"We're back from the prosecutor's. There were some things missing from my statement..."

"Oh, no. Sorry about that, Caner. You've had a rough time."

He doesn't humor me.

"That's true, Chief. I'm hoping it's behind me now."

I feel guilty.

"Are you going home? Shall I give you a lift?"

He hesitates. "I'm going home, but it's out of the way. My house is on the ridge of Sarıyer."

It's far all right, but I have nothing to do, and I could chat with the guy a bit.

"Never mind. We'll keep each other company."

We head towards my trusty old car. "Is this it?" Caner says when we come to it. Is he contemptuous, surprised or pleased? With his one eye closed, his scraped-up nose and swollen lips, it's hard to read the expression on his face.

"Sure, it's a bit old, like me, but it does the trick," I say.

"I love it... So then you can't give up on your old things either. Don't think I'm criticizing. I'm like that too. I'm incapable of throwing out any old item. I suppose my house will be filled with junk by the time I'm old."

I'm no hoarder; nevertheless, I am pleased he feels this way. I open the car door for him and usher him in. The poor guy holds his aching back like an old man as he sits down in the seat. It'll take at least a week for him to recover. I get in too, behind the wheel. "Thank you," Caner says as I start the car. It's cold inside so he wraps his coat around him and hunkers into his seat.

"No problem. I'll get a bit of sea air this way."

"You got me wrong, Chief. Thanks for taking me home, too, but I'm really thanking you for getting me out of this homicide accusation. If it weren't for you, I would still be inside."

Look, our profession wasn't so bad after all. Like Evgenia said, there are people we make happy too.

"I just did my job," I say, pulling the car out.

We easily get out of the back streets and on to the main road. That's when the madness begins. The main street is horrific. Evening traffic has descended on the artery like a bad dream. I'm a thousand times regretful I've told Caner I'll give him a lift, as the day's fatigue presses in on me. But it's too late. I've already offered. The car barely manages to find a place among the bumper-to-bumper vehicles, and as it starts to inch ahead, Caner breaks the silence.

"The murderer was that man, wasn't it? I mean Cengiz..."

I answer without turning my head.

"I suppose so..."

"You suppose?" Caner's voice grows taut. "I saw him go in with my own eyes."

I leisurely turn towards him.

"But you didn't see him as he was cutting Malik's head off with a sword."

"You are saying the man is innocent?" he says with dismay.

"I never said that," I reply calmly. "It's just, murder is a serious accusation, is all."

"Do you think I'm falsely accusing him? When I left the house, Malik was alive. After that Cengiz went in and then we found the man's body. What would you think?"

"You're right. I would have thought the same, but we need more than that to convict him. As it happens, we have gathered a fair share of material on him. For instance, he was also good friends with this Yusuf of yours. And you know Yusuf had that friend Timuçin? We asked you about him."

"Yes..." His one open eye is focused on my face. "What about him?"

"Well it turns out that Timuçin is Cengiz."

"What?" He slaps his battered right hand on his knee. "Of course! Timuçin, the other name of Genghis Khan. So why was he using an alias?"

I don't intend to explain all that's happened to him.

"There was some dirty business," I say, evading the question. My aim is to bring the conversation round to the Yusuf imposter. "And Cengiz wasn't the only one using an alias. Your Yusuf Abi also went by an assumed name."

"Yusuf Abi, too?"

Right then, the driver of the car behind mine starts honking. The man is right. The dark blue Opel in front of us has moved forward, opening almost a hundred meters of road. After pulling my car forward, I answer Caner's question.

"Yes, the man's real name is Selim. What's more, he's not Christian. Just your average Muslim..."

"Muslim?"

"Yes, Muslim. How could you believe he was a Christian?"

"That's what he said. How should I know he's lying?" His one eye is on my face but he's weighing things over without seeing me. "So that's why he said he doesn't know much about Christianity. To not stir up suspicion. But what about that dream he told us about? Mor Gabriel... The guy isn't Assyrian, so then why would he have a dream like that?"

"Twist of conscience. He felt guilty. Because he was trying to sell a book stolen from the Mor Gabriel Monastery."

"The Diatessaron..."

"Yes, the Diatessaron. If I'm not wrong, Yusuf told you the book was passed down through his family."

"That's what he said."

"And you believed him."

My voice sounds full of innuendo, so he tries to explain.

"What would I gain from not believing it? Malik Amca brought Yusuf Abi around; I mean, the self-proclaimed Yusuf. I trusted him."

"What did Malik tell you about Yusuf?"

"Nothing much. When he first introduced him, he said that Yusuf had strong nationalistic sentiments. He was right; I witnessed it myself later on."

"Nationalism? You mean, as an Assyrian?"

"As a Turk."

"How is that? You're going to be a Syriac and do Turkish nationalism? Weren't you surprised by that?"

"I wasn't, because Yusuf Abi believed all the Assyrians, Kurds, Greeks and Armenians living in this country are Turks."

"You must not have liked that."

He doesn't understand. He's staring into my face.

"Wasn't it these nationalists who killed your mother and father? I'm not mistaken, am I? Your father was a leftist?"

"Oh, I see," he says, appearing relieved. "Yes, my father was a leftist. Most likely they killed them because he was leftist. But those days are past. My mother and father never even occurred to me while Yusuf Abi was explaining his nationalist stance."

As for me, I could never forget my wife and daughter's murders. Even the smallest detail jogging my memory of them drew my attention to that point. Despite thinking about it hundreds of times and never coming up with a conclusion, I still find myself thinking about my wife and daughter's deaths all the time. How can Caner be so nonchalant as this? Maybe it's due to his young age at the time they were killed. To not having felt the heat of events. He'd been nine at the time. But a nine-year-old child can't be considered that young. Maybe his brain chose to forget, as some kind of defense mechanism. Just look, he doesn't even remember what happened so well. Caner continues, oblivious to my thoughts.

"But whenever Yusuf Abi said about nationalism, I would think how these views weren't valid anymore. Because the world is in the hands of multinational corporations now, rather than dominated by nations or even national companies. And their problem is less about getting the world to kneel before any one country than maintaining their own exploitation schemes. All calculations are made on this now. All scenarios are written to this purpose, including violent conflicts."

"So, what do you think about Turkish nationalism?"

He suddenly grows tense. He moves his one eye away from me and looks at the road.

"The Opel has gone ahead again, Inspector."

As I pull up to the car ahead once more, Caner explains. "Actually, it's hard to talk about an independent Turkish nationalism. Especially during the Cold War era, Turkish nationalists became an extension of America's applied policies within the country. Its intelligence agencies and this government have always maintained close relations. American secret services used them in both internal Turkish operations and abroad. But it wasn't just civilian Turkish nationalists. At the same time they blatantly used the army. Recently, a retired general explained how for years the expenses of an organization called Özel Harp Dairesi, or the Special Warfare Department, were covered by America. The Turkish nationalists' Special Warfare Department, Contra-Guerilla, Ergenekon... Whatever you want to call it, it's not a secret anymore that they worked with this kind of organization. After the fall of the Soviet Empire, Turkish nationalists were in for a big shock. Because America's dependency on them dwindled. They are now supposedly trying to form a foundation of anti-Americanism based on their strategies of anti-communism, but it's hard for them to do that with their dependency on the relationships of the past. So now they are leaning on the government. Not on the government, but on certain groups within the state. These days, they are trying to stay afloat by defending territorial integrity against Kurds who want autonomy, which would supposedly divide the country. And it's hard to say they failed. But their justification for existing is the armed actions of the Kurds. Yes, it may be a paradox, Inspector, but the activities of Kurdish nationalists strengthen the fanatical Turkish nationalists. When the armed actions in the Southeast stop, Turkish nationalism will surely be condemned to become a marginal group."

"You have an interesting take on this," I mutter. "Seems like you are pretty well versed in the subject."

"No, not so much. I'm just stating the obvious. You need only be slightly mindful of your country, or the world, and you'll know that's how it is." He goes quiet and watches the road for a bit. Then he must think he's left something out, because he starts up again. "Don't look at what I've said and assume I enjoy politics, Inspector. I like history better than politics. For example, this thing they call a nation state is neither a natural law nor God's edict. The formation of nation states is a matter of a few hundred years at best. They'll probably all but disappear in another few hundred years. What really interests me is culture. Especially the historical culture of this country. It's so rich, so deep and varied. I mean, I'm not talking about ancient remains, fallen cities, palaces where only pillars remain standing and temples sacked by the West. I'm talking about the die-hard habits of our old cultures, which define our daily behavior and still live within us. This being the case, isn't it wrong to restrict ourselves to only Islam, to only Turkishness?"

"But that's how we are, Caner. The majority of the country is Turkish, and an even larger majority Muslim."

"I have no objection to that. That's just how it is. But a great many tribes lived on these lands before the Turks: Hittites, Byzantines, Ottomans... Yes, Ottomans. We couldn't even claim that inheritance properly. And before Islam, a plethora of other faiths were adhered to in this country: Paganism, Judaism, Christianity... And even if our nations and our religions differ, we've inherited a great many habits from those who came before us. We continue to live in cities they built. We drink from the same water sources they did. We cultivate the land they cultivated, and uphold their traditions. And that is the natural order of things. Yet we still - because we are Turkish, because we are Muslims - continue to ignore the cultures that predate us. But this isn't right. Today, in Turkey, is it possible to distinguish just how Turkish someone is, how Armenian someone is, how Kurdish or Greek or Assyrian? And besides, why would we want to? Yet there are hundreds of thousands of fanatics living in this country who would stone me for these sentiments. People who only find meaning in life through their national identity or their religion. People who wouldn't hesitate to take a life, or give their own, for this."

I'm not crazy about fanatical nationalists or religious extremists, truth be told. But something about what Caner is saying gets to me. "So what is the meaning to your life?" I say, unable to hold back.

He tries to laugh, but when he can't, he chooses to explain, a wry look in his single eye.

"There is no meaning to my life, Chief. Once upon a time, there was. First, I got interested in Christianity. Even if not a faithful Christian, I was going to be a scholar in theology. But my mind wasn't having it. It presented so many questions that the religion I chose for life's meaning was riddled with holes. After that it was Western civilization that got my attention. Philosophy, science, and the ideologies that arose from them. Still, this damn brain of mine wouldn't leave well enough alone. While everything was sailing along smoothly, I saw what my eyes weren't meant to see: lonely, alienated and unhappy people. That's why I came back to Turkey, because I understood there was no hope in the West."

"That Italian girl's name was Alessandra, right?" I immediately insinuate. "The Islamic philosophy expert, who ran away with the American professor with the goatee?"

"Yes, Alessandra... No doubt I was also affected by her leaving me," he says, taking my comment on the chin. "Situations like these influence people's world view. One way or another, I came back to Turkey. But I couldn't find any meaning for myself here either. You might call it intellectual despondency, or egg-headed caprice, and you'd probably be right about that. People like me usually sever their ties with everyday life. They live in a kind of world of ideas, in a dream world even. A world of dreams that are unattainable, at that. But this country is merciless, Inspector. This land is hard, its people really rough, and this country really is merciless, Chief Inspector."

I look into his face; the wounds are so fresh, I don't know what to say.

Chapter 30
For me friendship is sacred. Like flag, like country.

When we get to Caner's house, it's evening. Meaning we've lost a lot of time on the road. Caner lives on the top floor of a two-story building on a large plot of land in the hills of Sarıyer. From within the property a dirt road stretches to the house. In front of the building, I see several black shadows. Like human silhouettes. I nod towards the dark forms.

"I guess your downstairs neighbors are out in the garden."

Caner laughs.

"No one lives downstairs, Inspector. It's a duplex. The downstairs is my sculpture studio. What you see are some statues I've made."

"That's right. You mentioned that. You said you were into painting and sculpture. I didn't realize how much."

"It's an amateur endeavor," he replies soulfully. "Just a whim. I have no pretensions."

He says he has no pretensions, but the sculptures appearing in the headlights don't look so amateurish. A dozen or so metallic pieces in white and black have turned this unkempt property into a veritable museum. Directly behind the statues, in front of the house, is a green vintage Volkswagen.

"Is the beetle yours?"

"It's mine. I got it the year I came back from Italy. It works if it feels like it, and doesn't when it doesn't."

I gently pat the steering wheel of my old faithful.

"Just like my old man."

"Yes, like I said Inspector, I can't get rid of my old things."

I pull my car up behind the Volkswagen.

"Here we are. Come have a tea, Chief," says Caner, getting out of the car. "If you're hungry, I'll make you an omelet or some spaghetti Bolognese."

In fact, I am starving, but I can't trouble this guy to make food when even wiggling his finger causes him pain.

"Thanks, Caner. Some other time, I hope. You're tired. Go get some rest, have a sleep. We'll have that spaghetti Bolognese later."

"I'll hold you to that, Inspector. I'll be expecting you. Maybe Zeynep Hanım and Inspector Ali will come too."

There was no innuendo in his voice when he said "Zeynep Hanım"; it was very unaffected. So I must have been wrong to think he was hitting on her. I never really thought he was, but I did worry Zeynep was falling for him. Looks like there was no such thing. And Zeynep and Ali have already started flirting in their own way again, bickering like cats and dogs.

I say goodbye, and as I'm pulling the car out, I glimpse a black form among the statues darting in and out of the headlights that makes my hair stand on end. It's like I've seen Malik. I slam on the brakes. Caner, who is waving at me from in front of his studio, is also taken aback. He comes towards the car. I pull the handbrake and get out. As soon as I do, Malik's life-sized statue confronts me.

"The statue of Saint Paul," says Caner, coming over to me. "You've probably guessed I used Malik Amca as a model. Malik was supposed to go to Tarsus to meet with some authorities, to exhibit the statue there. I told him they wouldn't accept it but he didn't listen. He said, 'Why not? Saint Paul is from those parts, isn't he? Don't worry; I'll convince them.' But it never happened." His good eye is on the statue and he mumbles, as if to himself, "Strange, isn't it, Inspector? However things evolved, in the end Malik died just as he believed he would." His eye, gleaming in the dark, is set on me. "Just as Paul did. I don't know whether that sword was actually the one that decapitated Paul, but Malik died in the same way."

I give him a teasing look.

"What's up, Caner? What happened to your skeptical agnosticism?"

"The agnosticism is still in place, but life sometimes messes with people's minds."

"And a good thing it does, or the world would be a very boring place."

As I say this, my gaze slips over to another statue behind Paul. This must be Jesus. The longhaired, wide-eyed prophet with the innocent face. But Caner has given the statue an air that's quite different from the religious paintings we are used to seeing. Jesus looks like a hippie. A band of daisies circles his broad forehead and a single collarless garment falls down to his knees. On the left side of the garment, right over his heart, is a peace symbol. Between Jesus's long, slender fingers is a cross in the shape of a four-leaf clover.

"Jesus, right?" I say admiringly. "Who did you do this for?"

"No one. I just felt like it."

"Nice... You are very talented, Caner. Good for you."

"Thank you, Inspector."

The road back is every bit as awful as the one there. After Maslak, I change my route, going down into Eyüp from the ring road and from there to Balat. It still takes me an hour. On the way, I mull over what Caner has said. In particular, his response to my question about the meaning of life. "There is no meaning to my life," he'd said. It was a heartfelt answer. If they asked me the same question, I wonder what I'd say? In fact, there is no meaning to my life either. There used to be. I believed in my job, and in justice. I thought there was such a thing as pure justice. Yes, at one time I believed that no matter how much evil there was on the planet, I could prevent it, however many criminals, I would deal with them all. But I'd learned my lesson. Life had taught me. It taught me through pain, sorrow and blood. I was tired now, very tired. Not just my body but my mind, ideals, my passions, my emotions, everything that makes me who I am, is tired. I can no longer believe in myself, nor people, nor the police force, nor the government. Not because I don't want to believe, but because after the myriad experiences I've been through, I've lost my sense of belief.

As soon as I've parked in front of my house, I make for Tekirdağlı Arif's restaurant. Arif's not there. His wife is sick so he's left early. His son Fikret greets me. Even if he doesn't know the business as well as his father, his etiquette is exemplary. I fill up on moussaka and rice with a salad on the side. The food is good but the Turkish coffee is terrible. Fikret doesn't understand how to make it. Well, that's just how it is. I drink half then take my leave. As I am re-entering my street, my eyes slide to the living room window for a moment. In the initial days of our marriage, when I'd leave the central station, I'd call my wife to tell her I was coming. She'd wait for me in that window. The table would be set and the radio would be playing. Maybe Müzeyyen, maybe Hamiyet, or maybe Zeki Müren would be singing. I suppose it wasn't always that way, but somehow it is the moment I always envision. It must be the most distinct memory I have left from those days. As I'm thinking of my wife Güzide, Evgenia also springs to mind. I still haven't managed to call her. Not that I haven't had time, I just couldn't collect my thoughts and don't know exactly what to say.

Tevfik catches me as I'm passing the coffeehouse. "Come inside," he insists. Apparently, Fisherman Necmi and Kebab Fettah have a backgammon match going. The loser has to take everyone at the table to a *meyhane*. Any other time I'd gladly have joined. Their banter would be very entertaining, but right now I have neither the head to deal with the hilarity nor the strength to sit even one minute in the coffeehouse. I escape Tevfik's clutches and rush home so as not to be caught by anyone else.

As I open the door, I can't help thinking how cold it is inside the house. Should I have hung out in the coffeehouse a bit? But no, I would have fallen asleep in my chair. I would've had to come back here eventually anyhow. I'll turn on the electric radiator and be done with it. I go inside, and as I'm closing the door, I feel the barrel of a gun on my neck.

"Hello, Nevzat. Welcome home."

I recognize the calm voice as soon as I've heard it: Cengiz. After the brief surprise, I try to adapt to the situation.

"Hi Cengiz. Welcome to you, too."

He lets out a guffaw, after which he says, "Bravo, Nevzat. You got my voice straight away."

"Well, we've been working together a long time. It'd be pretty disloyal to forget simply because you don't come into work one day."

I try to turn towards him. He presses the barrel into my neck.

"Not so fast. Let's relieve you of this gun first. It was a Smith and Wesson, wasn't it? A revolver?"

"That's right. You know what I'm packing, so then you must also know where."

"I know, I know. Don't put yourself out," he says, putting his hand down to my waist. He pulls my gun from its holster and stashes it.

"And the spare?"

"There isn't one. But if you don't believe me..."

"Of course I believe you, but sorry, I still need to search."

He takes his gun in his left hand, and with his right he pats me down all over. While Cengiz is looking for a gun that's not there, I consider how he could have got into the house. It isn't hard to figure out. By breaking the kitchen window, through the empty space behind it. How many times had Güzide told we should have metal bars put up? That's what happens when you don't listen to your wife.

"You were right," says Cengiz, finishing his search. "No other guns."

I slowly turn around.

"I told you there weren't, Cengiz," I say, looking into his smirking face. "Or should I say Timuçin?"

His smirk freezes on his lips.

"Go on, have a laugh, Nevzat. Life is like that. You use an alias in the line of duty at some point, for security, and the day comes when it's the butt of a joke."

"It's not your line of duty that makes you the butt of a joke. It's the murders you've committed."

"I didn't commit any murders," he snaps.

"Of course not," I say sarcastically. Then I point to the living room. "Let's go inside if you'd like. We can speak more comfortably there."

He gets a wisecrack expression again.

"All right. I am the guest is all; I'll go wherever my host wants. But I wouldn't want to be disrespectful, so after you, please."

As long as he's holding his Beretta, I have to comply. I go obediently into the living room like a good host. "There's a switch on the wall," I say, so he won't misunderstand and shoot without reason. "I'll turn on the light."

"Sorry to inconvenience you. I'd do it myself but my hands are full."

I reach out and flip the switch, and it lights up inside. Now I can see him better. He's still wearing the navy-blue cashmere coat.

"You didn't change your coat? If it were me, I'd have long since burned it. It's got you into a lot of trouble."

"I didn't have the chance. And so what if I did? You've already collected threads from my room."

"Sorry to say but that's true." I point towards the electric radiator. "Shall we plug it in? It's cold in here."

"That'd be nice. I froze while waiting for you."

Once I've plugged the radiator into the socket, I say, trying to keep up my cheerfulness, "I wish you'd turned it on. You're no stranger, Cengiz. In any case, the next electric bill won't cost as much as the kitchen window you broke."

A sheepish look settles onto his face.

"Sorry, Nevzat. I wouldn't have wanted to come in this way. I had no other choice. I am a fugitive, don't forget."

I gesture towards the sofa.

"Look, you can sit there." Then I point to the armchair opposite. "Or here. Wherever you want."

"I prefer the armchair. You take the sofa."

"Before we sit, tea or coffee?"

"Neither, thanks. You really are a good host. But I just want to talk."

"Okay. As you wish."

I go over to the sofa and sit down. Cengiz settles into the armchair opposite me. He glances over at the photo of my wife and daughter smiling at us on the side table next to the armchair.

"Actually, I wasn't planning on coming here," he says, "but today you visited my house and I thought it would be a shame not to return the visit." He gets serious. "Were you really hoping to find me at home, Nevzat?"

"No. It was a routine search, you know. We couldn't not do it. My apologies if we disturbed you, especially your wife."

He realizes I'm sincere.

"It's not important. She was a little perturbed, naturally. But you were polite, you went out of your way to be conscientious, and I thank you."

"It was my duty." I leave the mocking and the joking aside and openly ask, "Why aren't you turning yourself in, Cengiz?"

"I should turn myself in, should I?"

"That way you don't upset anyone. And we'll do whatever we can to..."

He suddenly hardens. No more wisecracks, no smiling.

"Stop this bullshitting, Nevzat. I'll turn myself in and you'll do away with me, isn't that right?"

"What makes you feel that way?"

He swings his Beretta towards my face.

"And now you're playing dumb. You and Sabri conspired. You want to get rid of me."

"Don't be paranoid, Cengiz," I say, in a voice at least as harsh as his. "I am not your enemy, and neither is Sabri. You even have him to thank for being able to sit here in my house and threaten me right now. This is not personal. You've been following events since the beginning too. And doing it without letting on to me. I was conducting an investigation and you made an appearance. And what an appearance! As a first-degree homicide suspect. My director, the man who killed Malik..."

"Malik's death was an accident," he interrupts. There's deep disappointment in his face. "I didn't want to kill him."

"So you admit you were in Malik's house."

"Yes, I was there, but his death was an accident."

This time I can't stop myself.

"Come on, Cengiz. What are you saying?" I snap. "Lay the man down on the stairs, crack his head off with a sword, and then call it an accident? Who is going to believe that?"

"It's hard to believe, but I'm telling the truth. Malik was dead before his head came off. I was interrogating him. We had a scuffle, and he hit his head on the stair railing."

"And you grabbed him and chopped his head off?"

"He was dead, Nevzat..." The desperation in his voice is conspicuous. "All right. I'm not proud of what I did. But the whole thing was an accident."

"What business did you have at Malik's house?"

"I thought he'd killed Yusuf. I mean Selim. I still think that."

"Why would Malik kill Yusuf?"

"The man was batshit crazy. He was completely hung up on Christianity. You questioned him too; I'm sure you noticed. The man believed he was Saint Paul."

I remember considering the same possibility. Malik fit the ideal profile for the murder of Yusuf's imposter. Cengiz carries on, unaware of my thoughts.

"This manuscript of Selim's, he knew he had taken the Diatessaron. For him, this was a big sin. I suppose he killed Selim to punish him."

Up till here is fine, but another murder weakens the probability of Malik's being the killer.

"What about Fatih?" I remind him. "Or should I say Mehmet Uncu?"

He doesn't ask, or try to deny, who Mehmet is. For that matter, he gets curious and asks, "What about Mehmet?"

Before answering, I first carefully study his face. Is he bluffing or does he not know what happened to his friend?

"Don't pretend you don't know. He's been dead four days, at least..."

"Are you serious?"

His voice is startled, aggrieved.

"Do I look like I'm joking?"

He doesn't say anything for a bit. His light brown eyes are on my face, just staring. It's not clear whether he is just thinking or if grief has got his tongue. "What's wrong?" I say. "You clammed up. Let's say Malik killed Selim because he was bonkers. Why would he kill Mehmet? Mehmet had nothing to do with either Mor Gabriel or the Diatessaron. Huh? Tell me, why would Malik kill Mehmet?"

Cengiz holds his tongue a bit longer. His eyes are still on me.

"So Mehmet has also been killed," he finally croaks. His voice comes out so deep, it's as if he's not talking to me but rather his own soul. "That is strange. Why would Malik murder Mehmet?"

Whether he is trying to work it out or steer me the wrong direction is impossible to discern. "You can't influence me with this attitude, Cengiz," I say without pausing.

"Why would I try to influence you?"

"To confuse me. You know this business as well as I do. If we don't count the poor shepherd you made minced meat of, or the six who suffocated in the cave next to the Mor Gabriel Monastery..."

"Those murders had nothing to do with me."

"Even if you didn't have a hand in it, the deaths of Selim and Mehmet are related to those murders."

His lackluster eyes brighten up.

"What, the Assyrians committed these murders?"

"Of course," I say flippantly. "The shepherd Yusuf's poor brother Gabriel secretly came to Istanbul. He determined it was Selim who had killed his big brother and had taken his identity, found Mehmet's address, and then killed them off one by one. Come on, Cengiz, are you kidding me? What Assyrian? You killed them. Same as you killed Malik, mercilessly, without blinking an eye."

"I don't murder my friends," he says, turning his gun on me again. "I don't know about you but for me friendship is sacred. Like flag, like country."

And they have the nerve to talk like this; it infuriates me. They torture, kill, steal, deal drugs, and then come out and say whatever they did, they did it for the country, for the nation, for the state. I feel like shouting into Cengiz's face to not even go there, but I know I shouldn't lose my cool so I hold back. My ex-director keeps talking.

"I would have given my life for them in a heartbeat. Do you know what I risked in order to protect them?"

I surprise myself by how calm I remain as I answer.

"I wish you hadn't. Anyhow, you were obliged to kill your friends because of the sacrifices you made, remember. You couldn't contain Selim anymore. And especially after he met Henna Meryem, he wouldn't listen to you. He got it in his head to sell the Diatesarron. Some day, somewhere, he was going to give the game away. And your bright career would be brought to an abrupt end. That is why you killed Selim. Of course, it wouldn't do to leave Mehmet behind. His psychological state was not good after all. His mental health was gradually deteriorating. Some day, somewhere, he was going to talk. Maybe you fought with him too. Malik was the first to suspect you. But he made a big mistake; he wanted to talk to you first. When he slapped you in the face with your murders, you killed him too. The religious messages, the underlined verses, the cruciform-handled knives and all that... All to give the impression of religiously motivated murders. Your first target was Malik. And since that didn't work, you're pinning the crimes on the poor Assyrians."

A deep enmity appears in his eyes again.

"That's a fine set-up," he hisses. "You found an angle on me and jumped at the opportunity, put the script straight into action, right? I never knew you were so ambitious, Nevzat."

"What ambition, Cengiz? I don't have any ambitions."

"If you didn't have ambitions, you'd have told me first that I was spotted at Malik's house."

"That would make me an accomplice to your murder."

"I told you it wasn't murder!" he rages.

"So then why are you running away?"

"Because you are the one investigating."

"You're running away because you don't trust me? Where did I misspeak? What I just said..." He narrows his eyes, not understanding. "I mean, the reason you committed these murders."

"I'm telling you, I didn't commit those murders."

"Okay, let's say you didn't. But put yourself in my shoes. Doesn't what I say make sense? Right now, you are the only one who stands to gain from the deaths of Selim and Mehmet. Isn't that logical?"

"It is logical," he says, but I see that the hate in his eyes has grown. "Very logical." He speaks with a voice full of resentment. "Once I'm ousted, Sabri will reward you by filling my position with you."

Perhaps it is dangerous for me to talk like this but I don't care. It's really starting to wear on me that this man has broken into my home like a thief, talking to me at gunpoint.

"You're like a broken record. I don't have my sights set on anybody's position. I was going to walk away; I only stayed here at your bidding."

As I raise my voice, the tension spreads to him too.

"Bullshit," he says, sitting up in the armchair. "You've had your eye on my job from the start. You're tripping me up with the greed not being promoted has given you. You planned to use my back as a stepping stone."

The man is wrong, yet sure of himself. His insults are really getting to me.

"It's people like you who make career and promotion calculations. Even if it comes to killing your friends."

My remarks infuriate him.

"Don't you talk about my friends!" he shouts.

I don't care one bit. Let the chips fall where they may.

"Why?" I say. "Does it give you a prick of conscience when I talk about them? You're reminded of how you killed them?"

"Shut up! Shut it, or I will shoot you."

"Of course you'll shoot." I rub salt in the wound. "After all, you have made a habit of shooting your friends."

"You are not my friend."

I should hold my tongue now, but I can't contain my rage.

"That's true. I'm not your friend. I'd need to be a murderer in order to be your friend."

The comment sends him off the deep end.

"I told you to keep my friends out of this," he says, launching at me. Before I find the chance to protect myself, the butt of his gun comes down on my head. Cengiz continues to yell as he hits me.

"Each and every one of them was a true patriot. Each and every one a true nationalist. Each and every one of them a true hero..."

Just before my eyes go dark, I see my daughter and wife still watching me and smiling from the frame on the end table. I wish I had listened to my wife and had those metal bars installed, is what passes through my mind.

Chapter 31
You've ratcheted up more adversaries, Nevzat.

I feel a wetness on my face, a warm breath on my left cheek, and I open my eyes. A pair of brown eyes is looking back at me with compassion. All at once I see a hairy face and a black nose, and I pull back, startled. It's Bahtiyar! Our street's stray, the Kangal crossbreed, Bahtiyar. What's he doing here? I suddenly remember what happened. Cengiz... Is he still here? I look around the room; there's no one but my wife and daughter smiling at me from the frame on the table. So he's gone, having left the door open, as well. Was it carelessness? I don't think so. It's to disgrace me in my neighborhood. I slowly try to sit up. I feel sick, my head is throbbing, and my left temple is numb. I reach up, there's a wetness on my fingers. I look at my hand in a panic: Blood. I try again to sit up. As I stand, my head spins and I feel like I'm going to fall over. I hold on to the edge of the sofa. My dizziness passes, and that's when I notice my gun. It's on the sofa where Cengiz was sitting not long ago. I reach over and take it, open it up, the bullets are in place. It's then that I know for sure that

Cengiz has left the house. Still, I can't help checking all the rooms one by one, with Bahtiyar in tow.

When I discern I'm home alone, I put Bahtiyar out then go to the bathroom. The cut on my temple isn't so deep but there is a walnut-sized lump on the back of my head. I wash my face and clean the cut with tincture of iodine and a cotton ball. And then there's this throbbing in my head. Before taking a painkiller, I ring Ali. I tell him to send a squad car to Caner's house. Cengiz isn't afraid to come to my house, so he won't hesitate to threaten the most important witness who can identify him. The sudden request raises Ali's suspicions.

"What happened, Chief? Is there some development?" he asks.

There's no point in agitating the kid at this time of night.

"It's not important, Ali. I'll explain tomorrow."

After which I call Caner. "A squad car will be coming to your house soon," I say.

Once I've said it, he gets worried.

"Did you get a tip-off or something, Inspector?"

"No, it's just a precaution. This is routine."

After I've hung up, I put the ice cubes I've taken from the freezer into a plastic bag and press them to the lump on the back of my head. The chill of the ice reduces the throbbing. Then I swallow one of those strong painkillers and stretch out on my bed.

In the morning I wake up better. My head still aches slightly but the horrific throbbing has passed. My left eye is bruised, and hurts when I blink, but it'll be fine. I wash my face and shave. I change the bandage on my left temple and go out into the street. First, I stop by Rafet Usta, the glazier on the corner. I give him my key and ask him to change the glass in the kitchen. And I tell him to find me a good ironsmith to make some bars for the downstairs windows. On my way to the central station, I drop into a patisserie and get a bite to eat. After my second glass of tea, I reach a state where I can deal with people again.

I find Ali at the station waiting for me. When he hears of the night's events, he gets upset, stressed out, and even scolds me. "Why didn't you let me know, Chief? What if Cengiz had come back?"

"Why would he do that, Ali? Killing me wouldn't solve his problem. Anyhow, let's get to work. We should piece together what's missing from the files. Where is Zeynep?"

"Zeynep went to the cemetery. I haven't seen her either."

"The cemetery?"

"For the DNA test. They're exhuming Selim Uludere's body, you know. To compare it to what they got from Gabriel. But Zeynep left us a note. It says that Mehmet Uncu and Selim Uludere were killed on the same day."

"Looks like our murderer was quite busy that day," I say. "I wonder what our Director Cengiz was up to the day of the murders?"

"If we'd caught him we would have found out, Chief. Shall we ask his wife?"

"She won't answer. Or she'll lie. Let's look at what we have for now. Do a little more research on these three."

"What three, Chief?"

"Cengiz and his friends. The photograph we found at Mehmet's house proves they were friends long before they started policing. If we find out when they met, how they became friends, maybe we'll get some new leads. And there's the issue with Malik. We still don't know what sort of relation he had to Cengiz and his friends."

"You're right," he agrees. "Why don't I talk to Malik's son then?"

"Good idea. You talk to Zekeriya. He knew both Cengiz and the Yusuf imposter. And we need to look in the newspapers too.

"Which newspapers?"

"Old editions. Now these men, they could be from the fascist team, or the nationalists or the like. It's also possible they were involved in some incidents in their youth. It'd help to look at papers prior to 1980. Let's assign a few officers to that duty. Have them scan the newspapers between 1976 and 12 September 1980. They should collect all news items with the names Cengiz Koçan, Selim Uludere, Mehmet Uncu, and Malik Karakuş."

"All right, Chief."

"By the way, we still have a detail on Caner, don't we?"

"Yes. They escorted him to the school this morning, sir."

"Good. Let's not leave him on his own for a while. Cengiz is rabid right now. You never know what he'll do."

"You be careful too, Chief. Don't get yourself hurt trying to protect this intellectual chump."

There's deep concern in Ali's wild eyes. This kid really loves me. Maybe he is putting me in his deceased father's place. No, that's too much. But why not? Don't I sometimes think of Zeynep as my daughter? It's a good thing Evgenia doesn't know I feel this way. "Your daughter Zeynep, your son Ali, it's obvious why you don't feel like you need a family," she'd say. She wouldn't be far off the mark, in fact. The bulk of my time is spent with these two.

Ali sees I'm lost in thought. "I'll get going now, Chief," he says, standing up. "I'll send some friends to the library and head to Zekeriya's."

"Go on then, Ali. Good luck."

As Ali is leaving, I pick up my phone. It is time for me to call Evgenia. I wonder if she's left for Greece. I suppose she has.

She's stubborn, and she'll do what she says. I dial her number. But Evgenia's phone doesn't ring, and instead a female voice says something in English. Probably something to the effect of "this number isn't reachable". Is she keeping her phone off? She must be so angry that she doesn't even want to talk to me. If she doesn't, she doesn't. What else can I do? I told her, "Don't go. Let's start over." She didn't listen. I lean back in my chair, perturbed. This isn't working; I need to put my nose to the grindstone. I open my desk drawer and try to go over the file I got from Nusret again, but it isn't happening. I can't take my mind off Evgenia. What's happened to me? Where did the relapse into this Evgenia sickness come from all of a sudden? Maybe it's because of last night's attack. Being knocked down and left alone that way. Only Bahtiyar came to my rescue, the loveable neighborhood dog. I had no one to ring and ask for help. How is that possible? Ali, Zeynep, my friends from the police force... they are different. In moments like these, people are searching for another kind of warmth. What's going on, Nevzat? You are coming apart at the seams. Pull yourself together. If Evgenia were here, you wouldn't have called her anyhow, not to frighten her or get her into trouble. It's true; this is not the reason I feel Evgenia's absence... Maybe it's because the murders are beginning to unravel. One way or another, we've made big headway. They say the idle mind seeks what it loves. What a yarn I've spun; there is no saying like that. Yet that doesn't make it wrong. If you have important work... Can there be any more important work than love? There can: Murder. We've come full circle; our subject is love and murder. I'd have liked to discuss this with Evgenia. No, that's a bad idea. Nice one. Now you're going to figure out where Evgenia is and talk it over. No, her anger will pass in time and she'll probably call. Would she just turn her back and leave like this? But knowing Evgenia, she would. She's capable of anything; both her ire and her love are unshakable. My gaze slips to the cell phone on my desk. Maybe she hasn't woken up, and I should call again. I myself am not convinced by what I'm saying, but hope makes a person foolish. I reach out, pick my phone up off the desk and dial again. And here you have your answer. Again, the woman speaking English. Evgenia has clearly turned off her phone and doesn't want to talk. I'd better get used to it, as there's no point in torturing myself. Easier said than done. I can't resist trying her a couple more times. That English-speaking woman always turns up. Like the ache in my head, Evgenia's absence grinds on me profoundly until noon.

I go out for lunch, and on the way back I run into one of the directors, Rasim. We have a good rapport, but this time he's acting cold.

At first I don't understand, but then it hits me. It's the thing with Cengiz. He sees the investigation I'm conducting as an internal operation, and also he likes Cengiz, so he is openly giving me attitude. You've ratcheted up more adversaries again, Nevzat. I don't give a damn. I'll take the peace of mind for doing the right thing at the expense of adding a few more enemies.

In the afternoon, Zeynep comes. They've taken the DNA sample from the grave. It appears Selim Uludere has no living relatives. He did have an elderly mother. The poor woman had a heart attack and died when she learned her son had been torn up in the thresher in Midyat. Selim didn't get the chance to tell his mother that he wasn't the one who died, or else for safety's sake, and probably also at Cengiz's behest, he hadn't wanted to tell her this truth. In this way, Selim was responsible for not only the deaths of the six youths and the poor shepherd, but also that of his own flesh-and-blood mother. It's obvious why the man got into cannabis and was seeing Mor Gabriel in his dreams. How could anybody live with a guilt trip like that? Murder doesn't just end with the taking of a victim's life, it stays with the murderer for a lifetime.

"It'll take a while for the DNA to finalize," says Zeynep. "The corpse was completely decomposed. They're going to work on the teeth, check the Y chromosome. So if Gabriel and the person in the grave are related, we'll find it out."

In fact we can both guess the results, but we have to prove it, substantiate it. As Zeynep is about to head to the lab, Ali comes in. When she sees him, she delays her exit. This thing with Caner has made them closer, I guess. Maybe Zeynep has turned back from the brink of a decision, or maybe she found the chance to test her feelings for Ali. And our loose cannon grasped that he would lose Zeynep. Good, no problem for me.

"I'm afraid I couldn't learn much from Zekeriya, Chief," says Ali. "His father didn't want him to come to the shop when he was young. It's understandable, because the guy was up to some dirty business. That's why it was only in recent years that he met the Yusuf imposter, that is, Selim Uludere, and Cengiz. He doesn't know how or where his father met them, or what kind of a relationship they had."

"Does he know Yusuf by his real name, the name Selim?"

"No, and that's also interesting. He knows him as Yusuf."

"But Malik," I say, "must know Selim Uludere by his true name. They've known each other for years. Probably since he met Cengiz."

Ali's head is also stuck on this question of Cengiz.

"That's another strange thing. While Selim was using a fake name in Malik's shop, Cengiz didn't have any qualms using his real name."

"Why should he, Ali?" says Zeynep. "Cengiz is not a wanted man."

"You're right... So then Malik also knew what these guys were up to. I wonder what their connection is?"

"Business," I speculate. "It must have come down to money. But we should find out what this business was. To shed light on the parts of this investigation that are still in the dark, it's a must."

"I sent our plainclothes officers Turhan and Haluk," says Ali. "They've gone to the city library. They're both smart. As of today, they are scanning the papers."

"Good work," I say. "I hope they come across something useful."

Ali finishes up his oral report and gently pats his stomach.

"I'm ashamed to say it, but I'm starving. Have you two eaten anything?"

"I haven't," says Zeynep.

"Bon appetit, kids. I've already seen to that business."

"Well then, let's you and me go get a bite," says Ali.

After they've left, the phone on my desk rings. It's the on-duty officer at the main entrance.

"Chief Inspector, there's a woman here by the name of Meryem Banaz. She wants to talk to you."

Henna Meryem! Where has she popped up from all of a sudden? Patience; we'll find out.

"Okay," I tell the duty officer. "Send her in. I'm waiting."

Chapter 32
The saturated voice of Müzeyyen Senar fills the meyhane.

Meryem doesn't keep me waiting long. A few minutes later she appears in my doorway. She must still be in mourning; she's dressed in black from head to toe. A long black coat, black scarf, and black gloves.

"Hello, Meryem Hanım. Welcome."

She removes her gloves and shakes my extended hand.

"Thanks, Nevzat Bey. Sorry to come without notice."

Her unmade-up face is pale and there's curiosity in the depths of her unsettled eyes.

"Never mind that. Come in and have a seat."

She takes off her coat and is left with a black suit. As she sits in the chair I've indicated, I ask her, "What would you like to drink?"

"Nothing for me, thank you. I know you are busy and I'd like to get straight to the point."

"Go ahead; I'm listening."

"Last night, near midnight, a man came to Nazareth Bar. He took out his ID. The name on it was Cengiz Koçan, and it said 'Chief of police'. He told me he was a police officer. And a friend of Yusuf's. To be honest, I blamed you. I thought you'd sent him.

"Anyhow, I told him that Yusuf didn't have any friends named Cengiz. If he had, I would have known. And he said, 'He probably called me Timuçin.'

"I asked him, 'Are you Timuçin?' and he said yes, he was, and that Yusuf wouldn't use his real name in the line of duty.

"That surprised me. My head was swimming. I asked him how he knew Yusuf, and he explained how it had come about. It turns out Yusuf was a former police officer. Apparently, his name was Selim. They used to fight terrorists in Midyat. A case had been opened against them after which Selim had to change his name to Yusuf..." Her black eyes stare at my face looking for confirmation. "Anyhow, you know all this."

"Yes, we've heard about it."

"Cengiz, I mean the man who said he was Timuçin, explained how you'd set him up. It seems he was your director, but you wanted to supplant him. You set out to put the blame for Selim's death on him. He claims the murderer was someone else. He told me, 'I will find the real killer within a few days.' He was going to do this not just to clear his own name, but also to avenge his friend."

"What did you say?" I ask.

"At first I didn't know what to say. I was struggling to understand what was going on. I spoke for two whole hours with the man. I asked lots of questions, and he answered them all."

"Did he say why he had come to you?"

"He did. He came to me because he was afraid of you."

"Afraid of me?"

"That's what he said. In his words, 'Nevzat realizes he won't be able to catch me, but he might come to tell you that I killed Selim. Nevzat knows you won't allow Selim's killer to live, and that is how he plans to take me out of the equation without getting his nose dirty.' He told me he didn't kill Selim, that Selim was like a brother to him. That they've been friends since childhood and Selim and Mehmet looked up to him. He said if you come to me and tell me he is the murderer, I shouldn't believe you. 'Nevzat has his sights set high. That's why he'll tell every kind of lie, get up to every kind of scheme.' The man hates you, Nevzat Bey."

"Even worse," I mutter, "he thinks I am like him. He thinks I'm just as low as he is."

"I didn't really fall for it either. That's why I'm here. Is Cengiz really Selim's killer?"

Without any explanation, I lean back in my chair, fold my hands on the table and scrutinize Meryem. An uncomfortable silence spreads through the room. Meryem is compelled to reiterate the question.

"You should tell me. If that man is the murderer, he may try to kill me too."

I maintain my silence.

"Why are you looking at me like that? Are you worried that I am going to kill Cengiz?"

"No. I don't think you'll do that. At least you wouldn't be bold enough to do it before his sentence is finalized and he's thrown out of the police force. Killing Bingöllü Kadir is one thing. Killing a police director, even if only a second-rate one, is another thing entirely."

"So then why aren't you telling me the truth?"

"I'm waiting for you to tell me the truth first."

She blinks as if she doesn't understand.

"What truth?"

"Don't do it, Meryem Hanım. You are still telling the same tall tales."

A flicker of rage suddenly appears in her black eyes.

"What tales?" she snaps.

"Calm down; you know very well what tales."

"Are you saying I knew Cengiz was this guy called Timuçin?"

"No. You didn't know this person by the name of Timuçin was Cengiz. But you did know Yusuf's true identity. You found out that he was Selim Uludere. A woman like you would never get into a relationship with someone you don't know, with an indeterminate past. Don't try to tell me otherwise."

"But...."

"Please, Meryem Hanım. We are both in the same world. We may be on opposite sides, but we breathe the same foul air, walk the same muddy and bloodied streets. I know every bit as much as you do how things go down on those streets. So don't spout these lies to me."

The rage in her eyes softens and she takes on an agreeable air.

"If you want to find out whether Cengiz is the killer, first you have to explain," I say, laying out the conditions. "And without holding anything back."

Now it is Meryem who stays silent. She just stares into my face.

"Can I smoke?" she asks.

"You can't," I say, adopting my strictest manner. "Sorry, but not here. If you're going to smoke, take it outside."

She crosses her legs nervously.

"All right, Nevzat Bey," she says, with a sigh of distress. "You're right. I did know Yusuf's true identity. But believe me, I learned about it much later on. My father's close friend, Seymen Nuri from Ankara, spotted me with Yusuf one day. He called me and asked, 'What are you doing with that cop Selim?' I told him I don't know anyone named Selim. I thought there must be some mistake. He said, 'What do you mean you don't know him? Then who was that guy with you at the restaurant in Yeşilköy today?'

"Naively, I told him, 'His name is Yusuf.'

" 'He's figured you out, my girl. That man is a cop. I know him from Ankara. And his name's not Yusuf, it's Selim Uludere. Ditch the guy.'

"Seymen Nuri is one of the most respected men in our world. And he loves me like a daughter. There's no reason for him to lie. So when it sank in, it was like someone had dumped boiling water over my head. I immediately called my lover Selim, the man I knew as Yusuf.

"I told him, 'I'm in the car. I feel like having a picnic. Let me come and get you. We can get out of the city.'

"He said fine, he's waiting. I didn't take any of our guys with me. I made this mess, and I would clean it up. So I picked Selim up and we set off for the mouth of the Bosporus at the

Black Sea. When I got to a place that was desolate enough, we got out for a breath of air. Selim's back was to me. He was peering out at the turbulent Black Sea waves. I drew my gun and put it to his back.

" 'Get on your knees,' I told him. He was taken off guard. He asked me what I was doing and I told him, I said, 'If you turn around, you'll eat a bullet. Now get on your knees!'

"He had no choice but to comply. I asked him, 'Who are you, Yusuf?' And he said, 'What do you mean?' I buried the barrel between his shoulder blades and shouted at him not to play games with me. I lost my mind; I really did want to kill him at that moment, to finish this thing. I asked him, 'Your name is Selim, isn't it? Are you or are you not police? What do you want from me? Are you going to have me put away?'

"He admitted that his real name was Selim Uludere. And that yes, he used to be an inspector. 'But this has nothing to do with you,' he said. 'This is not an operation. I live outside the law, like you do.'

"I didn't believe it. I thought he was trying to trick me. I shouted at him. 'Stop bullshitting! You mean to pull the wool over my eyes. You are using me to leak information to you from our world.'

" 'I'm not. I swear I'm not,' he said, and then he started to explain what had happened, about the shepherd Yusuf and the fight in Midyat. The only thing he didn't tell me was Timuçin's and Fatih's real names. When he'd finished his story, he said, 'But you are right to shoot me. I should have told you all this from the start.'

"I didn't know what to do. I should have killed him on the spot, but I didn't. I tried to but failed. You don't believe me, Nevzat Bey, but I really loved Selim."

Her velvety black eyes grow moist. Evgenia springs to mind again. When a woman loves a man, really loves a man, a strange power comes over her. A force that is just as constructive as it is destructive. At that moment, they could kill you, or go to their death for you without blinking an eye.

"That's why I hid his identity," says Meryem, by way of explanation. "Even if Selim died, at the very least I didn't want his name sullied. Sorry, but I couldn't have told you his real name."

"This matter of the Diatessaron," I say. "I suppose you wanted the book sold? That's why things went sour between you and Selim?"

"That's stupidity. I got bent out of shape over a few pennies, and I broke his heart. I could have found that money from somewhere else. But the book was there for the taking so I thought, let's sell it and put this thing behind us. I couldn't grasp Selim's state of mind. Malik was luring him in with that Christian nonsense. His conscience got to him. He was having weird dreams. I couldn't understand it. I couldn't support him. 'If only...,' I keep saying, but what good does it do?"

She wipes the tears dampening her cheeks with a tissue from her bag.

"And that's how it is, Nevzat Bey. These are the things I hid from you. Now you've heard all of it."

"What about Bingöllü Kadir?"

She gets an indignant look in her eyes.

"That's not what we agreed on. The subject was Selim, not Bingöllü."

"But Bingöllü died because of Selim. You killed him by mistake."

"If it'll make you feel better, let's say that I did. Let's say Bingöllü's death was a mistake. But if you don't level with me, perhaps others will die by mistake."

Meryem's veiled threat doesn't affect me one whit. In fact, I find it amusing.

"If this keeps up, we'll lock the courthouse doors, Meryem Hanım," I tease. "Turn the business over to people like you."

"Don't joke, Nevzat Bey. I'm quite serious."

"So am I... Anyhow, let's get back to our deal. A promise is a promise. You did your part, now it's my turn. I can tell you this much, we weren't able to prove that Cengiz killed Selim. I'm sure he killed Malik, but I can't say the same for Selim and Mehmet. The picture is still incomplete."

"So then why do you suspect Cengiz?"

"Because he's the only one who has a motive for killing Selim and Mehmet. As far as we know, of course. New facts could create new suspects. It's hard to know for sure right now."

Meryem stares into my face for a bit, trying to establish the truth of what I've said.

"I'm being straight with you," I say, my tone trustworthy. "That's why you shouldn't go doing yet another foolish thing like shooting Cengiz, okay? You might kill the wrong man again."

She's finally convinced, and she pulls herself together.

"Thank you, Nevzat Bey. What you've said is very helpful."

"I'm sure it is. Whether or not I like Cengiz, saving a life is a good feeling."

Meryem gets up; it must be she doesn't want to listen to my sarcasm anymore. She minds her manners, however, and after asking my leave and shaking hands, she walks out of the room. After Meryem, Ali enters. He's seen her depart.

"What's up, Chief? What is the queen of the damned doing here?"

She really does look like the queen of the damned with that red hair of hers. I tell him about our conversation.

"Are we going to let this woman go strolling about like this, Chief?" he protests. "She's just looking for someone to kill."

"So, what if we took her into custody? What would we accuse her of?"

"I don't know, Chief. There must be something we can do."

"Nope, Ali. We can't do a thing. Forget about Meryem for the time being. Let's concentrate on our work."

I say to concentrate, but I don't have the mental capacity for work today either. Once I'm alone, Evgenia comes to mind again. Why am I like this today? Where did this Evgenia affliction come from? My hand goes automatically to my cell phone again. I tell myself to stop, that I'm not going to call. All right, I won't call, but what if Evgenia hasn't gone to Greece? What if she's still in Istanbul? And why not? Maybe she didn't go. It's possible she hasn't tied up all the loose ends yet. The prospect softens my resolve, and this time I dial her house. It rings deep, but no one answers. Just as quickly as it's sparked up, my mood is snuffed out. Yet my heart just keeps hopelessly hoping. I wonder if maybe she has gone to Tatavla. I could call there, but then if she really has gone... Wouldn't I look silly? Won't they say, "Evgenia left him, so now Chief Inspector Nevzat is looking all over, not knowing what to do." I don't want to suddenly become the object of gossip among Tatavla's employees. Which is fine, but how am I going to find out whether she's left or not? If I get up and go to Tatavla, not to see Evgenia, but just to have a drink? I did take friends to Tatavla last summer when she went to Greece after all. I can do the same. Yes, this makes sense, but then who am I going to take? What about Ali, and I could even invite Zeynep? Am I being overly familiar with these kids? Is there any such thing? Besides, they're doing a great job, and it'd be a small reward. We could talk over the case. Yes, it's a good idea. I'll invite the two of them to Tatavla.

Unfortunately, Zeynep can't make it. They had plans to visit relatives this evening and it would be rude to cancel. But Ali loves the invite. When I say we'll go together, he hesitates.

"Um, Chief, can we meet at Tatavla? I have a little something to do."

"Sure," I say, "We'll meet at the *meyhane*."

As I'm leaving the central station for the evening, I see Ali and Zeynep walking out together. So this is our maniac's little something to do. I guess he's going to drop her home. Or have they become boyfriend and girlfriend and not told me? I doubt that; when would they find the time to talk, to start a relationship? We've been running around, you take this crime scene and I'll take that one, for four days now. Yet when two hearts beat as one, they'll find the time and the place. If that's the case, good for Ali. He's more adept than I am. Or good for Zeynep; perhaps she made the first move. Zeynep could have initiated the affair before our swaggerer could swallow his pride and talk to her. In the end, whoever it was, it's a good thing.

I enter Tatavla with a peculiar excitement. Inside it's crowded, and most of the tables are already filled. I search the crowd for Evgenia in vain. As I stand gazing around, I spot Chef Ihsan. He hurries over.

"Chief, welcome! It's an honor." He gestures toward the table I sat at with Evgenia the other day. "Here you are. Your regular place."

"Nice to be here, Ihsan," I say, walking to my customary table. "How is it going?"

"It's okay, Chief. We're trying to adjust."

His words clarify the situation, but I ask in order to be sure.

"What are you trying to adjust to?"

He gives me a look like, don't you know?

"Evgenia Hanım's absence... You know, she's gone to Greece..."

"Yes," I say, trying to hide my disappointment. "She's left, hasn't she?"

"Seriously? You didn't go to the airport?"

I don't have it in me to tell him she never invited me.

"Work is really busy these days. A murder investigation... It's quite a complicated case."

"You'll solve it. No one's got away from you yet."

That's true. No one's escaped our clutches. One by one we've caught our criminals, but we have lost loved ones along the way. We have the right to be proud of ourselves. Of course, we don't say that.

"Let's see, Ihsan. We're doing what we can to solve it."

As I settle into the table, Ihsan asks, "Is anyone else coming, Chief?"

A friend of mine, but go ahead and bring the *rakı* and some white cheese, *meze* and whatnot. Let me slowly get started."

"Sure thing, Chief."

Ihsan has the table set in the blink of an eye. A plate of white cheese, another of sliced tomatoes, winter melon, salted bonito... Once he's put down all the *mezes*, he fills my *rakı* glass himself. I squirm with uncertainty while he pours. In the end, my eagerness is defeating my will power once more. Even so, I maintain my dignity, and instead of directly asking about Evgenia, I ask, "Is the Tatavla in Crete bigger than this one?"

"Supposedly, Chief. We talked to Evgenia Hanım an hour ago. She called a couple times before that, anyhow."

My heart twists. Evgenia doesn't hesitate to take an interest in the employees which she begrudges me.

"The *meyhane* in Crete," Ihsan continues, "is twice the size of this place. And it has a fair few customers too. Things are run differently there. Evgenia Hanım is trying to learn them."

"She'll learn," I say. "She just got there."

"Can I tell you something, Inspector?" he confides, adding water to my *rakı*. "Evgenia Hanım isn't too happy. I've known her since she was a child. Her voice sounds glum."

"I hope you are wrong, Ihsan," I say, reaching for my *rakı* glass. "I hope she'll be happy there."

Ihsan is more forthright than I am.

"I don't, Chief. If she's happy there, she won't come back. Evgenia should come back and be happy here. This *meyhane* isn't the same without her."

There's implication in his face as he speaks. These guys are all aware of everything that's happened. God only knows they are blaming me, inwardly saying, "You left the woman alone, and look, she's gone."

"Well in that case," I say, raising my glass. "To Evgenia's happiness, Istanbul or Crete, wherever she wants..."

Ihsan makes the rounds to see to the other customers, while the emotive voice of Müzeyyen Senar fills the *meyhane*.

Are these bastards playing these songs on purpose? As if I haven't suffered enough. Keep it to yourself, Nevzat, this is nobody's fault but your own. This is what happens if you get up and come to Evgenia's *meyhane*. Where the hell is Ali? My phone starts to ring as if in answer to the question. He'd better not say he's not coming; the donkey is late enough as it is. I don't want to sit here all alone like an orphaned child. But it's not Ali. On the screen is an unfamiliar number.

"Hello?"

"Hi, Inspector," says a cowed and panicky voice. "This is Caner. I'm sorry to disturb you."

"Caner, it's you? I couldn't figure it out for a moment."

"Inspector, there's something strange here. The squad car is gone from out front. And my landline rang a few times. I picked up but no one answered. Maybe I'm worrying over nothing, but..."

Cengiz comes to mind.

"All right, Caner. I'm coming. Lock the doors and don't let in anyone you don't know. We're on our way."

"I'll be waiting, Inspector."

I hang up with Caner and ring Ali.

"I'm almost there, Chief," he says sheepishly. "I'm coming up the slope."

"Don't come here," I say. "We'll eat in Sarıyer. Let's meet at Kurtuluş Square."

Chapter 33
I take cover behind Paul, and Ali behind Jesus.

We've lost an hour by the time we meet up with Ali and get to Caner's house in Sarıyer. As we approach the plot of land where the house is, I call Caner on the cell phone. There's no answer. This is bad. We need to hurry. Ali looks around and says, bewildered, "There really is no squad car. Where did these idiots go?"

"It's Cengiz's stunt, Ali. You didn't understand? He's much loved in the police force. He's using all the leverage he has."

"Maybe we should have asked for backup."

"Never mind that. I don't know who we can trust right now. The two of us can handle this."

"We will, but this is a lousy thing these men have done, Chief."

"Don't worry about it. It isn't the first time and it won't be the last. Look, let's park the car there." I point towards some half-finished construction. "If Cengiz is inside the house, he shouldn't know we're here."

Ali does as I've instructed. We quietly exit the car. Outside the night is like glass. Cold but bright. A huge full moon lights us to the door. If it were Evgenia with me and not Ali, if we were going to dinner rather than a raid, this silver light could have been the source of romance for our evening. Presently however, the full moon that shadows us step by step is a grave danger.

"Shall we try ringing Caner again, Chief?" Ali asks.

"No, let's not tip off Cengiz unnecessarily."

"Are you saying Cengiz is here?"

"We have to prepare for the worst."

"But maybe Caner didn't hear his phone. He was in the bathroom or wherever."

As Ali is talking, a black Ford parked on the side of the road grabs my attention. I point to a logo on the windshield.

"What does it say there, Ali?"

My assistant squints and tries to read it.

"It's a rental car logo..."

"There you have it. Cengiz is here."

I take my gun from its holster. My assistant isn't asking questions any more. He's also probably getting his gun ready for a confrontation. Before entering the property, I point to the building hidden behind a not so tall garden wall.

"Look. That's the house."

"There's a light on the second floor, Chief."

"You're right. They're upstairs." I point to the empty plot of land. "We'll have to go through this property to get to the house."

"About five hundred meters of open space," Ali mutters. "We'd better get across it fast, Chief."

"Fast and quiet. I'll go first and you come behind. And you can be my back up. As you approach the house, you'll see some statues, so don't be startled. Anyhow, once we get there it'll be easy. The statues will conceal us. The house is a duplex; the entrance is on the ground floor. I told Caner not to open the door for anyone. Well, I doubt Cengiz rang the bell to get in. If that had happened, Caner could have found an opportunity to call us. He probably entered from below. He must have found a kitchen window or a garden door or something. We can go in the same way."

Ali has quit surveying the property and is listening intently to me.

"No shooting unless we have to," I warn. "You know, we need a live Cengiz, not a dead one."

"I know, Chief."

"Okay then. Cross your fingers."

"We forgot about the cell phones."

He's right. We turn off our phones so there are no untimely rings to blow everything up. We're now ready to face Cengiz.

I come out from behind the wall and bolt across the plot of land. It's so light out that I can even make out the crowns of dried-up spiky thorns from last summer on the ground rushing beneath my feet. If Cengiz were to raise his head and look out the window, he would see us straight away. However, we get lucky. We reach the statues with no problems. Once we are among them, we stop. I take cover behind Paul, and Ali behind Jesus. For now, there is no movement, no sign that we've been spotted. Well, in any case, Saint Paul and Jesus are by our side, so God is with us tonight. After catching our breath, I gesture towards the back of the building. Ali nods to show he comprehends. We keep to the shadows as much as possible and advance to the rear of the house. I scope out the lower floor from between two unfinished statues. It's dark inside and nothing is visible. If Cengiz has set a trap there, he'll hunt us both like a hawk. If he does, he does; there's no stopping now. I slink between the statues and throw myself to the side wall of the lower floor. Ali falls in line. As we get to the window, we stoop down and slide behind the building. I wasn't wrong. The glass in the window of the door that opens inward from the small back garden is broken. Cengiz must have smashed the glass first before sticking his hand through and opening the door. I also reach my hand through the broken glass and turn the key on the back of the door. It gently opens. We need to be much quieter now. We slip in with the wind from outside and lean against the wall for a bit, waiting for our eyes to adjust to the darkness. Once we can discern the objects inside, we see that the place we've entered is the cellar. We tread lightly as we come out. A vast room opens in front of us. From somewhere comes the stench of wet soil mixed with mildew. There's a fairly big worktop in the middle of the room, around which are uncut marble slabs, iron molds, open-mouthed burlap bags and an array of other effects. Ali touches my shoulder and points to the stairs going up. We both approach them. And that's when we hear Caner cry out.

"Ahh! No, don't!"

"Hold on!" says Cengiz, in that voice I know so well. "You're already shouting. We're just getting warmed up. We're here till morning, son. There'll be other surprises as the night wears on. We can go downstairs for example. I'm really interested in that paraphernalia there. The chisels, the pinchers, there are even nails. The kind they hammered Jesus to the cross with."

"Please, don't," Caner pleads. "What do you want from me?"

"I want you to explain."

There's the sound of a slap on bare skin.

"Ahh! Don't hit me! Please stop it! I'll tell you whatever you want."

"Of course you will..." says Cengiz's deadpan, pitiless voice. "You'll explain your whole life. I want to know even about the moment you fell into your mother's womb. How your father huffed and puffed and your mother screamed with delight. You'll remember all that, and then you'll humbly explain it to me."

A slap stronger than the last one reverberates through the house.

"Ahhh!"

"You understand, Caner? I'll show you just who you are dealing with."

We have to get a move on or else this animal is going to pulverize him. We ascend the stairs, nice and easy.

"So you saw me going into Malik's house, did you? Huh? Tell me, Caner. Why aren't you speaking up? That's what you told Nevzat. Is it a lie?"

"I don't know," says Caner's timid, frightened voice, "I saw someone but... Stop, don't..."

The voice cuts out with another smack, after which the sound of a chair crashing to the floor can be heard. Ali and I exchange glances and then, maintaining our silence, we quicken our pace.

"Look, you fell down," says Cengiz, continuing to belittle him. "You can't even manage to sit in a chair, yet you've taken on something bigger than you."

When we get to the top step, we find Cengiz righting the chair with Caner tied to it. Unfortunately, he is facing the staircase, but he hasn't seen us for now because he's struggling with Caner's chair. Caner notices us immediately. As soon as he does, he gets excited and starts wriggling around in his chair with hope. Cengiz looks up in a rage.

"Sit still!"

That's when he sees us. He doesn't panic at all, his lips just break into an impertinent grin. He pulls his gun and ducks behind the chair.

"Well, look who's here," he says, pressing the gun to Caner's head. "Take another step and I'll kill him."

Both our guns are trained on Cengiz, or rather Caner's chair, although we don't have much of a chance. But Cengiz's situation isn't so bright either.

"Surrender, Cengiz," I say. "It's not possible for you to get out of here."

"We'll see about that. If I can't get out, you can't get out. I'll take this intellectual highbrow and one of you out with me." For a moment, he points his gun at me.

"You, for example, Nevzat."

Ali takes a step forward.

"Touch that trigger and I'll waste you."

Cengiz watches him, his eyes full of scorn.

"Oh, and our loose cannon is here too! Seriously, why is it you are always stuck to Nevzat like glue, Ali?"

Ali's tense face softens and a cheerful expression sets into his eyes.

"Because it's a big job," he says flippantly. "The orders come from above. High above, and very deep. They've changed their minds and they're going to clean everyone like you out of the police force. And they've tasked us with it. The operation will take a while, of course. But when it's done, Chief Inspector Nevzat will be the interior minister and he's gonna make me the Chief of Police. That's why we're together."

Cengiz, listening with great solemnity at the start, finally realizes Ali is just making fun of him.

"That's not what I heard. I heard Nevzat is your biological father. That's why your other daddy handed you over to Child Protective Services. What do you say to that, small fry?"

"What can I say? I'd say you got your own life story mixed up with mine, you son-of-a-bitch."

Cengiz guffaws.

"Disgraceful, swearing at your director like that. You didn't raise this kid too well, Nevzat. Once this thing has simmered down, I'll give you both some discipline. That is, if you come out alive." This time he turns his gun on Ali. "No, Nevzat, I won't shoot you. I'll shoot this nursling. I understood yesterday, you've really lost your marbles. You aren't afraid to die. Killing you would be a blessing. I have no intention of reuniting you with your wife and daughter. But if I kill this babe in the woods, your guilty conscience will double."

"Listen to reason, Cengiz," I say, knowing full well he won't. "Surrender. If you are innocent, we'll back you up."

"You will back me up, huh, Nevzat? Back up the man you tried to pull the rug out from under?" He gently slaps the back of Caner's head with his left hand. "Give up on the devious plan you made with this punk? With success just around the corner?"

"You've lost your mind, Cengiz," I say. "You really are a paranoid. That's why you killed Selim and Mehmet, anyhow."

He suddenly rages.

"I did not kill Mehmet and Selim!" He brings the butt of his gun down hard on Caner's head. "This bastard killed them." Caner's head swings forward. Cengiz ignores it and keeps talking to me. "But why am I telling you this when you already know it. Your scheme is built on it."

"You're mistaken," I start to say, but he's not listening anymore.

He puts the gun barrel to Caner's head again. "That's enough! Either pull the trigger or throw your guns down."

"We won't throw down our guns. You know we won't. But we don't want to shoot you, either. Let Caner go."

"Sure thing. I'll let him go and you can put me down like a dog. No, I don't think so. It's you who will drop your weapons."

Ali turns to me.

"This isn't working, Chief. This guy is going to shoot Caner either way. Let's shoot him and be done with it."

Whether he is bluffing or serious, even I can't understand. My gaze slips to Caner. The wound on his nose has opened up and the blood streaming from his lip has painted his chin red. He's shaking like a leaf.

"No, Ali. Everything will be by the book."

"Bravo, Nevzat," says Cengiz. "Now here is a sensible man."

"Don't get ahead of yourself, Cengiz. We aren't dropping our guns. If you want to shoot Caner, shoot him. It'll make our jobs easier."

"You're making a big mistake," he says, but the indecision in his voice gives him away. He won't shoot Caner. His eyes wander over Ali and me a bit. "Let's not shed police blood unnecessarily. Even though you set me up, my hand's not going for the trigger. But if I have no other choice, I'll do it. We're going to walk out of here." With his free hand, he begins to undo the rope tying Caner to the chair. "If you attempt to stop us, I won't consider that you're police, and I'll fire."

Once the ropes are untied, he instructs Caner. "Get up real slow. Any false moves and I'll polish you off."

He straightens up as Caner gently gets to his feet. Both are now standing. His hostage's chest is protecting him from us.

"Move it," he shouts. "Move aside from the stairs. Quick."

For a moment, our eyes meet. If any of the three of us pulls a trigger, it'll be a bloodbath. Ali's eyes are on me. I signal with my head for us to step aside. I move to the left of the stairs, and Ali to the right, opening a path.

"No! Both of you on the left."

Seeing us hesitate, he puts the gun to poor Caner's nostril.

"What did I tell you? You hear me? Shall I blow his head off?"

Helpless, we do as he says.

"Bravo. You finally both remembered I'm your boss."

Things are going his way, so the lowlife's mood is good. He drags Caner along with a slightly limping leg. When he gets to the top of the staircase, he turns the hostage to the left, that is, towards us.

"We'll go down the stairs side by side," he says. Watch your step, Caner. If you make a wrong move..."

Cengiz's eyes are on us, his gun barrel to Caner's neck, and they begin to descend together. While they do, he keeps talking.

"The next time we see each other, I'll have proof. And then I'll fuck you both up."

The swearing sets Ali off again. Ignoring the consequences, he takes a couple steps towards the staircase and shouts, "It's us who are going to fuck you up, you son-of-a-bitch!"

Cengiz, thinking Ali is going to attack, takes his gun off his hostage's neck and turns it on him. And that is when Caner makes a completely unexpected move. He head butts Cengiz with the back of his head. As Cengiz swings back, he hits the trigger. The bullet whizzes past within a few centimeters of Ali's head. Caner turns round with one agile motion and, before Cengiz has the opportunity to recover, he grabs hold of him and drags him down the steps. The two of them start to tumble. With Ali in front and me behind him, we follow them down. When we get to the bottom, we find Caner first. He's writhing in pain at the foot of the stairwell. We hear a door open. We look to where the noise has come from and see that Cengiz has escaped through the front door. Ali immediately pursues him, and I fall in after. But I must have twisted my ankle or something as I was going down the steps, because there's a shooting pain in my foot when I step on it. I can't move too fast. I get to the door and a gun fires. I hear someone cry out. It's Ali. In the light of the full moon, I see the blood running down his hand, and his gun is on the ground. At that same moment, I notice Cengiz. He hasn't seen me yet, and he comes out from behind the statue of Paul, his gun trained on Ali. He's going to fire a second time. I take aim.

"Freeze!" I shout out.

Cengiz first turns his head and we come eye to eye, then he aims. I fire. Both our guns go off at the same time. I hear the sound of shattering glass behind me. Cengiz stumbles in place, then falls at Saint Paul's feet. Keeping my gun on my adversary, I go over to Ali.

"Ali, are you all right?"

"I'm okay, Chief. I'm fine. Don't worry. Only my hand is wounded. You worry about Cengiz. The guy has nine lives. Don't let him get another shot off."

I don't take my gun off Cengiz even for a moment as I go over to him. He's lying still, his gun has landed in line with his right shoulder. Just in case, I kick the gun aside. Because his face has fallen into Paul's shadow, I can't make it out. I watch him for a little while. There's no movement. I slowly draw closer. I take him by the feet and pull him into the moonlight. His head slumps to the left from the force of the tug. His bewildered eyes stare up at Paul from where he lies at his feet. There's a black hole in his forehead, lit by the full moon.

Chapter 34
Either you will spill blood or your blood will be spilled.

The hospital is quite busy. A minibus carrying English tourists to the Bosporus Strait has nose-dived into the sea; two elderly Englishmen drowned and there are many injured. The doctors and nurses are bustling about. Despite the congestion, they find the time to deal with us. In fact, neither Ali's nor Caner's life is in danger. The bullet grazed Ali's hand, and it's a deep gash but his tendons weren't damaged. They treat it and wrap his hand. Caner's condition is a bit worse. He hit his head when he fell. He's dizzy and feels nauseous. He's having a CT scan and X-rays and the doctors are trying to figure it out. There doesn't appear to be hemorrhaging. Still, they're worried he could have concussion. They'd need to keep him under observation for twenty-four hours. The wounds on his face are being tended to, and they have him on an IV drip.

We don't leave Caner alone. Just in case; because we don't know what relationship Cengiz has with whom and don't want any harm to come to Caner at the last minute. While

I'm leaving the room to grab us something to eat, Sabri rings. His voice is panicky.

"What's going on, Nevzat? They're saying you shot Cengiz."

"Unfortunately, that is the case, Sabri."

"Damn!" he says. "So it's true. This is bad."

"If I hadn't shot him, he would have shot us. Ali's hand was wounded, and if I hadn't got there in time Cengiz would have killed him."

"You mean he shot first?" Sabri asks hopefully.

"Three times, no less. We just defended ourselves."

"That's good..." he says, relaxing. "Otherwise everyone would have pegged you a cop killer."

He isn't the least concerned about me. He's afraid he'll get into a bind because he supported us in the case. But my words are a relief. Now he has a solid reason to present to the ministers and the management. Even so, he's looking for an excuse to reprimand me.

"Why didn't you call for backup?"

"First we wanted to make sure the intelligence was correct. And when we got to the house, we had to act fast. Cengiz had started the torturing upstairs. If we hadn't got there on time, he was going to bludgeon the hostage to death. You should have seen the man's face. You'd have been mortified."

Sabri doesn't push the subject anymore, but before he hangs up, he says, "I'm going to send an independent investigator. You know the drill. We can't default on that."

"Send whoever you want. They'll tell you the same thing. The incident unfolded exactly how I said."

Once he's hung up, I get a couple toasted sandwiches from the hospital canteen, cola for Ali, *ayran* for myself, and then I go back to the room. Caner is lying in his bed, his open eye planted on the ceiling, waiting for the drip they've stuck in his arm to finish. As for Ali, he's afoot, talking on the phone, holding it in his good hand.

"No, Zeynep," he's saying. "You don't need to come down here. Someone will try to tamper with the evidence or something. You stay at the scene." He notices me and collects himself. "The Chief is also fine. He's here with me now."

"Give her to me," I say.

Ali holds out the phone.

"Hello, Zeynep, my dear."

"Chief, how are you? Are you okay?"

Her voice is fraught with concern.

"We're fine, Zeynep. There's nothing to worry about. All three of us are good. Ali is right. You should stay there. You be the last person to leave the crime scene. And keep a record of all the evidence, documentation, bullets and cartridges... Got it?"

"I understand, Chief. Don't worry."

"We'll see you at central station tomorrow."

As I hand the phone back to Ali, the thought occurs to me, why am I keeping him here? If one of us stays with Caner it's enough. The crime scene is more important, and then we wouldn't be leaving Zeynep alone. Despite my scolding the other day, I don't think Şefik has it in for me. Even so, it'd be better to send Ali.

"Ali, both of us being here is excessive. Why don't you go over to Zeynep."

He likes that, the rogue, but he doesn't want to make it obvious.

"As you wish, Chief."

"Finish your toast first."

As we're eating our humble meal, I smile and shake my head.

"Things never turn out as intended, Ali. We were supposed to be having ourselves a little feast this evening."

"Sorry," says Caner, eavesdropping on us from the bed he's lying in. "I ruined your evening."

A reflective expression appears on Ali's face. He looks at Caner amicably for the first time.

"Never mind. If it wasn't you, someone else would have come along to ruin our night. It's par for the course."

Caner smiles with gratitude.

"I owe you both huge thanks. You saved my life."

"You weren't so bad yourself," Ali mutters admiringly. "I had you pegged as a sissy. You're a pretty solid guy. The way you threw Cengiz down..." He finishes chewing the bite in his mouth and continues. "And those two kids you gave a beating in the chapel... You're really something."

As Ali keeps talking, my eyes slide over to the young assistant professor. I suddenly remember Cengiz's words. "It's this bastard who killed them," he'd snarled. For a split second I think to myself, could it be true? But no, of course not. Why would Caner kill them?

"There used to be a karate studio below my Uncle Daniel's house in Antioch," says Caner, elucidating. "That's where I learned how to fight. But I hate fighting. Even the thought of hitting someone is anathema to me."

Our Ali is not of the same mind.

"Don't say that. Sometimes it's necessary. If you hadn't acted so quickly tonight, for instance... Just think what Cengiz would be doing to you now."

"You have a point. I really do owe you both thanks."

My assistant turns to me. His gaze has softened, his eyes almost moist.

"And I should thank you, Chief. You also saved my life."

I take a sip of my *ayran*. "Never mind, Ali. You would have done the same."

For a moment, I fancy I see Cengiz in the depths of his companionable gaze. "You betrayed me, Nevzat," says a whisper in my ear. "You saved Ali, but you killed me."

I close my eyes to rid myself of Cengiz's ghost.

"What is it, Chief? Are you okay?"

"I got lightheaded for a moment. I'm fine now; it's passed. Too much excitement. I'm getting old, Ali."

"Whoa, hold on, Chief... You can still run circles around younger men."

"That's a bit of an exaggeration."

"I can stay if you want. Zeynep can handle things anyhow."

"No. No, I'm fine. There's no need to stay. In the meantime, find us a good team for tomorrow. We shouldn't leave Caner on his own for a few more days."

"Don't worry, Chief. I'll call Inspector Tayfun. He's on the level, you know. And he really likes you, too.

"Tayfun is a good idea. Although, I don't think anyone will make problems for us anymore. Cengiz is dead. It's over and done with. Still, we'd better stay vigilant."

Once Ali's gone, I turn out the light and lie down on the other bed. Moonlight spills inside. Caner is so tired he passes out. For me, a restless night of half-sleep, half-wakefulness commences.

In the darkest part of the night, I hear the door open. I open my eyes. The white light from the corridor splits the blackness and the shadows of three people near a stretcher fall inside. I sit up in bed. Two male nurses are wheeling a patient in on the stretcher. Behind them is a doctor. The light hits them from behind, so I can't make out their faces. I immediately warn them, "You're in the wrong place. This room is full."

"It's not the wrong place, Nevzat," says the doctor. I know that voice. If he talks a little longer, I'll figure it out. But he doesn't need to talk after all. When the door closes, it cuts off the backlighting and a face burnished by death emerges: Cengiz. Yes, this is Cengiz, the bullet scar still in the middle of his forehead, a self-assured smile on his lips. My hair stands on end.

"Are you surprised, Nevzat?" There's no hatred in his voice. He's speaking conversationally. As he did before these events, like a superior and a subordinate on good terms. "Don't be. Don't you know there is no death in this world for us? We are martyrs, Nevzat. We were martyred for this nation. Those who are martyred for this nation will never die."

As Cengiz says this, I look at the nurses. Their faces ring a bell, as well.

"Do you recognize them?" my ex-director elucidates. "It's Selim and Mehmet. Or Yavuz and Fatih... You don't deserve it but we've come here to help you. To open your eyes through tradition, to enlighten you with holy light."

His gaze goes over to the patient in the stretcher as he talks. I look over too, fearfully. The patient is completely covered. Except in the middle of the shroud is a large cross drawn in blood. Above, around where the man's neck would be, is dark red. It seems the bloodstains are concentrated here. Concentrated is the wrong word; the man underneath is bleeding profusely.

"Don't worry," says Cengiz. "He's still bleeding, but he has the strength to speak the truth." All at once, he reaches out and pulls the sheet back. Under it appears Malik, his decapitated head fixed in a makeshift way on to his neck. His whole body is bloody. I gasp. But the old man sits up, paying no heed to the blood seeping from his neck. I'm afraid his head is going to fall now and roll down to my feet. But his head doesn't roll, and he starts to talk, as easily as Cengiz said he would, ignoring the horror on my face.

"Jesus Christ has appointed us, Nevzat Bey." He takes out a crucifix. "God has appointed us." The voice is wheezy, but intelligible. "Not Jesus Christ himself, but his agent, Mor Gabriel... You remember Mor Gabriel, don't you? Mor Gabriel delivered the message. This is a divine project. A project to save people from meaningless lives. A person who has lost the meaning in their life is more treacherous than a demon, Nevzat Bey."

"Like you," says Cengiz, looking at me. He isn't accusing, he's just calmly trying to explain to me. "There was a time you also had meaning to your life: Justice. Then you learned that it would never come to pass. Because you understood people are evil. Yet you still didn't give in. You maintained your pure belief that you could carry out justice. Right up until your wife and daughter were taken from you. Not that this was without benefit to you. In this way, a new meaning came to your life. Finding your wife and daughter's murderer, taking their revenge. You furiously went after evil people."

"What a beautiful meaning," Malik drones. To see him, you'd think he was jealous of me. "Wrath is sweeter than honey, Nevzat Bey. But it is also one of the seven deadly sins."

"Even the greatest sin is better than a meaningless life," says Selim, who has been watching us all along. That's when I notice the knife with the cruciform handle still stuck in his chest. "Those who live without meaning should abandon this world."

"Love it or leave it," says Mehmet. Amazingly, he's free of paralysis and stands straight up in front of me. As he speaks, the cruciform knife buried in his chest sways rhythmically. "Love it or leave it. Love it or leave."

"Those who live meaningless lives are a virus that blows about on the wind," Cengiz says, employing another metaphor. "They reach everywhere, plague everyone."

"You are absolutely right, old friend," says Malik, smiling at his murderer. "Meaninglessness is the denial of God. Whereas meaning is the source of life, its joy and its driving force. And it is also what unites us. We all have a meaning that we choose for ourselves." He turns his lackluster eyes on me. "It's only you who doesn't have one, Nevzat Bey." He nods towards Caner's bed. "And your sinner lying there."

Cengiz's pale face chimes in.

"But unfortunately we cannot save both of you. It's either you or him."

"Our choice is you, Nevzat Bey," says Malik. "He is a hopeless case." He throws a condescending look towards Caner. "Agnostic."

Cengiz reaches out a hand and first pulls the cruciform knife from Selim's chest, and then from Mehmet's. He turns both knife handles towards me.

"Take them, Nevzat. Don't be afraid; take them. These knives will save you."

Malik, realizing my indecision, takes the knives as if to say, look how easy. He weighs them in his hands and then holds them out to me again.

"Take them, Nevzat Bey, please. Believe me, you will attain peace. You will instantly be free of the weight of this world and will be illuminated in the light of the true world. Take these knives, and like the dragon-killing hero Saint George, boldly stab the heart of the sinner who is guided by meaninglessness."

"No," I say. "I don't want to. I don't want to kill anyone."

A pained expression appears on Malik's face.

"Why don't you understand, Nevzat Bey? This is a condition for your salvation. Either you will spill blood or your blood will be spilled. In order to distinguish yourself from the others, to forge an identity, this is a condition. You need to disavow them. You must understand your importance. And the simplest way is to render the others invalid, to discount them, or better yet to annihilate them."

"By killing in this world..." Mehmet says, starting another cadence. "...by burning in the other world. By killing in this world, by burning in the other world."

"No," I say. "I won't do it. I won't kill anyone."

"But you killed me, Nevzat," says Cengiz, in the bewilderment of someone who has suffered an injustice. "You didn't hesitate to put a bullet in my brow."

"I protected myself. Myself and Ali."

"You don't leave us any other choice," says Cengiz. "I wouldn't want to do this to you." He shifts his expression of hopelessness to Malik. "No, Malik Abi, this one won't succeed. Let's try the other."

"No," I say. "Leave him alone."

"That's enough," Cengiz shouts. "Come on. Let's get him."

The three simultaneously jump on me. Selim and Mehmet hold my hands, Cengiz my feet. I thrash about trying to break free, but they are so strong that I can't move my hands or my feet.

"Stop it!" I cry out. "Don't touch me!"

In the meantime, Malik approaches Caner. He presses the tip of the knife in his right hand to Caner's forehead. With the touch of the knife, Caner opens his eyes. Strangely, it's as if his wounds have healed and there's not a single scratch on his face. Malik doesn't say a thing to him; he just holds the knives out the same way he did to me. Caner doesn't object at all. He gets up from the bed and takes the knives. Then just like a robot, he starts to slowly come towards me.

"Wake up, Caner!" I shout out. "Wake up. Snap out of it!"

But Caner neither wakes up nor snaps out of it. There's a look of grief on Malik's face as he walks alongside him.

"What are you afraid of?" he asks, looking at me. "Don't be afraid. You have failed at living. If nothing else you'll deservedly succeed at dying. And your wife and daughter are waiting for you. Don't you want to be with them?"

"No," I shout. "No!"

Malik pays no mind; there is neither pity nor hate in his eyes. He watches me with the profound peacefulness of a religious man performing his sacred duty. As for Caner, he comes and stands at my bedside with the two knives in hand. Cengiz, Selim, Mehmet and Malik all stare at me with the same peculiar gleam in their eyes. Caner's hands rise into the air. Malik gives an order, his voice reverberating in my ears.

"Come on, son. Save him!"

Caner plunges the two knives down on me at the same time.

I wake with a scream.

When I open my eyes, I see Caner above me. I look straight at his hands, but no, there are no knives. He is at least as scared as I am. His one eye, grown wide with dismay, is trained on my face.

"Inspector... Chief Inspector..."

His voice is anxious, agitated.

"All right, Caner," I say, sitting up in bed. "Okay, it was just a dream."

Chapter 35
"State Terrorists."

As soon as I've left Caner's protection to a trustworthy team, I waste no time getting to the station. From the moment I step through the door, the questions begin. Supervisors, directors, chief inspectors and officers, friends and enemies alike are all curious about last night's altercation. Ali has arrived before me, so he met the first wave of questions. It's a good thing too - all that's left for me is to explain the result. The fact that Cengiz fired the first shot softens the reaction towards us. Like Director Rasim's hatred of us, doubtlessly Cengiz's friends also increasingly hate us. But it's plain that we are in the right so they can't openly take a side. And it is known Sabri supports me, which also makes things easier. Nevertheless, Ali and I both give our written statements. And an inspector is sent to the hospital to take Caner's.

The moment I'm back in my office, the phone rings, before I've even had my morning coffee.

"A woman is calling you, Chief," says the officer at the switchboard.

"Who is it?"

"The wife of a friend of yours. She said it's urgent."

"Fine, put her through."

"Hello," says a woman's voice. "Am I speaking to Chief Inspector Nevzat?"

"Yes, that's me. Who am I talking to?"

"It's Neslihan. Cengiz's wife."

I don't know what to say. I freeze there with the phone in my hand, like I've swallowed my tongue.

"They say you shot Cengiz..."

I want to melt into the depths of my chair.

"Say something, Nevzat Bey. Is it a lie? It wasn't you who shot him?"

This must be what they mean by hell. There's no escaping this confrontation.

"I am so sorry..." I manage to say. "I didn't want it to be like this. He fired first. I had to defend myself."

I wait for Neslihan to shout at me, to throw insults, but her voice is composed. Too composed.

"It's not important, Nevzat Bey. I just wanted to say congratulations. You have two children now."

I can't understand what she means. I guess the poor woman has lost her mind from grief.

"We have two children, Nevzat Bey. Seeing as how you killed their father, you can look after them from now on. You know, Nevzat Bey, I felt sorry for you. You lost your wife and your daughter. Whenever I saw you, I would grieve. But I couldn't understand the magnitude of your pain. I thank you; now I know. You gave me a taste of that pain."

Neslihan is repeatedly and relentlessly stabbing me with the knives Caner couldn't stab me with last night in my dream.

"I... I never wanted it to be this way."

"Cengiz, the man you shot, do you know that he liked you? I think I told you that before. But he really did like you. He said you were different. Turns out you were. You really were. Slyer, crueler, colder." For a moment she struggles to find the words. "Despicable. You are despicable, Nevzat Bey. Someone not beyond killing their own supervisor in order to get ahead..." Her voice has got hoarser and begins to quiver. She can no longer control herself. "You are a murderer, Nevzat

Bey. You know that, don't you? A murderer who has killed my husband for your own gain. A monster..."

I don't hang up. I listen to this bereaved woman's insults till the end. I'm listening, so that she can get it all out, listening so she can spew out her anger, so she can get some relief. Perhaps she'll get used to the pain more easily this way. Perhaps she'll more readily accept the situation. I listen to her knowing full well she'll never accept it, in order to make myself feel better. I more than deserve this. Even if I've been trying not to dwell on it since last night, I have killed a man. Whether I did it defending myself and Ali doesn't change the fact that I'm a killer. The woman is right. I killed Neslihan Hanım and her two children along with Cengiz. And I killed a part of myself along with Cengiz. I got a little closer to my own death, added more to the dead.

Neslihan Hanım curses me until she's spent, and begins to sob. Then there's the sound of the telephone falling to the floor and the phone hangs up unbidden. But I just stay there like that, with the receiver in my hand. That's how Ali` finds me when he comes in with renewed excitement. Sitting at my desk gripping the receiver.

"What happened, Chief?"

I exhibit the phone.

"Cengiz's wife. I just talked to her."

He grasps the situation straight away. He throws out his wrapped hand angrily.

"That's not fair!" he says. "What were you supposed to do, Chief? Let the guy shoot us?"

"He had two kids, Ali."

"So what? He should have considered that before he got involved in this dirty business."

We come eye to eye. "It is no fault of yours, Chief," he says as if he were my elder. "Don't you dare think so. Cengiz was a criminal. You even offered to help him. It all happened in front of my eyes. The man didn't accept your help."

"But ultimately, I killed him.

"You didn't kill Cengiz, Chief. Sure, you shot him. But he killed himself."

My brain is saying Ali is right, but this gruff voice inside me vehemently disagrees: *None of this changes the fact that you are a killer.*

Ali comes over and plunks down in the armchair in front of my desk.

"Look, Chief, maybe you'll say I'm heartless or selfish or whatever, but I don't care. I'll be frank. I'd rather listen to all the woman's complaints or insults or whatever she said to you ad infinitum than get news of your death. So long as nothing happens to you."

I just stare. Ali sees his words are ineffectual and starts to protest. "What, instead of listening to the woman's complaints would you rather be crying over my coffin? In that case, I wish you hadn't fired."

"Don't say that, Ali. That's nonsense."

"Sorry, but Chief, you are the one who is talking nonsense."

Much more of this and I'll be getting a proper kick in the teeth from him. I frown and replace the receiver. But Ali is already caught up in it.

"What's going on with you? As though it's the first time in your life you've been in a conflict. What's with this moodiness, like some rookie officer?"

I start to laugh out of irritation, but the kid keeps a straight face.

"Why are you letting it get to you? If we get depressed over every criminal who dies..."

"I wish we could," I say, "but we can't. Even if we wanted to."

Ali, thinking I still haven't come to my senses, is about to take up his sermon again. "All right," I say. "All right, it's over. Let's get back to work."

He studies my face carefully. Seeing that I'm sincere, "Ha, that's it, Chief," he says. "Back to work."

That's when I notice the envelope he's holding. He takes a few photocopies out and hands them over.

"What are these, Ali?"

"You're going to love it, Chief. Turhan and Haluk stumbled onto something relevant in the newspaper archives."

As I take the photocopies, I realize he's talking about the officers we sent to the city library. We'd told them to scan the papers in the period between 1976 and 1980. Before looking over the photocopies, I ask, "Is it about Cengiz?"

"Not just Cengiz, all the men are here. You know how we were saying, how do Cengiz, Selim, Mehmet and Malik know each other? All the explanations are here..."

I look over the photocopies and he continues . . .

"Oh, and Chief, our guys saw Cengiz at the entrance to the library yesterday. He was on his way out. He had some papers and whatnot in his hand."

"Why didn't they arrest him?"

He winces as if he himself were responsible.

"They didn't have the nerve, I guess. The man is a director and our guys are quite young. It's not easy, Chief. But don't worry. I reprimanded them anyhow."

There was no point in pressing Ali anymore. When even the big boss Sabri couldn't arrest him, how could we blame two young cops? I wonder what Cengiz had been looking for there. Well, I'll get to these first. The photocopy I'm holding was taken from a credible newspaper's edition of 24 January, 1980 . The first of a series of articles. The man who had put it together was a renowned journalist, fearless, who years later died in an assassination that is still unsolved. The title of the article: "State Terrorists." Directly under the headline is a man's photo. Big forehead, thin face, and connecting eyebrows. He looks familiar but I can't place him.

"He's changed a lot, hasn't he, Chief?" Ali says.

"Who is this?"

"It's written under the photo."

"Malik Karakuş. This is Malik? It doesn't look anything like him. He sure has changed!"

"That much is to be expected. The man went through a big spiritual conversion. He went from being a sleazy arms smuggler to Saint Paul."

I suppose we will finally be able to learn the real story. But where my reading glasses are, who can say?

"As per your smart-alecky grin, I'm going to venture that you've read it. Tell me and save me the bother."

"Now Chief, these guys..."

"Wait. Wait a second. Where's Zeynep? She should hear this too."

"She's almost here. She's also come up with some interesting results. While I was leaving to come here, she was organizing reports from forensics and..." Before he can finish, Zeynep turns up at the door. Look at the gleam in that rascal Ali's eyes. They seem to be well past the flirting phase. Ah, youth! Love is a wonderful thing! I feel overcome with sadness. Evgenia! I still haven't spoken to her. Perhaps we'd never speak again...

"Hi, Chief." With the sound of Zeynep's voice, Evgenia's bright face recedes from the darkness of my mind. "I got the autopsy report. There are some significant conclusions."

"Very good, Zeynep. Come sit. Ali also has some interesting information. From years ago. I suppose we've reached the end, nothing will be left in the dark anymore."

"I'm not sure, Chief," says Zeynep, as she sits down. "There are some questions weighing on me. Things I couldn't answer."

Now what does she mean? Just when all the pieces are falling into place, what have we overlooked?

"God forbid, Zeynep. What did you find?"

"It's not what I found, Chief. It's a hunch. We need to talk."

Maybe she is just stuck on some insignificant detail generated by her meticulous work.

"We will, but first let's start with the relationship between Cengiz and Malik. Yes Ali, what's the situation?"

Ali pulls the photocopies over. "Their relationship goes back years," he says, launching into an explanation. "I mean, Malik said as much in his police statement."

His police statement comment sounds loaded.

"What do you mean by 'police statement'?" I ask. "He didn't say it anywhere else?"

"He didn't. Or rather, he rejected the statement. I'd better explain from the beginning, Chief. Now the journalist who prepared this article had come into a good few documents, from court records to police statements. He drew up the series of articles based on those. Some of the people, he interviewed. Others, including Malik, avoided talking. Anyhow, Malik rejected what he'd said in the police statement, both to the prosecution and in court, saying 'While in custody, I was tortured by the leftist Pol-Der police.' But so many weapons were found in the shop's warehouse that he couldn't save his skin. Yes, it was that warehouse raid that lead to Malik being taken into custody. That's also an ironic story. Now, some thief got into this guy's warehouse. He started collecting anything that was light in weight but heavy in value, but then he got distracted by a chest full of guns. He took one of them out and stuck it in his waistband. As luck would have it, when the thief left the warehouse, he fell in between two rival groups who had started to clash while flyposting the walls. This idiot thief couldn't get away and the police caught him. The police assumed he was a leftist and started beating on him, and this halfwit came clean, saying, 'I swear I'm not a leftist. I'm a thief.' After that, the warehouse he'd robbed was raided. Fifty-three guns, thousands of bullets and two dozen hand grenades were confiscated. Malik was immediately taken into custody. In his police statement, he claimed he had brought the guns from Syria, and the buyer was Senior Officer Orhan Çimender. When the police pressured him a bit more, he admitted that he'd given a portion of Senior Officer Orhan Çimender's guns to Cengiz Koçan, Selim Uludere and Mehmet Uncu. However, and here it gets really interesting, the police never brought in Senior Officer Orhan Çimender or the other three. These people were only summoned to court, and they gave their statements there as witnesses. Of course the four of them rejected the accusations. They said they knew Malik from his shop in the Grand Bazaar, and that they had gone there as customers. And Malik changed his statement, saying, 'When the police tortured me and coerced me to name my friends from the outlawed organization, I gave them the names of these four people I knew.' In the end, while Malik was condemned to a ten-year prison sentence for arms smuggling, these four were acquitted."

"Now it's clear," I mutter. "These guys were a gang from way back when."

"Okay, but then how did they become police officers?" says Zeynep, her eyes wide open in amazement. "These guys are all terrorists."

"The same way they avoided arrest when Malik gave their names," I explain. "There were powers protecting them. Powers inside the government."

Ali shows the photocopies to Zeynep.

"The articles are entitled 'State Terrorists' after all."

"Kids, this officer," I say, "Could Cengiz have killed him too?"

"No, Chief," says Ali. "We looked into it. Orhan Çimender died of natural causes. Three years ago, from prostate cancer. But you're right; if he hadn't died, Cengiz would probably have rubbed him out too. Because Orhan Çimender was the gang's leader, most likely."

Zeynep squirms uncomfortably in her chair.

"That's what I wanted to talk about," she says. "I'm not sure Cengiz is the murderer."

All at once, an icy wind blows over the table. What is she saying? Both our gazes are riveted on her face.

"The man confessed, Zeynep," I say. "Well, he did claim it was an accident. But he accepted that he'd killed Malik."

"That's exactly what I was going to say, Chief. Cengiz may have killed Malik. I suppose he was telling the truth by calling it an accident, too."

Ali is every bit as stunned as I am.

"What do you mean he was telling the truth, Zeynep?" he protests. "We all saw the crime scene. He laid the man down and chopped him. What kind of accident is that?"

"Take it easy, Ali. What I'm saying is supported by my findings. Malik's autopsy reports came back. Before his head was cut off, he'd struck it on something. He'd suffered a brain hemorrhage due to the impact. A fatal cerebral hemorrhage."

The two of us are trying to make sense of this. Ali beats me, as usual.

"How can you be so sure? What if Malik's decapitated head got a brain hemorrhage from hitting the door after rolling down the steps?"

"That's not how it happened. When I got to Malik's house, I came across something that nagged at me. Where the head was taken off was at the top of the stairs to the chapel. But I found blood at the bottom of the iron staircase that leads to the floor above. It wouldn't be possible for the blood to splatter all the way to the other staircase. I couldn't find an answer to that question until I read the autopsy report and understood. Cengiz and Malik fought. Or more precisely, Cengiz was manhandling Malik. The icon of 'Meryem and the Child Jesus' that fell over also corroborates this scuffle took place. I suppose Cengiz wanted to find something out from Malik."

"Or maybe he was threatening him," Ali says, putting his own theory out there.

"Okay, maybe he was threatening him. And meanwhile he hurled Malik down. The old man hit his head on the rail of the iron staircase. His brain hemorrhaged and he died. After being briefly disoriented, Cengiz decided to frame Selim Uludere's murderer for the death. Because Cengiz knew Malik, he knew that he'd thought he was Saint Paul. He laid the corpse down on the stairs to the chapel and cut off his head with the Roman broad sword. And he knew about the rituals of the first murder, so he wanted to underline a verse from the bible in Malik's blood. However, he couldn't recall which verse had been underlined in the Selim Uludere murder. He searched for a verse that would lend meaning to Malik's death. He found one, but it wasn't in the Zachariah chapter, but rather from the chapter called 'Revelation' which John wrote. 'And the beast was taken, and with him the false prophet.'***[1] The line describes Malik's situation very well. His depiction as a 'false prophet' is a reaction to Malik's belief of himself as Paul, and was a kind of accusation directed against him. But there's no connection to the verse in Selim Uludere's murder. And if the second line of Zachariah's words hadn't been in the case of Mehmet Uncu's murder, we might not have seen the peculiarity of this situation." Zeynep flips through the documents she's brought with her. "Look, this is what was written in the verse the murderer used.

" 'Awake, O sword, against my shepherd, and against the man that is my fellow, saith the Lord of hosts: smite the shepherd, and the sheep shall be scattered: and I will turn mine hand upon the little ones. And it shall come to pass, that in all the land, saith the Lord...'***2 And the verse goes on from there.

"In the first murder, I mean after he killed Selim Uludere, our murderer underlined, 'Awake, O sword, against my shepherd, and against the man that is my fellow.' As for the second murder, that of Mehmet Uncu, he underlined, '...smite the shepherd, and the sheep shall be scattered.' But in Malik's murder, it suddenly leaps to John's 'Revelation'. What's more, the lines under the verses are different. The lines in Selim's and Mehmet's murders are as straight as if drawn with a ruler. Whereas in Malik's murder, the line is drawn by hand, and a shaky hand at that."

Zeynep's remarks are compelling. They have stirred up some of the doubts in my mind again. But Ali doesn't seem inclined to change his view so easily.

"It's a possibility. Maybe Cengiz changed his mind. Tried to find an appropriate verse for each murder. If we read the lines that way, there's no inconsistency. In the line he chose for Selim, he wants to imply that all the negativity starts with the killing of the shepherd. Then for Mehmet, with 'smite the shepherd, and the sheep shall be scattered,' he tries to explain how the incident is tied to poor Yusuf's death. And Malik's is obvious: The false prophet."

We could use that reasoning too, of course. But what Zeynep says seems more credible. In any case, Zeynep keeps stubbornly expounding her theory.

"Sorry, Ali. That's a bit of a stretch. Even so, I could accept it if it weren't for one more discrepancy. Mor Gabriel. In both Bibles we found at the murders of Selim and Mehmet, Mor Gabriel was scrawled in the right-hand margin in the victims' blood. But in Malik's murder, there was no Mor Gabriel."

"So he forgot," says Ali. "I don't know, he overlooked it."

"He wouldn't overlook it," Zeynep resolutely explains. "These signs are like the murderer's signature."

"Maybe he didn't have time," Ali doggedly continues. "Maybe our murderer isn't that thorough. He just gave an implied signature this time."

"It's possible, but there is a distinct difference in style between the murders of Selim and Mehmet and that of Malik. All three of us saw the crime scenes. The perpetrator of Selim's and Mehmet's murders worked meticulously. Even though Mehmet had a messy house, our killer painstakingly executed his routine. But Malik's murder was a disaster. Cengiz's work was all over the place, fallen icons, blood splattered all around..."

As Zeynep expounds, I recall that Cengiz had left his car in the parking garage. If he really had come to kill Malik, why would he leave his car there? Could Cengiz really be so stupid as to make such an obvious mistake?

"No," Zeynep continues. "I don't think the same person committed all three murders."

Disappointed, Ali asks, "So Cengiz is innocent now? We've accused him for nothing?"

"Not for nothing, of course. Whether it was an accident or not, Cengiz killed Malik. And don't forget the shepherd murdered five years ago. In that murder, he conspired with Selim. Cengiz is not innocent. What I mean to say is, someone else killed Selim and Mehmet. I mean, the murderer is still out there."

If that is so, it is time to reshuffle the cards. A new game is starting. One that requires us to be smarter and calmer in order to win. But when Ali understands that Zeynep may just be right, he can't manage to keep his cool.

"So then who the hell is it?" Desperation is making him stressed out. "Are we going back to the beginning? Chasing after a secret Christian cult again? Because we have no one left as a suspect."

Unlike Ali, Zeynep is remarkably calm.

"Don't forget Meryem. We know things were bad between her and Selim. The woman was in a financial pinch. And we know she attempted to kill Selim before."

I think back to the conversation I had with Meryem. I'm trying to remember her words, bringing her face to mind.

"I don't think so, Zeynep," I say. Meryem didn't kill Selim and Mehmet. She took a hundred thousand dollars off Selim, anyhow. I mean, we can't approach it as a matter of money between them. More importantly, why would she want to kill Bingöllü if she herself were Selim's murderer?"

"To throw us off the trail..."

"Then she should have had Selim killed off instead of Bingöllü. Since Tonguç took the fall for the murder, she could have carried on her own dirty life from where she left off." I remember something Meryem said when she came here yesterday.

"Wait, wait. You know Meryem came here yesterday? Well, she mentioned something Cengiz had said."

"What's that, Chief?" Ali interjects. "Did he give another name?"

"Not another name but, apparently what he said was, he would find the real killer within a few days."

"Meaning Cengiz was also looking for the killer," Zeynep surmises. "This indicates that Cengiz wasn't responsible for the two murders outside Malik's."

"Of course..." says Ali, standing up. "The library thing. You know our guys saw Cengiz leaving the library. He was probably there searching for the killer."

It makes sense.

"Come on then. Get up; we're going." They both stare blankly into my face.

"What are you looking at? The truth is hidden in recent history. And recent history is in the library, in the newspaper pages our ex-director was fishing around in."

Chapter 36
A red stain on the chest of her white turtleneck sweater.

As we step inside the wooden doors of the library, a smell I haven't encountered in years greets us. The smell of paper and ink, cardboard and glue, wood and dust all combined and aging. My father would have called this the essence of civilization. A scent you can only perceive in a library.

In contrast to the crowd and the noise outside, there's a deep silence, a calm peacefulness in the library. Like a mosque, church or synagogue, but brighter, a tranquility more of the present than of the other world. The librarian is a young man with a pimply face. He's busy with a mountain of books in front of him, cataloguing them in his computer. When he notices us standing there, he says, "Yes?" But he looks dismally at us as if to ask where we came from all of a sudden. "How can I help you?"

Ali flashes his ID.

"Police! We want to see the newspaper archives."

The librarian stops his work at the computer and smiles.

"Again? For two days now we've been inundated with police. We'll be opening a police station corner soon."

He can't help his eyes wandering to Zeynep as he says this. It doesn't escape Ali, of course.

"Come on, brother," he says. "We're in a hurry. Show us where these archives are."

The librarian's face falls but what can he say; he gets up without a complaint.

"All right. Newspapers from which period?"

If we try to comb decades of newspapers, we'll be here till evening.

"Just a minute," I say. "This officer in the navy coat that came in here alone yesterday..."

He immediately remembers Cengiz.

"The Police Director."

"That's him. We want the papers he was looking at. Can you find them?"

A relaxed smile spreads across his face.

"You're in luck, sir. They're here; I still haven't put them back."

He turns round and goes towards the large table behind him. He takes the largest of the volumes scattered on the table and brings it over.

"Here's the one he was looking at. But which day, which edition, you'll have to find that yourselves."

"Thanks."

Ali takes the volume and we all walk together to a table in a nook at the back. The radio in Ali's pocket starts to buzz. At a table we're passing, a white-haired man with his nose buried in a thick book raises his head and throws us a reproachful look. Without a pause, Zeynep sticks her hand inside the pocket of Ali's leather jacket and takes out the radio.

"I'm turning it off, Chief," she says.

"That's good, Zeynep."

Ali and Zeynep sit next to each other at the table and I settle in crosswise. This way, the three of us will be able to read. Ali opens the volume, with its black cover and 1979 WINTER written in yellow gilding.

"Let's look at the front pages, Ali," I whisper. "There should be news of a murder or an assassination."

"Okay, Chief."

"How are we going to know if the incident relates to Cengiz?" Zeynep asks.

She's speaking in low tones like me. In fact, the library is relatively deserted. If we don't count the old man we disturbed, there are only two other tables taken, and those are quite far from us. I mean, there's no need to lower our voices so much, but for whatever reason Ali also expresses himself in a whisper.

"Maybe his name will be mentioned. Or we'll find someone else we know," he says, starting to flip pages. As he turns the pages, the three of us read the headlines for the news on homicides and try to find someone familiar in the photos. I say three, but really it's just the two of them, and at breakneck speed. While I'm still trying to make out the script beyond my spectacles, they've flipped to the next page. Eventually, Zeynep places a long, thin finger on an article.

"Stop. Wait, Ali. One minute."

The headline from the news she is pointing to is at the top of three columns: "Killed in Front of Child's Eyes". In the photo next to the article is a yellow car, a Murat 124 with its doors open. In the car is a woman, a man... The man's head is on the steering wheel, and if it weren't for the blood on his temple, you would think he was just tired or sleeping after a long trip. The woman's head has fallen back, her long hair spread across her seat, a red stain on the chest of her white turtleneck sweater. A child stands in front of the open door. Blonde, with glasses - a child who cannot believe, doesn't want to believe what he's seeing. He's nine years old at most. Horror on his face, a desperation impossible to convey.

"Caner," says Ali, with his usual acuity. "Isn't this our highbrow Caner?"

Zeynep must have already identified him too. In place of an answer, she begins to read a section:

"*TÖBDER teacher Emir Türkgil and his wife Elizabeth Türkgil were killed in front of their son Caner's eyes... The only eyewit-*

ness to the event, young Caner, has said the murders were perpetrated by three people. The boy, who helped officers with police sketches of the suspects, specified that one of the perpetrators had a strawberry birthmark on his wrist...

"Selim's wrist..." Ali mumbles excitedly. "And we were discussing whether it was a birthmark or a tattoo."

"Yes. I asked the medical examiners about it and they confirmed it was a birthmark," Zeynep clarifies.

"Wow!" says Ali. "Caner's parents' killer is Selim...."

"Don't forget about our former director Cengiz and Mehmet," I add.

"The men are a death machine," says Ali. "Who knows how many people they took out before getting to the six guys from the Mor Gabriel Monastery."

"Would you look at this man who supervised us!" says Zeynep, joining in Ali's amazement. She's grave, and sad. She repeats the question she never quite found an answer for. "How could these men infiltrate the police force?"

I should be the one to answer it, and I do know the answer. But I don't think my explanation will do any good, so I go back to the case at hand.

"Unfortunately, it's easy for them, Zeynep. Maybe one day," I say, although I'm not so sure that day will ever come, "one day we'll be completely rid of these men. But it seems for now someone else is dealing with them. This time they've met their match." I look Ali in the eye. "This kid we all looked down on as an intellectual snob, he has balanced accounts. He even managed to fool us." Now my gaze is on Zeynep. "Toying with us, convincing us all he's innocent. Yes, I think we have finally found our killer. It looks like Caner is our man."

I expect Ali to say he suspected him from the start. He doesn't say it. "You have to give him credit. He really hid himself well," he says, almost admiringly.

I consider saying that luck was on his side; if Cengiz hadn't gone and stupidly attacked Malik...

Zeynep's pensive voice scatters my thoughts.

"I can't understand the desire for a cultured man like Caner to take revenge. Is this a blood feud? If he found his family's killers, why didn't he go to the law? Why would he ruin his life, and when he has such a bright future ahead of him..."

"I don't know about that," says Ali, all but cheerfully. "Must mean the saying about murderers always returning to a crime scene is true. Caner was the first to come to Selim's house. And me, like an idiot I told him, 'A murderer always returns to the scene of the crime,' pretty much trying to scare him. Turns out he was toying with us."

It was time to wrap up this conversation.

"Come on, kids. We'll continue to talk this over later. Right now, we have work to do. Ali, you call the officer on security duty at the hospital. As soon as Caner's period of observation is up, have them bring him down to the station. After that, you can go over to Mehmet's house and give Caner's description to the neighbors. Let's see if he ever came round to the building. Seeing he got in so easily, maybe Caner and Mehmet knew each other. Zeynep, let's you and me get a warrant from the prosecutor's office and search Caner's house. Although I don't expect it, he may just have overlooked something, left evidence behind, a document, a trophy from his victims, or who knows?"

But in the afternoon when we get to Caner's house, I realize I wasn't wrong. We find not a single clue. *In the atelier, the metal for the cruciform-handled knives is right there in front of us. The steel scissors, files, welding machine... the whole apparatus that turns iron into crosses is here. But we find neither a piece of iron nor a draft of the model that proves Caner made them. So it'll be difficult to accuse Caner of the murders with such ambiguous evidence. And let's say we do, it'd be impossible to prove beyond the shadow of a doubt that he committed them. If we take him into custody, prosecution will release him straight away. Of course, that won't stop us taking him in. From his expression, his bearing and tone of voice, we'll try to piece together what's missing. We'll ask him about the murders and try to get him to confess. I don't know if it'll do any good, but we'll have a nice long chat with him.

Ali gets to the station before us. He also got lucky. Sıdıka Teyze, Mehmet Uncu's next-door neighbor, identified Caner from his description. In any case, she knew his name. He used to come with Yusuf to visit Mehmet. That's also strange; why would Caner knowingly give himself away? Why would someone who commits two near-perfect murders do something stupid like that? But the why is not so important; what's important is that we have this information. Because Caner said he didn't know anyone like this. It is possibly the only contradiction in his statement, if we don't count his concealing the truth about his family's deaths. Naturally I'm going to work on this inconsistency, like a boxer trying to take down an opponent by punching at his weak spot.

Chapter 37
Unfortunately, justice is not so easily realized with us.

The interrogation room is dim. Caner is seated at the end of the long table. I'm on a chair to his left and Ali is standing, planted directly behind Caner. The overhead lamp only illuminates Caner's head; his blond hair gleams like gold and the swelling and cuts on his face look more distinct in the shadows. One eye is still closed. His open eye looks out with concern, but it's hard to tell if it is genuine or if yet another scene from his acting performance is starting. With his bruised face, slumped body and anxious demeanor, he looks more like a poor, helpless victim than a murderer who skilfully killed two people. But we know that's not the case. It's a contradictory situation. Despite not having found any certain proof, we know that he has killed Selim and Mehmet. Whatever good that does.

Zeynep is outside the interrogation room and there's a two-way mirror between us. We can't see her but she can comfortably watch the inquiry. If we miss any detail, we'll evaluate it later together.

Neither Ali nor I have spoken since we came into the room. By means of our silence, we accuse Caner. He can't stand it for long.

"What's going on, Chief?" he asks impatiently. "What am I doing here?"

"You tell us, Caner. What are you doing here?"

"I don't know. The police from the hospital brought me. I told them I wanted to go home. They said, 'Chief Inspector Nevzat wants a word with you.' "

Ali leans down from behind him and rests his chin on Caner's right shoulder. "We decided to keep you safe," he murmurs in his ear. "No objections. You more than deserve this."

Caner doesn't understand. He tries to turn around. Ali catches his head in his left hand.

"Keep still. This room has its own rules, Caner. Wait, let me explain it in a way that's appropriate to your level of culture. Just as the moon has less gravity than Earth, this room has less freedom than the outside. You can't just go turning your head back and forth however you want. And you can't go telling whatever lies you want either. Outside this room, you can lie, trick people and even commit murder. You can even kill two people and try to frame someone else for it."

The concern in Caner's single eye grows; when he's sure of the gravity of the situation, he throws his hands up and says, "I don't understand what you are talking about."

Because his right hand is still bandaged, Ali slaps Caner's hand with his left.

"What did I say, Caner? Aren't you listening to me? Not one move without permission in this room!"

Caner turns his eye on me.

"What's going on, Chief?" he asks again. "I don't understand any of this. Please won't you explain?"

I give him an offended look.

"You're still acting, Caner. Ali is right. We've decided to hold on to you. Because you managed to cheat us. You've been toying with us for days. Don't be humble, this is not an easy thing to do. It takes talent, and at the same time courage and intelligence. You were great up till now. But it's over. We figured everything out, Caner."

The surprise in his eye gives way to strong determination. This guy won't fold easily.

"What did you figure out, Chief?"

"What do you think?" says Ali, coming alongside him. "Your potential. We've been lamenting that for years there have been no serial killers in this country. You put an end to that. Although, you did only kill two people in total..."

Caner finally gets angry.

"What are you saying? I don't understand!" he protests.

With one sudden move, Ali reaches out and takes Caner by the collar, shaking him hard.

"Keep your voice down!" Then he softens, lets go of Caner's collar and continues calmly. "Remember what I told you. There's less freedom in this room than outside. That includes the freedom to raise your voice. What'll happen if you raise your voice? Well then, that life we saved last night, we'll be forced to take ourselves. Got it?"

Caner pays no heed to Ali's erratic behavior anymore.

"I don't understand," he shouts. "What are you trying to do? Just tell me. Who have I tricked? Who have I killed?"

"I'll tell you right now," says Ali, keeping up his sarcasm. "Selim Uludere and Mehmet Uncu... You'd have killed Officer Orhan Çimender too if he hadn't died of prostate cancer. You attached particular importance to our former director Cengiz Koçan. You had other plans for him. Like framing him for the murders."

"This is all nonsense. I'm sorry but you are all out of your minds. Why would I want to kill those people?"

I look into Caner's open eye and articulate, "Because they killed your mother and father."

There's phony amazement in his beat-up face again. I ignore it.

"Don't deny it, Caner. We know everything. You were also in the Murat 124 while your parents were being murdered. You were sitting in the back seat. We read it in the papers; there's your very own statement. You say there were three people. One of the shooters had a strawberry birthmark on his right wrist..."

He's still feigning ignorance.

"Fine, but what does that have to do with the murder of Selim, or as I knew him, Yusuf Abi?"

Ali lands a vigorous smack to the back of his neck.

"Didn't we say no lying, Caner? Look, you are asking for it."

"I'm not lying... And I don't know what you are talking about. You aren't explaining clearly..."

Ali gets ready to slap him again but I stop him. We aren't in any position to torture Caner into talking.

"Leave him, Ali. Come sit over here." I turn to our suspect, who has pulled his neck in to protect it. "Look, Caner, you know very well what we are talking about. Save your breath. We got hold of some very powerful evidence. You can't get out of this. There's no escape. Your only resort is to cooperate with us. We understand why you committed these murders. Cooperate with us, and we can help you."

He is so certain that he's left no trace behind that he calls our bluff.

"I don't know what you're talking about. I don't even know what you're accusing me of."

He wants to find out what we know. Or if he left some stone unturned. That's the thing that is eating at him right now. Without mentioning what we have, I start to explain in the manner of a detective who has wrapped up a case.

"Listen up then. Let me tell you your story. Everything started with Malik introducing you to Yusuf, that is, Selim Uludere. Or more precisely, with your seeing the strawberry birthmark on Selim's arm. Malik was oblivious to everything, of course. Selim was trying to understand the value of The Diatessaron stolen from the Mor Gabriel Monastery. Because he was incapable of holding down any job. His money would melt away like thawing snow, and the help he got from Cengiz and Mehmet wasn't enough anymore. He was hanging in there for the time being, and could possibly have endured another year or two, but then he planned to sell this book and build a brand-new future for himself. He found Malik, the man who had supplied them with guns back in the days of terrorism. He knew that he had once dealt in smuggling historical artifacts. I don't suppose Malik was happy to see Selim there. The old man didn't want to get involved in that business anymore. But he couldn't manage to completely extricate himself from his dirty past. Or maybe he was doing it to have his back covered. Because he was completely convinced he was Saint Paul. In a country where the population is ninety-nine percent Muslim, this delusion was quite a dangerous thing. It must have been why he kept his relationship up with both Cengiz and Selim. But Malik, learning Selim's intentions, had mixed feelings. It saddened him that a holy book like the Diatessaron had been stolen from a monastery. As Saint Paul, it suited him to return the book. That's why at every opportunity he reminded Selim that selling the book was a big sin. Likewise, Cengiz and Mehmet also kept warning them not to sell the book. So they wouldn't get into trouble, raking up the past. Anyhow, Selim was in no hurry. First, he wanted to find out what the book was worth. That's why they went to Malik in the first place. But Malik was confused. He couldn't yet figure out what to do. He decided to throw the ball to someone else, that is, you. 'There is someone who knows more about this than I do,' he said, introducing Selim to you."

"So far, everything you've said that relates to me is true," says Caner, with a positive shake of the head. "It happened jus as you say."

I smile and shake my head too, albeit negatively.

"But maybe it didn't happen that way, and maybe you recognized Selim the moment you met him. We'll know better once you've confessed."

My two eyes meet his one. His single eye reflects nothing, like an old mirror.

"Yes, that is how you met Selim," I continue. "When Selim heard you were knowledgeable on the subject of Christianity, he wouldn't leave you alone. He didn't want to sell the Diatessaron for less than its worth. Meanwhile, under Malik's influence, he may also have taken a secret interest in Christianity. As for you, initially you were bothered by Selim's preoccupation, because for you this was just a small-scale consultancy job to earn some extra cash. That is, up until you saw the birthmark on Selim's right wrist."

"You're wrong there," he interrupts. "I didn't see any birthmark..."

"Come on Caner," says Ali. "Don't insult our intelligence. You knew Selim for almost two years. There are summers and winters; the man wears short sleeves, t-shirts. How could you not have seen the birthmark? We saw the man once and immediately noticed it."

"I don't know. If I saw it, it didn't register."

"Let's see what else will arise that you didn't register," I say insinuatingly. "As soon as you see that birthmark, you harbor suspicion. You think Selim might be one of the murderers who killed your parents all those years ago."

"No, I never thought that..."

"You didn't think that but then why weren't you surprised when we said Selim and his friends were your parents' murderers?" Ali hits the nail on the head.

"They're the ones that murdered my mother and father?" he asks, as if I hadn't just said as much, and he were hearing it for the first time.

His reaction is so exaggerated that even I smile.

"Holy cow! It was them!" says Ali, mimicking Caner. He gets serious and continues. "Come on, Caner. Now you are insulting your own intelligence. You aren't going to say you haven't understood anything discussed all morning, are you?"

"I don't understand, of course. First the Inspector talks, then you. You are accusing me of homicide but there's no solid motive for you to base it on, nor one shred of evidence."

"Not one shred, but many shreds, and a whole lot of motive, actually," I say calmly. "It is so clear you committed these two murders that the prosecution won't have the slightest uncertainty when they hear it."

He gets an arrogant smirk on his split lips.

"How is it clear?"

"Shut up and listen, and you'll understand."

He goes quiet because he needs to know our thoughts.

"When you first saw the strawberry birthmark, you couldn't be sure," I start to explain again. "With a secret curiosity, you began to research the man who called himself Yusuf. This is why, even though you really had nothing in common, you became friends with the phony Yusuf. You got him to trust you. You went all the way to Mardin to find out how the Diatessaron was stolen and perhaps to research Yusuf Akdağ. You're not going to deny you know the area well I suppose..."

"Why would I deny it? I know the area well. I've traveled around there a lot. Anyhow, Inspector, why don't you finish what you're saying and then I'll explain?"

"Your findings confirmed your intuitions. The man with the strawberry birthmark was not the real Yusuf Akdağ. You read the papers from that period, learned the story of the six youths who suffocated in the cave after being taken from the Mor Gabriel Monastery - and that an inspector by the name of Selim Uludere had died in a thresher. You tracked Selim and came across Cengiz and Mehmet. And let's not forget Senior Officer Orhan Çimender, although unfortunately he was long dead by the time you found him. Cengiz, Selim and Mehmet, or if we call them by their code names, Timuçin, Yusuf and Fatih. This is how you uncovered the gang that killed your parents."

There's a mocking expression to Caner's battered face.

"Nice story. So why would I want to kill them when I could hand them over to the law? Would a man like me be motivated towards a blood feud?"

"Good question," I say. "But you've already given us the answer."

He narrows his eye and racks his brain.

"While I was taking you home... You know, we were talking in my car... You were saying how life had no meaning. That's why you came to Turkey, you said. To find meaning. But you talked about how this country was so cruel. Strangely, it's this cruelty that gave your life meaning too. You thought you couldn't get any results in this country with the methods you knew. I mean, if you had gone to the law saying these people are my parents' murderers, you thought nothing would come of it. And I should say you are partly right. Unfortunately, justice is not so easily realized in Turkey. The reality of this became one of your main motivations. And suddenly, or maybe after days of deliberation, you made up your mind to punish the killers yourself."

His face lights up with a sarcastic expression.

"And this is how I found meaning to my life."

"Wipe that look of ridicule off your face. It is exactly what happened. Maybe when you were going to Italy you were full of hope. Christianity or the education you got there could have made you forget the trauma you experienced as a child. But that wasn't going to last forever. Your frustrations on the subject of Christianity, your life in Italy and your return to this country dragged you into a void. And that's right when you ran across Selim. You realized he was one of your parents' killers. Your childhood trauma was rekindled. Perhaps you related your present unhappiness and lack of meaning in your life to your parents' deaths. It was Selim, Mehmet and Cengiz who paved the way for this. And you wanted to turn your life around, so to speak. Yes, revenge was not your sole motive for these murders. You wanted to give meaning to your life. And in this way, you were going to obtain the justice that for years had eluded you. That's why you killed them. And it wasn't hard. Because you'd gained Selim's trust, you succeeded in influencing not just Selim, but Meryem and Mehmet too. Selim's cannabis habit made things much easier for you. By the time you'd finished your preparations and entered the house, Selim was already high as a kite. You wrote that scenario well beforehand. Selim's recurring dream would make for a suitable murder. While he was unconscious, you took out the cruciform-handled knife you'd made in your atelier and stabbed him twice in the chest. You wrote 'Mor Gabriel' in the margin of the Bible, then underlined the lines in Zachariah with Selim's blood. That same day you went to Mehmet's. You killed him with a cruciform-handled knife as well and nailed his hands to the cabinet. Once more, you wrote Mor Gabriel in the margin of a bible you left in his lap, and then continued with the second verse from the prophet Zachariah, underlining it in Mehmet's blood. That wasn't enough, and you wrote this message on the television too. Your aim was to bring Yusuf's true identity out into the open. So you wrote 'Mor Gabriel' and underlined the two verses where the shepherd's name was mentioned. You wanted to draw attention to the murders Selim had committed in Mardin, which would lead us to Cengiz. It would raise our suspicions. But something went wrong. Cengiz found out Selim had been murdered and suspected Malik. He went to his house to make him talk. While they were arguing, he slammed him too hard, and poor Malik hit his head on the iron staircase and died. At that point, you were in the coffeehouse, waiting with bated breath for the outcome. You were itching to go into the house. But then you got caught inside. Malik had been killed and you looked like the culprit. But you managed to tip the scales in your favor because you were telling the truth. However, Cengiz started to realize there was more to it. He thought the murderer was Malik or some Christian sect around him. When he came to my house, he was very surprised to learn that Mehmet had also been killed. There was no reason for Malik to kill Mehmet. After that, he scrutinized everyone who had had a relationship with Selim one by one, and when he understood that it couldn't have been Meryem, he concentrated on you. He did a little research on you. He came across some interesting findings. You were the son of a TÖBDER teacher who was killed years earlier. He had no doubt anymore that you were the murderer. He went to your house to make you talk, and if we hadn't got there, he might have succeeded. But you were on the ball again, and you called us as soon as you saw the squad car in front of your house was gone. We came and saved you. How thrilled you must have been. You killed Selim and Mehmet with your own hands, and had us kill Cengiz. You finally avenged your family. More importantly, you gave your life meaning."

"I wish I could have," says Caner. His one eye gleams with hatred like a steel pea. "They deserved death a thousand times over." He looks at Ali. "You were just saying there hasn't been a proper serial killer in this country for ages. But there has been. And the state rewards them by taking them into the police force. I'm sure there are dozens more like Cengiz. If you really want to take on serial killers, go look at the old files. The files before the military coup. Files cooked up by the deep state in collaboration with American intelligence, in which fascist nationalists directly, and certain armed left-wing organizations indirectly, played a part. You will come across some of the world's most interesting serial killer cases in those files." He turns his eye on me again. "And when it comes to you, Inspector, I know you are an honest man. You have your own sense of morality and justice. But stop messing with me. It'll be a futile effort. I didn't kill them. No matter how hard you try, you won't be able to prove it. Because you have nothing on me."

Ali is wired, but he can't put his energy into words. He's simmering, just staring Caner down.

"We do," I cut in. "We found the iron you used to make the crosses in your studio."

"Come on now, Inspector," he says, laughing confidently to himself. There are thousands of those in ironwork shops. Anyone can get it."

"You lied to us. That is also important proof."

"What did I say?"

I list it all out in one breath.

"You hid your past, you misdirected the investigation..."

"I didn't hide my past. Whatever you asked, I explained it all. I knew Yusuf Akdağ as Yusuf Akdağ. You told me that he was Selim Uludere, and that he was my parents' murderer. After he was dead, in fact."

"What do you have to say about Mehmet's neighbor, Sıdıka Hanım? She's identified you."

He doesn't panic at all.

"That's normal. It's normal that Sıdıka Teyze knows me, because Yusuf Akdağ introduced me to Mehmet. We came and went from Mehmet's house together. Isn't it a humanitarian duty to help people with disabilities?"

In the end, Ali's anger defeats him, he can't take it and he slaps Caner hard across the face.

"Stop lying!" he shouts. "Did you not say you didn't know him? Did you not say Yusuf never talked about his friends?"

Ali's slap reopens the cut on Caner's lip and a thin string of blood dribbles down his chin. But he doesn't care. He just brazenly smirks and answers.

"No, we never spoke about Mehmet. You simply asked me about someone called Fatih. How should I know Fatih was Mehmet's code name?"

Ali is about to lose it. He clenches his teeth and prepares to hit Caner again. I stop him.

"Don't, Ali. Leave him."

Ali, his face red with rage, stifles himself with difficulty. Truth is, he also realizes we are helpless. That's why he's so enraged. He's thinking this highbrow intellectual has beaten us. He's right, but anger won't solve a thing. All we have to do is to wait. Wait patiently until we find new evidence or another eyewitness.

Chapter 38
Justice through death serves no purpose at all but to glorify death.

We keep Caner in a holding cell that night. Zeynep, Ali and I sit for hours preparing a detailed summary of proceedings, containing our findings, our thoughts and impressions, and Caner's statement denying all charges. The next morning, Ali and I take the summary to the prosecution together. As for Zeynep, she gathers all the files and begins to review them to see if there is any point we missed. Prosecutor Mümtaz Bey is a young man. Young, but a whiz kid legal expert. We've worked together on a couple cases and I couldn't fault him on any thing. Anyhow, because it piqued his interest, he's followed this case from the beginning. He reads the summary and questions Caner. He must be quite baffled in the end, because he asks to speak with me as well. I explain what happened in detail. He asks question after question. He listens intently, taking notes. Our discussion lasts two hours. When the questions are exhausted, he sighs deeply.

"We cannot arrest this man, Nevzat Bey," he says reluctantly. "I suppose you are right; the individual is most probably

Selim and Mehmet's killer, but we have neither the evidence nor the witnesses to justify arresting him. Even if I do, the courts will just release him immediately. So we'll have to let him go. But don't worry; I will request that he stand trial as a defendant. Maybe in the meantime you'll come up with some new testimony or witnesses."

When I come out of Prosecutor Mümtaz's office, I find my assistant at the door of the room where we're holding Caner. From my face, he understands what happened.

"He's getting off, isn't he, Chief?"

"Not completely. He's going to be tried, but he'll be on the outside."

Strangely, Ali doesn't get upset.

"What can we do? If the judiciary says so..."

We have the guard open the room, but I go in alone because I have something to discuss with Caner. He's won this round but I want him to know how I feel. I don't know why. Perhaps because like Malik, I still haven't given up hope on him. I don't take Ali with me, afraid he'll continually butt in.

Caner's one eye is on my face. The other eye has started to open a bit. He's a clever kid and he grasps the situation straight away.

"In the end it's been determined that I'm innocent, hasn't it, Chief?"

"Nothing's been determined yet. Because you're not innocent. No matter how merited your reasons, you're a murderer, Caner. Nothing can change that fact. From now on, you will live with the burden of those you killed..."

He starts to get insolent, certain that he's won.

"You mean like you?" he says, reminding me of Cengiz.

"Yes, Caner. It's true; I'm a murderer just like you. I'm the one who killed Cengiz. Except that I didn't plan it out or set it up. It was just how things developed. I didn't want to kill Cengiz. Not Cengiz or anyone else. Because when you kill someone, you kill a little of yourself too. A little of your life, your soul, your innocence. The dead are strange beings, Caner. After we bury them, even once they've rotted away and their bones have disintegrated, they continue to live among us. They'll seep into our dreams, cast shadows over our imaginations and blacken our hopes. That's why I don't want to kill anyone. Because after killing someone, I know that life won't be the same again."

My words have no effect. The delight in his face doesn't decrease one iota. But he continues to keep his silence.

"I'm wasting my time, aren't I?" I say. "Maybe you'll go back to living the same way, or more peacefully, more contentedly, for that matter... But don't you think you resemble the people you've killed? The people who make this country unlivable?"

The merriment in his bruised face vanishes for a moment, but just for a moment.

"I don't resemble anyone," he says, blinking his good eye cleverly. "Because I didn't kill anyone."

"Stop lying, Caner. You did kill them, but we can't arrest you because you were so crafty about it. I won't say intelligent, because intelligence doesn't require darkness or secrecy. I have no respect for intelligence that requires secrecy or darkness. I call that deviance, or cunning.... Sure, you appear to have won, and the prosecution is letting you go for now. But only for now. And soon, believe me it'll be very soon, we are going to turn up some evidence that will put you away for years. Be sure of that, because there is no such thing as the perfect murder. You have absolutely overlooked something. And we will find that thing."

A shadow falls across Caner's face; foreboding extinguishes the gleam in his eye. He's trying to understand if I have something on him. But it doesn't last long and he recovers.

"You're wrong, Chief. You won't find a thing. No evidence, no witness, no lead. Because I haven't killed anyone."

I run out of words. And he has nothing to say anyhow. He's made his case through murder rather than words. Now he just wants to escape these four walls and get back to his freedom as soon as he can. I could tyrannize him, take him down to the station, maybe keep him for one more night, but it wouldn't do any good. We have no other choice but to release him. And that's what I do. I take off his handcuffs, open the door and step aside.

"You're free to go, Caner."

"Thank you, Inspector," he says. As he approaches the door, he suddenly stops. His eye is on me. "If it really had been me who killed them, wouldn't you give me any credit at all?"

I shake my head resolutely.

"No. Justice through death serves no purpose at all but to glorify death."

He laughs quietly.

"That is true. I would have felt exactly the same."

We step through the door, and amazingly Ali's not around. Where did the kid go? Caner reaches the outer door, and I walk beside him. All at once, Ali pops out in front of him. Caner must still be leery of him because he takes a couple steps back. Ali is jovial.

"So, you're off scot free, Caner Efendi," he says. "Don't get too used to the feeling. We'll be seeing you again soon. Actually, it'll be like you never left us. We really like you, so we'll always be breathing down your neck."

Caner, taking care to keep his distance from Ali, takes one or two more steps towards the door, although he can't help heckling him.

"Actually, I like you too. You should come over for dinner. I've already invited our Chief Inspector. I'll make you some spaghetti Bolognese."

"We'll be there, my friend, don't you worry. But you'll be making your best pasta after prison."

Caner's face is flustered. Are we not going to let him go?

"Don't be scared, friend," says Ali, delighting in this little temporary deception. "We're not throwing you in right now. Later I mean, when we catch you again. One way or another, you will fall into our clutches." His gaze shifts to me. "Although, we'd throw you in now if the Chief would let us. Man, how I'd make you sing. Like a nightingale, I tell you. Anyway... this is also nice. Just when you've got used to your freedom, we'll come for you. At midnight, in the depths of your sleep, or right as you are savoring a meal, or else in your lover's embrace. Or maybe while you are lecturing your students. Just as you are reciting, like it says in the Bible, 'Thou shalt not kill.' It'll be a moment you never forget, of course.

Same as the moment you stabbed a knife into your victim's chest..."

Caner frowns. His mood is completely ruined now. He picks up his steps and rushes for the door.

"You're mistaken," he says. "You will understand you were mistaken..."

"We've already understood all there is to understand, Caner Efendi," Ali calls out behind him. "Go on. Godspeed! But as I said, we'll be seeing each other again soon. Very soon."

Caner hurries out the door. We follow him out. Once we are outside, we see the crowd circling around him. An army of reporters with cameras in hand... Apparently, someone from the inside has leaked the news again. As I'm considering how we'd do best not to be spotted, I fancy I make out the long face of Henna Meryem's man Tayyar among the crowd. I bolt into the crowd in a panic. Before I even have time to warn Ali, a gun fires three times in succession. The crowd of reporters scatters like a clutch of chicks. Ali and I draw our guns and head towards Tayyar's stout form, standing there in the middle of the dispersing crowd. He sees us too.

"I surrender, I surrender," he says, dropping his weapon.

We get Tayyar down on the ground and cuff him. Caner's lifeless body is lying a few meters beyond. The front of his coat is open, and three bloodstains spread slowly across his blue shirt. I go over to him. His one eye twitches and there's blood on his lip again. He notices me, and a pained yet victorious smile appears on his face.

"It didn't work, Chief," he struggles to whisper. "It didn't work. Look, now you'll never get me."

Chapter 39
The meaning of life is people, Nevzat. People.

A pungent odor woke me. I knew this smell. The smell of a church that had remained shut for years. Of oil lamps, crumbling stone, corroded marble, rotting wood, tattered pages and molding corpses. I should have been horrified but I merely gazed around. First, I saw a man, sleeping on the sofa. Then a gently stirring black figure. A formless, vague shape... A jet-black silhouette... The man on the sofa saw the stain too. He slowly sat up and smiled at it.

"Mor Gabriel," he murmured.

"Mor Gabriel," I murmured. Where had I heard that name before?

With silent steps, the figure all but flew over to the man on the sofa. As it drew closer, it assumed human form. A person in black, with a long white beard and a cherubic face. And he came up to the man on the sofa, and leaned in to his ear.

"Do you know me?" he asked.

"Mor Gabriel," the man on the sofa murmured again.

"Mor Gabriel," I said. As the name Mor Gabriel spilled from my lips, I heard music: Liturgical music coming from deep, deep within. A mumble of recurring passion in a language I didn't know, the rhyme of a person in rapture. Just then I noticed the cross. A cross of silver. As I tried to discern whether Mor Gabriel carried it in his hand or chest, a flash of light split the emptiness in two. The man on the sofa felt a stab of pain. I felt a stab of pain in my chest. The light flashed again and the pain disappeared. Relief spread throughout the body of the man on the sofa. Relief spread throughout my body. The sound receded. First the colors in the room faded, then the black shape vanished, and then the room, and then the light... And then the sound of a bell. Without fading, without letting up, a bell insistently ringing.

When I open my eyes, colors crystallize, light returns, the room comes back. But there is no man on the sofa, nor is there Mor Gabriel. However, the bell continues to ring. I sit up in bed, and it's my room, and the ringing is my phone. Even if I can't yet fully shake off the effect of the dream, I reach for the phone and answer it. It's Ali.

"Hi Chief." His voice is serious. "Did I wake you?"

I look at the sunlight seeping through the window.

"No, Ali. I was going to get up anyhow. What's up? Has something happened?"

"Caner died," he says, with his usual terseness, like dropping a brick. "An hour ago."

We were expecting that, in fact, as he's been in a coma for three days. After he was shot, we rushed him to the hospital. They took him into surgery straight away. They removed three bullets, but his internal organs were damaged. He never woke up after surgery, and fell into a coma. The doctors said his situation was dire, but Caner was a tough kid and he hung in there, exactly three days. Then he finally gave up. Strangely, I am saddened. Whether about Caner, myself, or life in general, I don't know. But a deep pain burns my nasal passage.

"May he rest in peace," I say. "He wasn't a bad guy, really."

"May he rest in peace, Chief." He sounds saddened too. "He was the most interesting murderer I ever met."

As we hang up, I look over at the photo of my wife and daughter smiling up at me.

"Another dead among us," I say. "Another death on our doorstep."

The pain in my nasal cavity becomes unbearable. I wish I could cry but I can't. I wish the anger growing inside me for days, the increasing pain within, would turn into tears and flow away, but it doesn't. The pain within me becomes a deeper misery, a deeper sorrow, a more profound sense of meaninglessness. I don't feel like getting out of bed. I don't feel like washing my face, shaving, getting dressed, going down to central station and running around after new incidents. These are all hellish punishments for me. I want to sit in bed all day without moving a hair. But that isn't meant to be. I can't do that. So although it's hard, I get up. I drag my feet to the bathroom, wash my face, shave, dress... I don't want to eat anything but I tell myself I can't skip breakfast. There's nothing to eat at home. I wonder if I should get something at Tevfik's coffeehouse. No, I don't have the energy to talk to anyone. I should just get in my faithful old car and go down to the seaside. Maybe it'll revive me. And just then, my house phone rings again, just as I'm about to grab my coat and leave. It must be Ali. He's probably forgotten something.

"Yes, Ali..."

"Nevzat!"

This... This is Evgenia. It is Evgenia's crystalline voice, like a water droplet. "Evgenia..." I say, as no other word comes out. It's taken me by surprise; this call is something so unexpected...

"Nevzat, are you okay?"

"I'm fine, Evgenia. You called so, you know, I'm really good now. How are you? How's Greece? Have you settled in?"

"I'm back, Nevzat... I'm at the airport."

"What?" I say, thrilled. "At the airport?"

"Yes, I came on the morning flight. I'm in Yeşilköy. Can you come and pick me up?"

"Of course... Of course, wait. I'm coming right now."

As I hang up, for one moment I'm free from the weight of my dark thoughts. That's how Evgenia is. In a heartbeat, she can take a day that's a nightmare and turn it into happiness. So she is here. She's come back. Meaning she couldn't make it without me. I quickly pull on my coat, and just as I'm about to leave, I suddenly stop. I go back into the bathroom and look at myself in the mirror. The cut on my temple has healed - only two small scratches remain. My face is tired, and it's drooping from sorrow, but there's a fresh new hope in my eyes. I approve of myself, and I'm sure Evgenia will approve too.

Amazingly, even my old car doesn't act up this morning. As soon as I turn the key in the ignition, it revs up. We're into the streets quickly enough, but oh, the Istanbul traffic. I do something I've never done in my life before. I place a mobile emergency light on top of the car. My apologies to Istanbul, but this time I can't keep Evgenia waiting. The vehicles that hear the siren pull aside, trying their best to make way. A traffic police car on the road even attempts an escort. I go down to the coastal road, try to reach Evgenia by means of the asphalt running parallel to the sea. I feel as happy as the winter sunlight spilling onto the water, but the dark clouds haven't yet fully dispersed. I'm aching to see Evgenia, but even as I go to her, my mind is still wandering through the details of the investigation. I somehow just can't pull myself away from this case. Ali says of Caner, "The most interesting murderer I've ever met," and for me this investigation was the most interesting case I'd ever had.

As it turns out, there is not one single point left in darkness. The DNA tests proved that the person lying in Selim Uludere's false grave was Gabriel's big brother, Yusuf Akdağ. All the same, when Gabriel saw the pile of bones exhumed from the cemetery, he was crestfallen and refused to have a funeral. "That's not my brother," he said. "My brother is with Mor Gabriel." That poor shepherd, Yusuf, was left alone in death just as he had been in life. The bones that weren't torn up in the thresher were buried in an unmarked grave in the cemetery. On the other hand, the DNA results also confirmed Selim Uludere had committed this murder in order to hide his identity. And it made it clear that Cengiz had aided and abetted him. After it was proved that Cengiz killed Malik, they dropped the case against Ali and me. Henna Meryem was taken into custody for two counts of inciting murder. Prosecutor Mümtaz acted more resolutely this time. He referred the case to a judge along with a request for Meryem's arrest, but our hell queen was let loose on insufficient evidence again. Maybe we would never get Henna Meryem behind bars, but she was certain to be the architect of her own downfall. Those who run in darkness fall fast. Just like her father, she would one day be taken out by a young new mafia don.

All this I think about right up until I pull into Yeşilköy Airport. After leaving my car at the door of International Arrivals, I go in to find Evgenia waiting with two huge suitcases. Her eyes are on the door. As soon as she sees me, her face lights up. Her green eyes are misty, and the teardrops, like sweet promises, are nearly spilling down her cheeks. I hug her without saying a word. I feel the heat of her under her clothes and greedily take in her scent.

"I missed you so much," she whispers.

"I missed you too," I whisper back. We stay that way in the middle of the hall for a while. We block everything out and surrender to the rhythm of the world, the will of our bodies and our souls. I let go first, and then she lets go of me. We take the suitcases to the trunk of my car and then we get in. Evgenia sits next to me, her eyes fixed on my face.

"You've changed, Nevzat," she suddenly says. "Something happened to you."

I contemplate telling her I've killed someone, killed my own director, Cengiz. No, let's not say that now and spoil the day. But I can't keep holding back everything I've been through from her anymore.

"I have changed," I say, steering the nose of my car onto the main road. "I've started to think about life, about myself. This latest case..."

"The Assyrian murder?"

"Yes, the Assyrian murder. We solved it actually, but the things I saw, the things I learned, have taught me to think about myself. There was a murderer, searching for a meaning to life, and that's why he did it. And that is how I also started to think about the meaning of life. Strange, isn't it? After all these years in this profession, a murderer affecting me so much?" All at once, I turn to her. "Evgenia, what do you say?"

She doesn't understand. She's still watching my face with curiosity.

"I mean, what do you think is the meaning of life?"

She smiles, keeping her eyes on me.

"You are the meaning of life, Nevzat," she says.

I think she has misunderstood the question.

I'm about to tell her, you say that because you love me, when she says, "You think I still love you?"

Shot down, I turn to face forward, like a sulking child. She leans in.

"I'm joking," she says, planting a huge kiss on my cheek. "And when it comes to the meaning of life, yes Nevzat, you are that meaning. I mean people, some of them find meaning in their work, some in love, some in religion, or politics, or art, even a large number in football. I don't know. Everyone creates meaning in their own way. If not for these people, none of these meanings would exist. Isn't that so? The meaning of life is people, Nevzat. People."

Right at that moment, there is a loud crash. A red van has rammed into a black jeep from behind. Thankfully, it's just a fender bender and there are neither dead nor injured. But the jeep's owner gets out in a rage and starts cursing. The driver of the van also isn't having any of it. They go at each other like two raging bulls. In a split second, the road is blocked. People are getting out of their cars and trying to separate the two fighting men. There's shouting and hollering, horns honking... Look at this madness; we'll be here at least another hour. I turn back to Evgenia, who is watching the fight from where she sits, like me.

"But really, Evgenia. Why did you come back to Turkey?"

To tell the truth, I'm expecting her to say, for you. But she says, "It didn't work out. I couldn't warm to the place. You may ask, wasn't it too soon to tell? But I swear from the very first day I thought of coming back. That place was not my country, Nevzat." She looks around out the car windows. "This is my country... I came back for this." Seeing the surprise in my expression, she explains. "Sure, this place is dirty.

It's crowded and vulgar. People in this country are brutal, and crude, and selfish. But this is my country, Nevzat. I was born here. My mother and father's graves are here. My work is here, Nevzat. And you. You are here too. That's why I came back."

Like Evgenia, I also look around me. It's not a nice view. The clamor outside has increased, and rather than calming the two fighting men, a few more people have joined the brawl. Honking horns, yelling and swearing, screams and pandemonium... But I feel warm inside.

"You're right, Evgenia," I say. "This country is brutal, the land is hard, the people here are crude and the country really is quite cruel. But this is our country. This is our nation, our homeland. This land is who we are, Evgenia..."

AHMET ÜMİT

Translated by Rakesh Jobanputra

A Memento for Istanbul

AHMET ÜMİT

Translated by Chantal Hamelinck

Ninatta's Bracelet